THE NOVELS OF SHAYLA BLACK ARE...

"Sizzling, romantic, and edgy!"
—Sylvia Day, #1 *New York Times* bestselling author

"Scorching, wrenching, suspenseful . . . A must-read."
—Lora Leigh, #1 *New York Times* bestselling author

"Wickedly seductive from start to finish."
—Jaci Burton, *New York Times* bestselling author

"The perfect combination of excitement, adventure, romance, and really hot sex."
—Smexy Books

THE NOVELS OF LEXI BLAKE ARE...

"Hot and emotional."
—Two Lips Reviews

"A book to enjoy again and again . . . Captivating."
—Guilty Pleasures Book Reviews

"A satisfying snack of love, romance, and hot, steamy sex."
—Sizzling Hot Books

continued . . .

$\mathscr{S}$EDUCTION IN SESSION

SHAYLA BLACK
AND LEXI BLAKE

BERKLEY BOOKS, NEW YORK

BERKLEY

An imprint of Penguin Random House
375 Hudson Street, New York, New York 10014

This book is an original publication of Penguin Random House.

Library of Congress Cataloging-in-Publication Data

Title: Seduction in session / Shayla Black, Lexi Blake.
Description: Berkley trade paperback edition. | New York :
Berkley Books, 2016. | Series: The perfect gentlemen ; 2
Identifiers: LCCN 2015035585 | ISBN 9780425275337 (softcover)
Subjects: LCSH: Bodyguards—Fiction. | Women journalists—Fiction. |
Man-woman relationships—Fiction. | BISAC: FICTION / Romance /
Contemporary. | FICTION / Romance / General. | GSAFD:
Romantic suspense fiction. | Erotic fiction.
Classification: LCC PS3602.L325245 S43 2016 | DDC 813/.6—dc23
LC record available at https://lccn.loc.gov/2015035585

PUBLISHING HISTORY
Berkley trade paperback edition / January 2016

PRINTED IN THE UNITED STATES OF AMERICA

10 9 8 7 6 5 4 3 2 1

Cover art: *Bedroom* © Jakub Karowski / plainpicture.
Washington, D.C. © Joe Ravi / Shutterstock.
Cover design by Judith Lagerman.
Text design by Laura K. Corless.

Penguin
Random
House

To Kim, for her tireless hours of effort in keeping track of this large fictional world and ensuring the two authors using it remain factually accurate. It must be like herding cats.

Thanks to Lina for her Russian translations in Cyrillic. We would have been lost without them. Thanks also to our favorite innkeepers, Brad and Marcia, for so graciously allowing us to work in odd places, at ridiculous hours, and leave behind many wine bottles. And to your goats for the inspiration.

Lastly, thanks to tequila for being so willing to become a margarita. Because of the way you bravely mix with sangria, two authors talked and bonded and decided, what the hell? Let's write books together.

PROLOGUE

Martha's Vineyard
Twenty-one years earlier

From the foot of the old pier, Connor Sparks watched his friends' revelry farther down the beach. After tonight, would he ever feel like one of them again? In a few days, everything was going to change, and it killed him. Since his first year at Creighton Academy, way back in the seventh grade, he'd known his friends would be a part of every single day—usually a big part. Since they'd formed a friendship in prep school, the "Perfect Gentlemen," so named by a sarcastic counselor, had been tight. That first Christmas, Dax had asked him what he was doing for the holidays. The conversation had ended with him accepting an invitation to spend two weeks with the Spencer family. In fact, he'd managed to worm his way into spending every summer break or holiday with one of their families for years. He wouldn't be lucky enough to continue that tight-knit shit during college.

What the hell was he going to do now?

Connor looked out over the beach where his buddy Gabe Bond had started a massive bonfire. It crackled and the embers promised warmth. The moon hung low, and Connor could hear their laughter, practically smell the hot dogs they were roasting. That wouldn't be the only thing smoking out there, but he rarely touched anything harder than a beer. He couldn't. He was a scholarship kid, which meant he had to prove his worth every second of every day or he would be right back in the trailer park.

Now that they had graduated and prep school was in their rearview mirrors, Connor refused to go back to that sad-sack single-wide with the cracked linoleum and broken stairs. But he also wouldn't be joining his buddies at Yale. Of course, they had no idea. All they knew was that he'd gotten his acceptance letter at the same time as the rest of them.

He alone had been forced to wait for more information to see if he could actually attend. Unfortunately, his financial aid letter had not been quite as cheerful. In fact, that letter had slapped him with the reminder that no matter who his friends were, he lived in a different world. He'd merely had a four-year reprieve from having to deal with that truth.

"Hey." Dax Spencer clapped a hand on his shoulder. He dangled a six-pack from his other hand. "Why are you hanging alone up here? The party is on the beach, man. Well, unless you're Roman, and then the party is in Gabe's parents' bedroom. I am not cleaning that up. What the hell is he thinking, taking twins in there?"

"Double the pleasure?" Connor quipped.

Roman had actually offered him one. A beautiful blonde from their sister prep school who would likely be headed straight to Yale and pledging a sorority closely tied to Skull and Bones. Hell. That wasn't exactly accurate, was it? She would serve the men of Skull and Bones because they would run the world one day.

No one ran the world from community college, and they didn't run it from where he was going, either.

There would never have been an invite to Skull and Bones in Connor's future, even if he could have afforded the Yale tuition. Bonesmen came from the elite. No matter how closely he was associated to these men, Connor could never forget where he came from. Neither would anyone else.

Dax winced. "I'm a realist, man. I think it's just double the trouble—even for a night. I'm with Scooter. I kind of wish Gabe hadn't sent out that invite. It's our first night of freedom. It would have been cool to spend it together. But hey, we've got all summer for that, I guess. One last blowout before the real fun starts."

Like the rest of the group, Dax was headed to Yale, though after his four years, he intended to join the Navy as his father had, and his grandfather before him, and so on, dating back to when the U.S. Navy had first been formed. Gabe and his ancestors were the first family of aeronautics. The rest of the Perfect Gentlemen came from equally pedigreed backgrounds. Maddox Crawford's family practically owned the Upper East Side of Manhattan. Roman Calder came from a long line of powerful D.C. lawyers. Zack, aka Scooter . . . well, he was being groomed to become president of the United States.

"Can't wait." Connor simply wasn't ready to admit that he wouldn't be staying here for the summer.

"Mad bought a brownstone off campus."

"I thought we were supposed to move into fraternity houses." It was tradition among this set. Each of their fathers had pledged influential frats.

"And live through all that hazing? Fuck that," Dax said with a shake of his head. "I'm with Mad on this one. We're our own frat, brother, and we take care of each other. Senior year at Yale, Skull and Bones will come for Zack. You know they will. And Roman's dad is legacy. Mad just wants them to have a place where they're not expected to be the next freaking saviors of the free world. He thinks it's up to us to keep those two grounded. Everyone else in the world is going to want a piece of Zack, and because Roman is never going to leave his side, they'll want a piece of him, too. So Mad wants to remind them who their real friends are."

Connor looked out over the dark water shimmering under the moonlight, then at the beach. Mad danced around the bonfire with total abandon.

Puck. Ever since Connor had read Shakespeare, he'd thought of Mad as Puck—impish and chaotic, yet truthful when a person least expected it. That brownstone was Mad's attempt to keep their little family together. They had four years before the world would separate and test them, each in their own way. Four last years to live together and influence one another. It was a good plan. Mad simply didn't know all the facts, and Connor intended to keep it that way because his pride wouldn't allow anything else.

"Your dad was in," Connor pointed out. "You're a legacy as much as Roman. You should be a Bonesman, too. It would help your Naval career. You want to make admiral, right?"

Dax shrugged. "Yeah, but who knows?"

"They're fuckers if they don't let you in," Connor insisted.

Dax was the best guy he'd ever met. Shit, he would miss Dax most of all. Like freaking Dorothy and the Scarecrow.

Connor frowned. Maybe he would get a little wasted tonight. He was sounding awfully maudlin.

"I'll be honest. I don't want in. I don't want to rule the world. I just want my own command someday. And one really hot woman to settle down with. Roman's insane. See you down there?" Dax was halfway down the steps, already moving away from Connor.

"Sure. I'll be there in a bit."

Unmoving, Connor watched Dax join the others.

Creighton Academy had been the best years of his fucking life. Likely, they always would be. But after tonight, it would be time to make his own way. He would claw out of poverty while he watched the rest of them soar into their wealth and power.

"You're looking lonely there, son," a deep voice to his left said.

Connor turned and spotted the man standing in shadow almost immediately. He was tall, his hair just starting to thin out on top while graying at his temples. He was lean, without the usual middle-aged paunch. He wore a three-piece suit and expensive loafers, which struck Connor as odd since they were at the beach. Even the businessmen who came out here changed before they left the city.

"What can I do for you, Officer? Or should I say Special Agent? The Bonds aren't here. If you're looking for them, you'll have to go back to Manhattan. Only the son and his friends are here now."

He quickly assessed his chances of walking into the house and finding Roman in any kind of position that wouldn't make Connor want to go blind. The odds were ridiculously bad. He'd had a good twenty minutes, so his freak flag was probably flying high, but he was also known as the teenaged law god in their circle. He'd ruthlessly used school code against their administrators on more than one occasion. If the feds were here for some reason, Roman would be the one to handle it.

The man chuckled and stepped into the light from the porch. "I'm not with the FBI, but I find it interesting that your mind went there. Any second guesses?"

If the man was carrying a gun, his tailor was impeccable because Connor couldn't detect the line of the man's holster under his clothes.

"FTC?" With really rich people, it was always a risk. The Federal Trade Commission watched over stock transactions, and he wouldn't put it past them to come after any of his friends' parents. "I would say IRS, but the shoes are too nice."

He recognized the Ferragamos. They were the same style Dax wore when meeting his parents for brunch. Most IRS officials couldn't afford thousand-dollar shoes. Mrs. Spencer had bought Connor a pair and some proper clothes when she realized all Connor had was his school uniform, some worn jeans, and a few T-shirts. After that first year, the woman had always invited him to shop for clothes with Dax. He'd felt bad about the expense until he realized how genuinely happy she was seeing to his well-being. He was going to miss her, too.

"Interesting observation for a boy whose mom was a trailer park whore."

A chill went up Connor's spine. "Or maybe you're nothing but a sleazy reporter. I think I'll call the cops and let them sort it out."

The man put up a hand. "I'm sorry. That was harsh. And you won't call the cops. That's not incense I smell. I'm afraid I've spent so much time in the field, I've lost all conversational finesse. I'm not a reporter. But I'll get to who I represent in a minute."

"You're here for me." He quickly reassessed the situation. College recruiter? For lacrosse? Any university that wanted him for their team would have contacted him long ago. He'd attended Creighton on a lacrosse scholarship, but he hadn't been good enough for the Yale team. "For the record, she wasn't a whore. My mother never accepted money for spreading her legs. Get it right. She was our trailer park's resident skank and full-time waitress at a greasy truck stop. What college do you work for?"

"I'm not with Yale and I suspect that would be a problem for you."

He shrugged. "I'm keeping my options open."

The man in the suit chuckled and leaned against the railing. "You're going to play it that way, huh? I know about your issues. I know the scholarship Yale offered you isn't enough. How much would you have to borrow?"

"Eighty grand." More if he went to grad school. And the truth was he didn't even know what he wanted to do.

"Ask Crawford out there for it. He won't miss the money. He came into his trust this year, right? Five hundred million, if I recall. He would write you a check and never miss a penny." The man was starting to sound a little like Mephistopheles, whispering his devil's bargains.

Connor had already discarded the idea. He knew what he was going to do, what he had to do. "Why are you so interested? Because I suspect you're not from a university. So what do you want?"

"Universities aren't the only institutions who recruit young people such as yourself. I represent a group with a singular interest in finding the smartest young men and women, people who possess both brilliant minds and a certain flexibility in their moral character. I need a young man like you who loves his country enough to sacrifice for it."

Since when did the military send out recruiters? "You're too late. I'm scheduled to see a Navy recruiter on Monday. I'll be at RTC in Great Lakes the week after that."

He'd picked the Navy because Dax would be there in a couple of years. Yes, he would be enlisted and Dax would be on the officer track, but he felt better knowing they would be in it together in some small way.

The man sighed. "I'm well aware of your meeting. Might I say that would be a waste of your talents, Connor? And I also believe you'll end up in the same place, just years later."

"And what place would that be?"

"Oh, I would rather you used that brain of yours to tell me."

What could he be talking about? Almost none of the big law enforcement agencies recruited directly out of high school. College was another matter.

He hadn't had any run-ins with the law, hadn't gotten caught doing anything he shouldn't. The only thing he'd ever done that might attract the attention of law enforcement was to send in his assessment that the terrorist groups Jamaat al-Fuqra, Gama'a al-Islamiya, Hamas, Islamic Jihad, and the National Islamic Front had put aside their differences and were working together to find a soft target in the U.S. He'd gotten involved in a group that tracked conspiracy theories. When he'd joined, they'd been all about the Kennedy assassination and alien cover-ups, but he'd whipped them into shape. They were smart and had simply needed a proper outlet. They'd combed papers and talked to people and come up with a conspiracy of their own.

He'd sent his predictions to the CIA but never heard back. Three weeks later, the World Trade Center had been attacked, killing six and injuring a thousand after a truck bomb had been detonated under the North Tower.

"So Langley finally read my report and figured out I was right?"

A smile split the man's face. "Oh, I read your report—after the attack, of course. You were right. What kind of high school kid follows terrorist groups?"

A perverse one. He knew a bunch of kids who were fascinated by serial killers. He'd always wanted to know what made a man do something crazy like strap on a bomb and walk into a crowded plaza. "It's a hobby."

"I'm afraid when we received your report, someone tossed it aside in the 'kook' pile. After we pulled it out and dissected it, your conclusions were so spot-on that a faction within my group assumed you were involved in the attack, even though we'd already prosecuted four of the perpetrators and were pursuing two others. They wanted to question you, but I got one of my tingles."

"Sounds like you need a shot of penicillin, buddy." Connor didn't like the feeling he was getting. Why would the CIA come out here? Why not give him a call? Why wait over a year to question him?

The man chuckled again. "I'm talking about instincts not STDs, but I enjoy your sarcasm. The Navy won't. I've been studying you and I've decided you have exactly what it takes to be an operative."

"So you're not here to accuse me of working with terrorist groups? Because I'm not. I follow them. I believe they're beginning to get sophisticated. There's this new thing. The Internet. I know DARPA has had it for years."

"Yes, you know that because you managed to hack into the system. You're the reason they're developing security to protect themselves. By next year, the Internet will be fully commercialized, and we need a new wave of operatives. You understand that communications is changing. The way we listen is changing, and analysis just got interesting. So you can join up and do the Navy thing for a couple of years, or you can let me pay your way to Yale. You'll get a degree in communications with a minor in world politics."

"Ivory-tower professors know nothing about real world politics," Connor said with a huff, but his brain was working overtime.

"No, they do not, son. But a degree from such an esteemed estab-lishment looks good on paper and will help you rise through the ranks." He smiled. "You're going to be a spectacular find. What do you say? While you're getting the degree I mentioned, you'll also begin a physical training program that will teach you everything you need to know to survive in the field. In exchange, you'll receive tuition and books, along with room and board. If you live up to your end of the bargain and join the Agency, you'll receive some information your mother has withheld that might lead to a turn in your financial for-tunes."

"What are you talking about?"

"Secrets, son. Information is power. Power can be turned into money. If you say yes, I can promise you you'll never worry about money again. And it will be so much fun helping you get your hands on it. You'll find I never do merely one job when I can do two."

The door opened, and Roman strode out wearing his swimsuit and a dress shirt he hadn't bothered to button up. He had a girl on either arm and a bottle of tequila dangling from his left hand. "You seen Scooter? I have to make sure he doesn't spend the entire night study-ing. We just graduated, damn it. Why does he have to go to freaking summer school?" He straightened up when he saw the man standing there. "Hello, sir. I was just taking this bottle out of the house so none of our underage guests can find it and drink it."

"Sure you are, Calder. Just make sure no one takes pictures, and don't talk where someone can record it. And make damn sure Zack Hayes doesn't inhale." He turned back to Connor. "Are you in?"

He didn't get time to decide? What was he thinking? He didn't need time to decide. He loved Dax, but fuck the Navy. He could be a CIA agent. He could have everything he wanted. "I'm in."

"I'll contact you." The mysterious man in the suit started to walk off, then turned, shaking his head. "And don't ever tell the story of how you boys came to call Hayes Scooter. It could really hurt the kid's chances when the presidential elections roll around. By the way, a patrol car was on its way out here to investigate the party, but I think you'll find the locals will leave you alone for the summer. Consider it my graduation present to you, Connor."

The agent walked back into the shadows as though he belonged there. Connor realized that he'd never gotten the man's name.

"Who the hell was that?" Roman asked. "That dude was creepy."

"I'm pretty sure he was my version of a fairy godmother."

Roman shook his head. "You're in a fucked-up fairy tale, brother." He grinned. "But we're going to Yale. We're going to take over the world, aren't we?"

For the first time since he'd gotten his financial aid offer, Connor smiled. "Yes, we are."

He followed Roman down to the beach and joined the party.

ONE

Washington, D.C.
Twenty-one years later

I don't really need a bodyguard." Lara Armstrong took a sip of her chai tea and sat back, staring out the coffeehouse window. Everywhere she looked, people bustled by, their briefcases in hand, cell phones pressed to their ears. They were lawyers and politicians, along with their aides, and anyone else who thought they were important on the political spectrum. Soon, one of the people moving along this street would be a man sworn to throwing himself in front of a bullet for her.

Connor. No last name. Or maybe that was his last name and he hadn't given her his first name. She wasn't sure. She only knew that enigmatic Connor had commanded she meet him here at three thirty. Did he realize how bad traffic was going to get?

"Look, someone knows what you've been doing, L, and that means you need a bodyguard." Her best friend, Kiki, traded a look with the only male at the table.

Tom sat forward, his hands around his nonfat latte as though he needed the warmth. "I don't know. I kind of agree with Lara."

Kiki rolled her dark eyes. "You always agree with Lara. You even agreed with her when she broke off your engagement. You're a doormat."

"I'm helpful and practical." He frowned. "Look, she's only received a couple of e-mails, and it wasn't as if the sender attached a bomb or anything. The contents simply stated that they 'know.' Know what? That could mean anything."

Lara sighed and lowered her voice. Only a couple of people in the world knew what she did for a living and she meant to keep it that way. "He knows I run CS."

Capitol Scandals, D.C.'s most fun and informative news site. Oh, most people called it a horrid tabloid rag that aimed to ruin the lives and reputations of politicians and bigwigs, but Lara liked her description better. And she never ran a piece about any deserving public servant that she couldn't verify. Well, at least not any serious piece. She didn't personally know the size of the current president's penis, though several confidential informants had used the words *extra-extra-large.*

"Shit." Tom's thin lips flattened further, and she knew she was in for a lecture. Unlike Kiki, who often wrote articles for CS, Tom thought the site was a horrible idea. "I told you something bad would come of this. You can't expose the powerful people you do and expect to get away with it. I thought someone had finally realized you spearheaded the effort to remove vending machines from public schools or something."

"Those vending machines never sell anything but processed foods. Kids should have healthier options in school," she began.

Tom shook his head and every strand of his light brown hair stayed perfectly in place. "People don't like it when you take away their sodas, L. They get crabby. Still, I was fairly certain no one would actually kill you over that. But running a tabloid that ruins high-powered careers? That might be a little different."

Kiki nodded. "Exactly. Have you told your father?"

Lara winced. Her father knew about Capitol Scandals. He'd been very supportive when it had been a little site that reported on things like environmental bills and ran essays on the Lilly Ledbetter Fair Pay Act. When she changed the contents to the current iteration, she knew she'd tested him. He'd called screaming when she ran a not-so-glowing story about one of his closest allies on the congressional floor. She'd detailed just how much money the congressman had spent on hookers outside his district while those actually working in his district had lamented about a drastic downturn in income.

She'd been perfectly right to publish the story since the congressman had been running on a platform to bring new jobs and opportunities to his constituency. All the while, he'd been making deals with businessmen to send jobs offshore to Korea. So it really was a true-life metaphor for all that was wrong in politics.

Shortly after she'd published the story, the late-night TV talk show circuit had picked it up. While the comedians and hosts had laughed about the hookers, their viewers had also heard the very true news about backdoor deals, too. Lara had learned early on that she needed to catch the public's attention if she wanted to do any good in the world. And she wouldn't do that with a protest or a well-crafted op-ed piece.

"I'm not telling my dad about this. He already blackmails me. If he found out that someone else knows and is sending me semi-threatening e-mails, he would likely strong-arm me into moving in with him or something. It would be awful."

It wasn't as if she didn't love her father. Her parents were amazing people. She couldn't think of another man in the world who would support her the way her dad did. He'd been angry when he'd learned about CS, but he hadn't outed her. And given that he was a senator from the great state of Virginia, he probably should have. Instead, he'd forced her to accept a condo in a swanky part of town. She could never have afforded her Dupont Circle pad on her own. She'd wanted a little loft in a more real part of town, but her parents had been insistent.

Luckily, she'd never had to decide whether or not to run a story about her father. He was madly in love with her mom and he played things straight. She'd never gotten a tip about him taking bribes or selling out his constituents. When she'd started Capitol Scandals, she realized a surprising majority of politicians thought they were acting in the public's best interests. It was just that rancid 10 percent who really screwed things up for everyone else.

She'd created Capitol Scandals to call them out.

"Maybe you should stay with your folks temporarily. Your dad has a serious security system." Kiki set down her mocha. "Not just a doorman named Moe who sleeps on the job."

"Moe has a serious case of narcolepsy. You shouldn't judge." She shook her head. "Besides, I can't risk working at Dad's place for two reasons: One, I don't know who's watching him. I've long thought the CIA, the NSA, or DARPA listens in on all elected officials."

Tom coughed but the noise sounded suspiciously like he'd called her paranoid.

She ignored him because she knew paranoia could be a lifesaver. "And two, if anyone ever learns my secret and outs me, I want my parents to have plausible deniability."

"I don't think they'd care. They would stand by you," Kiki said.

Bringing trouble down on them was Lara's only real fear. Well, that and global climate change. She fought for what she believed in, but she loved her parents, too. She didn't want to cause her dad issues.

"I have a plan," Tom said, getting serious again. "Hear me out. You close down the site for a while and come stay with me. I have a second bedroom. I can watch out for you. I am a Krav Maga god. We'll hang, and the heat will die down. Then you can go back to fighting the good fight."

She loved Tom, but she wasn't going there again. There was a reason she'd broken off their engagement. There was also the fact that Niall thought she needed someone to watch out for her.

Niall Smith. Her heart gave a little shiver as she thought about him. Since he ran a small site that called for transparency in California politics, he'd come to her as a confidential informant. Nothing he'd sent her had actually panned out, but that wasn't so surprising. Ninety percent of her leads were dead ends. But Niall had come to mean more to her than just a source. Over the course of a few months, she'd come to view him as something of a soul mate.

"No," she said with a sigh. "I need to meet this bodyguard. I'll talk to him and see what he thinks. He's supposed to be a professional. He can give me advice."

"He can give you protection," Kiki argued. She was dressed in her normal Bohemian garb, a peasant blouse and a flowy skirt. She somehow managed to make it sexy. "You have to take this seriously. Whoever sent you that threat knew your personal e-mail."

"But there wasn't anything specific about the threat," Tom argued, then turned to Kiki. "In fact, I'm not even sure it was a threat. Maybe we're freaking out about nothing. What are the real odds that someone's put all the pieces of the puzzle together? There are rumors everywhere about who runs CS, and not one of them mentions you, Lara."

She wasn't sure that was true. What might someone else know about her? She was Senator Armstrong's vegan hippie daughter, whom everyone in the Republican party knew not to put on camera because she would use the opportunity to talk about policy as she saw it.

There really wasn't anything else about her that would be considered even slightly gossip-worthy. Good grades in the right schools. A degree in political science that would probably lead to law school when she found the time. She'd broken her engagement an acceptable amount of time before the wedding. She hadn't even dated in the two years since she and Tom had broken up. Capitol Scandals was the sum of her "nefarious" existence. She'd put everything she had into it, and she was finally scenting something big.

Could this new threat have anything to do with the anonymous stranger who claimed to know what really happened to Maddox Crawford? He'd hinted that if she figured out the truth, the trail would lead to something much bigger.

She merely needed to find a woman named Natalia Kuilikov. Just find one Russian immigrant, and the yellow brick road would open up and take her straight to Oz.

Lara found it interesting that her first big case and her first potential death threat had come so close together.

"I don't know that there's no threat, but simply figuring out who I am doesn't mean someone intends to kill me. I might have overstated that," she admitted.

"To your Internet guy?" Kiki wasn't Niall's biggest fan. She might have suggested on more than one occasion that he was likely a middle-aged creep looking for an online hookup. "He's the one you told, even before you told me. Before you told Tom. I hate to say it, but you seem to have some stake in the guy and that's why you're listening to him."

"Maybe you should listen to the people who have been with you for years. What do we know about this Niall guy? Next to nothing. You can't just let this random dude start to dictate your life." Tom hopped off his barstool and straightened his V-neck tee. "I've got to run. We have oral arguments on the McNally case tomorrow. Lara, call me if you need me. You know I'm always here for you." He walked away.

Tom clerked for an appellate judge, so he was always talking about oral arguments and drafting opinions. She had to admit, watching Tom was one of the reasons she hadn't given in to her parents' pressure and gone to law school. He was endlessly writing other people's opinions. She wanted to make up her own mind.

"Holy jeez. My mouth just watered." Kiki's eyes went wide as she stared beyond the door through which Tom had exited moments ago. "I finally understand what that means."

"What?" Lara turned and caught sight of a man in jeans and a black T-shirt. He stood right outside the coffeehouse, his cell phone pressed against his ear.

His shoulders were so wide they almost spanned the window. He had to be six and a half feet tall, and his T-shirt molded to every muscle and sinew of his lean form.

He turned slightly, his profile coming into view. Lara realized then that *mouthwatering* was really just an elevated term. *Drooling* was more accurate. The man was stunning. His jaw looked perfectly square, though the lines of his face were far too angular to be beautiful. His dark blond hair was cut in an almost military style, accentuating his features. Manly. Handsome. Sexy.

His lips suddenly curled up in the hottest smirk she'd ever seen.

Caveman. Alpha male. And probably straight off some military base. While she could appreciate him on an aesthetic level, Lara preferred her men a little more civilized. "He's very nice looking, Kiki."

Kiki groaned. "Nice looking? There is nothing 'nice' about him. He's dirty. He's bad. And you can't dare call him a boy because he's all man."

Lara adjusted her glasses. "I like Niall more."

Niall had perfect surfer hair and the sweetest face.

"You've never met Niall."

She shrugged. "But I know Niall's soul. He's more my type."

"And by that you mean a thousand miles away and safely unobtainable." Kiki slapped the table. "Damn it, it's time you got laid. How long has it been?"

"Not long." She put her head down and mumbled. "Two years."

Kiki gasped. "You haven't slept with anyone since Tom? Oh my god. I never imagined it was this bad. I thought you just didn't want to talk about it."

"I talk to you about everything and you didn't think I would mention a couple of one-night stands?"

Her stare trailed back to Caveman Hottie. He really was amazing to gawk at. The slightest hint of a beard spread across his jaw. Though he'd probably shaved this morning, his masculinity wouldn't be tamed or denied.

"It's a muscle, you know. You have to use it to keep it healthy. I think your vajayjay has atrophied. That's why you can't think straight about this death threat stuff."

"It's not a muscle," Lara argued. But it probably had atrophied . . . and maybe grown a few cobwebs because she hadn't even played around down there herself in the longest time. She hadn't had time. Even in her head she sounded prim, like she was already hoarding cats and newspapers in preparation for old maid–dom.

She had a sudden vision of that caveman putting his big hands on her. They wouldn't be soft. When he touched her, she would be able to feel every callus and rough edge of his skin. He would have working hands, hands that had built things and protected people. He wouldn't ask her what she wanted . . . but he also wouldn't hesitate to give her exactly what she needed.

"Um, do you want to borrow my sweater?" Kiki's question forced her out of her daydream.

"No. Why?" Lara turned, not wanting her friend to catch her staring.

"Yours is really thin and your nipples are giving everyone here a show," she pointed out.

Lara crossed her arms over her ridiculously erect nipples. "Guess I was a little cold."

Kiki gave her a skeptical glare. "How about we go and introduce ourselves to the hottie and see if we can buy him a coffee. Or better yet, we could take him to the bar next door, get him tipsy, and have our wicked way with him."

"Our?"

"There's a reason I'm known as Kinky Kiki, hon." She grinned, looking back at the caveman. "I'll go talk to him, and you can join us after you interview the bodyguard." She glanced down at her watch. "He's late."

Lara checked her phone. Sure enough, she was supposed to have met the mysterious Connor five minutes ago. She'd gotten here early enough to have a cup of tea and assumed he'd join her. But now that she thought about it, he'd actually instructed her to meet him outside.

She nearly fell off her seat. There was only one person standing outside the coffeehouse.

That glorious hunk of man.

"Kiki?" she squeaked.

Her friend settled a designer bag over her shoulder. Lara had tried to convince her to buy a purse from a Nepalese women's organization that supported indigenous children, but Kiki had replied that when Louis Vuitton supported them, she would, too. "Yes?"

"I think he may be my bodyguard."

Kiki's jaw dropped. "Holy shit. That man is supposed to be your close cover for the next few weeks? Why can't someone want to kill me?"

Lara shook her head. Nope. She didn't need a bodyguard. At least she didn't need one as gorgeous as him. "I'll call you later."

"Make sure you do and it better be juicy." Kiki's gaze was still glued to the man outside.

Lara took a deep breath and strode toward the door to fix her problem.

Connor stood outside the coffeehouse, his stare traveling the path he'd just walked from Union Station. He'd picked this as their meeting spot because he could walk. Three hours on a train from Penn Station to D.C. had done little to elevate his mood. He would rather have had Gabe fly him here, but if Lara had seen him, he wouldn't resemble a sad-sack ex-military man looking for a job, carrying everything he owned in the world in his beaten-up duffel.

He fully intended to play on the woman's soft instincts. If she had them . . .

A chalkboard sign beside him proudly announced that someone named Goldie Starshine would be performing tonight, and all proceeds would go to the global fair trade initiative.

Yeah, it was that kind of place.

He really would have preferred some seedy bar. He'd come to like the dark places of the world. He felt far more at home there.

Lara Armstrong probably never went into bars. Or if she did, she only frequented hipster bars where the craft beer and red wine flowed like a river and no one ordered Scotch because it might get in the way of their deep political discussions.

Of course, he could be wrong about her. She also ran one of the most infamous tabloids D.C. had ever seen. She qualified it by saying she only ran the nasty stuff so people would maybe pay attention to her op-ed pieces on saving dolphins, but he wondered. He was going to scratch under her carefully built exterior, and he knew what he would find. She would be everything he expected—a naive, vain little rich girl who didn't know a damn thing about the real world.

Hell, she'd fallen for a cipher. Niall Smith, brave warrior for the California environment. Connor had created the online persona when he'd discovered Lara Armstrong ran Capitol Scandals. She, along with her site, were ass deep in the game he'd been playing for weeks—a game that had already cost one of his best friends in the world his life. Maddox Crawford had died to cover someone's secrets. Gabriel Bond and his fiancée, Everly, had almost died, too. Someone was weaving intricate threads of deception and half-truths in an attempt to throw him off, but Connor Sparks was like a bloodhound. Once he caught the scent of something, he never let go. If someone had brought Lara Armstrong into this chess match, Connor had no compunction about using her like the pawn she was, because he refused to lose any more friends.

And he would not lose this game.

His cell phone buzzed in his pocket. Since his intel on the girl indicated she was often late, Connor figured he still had a few minutes. He pulled the device free and glanced at the display.

Dax.

"Hey." He never refused Dax's calls. He could likely be in a fight to the death with a foreign operative and would stop in the middle to shoot the shit with Dax. Sometimes he was fairly certain Dax was the only thing in the world that kept him grounded. He loved his friends—Dax, Gabe, Mad, Roman, and Zack were the only people he gave a damn about.

Except he kind of liked Everly. She was a good kid.

"Hey, buddy, you make it to D.C.?" Dax's jovial tone belied the reason Connor was here, but then that was just like Dax.

He was careful with his wording in case she showed up and overheard any of his conversation. "I did. I'm starting the new job in a few minutes."

"Are you sure you don't need backup? I'm off for another couple of weeks. I could be down there in a heartbeat. If someone's really trying to kill this girl, you could use an extra pair of eyes."

"I don't think that will be necessary." He was certain the threat wasn't real. He'd hacked her system and checked the security. He hadn't found a trace of anything that shouldn't be there. The "threatening letter" had been very vague. It was more than likely this was all a ploy to get her daddy's attention and milk him for cash.

Poor little rich girl.

"Okay, but I'm ready to back you up. Hanging out here with Gabe and Everly is giving me a sweet tooth. Maybe I'll go to a bar tonight and see if I still have some of the old magic."

Connor shook his head even though Dax couldn't see him. "Absolutely not. Let me call in some hookers. You won't wake up in Vegas married to one of them. I hope."

"Ha-ha. I only eloped once," Dax insisted.

But Connor knew what that "once" had cost him. "Yeah, I'm trying to avoid horrific divorce number two. Do you ever think about her?"

Why was he getting so sentimental? Maybe he'd spent so much time pretending to be gentle Niall that he was actually growing a vagina. Or maybe it had been sitting next to a family of three on the way down here from New York. Young mom and dad with their infant. They'd been so careful with the tiny girl and with each other. He'd watched as they passed the baby between them.

He wondered if he'd ever have anything so fragile. Not likely. He was far better at wet work.

"I try not to think about it, but then I look at my bank account," Dax replied with his usual dry wit.

"I wasn't talking about your ex-wife. I meant Holland." The woman Dax actually loved. The one he'd lost.

Dax was quiet for a moment. "All the time, man. Not a day goes by that I don't regret what happened. Which is exactly why you should be careful with the Armstrong girl. I don't think she's what you think she is."

"Because you've spent time with her?" He knew the answer to that one.

"No, obviously I haven't, but I'm also a way better judge of character than you are."

"I seriously doubt that."

"Dude, you pretty much just shoot everyone."

"Everyone deserves it." He turned slightly and caught sight of a brunette wearing hipster glasses and what looked like a vintage sweater staring out at him, her mouth slightly ajar. He couldn't help the smile that curled his lips up slightly. Little Miss Vegan was staring at him like he was a juicy steak and she wanted a bite. So much for her unrequited love for tender Niall. His sad-sack persona would have to strum his guitar on the Internet forever because Lara Armstrong might say she was attracted to good boys, but it looked like a bad one could tempt her. "And our girl is here. It's showtime. Is Everly still working on her end?"

Recently, they'd discovered a trafficking ring operating under the auspices of a women's charity. The International Women and Girls Education Foundation had been a front for the Russian mob. One of their big corporate sponsors had been Crawford Industries, run by their late friend Maddox Crawford. As far as Connor could tell, once Mad had found the connection, they'd killed him for it.

They'd also realized that one of the women who had been trafficked had worked as Zachary Hayes's childhood nanny. The president of the United States had most likely been raised by a sex slave, and according to their lone lead, the only person who might be able to find her was Lara Armstrong.

He glanced back and she appeared to be arguing with her friend. The friend was much more his type. She was tall with lush breasts and looked like she knew what to do with a man. So why could he not take his eyes off the little intellectual fairy? That was what Lara reminded him of. A pretty little fairy with too-big blue eyes and bright thoughts and so much dark hair he wasn't sure how she handled it.

"Yes, Everly is trying to track Deep Throat."

He winced at that expression. Though he knew its historical context, it really did sound like a porn film. "Has she found anything?"

"Yes, but you're not going to like it."

He turned back because it looked like he was about to have some company. Lara had anchored her purse on her shoulder and seemed to be drawing her courage. He knew exactly what Dax was about to say. "He contacted Lara Armstrong."

"Yes. We believe he's sent her three e-mails in the last week. In the most recent, he told her to move to their backup means of communication. I don't know what that is."

So Deep Throat knew they were onto him. He would be looking for letters or faxes or perhaps a disposable cell phone. He needed to get into her condo, embed himself in her life. "I'll figure it out. I need to go. I'll call you if I need you, brother."

"See that you do." The line disconnected just as the door swung open and his quarry made her appearance.

Vintage sweater, check. Yellow dress, check. Purse that looked like she could shoulder the cares of the world inside, check. He'd expected her to look a little like the greenie version of Snow White. He hadn't expected her breasts to be quite so round. They didn't look that hot in her pictures. She always wore one of those damn sweaters that hid her body. Now he wanted to get a look at her ass to see if it matched her chest.

Instead, he raised a brow, looked her over, and used his deepest voice on her. "Miss Armstrong? You're five minutes late."

Her mouth opened, then it closed again. She had to crane her neck to meet his gaze when they were this close. A gentleman would have moved back and given her some space.

Connor Sparks wasn't a gentleman.

"Mr. Connor?" She squared her shoulders as though she was preparing for battle.

"Just Connor." He wasn't about to give her an inch.

"Is that your first name or your last name?" She shook her head. "It doesn't matter. I wasn't actually late. I was waiting inside so I wouldn't be late."

"Our meeting was out here."

"I assumed we would go in the shop."

"You assumed wrong." He'd meant to sit down with her in the coffee shop, but now it seemed like a better idea to keep her off-kilter. She would be comfortable in the coffee shop. It was her kind of place. She would be uncomfortable in a dark bar, and he saw just what he wanted across the street. "I was on a three-hour train ride with screaming children. I need a beer. Let's go."

He started across the street toward a bar with no windows. Dank. Skanky. Perfect. He didn't look back, but knew from the sound of kitten heels clacking on the pavement that she was following as fast as her petite legs could take her.

"Connor, we should talk," she said as she tried valiantly to keep up.

He gripped his bag and was gentleman enough to open the door for her. Hard rock throbbed from inside the joint. It looked dark, like the kind of place where secret meetings happened or where D.C.'s citizens went to drink when they didn't want anyone they gave a damn about to know. It was definitely the kind of place where a fairy would need an escort.

His world.

"We can talk while I grab a beer."

She stared at the door like it might be an opening to hell. "I think we can have a very quick talk out here."

So she intended to back out of their arrangement. Connor couldn't allow that to happen. He let the door close and looked down at her. What tack to take? He played out a few strategies in his mind but quickly settled on guilt. Anyone who gave as much of a damn about dolphins as Lara must have a well-developed sense of guilt. He could definitely use that.

"I'm sorry," he murmured. "I'm being selfish. I'm just really tired after that long trip. I should have taken the flight straight to D.C. from L.A., but I wanted to see my mother. She's in a home in the Bronx and I rarely have the money to get back there, you know what I mean? I didn't mean to inconvenience you."

Just like that, those blue eyes went wide with sympathy. "Oh, you didn't. Not at all."

His mother was likely fucking her way through some Southern Florida trailer park. The last time he'd seen her she'd had the temerity to ask him for money. He'd given her two hundred in cash and told her to never contact him again. Ah, the joys of family.

"Niall said you were a really busy lady." He grimaced like he knew he'd done wrong.

The minute he said Niall's name, she flushed. "No. I mean, I am busy, but I'm definitely not too busy for a friend of his."

"He really thinks a lot of you."

Another flush and he could tell she was feeling guilty about staring at him. What had she been thinking to get her to blush like that? He could play on that as well.

"I think the world of him, too. He's really the smartest guy I've met in a long time. So emotionally intelligent. Um, maybe we should get that drink." She straightened her shoulders again. Mentally, Connor added that gesture as another one of her tells.

Life was a lot like a poker game. A smart man didn't play his cards. Instead, he played the players. Lara Armstrong would be a horrible card player. She telegraphed everything she was feeling, held nothing back. Oh, she probably thought she was good at hiding her emotions. Most people did. And most people were wrong. That little shoulder shake told him she was doing something she thought unpleasant for the sake of the overall good.

If she thought for a second that he was letting her slip out of his carefully laid trap, she was so wrong. He was close to figuring out her part in this mystery. Through her, he would locate Deep Throat and the mysterious Natalia. He needed to find her, talk to her, convince her not to talk to the press.

He would protect Zack one way or another.

"You don't mind?" He opened the door again.

Her chin came up. "Not at all. It looks lovely."

He had to smile as she strode through the door because it looked skanky, but he could see she was going to pretend this dark bar was perfectly respectable. She held her head high as she moved past him.

Then he got his first view of her backside.

Lush. Round. Perfect. Maybe this job wouldn't be so bad after all. His palms itched to cup that sweet ass and force her flush against his body. He would bet any sex she'd had was polite and deadly dull. Intellectual. *There, dear, I've had my requisite physical release. Now you may have yours, then we'll take tea.*

Connor held in a chuckle. He would bet she'd never had a man hold her down and eat her pussy until she screamed, begged, and pleaded for him to give her his cock.

Damn. He was getting hard. He moved into the darkness where he hoped she wouldn't notice he was suddenly sporting some serious wood.

The corner of the bar he led them to was surprisingly quiet, with the only illumination coming from neon signs and televisions showing every sport known to man. Lara looked around and seemed to select a table based on its cleanliness. She still opened that gigantic bag of hers and pulled out what looked like a set of hand wipes and gave the table and her chair a scrub. She looked up at him, offering one.

"I'm good." So she was a clean freak, too. He'd been to the world's worst places and likely exposed to just about every horrific disease he could think of. He could handle a little bar dust. He planted his duffel, and the waitress joined them.

She was dressed in the sexy version of a ref's uniform. He ordered whatever was on draft and Lara actually asked about the wine.

"Red or white."

"Sometimes the tannins in red upset my stomach, so bring me the white menu. Thank you so much." She gave the waitress a smile.

The waitress shook her head and walked away.

"You know there's only one white, right? She's not bringing a menu." He frowned. "I should have known. This isn't your type of place, is it?"

"Oh, no. I come here all the time. Absolutely. I love it. Sports. They're great. And I was joking about the menu. How was your mom?"

His mother was a craven bitch. "She's getting along. She's made friends. That's good."

"That's great. Niall told me you were in the Army."

"Navy," he corrected. If she looked into his background, she would discover he'd been honorably discharged after fifteen years. He'd served under one Captain Daxton Spencer, who'd written Connor a stellar recommendation. "I was planning a career, but then my mother got sick and I had to come home to take care of the family business. I put all the savings I had into it, but unfortunately, our store still went under. You know how it is. Mom-and-pop stores can't compete."

A fire lit in her eyes. She'd written several articles about the demise of Main Street America so he'd planned his backstory accordingly. "No, they can't. Big-box stores come in and undercut everyone else until they're the only game in town. What's going to happen when there's no more competition? Monopoly. That's what." She stopped. "I'm sorry. I'm sure you would rather talk about something else."

The waitress returned, placing a mug in front of him and a wine-glass in front of her. It wasn't exactly white, more of a blush color. She sighed and picked it up anyway, likely looking to make sure the glass was clean.

"Let's talk about the job," he suggested.

Even in the low light, he could see her bite her bottom lip as though trying to find a way out of this. "Yes, I'm afraid there's been a mistake. You see, Niall acted very quickly and he really didn't talk to me about this job. He just told me he was sending you out here."

"He acted so quickly because he cares and he wants you safe." The beer was passable, but then he wasn't a snob.

She nearly spit out her first taste of the wine. She somehow managed to swallow it, but moved the glass out of reach. "I am safe. This is really all a big mistake. I got a silly note and I overreacted."

"I don't know about that. Given the website you run, any number of individuals could want to hurt you. And I understood it wasn't a note. It was an e-mail and it was sent to your personal address. I don't think that's silly. It's serious."

Her eyes had widened, giving her an even more fey-like appearance. "You know about the site?"

"Of course. Niall trusts me. I have to know everything or I can't effectively protect you." He enjoyed watching her sweat.

"I didn't realize he would tell you that. It's supposed to be a secret, for obvious reasons."

As much as he loved making her squirm, he needed her comfortable for the moment. "Niall made me sign a confidentiality agreement. He said it was the same one your friends sign. You don't have to worry that I'll say anything. But someone knows or they wouldn't have sent you that message."

She sat back in her chair. "The e-mail doesn't actually say anything at all about the website. It's very vague, which is why I've changed my mind. I'm sure there's nothing to fear. The truth is, I don't need any upheavals in my life right now. I'm sure if I ignore it, this guy will go away. He's very likely another journalist looking for a story. You know who my father is, right?"

Senator Armstrong. He was a fairly staunch supporter of Zack's, who would likely recognize Connor's legal name but the senator couldn't possibly know what the hell he looked like now. The last time he'd had his photo taken was for his senior yearbook and he'd changed much since then. He was more muscular than he'd been as a teenager. His nose had been broken three times. He had a few scars and always wore his hair in a military buzz. He could meet any of Lara's friends and family without them recognizing him.

"Of course." He nodded. "Niall told me everything. You have a good relationship with him, right? Despite the fact that you're on two different sides of the fence politically?"

"My dad is a good man. He just has this thing about taxes and small government. It doesn't mean we don't love each other. My point is that there are always reporters out there hoping to get something on my dad. That's probably what this is. We have no idea what he's referring to. He never actually mentions the website or my work. More than likely he's fishing and he hopes I'll freak out and do exactly what I'm doing. So I really think you coming out here was a mistake. There's no job to do."

"I wish you'd told me that before I traveled all the way from California." Time to lay on the guilt. Then he shook his head as though he wished he hadn't said anything. He gave her a slight smile. "Not an issue. I'm sure I'll find work out here somewhere."

"You're not going back to California?"

"No return ticket, sweetheart."

She softened immediately, leaning toward him as though she could understand for one second what it meant to be in a strange city with no resources. "I'll buy you one. It's my fault you're here."

That would salve her conscience? No way. He would need to figure something else out. Possibly Niall could convince her, but only if Connor stayed in D.C. He owned a lovely home in Langley that he wouldn't be visiting because he needed to appear cash-strapped. It was a no-name motel for him. He threw some cash on the table and stood.

"No, thank you, Ms. Armstrong. I don't accept charity. I'll be fine. I've got a couple of bucks. I'll find a place to stay. I wish you well."

As he started toward the door, he felt her hand on his arm. "Connor?"

He turned, cocking an eyebrow. "Yes?"

"I really wish you would let me send you home."

He bet she did. "It's not an issue. You don't need my services so I'm no longer your problem. If you change your mind, contact Niall. He'll know where I'm staying."

Maybe he should go for broke and hit a homeless shelter. Was that overkill? He stepped outside, knowing damn well she'd be hard on his heels. He needed a finishing touch. Ah, there it was. Perfectly placed, as though someone had known he would need it. *Thank you, city planners.* He walked a few steps to the bus stop and dropped down on the bench under the sign denoting it as a bus stop.

Sure enough, she practically ran out of the bar, all that hair flying behind her. Damn, but he was fascinated by her hair. It looked ridiculously soft and he wondered if she would gasp a little when he pulled it. Not too much. Just enough to sensitize her scalp, to let her know he could make every single inch of her bend to his will.

And there went his dick again. Unruly thing and yet it was kind of nice to know the fucker still worked. More than a few months had culminated into what could only be called a dry spell. He hadn't picked up a woman like he usually did when he needed to burn off stress. It had been even longer since he'd spent more than one night with any woman, but if this worked the way he thought it should, he would be with Lara for a few weeks. He could be in her bed in a couple of days, if her interest level was any indication. Every report he had on her stated she practically lived like a nun. She hadn't had a single serious boyfriend since she'd broken it off with her lawyer fiancé. She'd thrown herself into work. All it would likely take was showing her a bit of interest and a little affection.

He didn't even want to try this without seducing her, Connor suddenly realized. He wanted her.

He really was a bastard.

She stopped at the edge of the street. 2nd Street NE was crowded at this time of day. Most of D.C. was crowded at any time of day. She looked up and down the street, obviously trying to find him.

She breathed a long sigh of relief when her eyes lit on him. "I thought I'd lost you."

You couldn't lose me if you tried, little girl. "I'm just waiting on the bus."

"Oh." A slow smile spread across her face. She sat on the bench beside him. "I take the bus, too. Though I prefer the Metro. It's faster."

"You don't have a car?" He was a little surprised. Given her upbringing, he'd half expected she had a driver on call.

Her head shook as she settled her bag on her lap. "I have a hybrid, but I don't like to use it in the city. There's no reason to. Public transit is faster and better for the environment. And you meet the most inter-esting people on the subway."

Yes, and also got to see a lot of public urination. Actually, he didn't like the idea of her being alone on the subway at night. It would be a little like a cupcake running around a group of toddlers, only she'd look tempting in the midst of thugs with rape and murder on their minds. "You shouldn't use the Metro late at night."

She waved him off. "It's fine. I have a rape whistle."

"You need a gun."

"I don't believe in guns."

Why wasn't he surprised? He was sure she thought that if the gov-ernment took guns away from good people, everyone would be safe. "Here's the bad news, sweetheart. They believe in you. You don't have to believe in a gun to get killed by one."

She frowned. "Do you have a gun?"

"Of course."

"How did you get it on the train?"

Because he had paperwork that showed he was allowed to carry any-where. It came with the whole high-level Agency gig, but he couldn't tell her that. "I have a license to carry concealed."

He had three guns within reaching distance, along with a couple of knives. He was practically a walking armory. But she didn't need to know that, either.

"Wow. I don't have any guns. I'm surprised Niall would be all right with them."

This was a delicate subject, but he'd already thought about it. In fact, he'd gone over just about every scenario possible. "Niall understands that sometimes you have to protect the things that are precious to you. If someone is trying to hurt you, he would want me to use everything in my power to make certain you were safe."

She sighed and turned to face him. "Maybe you could take a look at the message I received. What could it hurt for you to just stop by my place and take a look? I'm not very security conscious."

He was in.

Connor put out a hand. "You've got a deal."

In the distance, he heard the sound of a motorcycle engine revving. Lara began to talk about where she lived and how long it would take them to get there at this time of day. She'd taken the Metro, but was more than happy to get on the bus if he preferred.

Connor turned and watched as some asshole on a crotch rocket started weaving his way in and out of traffic. It was an annoying little bug flying around the stopped cars.

"I guess we could find you a hotel close to my place," Lara said.

Was she high? "Ms. Armstrong, if I work for you as a bodyguard, I need to stay with you."

Someone honked as the motorcycle cut them off, making it across the intersection before the light changed. Lara completely ignored the little drama playing out on the street. "But I only have one bedroom."

And he intended to be sharing that bed with her damn quick. "Hey, your couch is probably better than the room at the Y I would likely be at. Look, even if you decide you don't need me, at least you can sleep well tonight knowing I won't let anything or anyone come through your door."

She bit that fucking gorgeous bottom lip, and he would bet she hadn't been sleeping well. Would she sleep well in his arms? Would she cuddle up and lay her head on his chest and curl like a kitten around his body?

"I guess it would be all right for a night. You should know, though, that I cook, but it's one hundred percent vegan."

Damn. He was willing to do a lot for his friends. "No problem. I'll eat anything you put in front of me and I'll do the dishes. You cook. I'll clean. We could be a good team."

He would be the team leader. She just wouldn't know it.

She smiled and he had to admit it was kind of breathtaking. When Lara Armstrong's lips curled up, the rest of the world sort of melted away.

Staring into her blue eyes would have rocked his world if that buzzing sound hadn't stopped with a hard squeal. Connor's instincts flared and he looked up just in time to see the motorcycle stop and its black-helmeted rider lift a hand.

Connor caught sight of a semiautomatic in the rider's fist—pointed right at Lara's head.

It looked like his job started now.

TWO

Lara looked up at Connor, an unfamiliar rush of excitement crackling along her skin. He was different than she'd imagined. When she'd seen him outside the coffeehouse, she'd assumed he'd be a big, gorgeous, unintelligent frat boy like the ones she'd barely been able to tolerate in college. They'd only cared about the next party and all that entailed.

But Connor was different. Yes, he'd taken her into the nastiest bar she'd ever seen, but because it looked as if he couldn't afford more. He didn't even have the money for a plane ticket home.

What had Niall been thinking? She chatted on, but it was nearly impossible to take her eyes off Connor. The man needed to stop the bodyguard business and go to Hollywood.

She had the distinct feeling that once he got into her condo, he wouldn't leave until he wanted to. Still, she couldn't find the will to tell him no and send him to some ratty motel. Her couch was pretty comfy. She'd fallen asleep there many a night.

It had been years since she'd had someone sleep over. She'd meant to jump back in the dating pool with another scared minnow like herself. Connor was a shark. A hungry, down-on-his-luck, might-munch-on-anything-he-saw shark.

But the good news was the two of them spending time together wasn't a date. She had to get her mind off that notion. Their interaction was purely professional and she intended to keep it that way because she was only interested in one man. Niall.

"Down!" He shoved her off the bench.

One minute she was talking about the Metro and how to avoid traffic, and the next Connor was shouting at her. "What do you mean 'down'?"

She turned her head and saw instantly. A man had stopped in the middle of traffic, his arm raised. She glimpsed the faintest glint of metal before Connor tackled her with his big body. Lara went down hard on the concrete to her right. Pain flashed through her shoulder. Her head knocked against the ground and the world went a little fuzzy.

Something was wrong with her hearing. A persistent ringing resounded in her ears. Her vision was tunneling, getting dark at the edges.

"We need to move, Lara." Connor was all around her. His arms enveloped her, his weight pinning her down. He was warm, so warm. Had she thought of him as a shark? Sharks were cold and she would bet they didn't smell delicious, like sandalwood and soap.

She shook her head because her legs didn't want to work. "No. I need rest."

"Shit." He cursed but kept on covering her.

Screeches and shouts sounded everywhere. The high-pitched engine revved again. Rubber squealed against the cement. Flashes of what seemed like hundreds of shoes rushed by impatiently. One of them even stepped right on Connor's hand and he cursed again. He knew a lot of cuss words. He was very creative with them.

Another pain flashed through her as something crushed her foot. The pain jolted her into clarity. A gun. She'd seen one just before Connor pushed her down. She'd hit her head and now he was literally covering her body with his own, protecting her from the mass panic the shooter had incited.

He was in danger. She had to get it together.

"We need to move before they come back." Connor's voice was deep and calm, as though nothing was really wrong.

She nodded but winced. Every single muscle in her body seemed to ache and her head pounded, throbbing to the beat of the feet fleeing the scene.

"Let's make for the bar and we'll hole up there until the cops come." He eased off her. "I want to make sure the shooter's really gone. Don't move."

It seemed as if the worst of the rampage was done, and the street had become eerily quiet. In the distance, she heard the sound of sirens, but the afternoon traffic clogged the roads, so it could be crucial minutes before they made it here.

Connor stood over her, stretching his hand down to offer his help. "The little fucker got away. I hope like hell some of these CCTV cameras caught his plate."

She started to reach for him, but her vision wavered once more.

"Damn it." Connor leaned down and wrapped an arm around her shoulders before tucking the other under her knees. He lifted her as if she weighed nothing at all. "You have to go to the hospital. There's a knot on your head."

When he cradled her to his chest, the pain didn't seem so bad anymore.

"What happened? Why did someone shoot at the bus stop?" she asked, trying to piece it all together.

He strode to the bar but someone inside had locked the door. "Bastards," he muttered under his breath and stomped back toward the bench, scanning their surroundings as if he expected more danger. "He wasn't shooting at the bus stop, sweetheart. He was shooting at you."

"Why would anyone shoot at me?" It didn't make sense. Nor did her exhaustion. How had she gotten so tired?

"Well, I think we can safely say the little e-mail you received is just the beginning. Ah, there we go." He hugged her against his body and carried her down the street. "I need an ambulance!"

He was still calling out when everything around her went dark.

still don't understand what you're doing here."

She could hear her father, but he seemed far away. And really annoyed.

"If my daughter needs help, by god, I'll be the one to provide it. How exactly do you know the incident wasn't what the police said?"

"The police will say what I want them to. We need to keep this quiet for obvious reasons, but it was hardly random, sir."

That dark voice tugged at her. Connor, her bodyguard. Her big, strong, cavemanny bodyguard. She shouldn't like his voice. It shouldn't sound so smooth and yummy. "The shooter stopped in the middle of the street and leveled that gun at her."

"How do you know he wasn't aiming for you?"

"Because I've been doing this for a while." There was nothing but patience in Connor's voice. "I spent fifteen years in the military and another year in private security. This is what I do and it's why your daughter hired me."

"Well, you did a shitty job since she's here in the hospital."

Lara forced her eyes open because it was obvious they weren't going to clear up this argument on their own. "I didn't get shot so I would say he's done a bang-up job so far."

Her father moved to her bedside, his eyes softening the minute he looked down at her. "Hey, muffin. How are you feeling?"

"A little embarrassed that you called me muffin." She licked at her ridiculously dry lips. "Connor protected me. He got me out of the way of that bullet and took the brunt of the crowd as they ran away. Am I in the emergency room?"

"Yes." Her father took her hand. "Your mother is going to cut her trip to San Francisco short."

Her mom was visiting friends. They were supposed to go on a tour of wine country. She never got to do anything for herself. "No. I'm fine. I'm sure it's just a bump."

"You have a knot on your head and the doctor says I'm supposed to watch you overnight, but other than that they're releasing you as soon as you're awake and feel strong enough to walk," Connor explained.

"You'll come back home, and I'll have a security detail for you in a few hours." Her father pulled out his phone.

If she let him dial those numbers, any freedom she had would be chucked right out the window. "Dad, no. I'm not going to Arlington. I'm going to my place and it's all right because I already hired a bodyguard."

Connor's eyebrow lifted in a quizzical stare. She shrugged because there was no way she wasn't going to hire him now.

Her father shook his head. "I don't like it. I don't like it at all. I don't know who this man is and I don't trust him. For all I know, you hired him off Craigslist and he's a serial killer. Maybe he set up the whole scenario to con a job out of you. Have you thought of that?"

She came by her conspiracy-theory tendencies honestly. Her dad could come up with some whoppers. "Dad, he didn't set anything up. I wouldn't hire someone off the Internet."

Connor cleared his throat. "Really?"

He had a way of making her feel dumb. "It's not the same. You came with a reference."

"From a man you met on the Internet," Connor replied in that annoyingly hot, arrogant way of his.

"Are you kidding me?" Her father was suddenly standing next to Connor, and she had the distinct sense that she was being ganged up on.

"Niall is a friend. He's an activist in California and I've been speaking to him for weeks. He's a good guy."

Connor shook his head at her dad. "He actually is a decent guy, but there's no way for her to know it. She's never talked to him in person."

"We Skype almost every day."

"Every day for a couple of weeks but you're only messaging. For all you know he's some creepy old dude looking to add to his harem of stolen brides."

Her dad turned, fully engaging Connor. "She always does this. She's far too trusting and I swear it's going to get her killed one day. When she turned eighteen, do you know what she did? She hopped a bus to Guatemala with a bunch of hippies to pray to some hippie deity and smoke god only knows what in the middle of the rain forest."

"We were building sanitation systems for poor villages." She sighed and kind of wished her concussion had been worse so she didn't have to sit through a recitation of her sins.

Her father gritted his teeth. "She left a note."

"Because there was no way you would have let me go," she pointed out.

Connor stared down at her. "Of course he wouldn't have let you go. You're the daughter of a senator of the United States of America. You're a high-value target to many South American groups."

Her father nodded. "That's what I explained to her. Kidnapping important people is big business in that part of the world, but did she listen?"

"I also didn't get kidnapped because I didn't run around with a sign that said, 'Hey, Daddy's got cash. Please kidnap me.' I'm not an idiot. I know how to blend in."

"You couldn't blend in if you tried." Connor's deep rumble made her wonder exactly what he meant by that.

She sat up and found her head surprisingly clear. "It doesn't matter what either one of you thinks. I'm going home. I have work to do."

Natalia Kuilikov was going to be a big story—if she could find out what had happened to the woman. Lara had come across a lead but she hadn't been able to act on it for a few days. She definitely didn't intend to be locked in her father's Arlington mansion with a bunch of Secret Service wannabes on her twenty-four seven.

"You're supposed to rest. And if you don't think I can force you to come home with me, you're wrong." Her dad's cell phone was right back in his hand, almost a bigger threat than that gun had been.

"Sir, if you force her to go with you, I think she'll run at the first opportunity. If you want to ruin what seems to be a perfectly fine relationship with your daughter, this is the way to do it," Connor pointed out.

There was the voice of reason. "Yeah, what he said."

Her father flushed, his cheeks going red. It was what he did when anyone backed him into a corner. "What the hell am I supposed to do? Someone took a shot at her. I can't let that go."

"I'm going to look into it. The cops are already checking all the cameras in a three-block radius. We'll figure out where he came from and where he's going. If we can get a plate number, we'll find this guy. But I think it's for the best that we keep the incident out of the papers. The last thing Lara needs is a bunch of media attention," Connor explained.

Her father huffed as though he hadn't even thought about it. He turned to her. "If they start checking into your background . . ."

Connor finished for him. "They'll very likely put together enough to out her as an infamous blogger."

Her father's jaw dropped. "He knows?"

"Of course I know," Connor replied simply. "I told you. I'm her security. I need to know everything. And in this case, one bodyguard is likely better than a whole team. No one will question what I'm doing with her. We'll say I'm her new boyfriend. She can't hide behind that if she's got three dudes in suits with communication devices in their ears. I'm easy to explain away, and I have the flexibility to protect her and work with the police to figure out who tried to kill her."

"Boyfriend?" It made her a little antsy. "Couldn't we say you're my cousin or something?"

"No." No explanation. Just no.

"Or you could be my life coach."

"No."

Fine. He didn't really look like a life coach. Maybe a personal trainer. She started to give him that option.

He simply looked down. "Whatever you're going to say, the answer is no. Now, if you're feeling up to it, go and get dressed. I want us gone before the press figures out where we are."

"I wondered why you took her to this place." Her father was looking at Connor with something like respect in his eyes. "There were closer hospitals."

"I think if your office releases a statement that you're so happy your daughter is safe after today's seemingly random act of violence, the press will back off. If they scent the truth, they'll be all over her and it won't take long for one of them to put the puzzle pieces together. It could certainly open her up to numerous lawsuits, and it could truly harm you politically."

Her stomach clenched at the thought of hurting her dad. It wasn't fair that her actions could blow back on him, but at least Connor had given them a viable alternative. "I'll say nothing beyond how scared I was." Although it would give her a good platform. "Then I can use it as a call to further protect citizens from guns."

Connor and her dad both groaned. Almost identically.

Connor ignored her very practical option, preferring to continue talking to her dad. "Have your staff draw up a statement for her, too. We'll nip this in the bud while I start trying to figure out what's happening."

Her father turned to Connor. "Look, I thank you for protecting my daughter and you seem like a guy with a good head on his shoulders, but I don't know you. I don't know a thing about you. I can't trust my daughter's life in the hands of a man I don't know anything about."

Connor withdrew a letter on very official crisp linen stationary. "This is a letter of recommendation."

The senator barely glanced at it. "It will take too much time to verify this is actually from Captain Spencer, whom I've also never met. Besides, I'm not much of a Navy man. My family's roots are Army."

Connor reached into his pocket. "I understand. I don't like to use this reference very often, sir, but I think if you call this number, you'll feel better about your daughter employing me."

Her father took the card, looked at it for a moment, and then stared back up at Connor. "Is this what I think it is?"

"I did some work for him back in the day. Please feel free to ask him anything you like about me."

Her dad held the card up. "Don't think I won't know if this is a fake. I'll be back."

He stepped out.

"Who's your reference?" Whoever it was had her father jumping to attention. Very few people could do that.

Connor shrugged. "An old acquaintance." His eyes hardened, his whole body losing that calm presence he'd had with her father and becoming predatory. "Now, we're going to talk about how this will work because I will no longer buy your bullshit that you don't need a body-guard. In fact, I'm fairly certain you need a keeper."

"A keeper?"

He leaned in, nearly pinning her to the bed. "Yes. You need someone to make sure you don't get yourself killed. The good news is I no longer have to hold back and hope you'll let me do my job. In about three minutes your father will walk back in here and he'll be completely on my side. There's nowhere left to run, little girl. From here on out, it's going to be my way all the way, and the first rule of this partnership is that I'm in charge."

"That's rude and I don't have to put up with it." She was deeply grateful for the blanket between them because her nipples were acting up again. "I'm your employer."

There was that sexy caveman smirk again. "No, you're not. As far as anyone knows, I'm your boyfriend and we'll have to keep up that pretense in public. I've found whenever I'm going undercover it's best to keep up the pretense in private, too. You're less likely to slip up that way. Now that I think about it, I should really thank that fucker on the bike since I hated the thought of sleeping on your couch."

His mouth hovered above hers, and suddenly her lungs didn't seem to function. He was close, heat radiating off his body in waves. All she had to do was lean forward a little before her lips would touch his and she would know what it meant to kiss him. "There's nowhere else to sleep at my place."

"Sure there is. Do you like the right or the left side of the bed, sweetheart? Actually it doesn't matter. I'll take the side closest to the door."

The thought of sleeping next to him was a little too tantalizing. It had been forever since she'd slept next to a man, and even then he'd been more of an overgrown boy who stole the covers and claimed he couldn't sleep if she was too close to him. Tom hadn't been a cuddler. Not that Connor would be. Somehow she couldn't see him wrapping that lean body around a female to sleep. What would it be like to turn over in the early-morning light and have him resting between her and whatever might come through her door? She would feel so safe. But she couldn't give in because she wasn't about to let him think she was some doormat. "Or I can fire you. Then I wouldn't have to pretend anything at all. I don't like your attitude."

"Oh, you might not like what I'm saying to you because you're not used to having to play by anyone else's rules, but I think you like me. I think you like me just fine."

She managed to shake her head.

With a little twist of his hand, he pulled the blanket from her, unveiling her rigid nipples against the superthin material of the hospital gown. He looked down. "Cold, sweetheart?"

She pushed against his chest. "Asshole."

He stepped back but didn't go far. He sat on the edge of her bed with a little sigh, as though he was sad their play was over. "I'll take care of you, Lara. I won't let anyone hurt you, but you might not always like how I do it."

She was feeling stubborn. Stupid, actually, because she was still thinking about kissing him. This was dangerous. She wasn't about to get involved with a meathead who thought he could be all nice and polite one moment then take-charge, protect-the-little-woman the next. Nope. She didn't care that her nipples liked him just fine. She was more than the sum total of her girl parts. Her biggest girl part was her brain, and her brain didn't like him. Mostly. "Or we could just call it quits here."

"Oh, we're past that choice. Unless you want your father to take over. I think you'll find he's very comfortable with handing you over to me now. And I'll allow you to work. Hell, I'll help you. If you go with your father, you can't work out of his place and you can't ever let the guards he hires know what it is you do for a living."

Damn it. Connor was right.

"I still think you should sleep on the couch."

When he really smiled, fine lines crinkled slightly around his eyes. She was already beginning to differentiate his smiles. There was the arrogant smirk that seemed to be the most common in his repertoire. There was a little half smile that seemed to come when she said something he thought was stupid. Yeah, she could read that on his face. And then there was the smile that kind of lit up the room.

"How about I promise not to make love to you until you beg me? Would that make you feel safer?"

She blushed and wished he wasn't sitting so close. "That's not ever going to happen."

"Then you don't have anything to worry about, sweetheart." He raised his hand and brushed his index finger against her nose, a sweetly affectionate gesture. "Who knows you were hiring a bodyguard?"

"Kiki."

"The girl from the coffeehouse?"

She nodded. "Oh, and Tom."

A single brow arched over his eyes. "Who is Tom?"

"He's a friend. He's cool. He clerks for a judge. Our fathers have been friends for years." For some reason, she didn't want to tell him that Tom had almost been her husband. She deserved to keep a few secrets.

"Tonight you're going to call them and explain our situation. If anyone asks, they need to say we met through mutual friends at a party and we've been talking online for a couple of months. We decided it was time to move this relationship to the next level."

"See, to me the next logical level would be on my couch. And there's no way they buy any of that story. We're really close."

The door opened and her father walked in, looking a little pale. He slid his cell phone into his pocket. "Lara, you do whatever this man tells you."

"He just said he intended to sleep with me. Should I do that?"

Connor rolled his dark eyes. "I believe I told her I wouldn't touch her in any physical way unless she begged me. Your daughter is apparently afraid that if I stay in her apartment, she'll be overcome with lust. I'm a little worried about it, too, but I think I can handle her."

"Connor." She hit him with her pillow.

"Senator Armstrong, I'm sorry. Your daughter brings out the sarcastic jerk in me. I'll keep it reined in. I'll step out and give you two a moment. Lara, we need to get moving if we're going to avoid those reporters." He left the room, not quite shutting the door behind him.

"Dad, who was his reference?"

"The president."

"Of the United States? POTUS? POTUS was his freaking reference?" Who the hell was this man?

Her father nodded. "I just had a nice chat with Zack Hayes. He claims Connor is one of the most honorable men he's ever met and that I couldn't be putting my daughter in better hands. He also invited your mother and me to a private dinner."

"But he usually ignores you."

"I don't know that I would use the word *ignore*. We've met on several occasions, but he's never met with me privately. Apparently your bodyguard is also a POTUS whisperer. Lara, do you understand what it would mean to become friendly with Hayes?"

It would mean backing from a popular president. It would mean taking a bigger position within the party. It would mean her father could get his agenda pushed through. Still, Lara didn't entirely trust Zack Hayes. She would likely never trust anyone who had reached such a pinnacle in politics, but there was something going on with this president. Her confidential informant had hinted that the leader of the free world was tied to some unsavory events. Then there was all the research she'd done on the murder of Joy Hayes.

She wasn't so certain the president hadn't had his own wife killed, and now it seemed her bodyguard was close to the man. And her father didn't mind that one bit.

"Wait. Are you seriously pimping me out to get to the president?"

"Of course not. I would never do that." He cleared his throat. "Although Connor is a very attractive man, Lara."

Lara laughed, her whole body shaking with amusement. Her father sat on the edge of the bed, a smile on his face that faded after a moment. She let go of some of her worry. How close could Connor really be to Hayes? It was unlikely the president was best buds with a guy who seemed to be a drifter.

"I could have lost you." He gripped her hand.

She squeezed his in return. "I'm okay."

"Promise me you'll let that man do his job. Baby, I couldn't survive losing you. Your mother and I would . . ."

She leaned against the man who had been her rock for twenty-six years. He almost never understood her, but he'd always loved her just the same. "I promise."

Now that the police had asked Lara "a few" questions and left, Connor could finally get her home. He looked up and down the hospital's sterile hallway. So far he hadn't seen a reporter, but it didn't mean they wouldn't show up at any moment. He'd half expected them to be waiting when they'd pulled into the ambulance bay.

He made a mental note to start files on Lara's friends. If they knew her secret, then they were as close as Lara claimed. They had to be pretty good friends if they'd known about her blog for this long and the secret still hadn't come out. Still, even well-meaning people could fuck up at any point.

In his pocket, Connor's phone buzzed. He slipped it out and walked just out of the Armstrongs' earshot.

The pain in his shoulder flared up as he swiped his thumb across the screen. He'd taken some blows when he'd covered Lara's body with his own. He would feel it in the morning. Maybe he could groan and whine a little and get her to massage his poor sore muscles.

Of course that turned another muscle of his hard and wanting. Damn, he had to admit they had chemistry. It was a dangerous thing.

"Hello?"

"So I just got a call from Senator Armstrong."

As Connor made his way out of the room and the door shut behind him, he couldn't help but smile. It wasn't every day the president gave him a ring. "I should have warned you."

"What? And made my day a little less surreal? Want to explain why I just gave you a sterling recommendation to an ally of mine?"

"I didn't know you were close."

"We're not, but you gave me a convenient way to remedy that. He's actually influential in a very quiet way. I invited him to dinner. So why are you protecting Lara Armstrong? I thought you were going to have Capitol Scandals shut down, not play bodyguard. Wait. He said she was in the hospital. Was she involved in the shooting on 2nd Street?"

He had to give his commander in chief credit. He wasn't slow on the uptake. "The police suspect it was random, but they were trying to get Lara, Zack. He pointed that gun straight at her head. She needs me, and I need access to her daily life if I'm going to find whatever information she knows. Now I have access, and in order to keep her cover, we'll play boyfriend and girlfriend. Don't be surprised if you see pictures of us. No matter what I do, a senator's daughter getting caught in the middle of gunfire is going to make the news."

So he would play her mystery guy. He already had everything in place. His cover would hold. The reporters who looked him up would see exactly what he wanted them to see.

"You really think she's going to lead you to Nata?" She'd been Zack's childhood nanny. From what Connor knew about Zack's upbringing, he was fairly certain Natalia had been more of a mother than Zack's biological mom. There had been rumors for years that Mrs. Hayes had a drinking problem. Her accidental death had been blamed on slick roads, but the whispers had never ceased.

"I think she's the only lead I have. We know the informant wanted Everly to reach out to Lara. He said Lara had another piece of the puzzle. I'm betting that piece is Natalia's location." In fact, he was betting a lot on that.

"I don't know, Connor. I've been talking to Roman about this. Maybe we should leave it alone." Zack's voice turned low, a sure sign he was uncertain.

In this case, he couldn't follow Zack's lead. This was Connor's area of expertise. "And potentially have this come back to bite you in the ass?"

"Me? Whatever happened was probably my dad's doing, but his dementia is getting worse every day. Last week, when I reminded him that I was his son, he told me he didn't have one." Zack cleared his throat, and Connor had no doubt his old friend was struggling with his father's degenerating illness. "So I don't think my dad will care what the press says. And it couldn't have been my fault. I was a baby. I don't think even the press can come up with a way to pin this on me."

Oh, but the press could be so creative. Besides, more than the media potentially threatened Zack. The Russian mob was somehow involved in all of this, and he wanted to make sure he put any connections between them and the White House to rest. "It doesn't matter and you know it. If you get mired in this kind of a scandal, no one will talk about anything else. Every drop of energy you have will go to changing the dialogue, so every bit of power you have could go down the toilet. We need to find her and shut this down now." And figure out who the hell the mysterious Sergei was. It was a name he'd come across more than once, and this mysterious Russian seemed to be at the center of everything. He didn't talk about it with Zack, though. As president of the United States, he had enough to worry about. "I'll take care of this."

"I know you will, Connor. I just can't stand the fact that Dax got shot and Gabe and Everly almost died over this. I could just come out with this info myself. Maybe if I directly address it, I can shut it down." A long sigh sounded over the line. "Roman's threatening to hang himself. Or he's trying to tell me I'm committing political suicide. He's not very good at charades."

He should have known Roman would be there. He was Zack's right hand. "He might suck at charades, but he plays the game of politics well. Let me handle this. I'll be fine."

"No, I'm not going to ask him . . . What is wrong with you?" Zack's voice got muffled for a moment. "Oh, all right. I want to know, too. Roman has a very vital question for you concerning the current operation."

"Shoot."

"You gonna do her?"

Connor snorted because even the most powerful political figure on the planet could still sound like a teenaged boy when he got around his friends. "That's none of Roman's business."

"She's kind of cute in a hipster way," Zack pointed out. "You have to admit, it's been a long time since you had a serious girlfriend."

"Yeah, I gave up on that when the last one nearly put a knife through my heart." He didn't like to think about Greta. The willowy blonde had been beautiful and exciting and about as different from Lara Armstrong as possible. She would have sold her unborn children for pocket change. She'd also been a double agent, and now she was god only knew where, being tortured for information. She could be dead for all he cared.

Maybe there was a reason his dick perked up around Lara. Unlike the last chick he'd fucked on a regular basis, the senator's soft daughter wouldn't attempt to carve him up.

"Lara Armstrong wouldn't know what to do with a knife," Zack offered. "She's too busy saving puppies and complaining about my immigration policies. On the upside, she did run a story calling me the best hung of all the modern presidents. Shockingly accurate information."

He laughed, but he didn't actually like Lara wondering about the size of Zack's package. Did she prefer slick politicians? Or was she all about the soft-looking dudes who played vagina rock and saved penguins? Maybe, but her nipples didn't lie. Connor knew they got hard whenever he came close.

"Yeah, I'm going to do her."

"I was joking, Connor. You really shouldn't do that." Zack's voice went low. "From what I understand, she's actually a sweet kid."

The door opened and the senator stepped out of the little room, followed by his daughter. He would do well to remember that sweet kid sometimes ran ruthless stories. Deep down, she wasn't so different from Greta. She just hid it better and masked her ambition under the guise of saving the world. But Lara Armstrong would publish any story she needed in order to further her agenda.

"But she's got another side," Connor argued. "She really does run that site and makes no excuses for it." She was smart enough to know that she didn't want her name associated with the sensationalist crap she published. That alone should tell everyone something about her. "She's ruined the lives of several people in this town."

Any one of whom could be attempting to kill her.

"Don't be so dramatic. Capitol Scandals is really only responsible for two resignations, and I think the bastards deserved to go. One of them was indicted for fraud. The trial is pending."

"Are you trying to tell me to let her go, Zack?" His eyes were on her as she thanked her nurse and took all the paperwork. The senator had brought her a change of clothes. She looked even younger in jeans and a simple red T-shirt. Her face had been scrubbed down and she wore a fresh, doe-eyed expression.

He wouldn't let her go. Not even if his president told him to.

"No. Do what you need to. Just be careful with her. I wouldn't want you to do anything you'll regret. Keep me up to date."

The phone clicked and he slid it back into his pocket. Zack didn't understand that, in his line of work, he didn't bother with regret.

THREE

Lara's eyes widened as she realized a crowd waited outside her tall, Beaux Arts–style building.

Connor sat in the backseat of her father's staid Benz and sighed. "I told you they would show up."

"Are those reporters?" Her dad peered through the windshield as dusk gathered while they waited at the stoplight about a block from her home. "Should I drive past them?"

It was odd to see her very take-charge father deferring to Connor, who still didn't have a damn last name. She'd meant to ask him, but Nipplegate had happened. Then they'd argued over where she would sit. She'd wanted to ride in the front seat by her father. Connor had insisted she treat her dad like a driver and stay in back with him.

So naturally she found herself plastered against Connor, who had curled his arm behind her, cupped her shoulder, and slid her across the leather seat, dragging her close. "Senator, I think the best way to handle this is to blast through quickly. The press is a little like a kid with a shiny new toy. We're only interesting until they've played with us a couple of times. Then something shinier will come along. I'll take

Lara upstairs. She's tired and she's been through a lot today. You'll make a statement that today's incident is simply proof that D.C. needs more funding for crime prevention."

They were missing an important opportunity. "And mental health screenings. And less motorcycles on the streets because they're dangerous and the people who drive them are crazy douche bags. Damn. He was wearing a helmet, wasn't he? I could have taken a real stand against people who don't follow helmet laws."

Connor's hand around her shoulder tightened as he chuckled. He was amused by her, and that honest smile did something to her insides. "Let's get through the night. Then you can start your campaign against motorcycle douches tomorrow. After getting run over by the herd, I'll join you in that one."

She hadn't even asked if he'd been hurt. What was wrong with her? He'd protected her, made sure she'd gotten to the hospital. Yes, he'd totally taken over her life and was trying to upend it from top to bottom, but she needed to know he was okay. "Do you need to see a doctor? Is anything broken?"

"I'm a little sore. I think I almost got murdered by some chick's Choo, but it didn't break the skin. Other than some bruising tomorrow, I'll be fine." He lowered his head to hers as her father lurched forward with the green light, toward her building. "It's sweet of you to worry. Look at me, Lara."

He'd maneuvered her so that even her thigh felt glued to his. His face hovered above her own as he pulled her even closer into the heat of his body. Somehow her right hand had found its way just above his knee. The softness of well-worn denim covered his muscular leg. Lara shivered.

She immediately pulled away, but he dragged her hand back.

"No, you were right the first time. This is why I wanted you back here with me. We're supposed to be together. Boyfriend, remember?" He pointed at himself.

"Connor, do you really think that's necessary?" her father asked.

"She . . . well, she hasn't dated much. I don't know that she's very . . . um . . . comfortable around men, if you know what I mean." He stopped the car in front of the building, ready to make a left into the circular drive where the vultures waited.

What had her father just implied? "I'm comfortable with men."

She settled in closer to Connor. There was that chuckle again, though this time she felt it go through his body.

"Your daughter likes men just fine, Senator. She's a little out of practice, but yes, this ruse is necessary. If the press knows she's hired a bodyguard, the story will seem so much more interesting, and we want to look as boring as possible. Senator's daughter and her bodyguard equals a story to tell. Senator's daughter has a loving boyfriend equals a big yawn."

She looked up at Connor, and he was staring down at her intently, as if he wanted her, cared about her. That expression—which couldn't be real—made her tingle in some very personal places. That just had to stop.

She turned back to her dad, their eyes meeting in the rearview mirror. "You thought I was a lesbian? Not that there's anything wrong with that, you know. But I'm not."

Her father turned a nice shade of pink. "Well, when you broke it off with Tom, I wondered a bit. And then you spent so much time with that Kiki girl."

"You thought I was sleeping with Kiki?"

"Tom?" Connor's whole body had tensed, his lazy affection evaporating. "As in your friend who knows everything, including your occupation? That Tom? You left him at the altar? Which altar was that, Lara? Please tell me it's the one where you sacrificed his soul to some dark lord."

"Tom knows?" Her father stopped the car in the middle of the damn intersection. "You told me no one knew. You promised."

It had been just one little tiny baby lie to make her dad feel better. "It's just Tom, and of course I didn't sacrifice him to Satan. I just called off our wedding. Oh, and Kiki knows, too, but I've never slept with her. Although she did offer to share Connor here with me."

Connor's jaw dropped, and she wondered how often he was left speechless. Probably next to never. But his shock didn't last for long. "Let me get this straight. You told your deepest, darkest secret to a man you betrayed?"

That was a little overly dramatic. "I didn't betray him. I just didn't go through with our wedding."

"I knew that Kiki girl was a bad influence," her father said, shaking his head. "Lara, I forbid you to get involved in weird three-way sex."

How the hell had this conversation gone downhill so quickly? She was glad she and Connor weren't in a relationship for real because she wasn't sure she could survive her dad and Connor working together to badger her.

Connor's jaw firmed into a tight line as he reached for the ball cap he'd pulled from his duffel before setting it in the front seat. "Senator, we need to move. I'll settle this with your daughter when we get upstairs. Keep the press off us and we'll call you in a couple of days. And there will be no three-ways while I'm in charge of her. We're going to talk about security, sweetheart. And decency."

Her dad turned and she watched as one of the reporters apparently recognized the car. "I'm glad that you have a healthy sex life, Lara, but you don't have to share men with your friends. There are more than enough to go around."

"Kiki mentioned it, but I'm sure she was joking." *I think.* "And I don't have a healthy sex life." She was doing that nervous word-vomit thing where she blurted out whatever came to mind. "The sexiest thing that's happened to me lately was Connor covering me when that douche bag started shooting. It's the first time I've had a man on top of me in years."

Why had she said that? She was fairly certain her whole body had gone pink.

Connor caught her hand, threading their fingers together, and then brought it to his mouth for a brief kiss that flashed another wave of heat through her system. "It was good for me, too, sweetheart. We're here. Follow my lead."

The door opened and she was nearly blinded by the lights flashing.

"Lara, do you think the killer was coming after you over your father's stance on welfare?"

"What was it like staring into the face of a man who wanted to kill you?"

"What were you doing at the bus stop? Planning a protest? Did you stage this danger to bring light to a cause you believe in?"

She whirled around because that last question was ludicrous. "The bus is a better way to travel than private vehicles. Do you know how much gas we would all save if just ten percent more people took the bus to reach their destinations?"

Before she could say another word, she found herself cradled against Connor's chest, her face nearly buried in his T-shirt.

Then her father stepped in. "Ladies and gentlemen, my daughter was having coffee with her boyfriend on 2nd when she was caught up in a random act of violence. It's been a long day, and she's tired. We ask you for some space and privacy so she can rest. The police know more about the incident than we do, but I believe this near tragedy should force us to look at funding for police officers and first responders . . ."

While her father went on, Connor expertly maneuvered her to the front entrance and had her through the door before she could explain her stance on gun control. He walked straight to the bank of elevators. "What floor? Quickly before they decide to follow."

"I'm on ten." She looked back out the windows. The reporters surrounded her dad, pointing cameras and microphones in his face. They seemed to be honoring his request to give her privacy—for now. She breathed a sigh of relief . . . before she realized something was wrong. "How did you get in? You need a keycard to have access to the building."

The elevator doors opened, and he hauled her in. She noticed that the way the ball cap sat on his head obscured his face. He set his duffel at his side, punched the button for ten, and turned to her. "I stole yours. You need to keep it in a better place than loose in your purse."

"Well, I didn't expect anyone to try to steal it."

"Because you're naive, and I'm convinced of that because you think it's a good idea to let the fiancé you dumped in on your secrets. Why don't you just take out a billboard? Put your secret in neon lights."

It had really been a hell of a day. "It's my life. I run it the way I want."

"Not while I'm in charge, you don't. And you need to relax around me. If your father hadn't distracted those reporters, there's no way they would have believed we're in a relationship. You were stiff. Hell, you barely looked at me. You certainly don't act like a woman who has an attentive lover."

Had he not heard a damn word she'd said? "Because I don't. This is all stupid. It will go away. I'll hide out in my apartment for a few days and this crap will be behind me. Then you can go back to California and order around all the women you like. And I'm stiff around you because you scare me."

He was suddenly in her space, and it felt as if all the air had been sucked from the elevator. His chest brushed hers and she couldn't help but tilt her head up to meet his demanding stare. He was so tall, so big and broad and manly.

"Then I have to make you comfortable around me in case this threat doesn't go away. You're stuck with me for a while. We might as well enjoy the time, sweetheart."

"What does that mean?" The question came out all breathy and come-hithery when she'd really meant it as an intellectual question. Mostly.

"It means follow my lead and we'll get along nicely. Relax, Lara."

His mouth hovered right over hers, and she felt his hands trail up her shoulders and caress her neck until he cupped her face. "I'll take care of you."

"They'll never buy it." She couldn't quite believe she was standing here with him, her heart threatening to pound out of her chest.

"I'll make them. And I'll make you believe it, too." His mouth descended, covering hers.

Connor was so hard. His lips shouldn't be that soft. But they were, as well as plump and sensual. It had been years since she'd pressed her body to a man's and felt his dizzying heat seep into her cold bones until she melted into him.

His hands sank into her tresses. "So fucking much hair. It's going to make me crazy."

She wasn't sure how her hair could do that, but then he kissed her again and she couldn't think about anything beyond the tingles she felt from having his hands and his mouth on her. He was utterly in control and she didn't care. So much of her sex life up until that moment had been unremarkable. She loved to cuddle, but the actual sex act hadn't thrilled her or even meant much. She'd certainly never just given over to a man. Her high school boyfriends had been too shy, and Tom had never liked kissing much. Lara hadn't minded because he'd been a little sloppy.

There was nothing sloppy about Connor. As he backed her against the cool metal wall of the elevator, he seized her in a slow, thorough melding of lips before he kissed his way over her cheeks, her forehead, and even the tip of her nose, as though he could explore her with his mouth.

"Open to me." His words sizzled along her skin.

The minute she parted her lips the slightest bit, he was on her. His tongue surged in, sliding against hers in a way that made desire spark and her body shiver. Without even thinking about it, she pressed against his until she could feel the masculine part of him thicken against her belly. He didn't do the gentlemanly thing and pull back. No. Connor actually rubbed himself against her as if he couldn't wait to get inside her.

She meant to do the ladylike thing and shove him away . . . except her hands seemed to have the same affliction as her nipples. Before Lara realized it, she'd wrapped his lean waist in her grip. Her left leg slid up his right. He gave a gentle tug on her hair and delved deep inside her mouth, his tongue dominating her.

Somewhere in the back of her mind she felt the elevator stop and heard the *ding* announcing the fact that they'd reached their destination, but it wasn't until she heard Tom's voice that she came out of her haze of lust.

"Lara? What the hell is going on?"

She finally found the will to push Connor away, to bring her leg—god, it was practically around his hip now since she'd been humping the man's thigh—back down to where it should be. She turned and saw not only Tom wearing a look of pure shock on his face, but Kiki grinning beside him.

"So you hired him after all?" She winked. "Good choice."

Connor picked up his bag. "See, they believe it, sweetheart. I told you I could make them believe it." He stared at them. "How did you two get in here?"

Kiki stared at him as if she exerted a conscious effort not to drool. "I live on four. Tom left work when he heard about the shooting."

"Excellent. Well, that was what I needed." He strode out of the elevator like nothing had happened.

"Lara, what are you doing with that idiot?" Tom asked. "We heard the news and got here as fast as we could. No one would tell us anything. Now we find you making out with the help?"

"I'm highly skilled labor if that helps any." Connor stepped back into view. "And I'm going to need to talk to both of you. Lara, let's go. I would prefer to have this conversation in private. Which door do these open?"

He dangled a set of keys in front of her. They were a mishmash held together with a SAVE THE ORCAS key chain. Yep, he'd stolen her keys . . . and she was pretty sure he'd just walked off with all the dignity she had left.

"1024."

"Excellent. The four of us should go have a talk because you're about to find out we're all one happy family. Lara, I hope you have Scotch."

She shook her head. "No. I have herbal tea."

"Then we'll send out for some when we order dinner. Let's go." He turned and walked down the hall like he owned the place.

Like good little soldiers, Kiki and Tom followed. Lara thought seriously about darting back in the elevator and fleeing the country.

"I'll find you if you run," he shouted down the hall.

With a sad sigh, she forced herself to move. And her nipples were hard again. Damn it.

Connor settled in after hanging up the phone. The minute everyone was in the condo, Lara's crew had hightailed it to the back of the unit. He was sure they were trying to talk Lara out of hiring him, but that ship had sailed the minute he got her father on board. Still, her friends could make things difficult for him. Connor wanted to get a few things in place before he dealt with the problems ahead. Namely, food and drink. He'd taken one glance inside Lara's fridge and known he would need help to survive. The woman didn't even have real milk. Apparently someone had decided to slap whatever the hell came out of almond teats into a milk jug. So he'd made a list of necessities and called a delivery service.

If connected to the right people, one could get just about anything delivered in D.C. A twenty-five-year Glenfiddich was on its way. He preferred the fifty-year, but he had a down-on-his-luck image to maintain. In addition to the Scotch, he had burgers and fries being catered in. He definitely wasn't going to be able to live on whatever tofu crap Lara intended to serve.

"I thought you were broke and stuff." Lara stood in the hall that led back to her living room. "That's an expensive bottle of Scotch."

Ah, that's where the senator had done him good since he couldn't use his own very-high-limit credit cards without blowing his cover. "Perks of the job. Your father gave me a healthy per diem. Don't worry about a thing. I'm all paid for. I have to say, I'm glad your dad stepped up because Niall was paying me next to nothing."

"I don't think my dad gave you that money so you could buy booze." She'd done nothing but frown his way since the moment that elevator door opened and his rival for her affections had entered the picture. Oh, sure, she and Tom were no longer dating, but from the nasty looks the other man sent his way, Tom was obviously still interested. Despite the guy's pale-eyed, metrosexual vibe, Connor didn't think Tom intended to simply give up. Not that he gave a shit about Lara's ex, but he was surprised to discover he didn't like her frowns. He'd definitely preferred it when she'd smiled at him.

"Your father understands the need to relax. Unless you can think of a more interesting way?" He grinned. Needling her was rapidly becoming his favorite pastime.

"Jogging," she shot back, crossing her arms over her chest. "It releases all kinds of endorphins."

He'd noticed she'd walked in and immediately covered her torso in a thick hoodie that proclaimed she was a woman earth warrior. Interesting wardrobe change since the thermostat was set to seventy-six in the apartment.

"That's not going to work." He shook his head. "Whatever activity I choose to relieve my stress has to be something we do together. I can't let you out of my sight, and I don't think it's smart to be out in the open until we figure out who's shooting at you. We'll need to find something we can do as a duo and in this apartment. Alone. Can you think of anything?"

"You're a jerk." She spun around, the sneakers she'd changed into earlier squeaking on the hardwoods as she stalked out of her very organized kitchen that apparently contained no meat, cheese, or alcohol beyond something called organic blueberry wine.

He stared at the opening she'd just huffed through like the little princess she was, that sweet ass of hers swaying. He hadn't gotten his hands on it when they'd kissed. He'd been distracted by the softness of her silken-spun hair and her plump lips. He'd been so consumed with kissing her that he'd forgotten to fill his hands with her lush backside.

He'd meant the kiss to prove that he could handle her and he would be in control. He'd intended to stake a claim, to shove his way into her life even more than he already had. She was too polite and used to deferring to the people around her, so Connor had known that if he simply pushed his way into her circle, she would accept it. Oh, she might frown at him, might use that pretty mouth of hers to spout shit at him from time to time, but she wouldn't kick him out. Hell, she hadn't been able to get rid of that fiancé of hers for years.

Yeah, the kiss was supposed to have been his show of power. Instead, he'd almost lost it. When he'd pressed his lips to hers, she'd sighed a little before completely giving over to him. Her reaction had been so open, so honest. She hadn't held back or prevaricated. She hadn't teased him. He'd fully expected the kind of flirty negotiations women often engaged in before sex. It was a little bargain between soon-to-be lovers. Women always wanted more, and the smart ones knew how to get what they wanted, whether it was money or introductions to his powerful friends or information. They would kiss him, press their bodies to his, and then pull back until he agreed to their terms. It had been that way ever since he'd lost his virginity during his Creighton days to a college girl who wanted an introduction to Maddox Crawford.

Lara Armstrong hadn't engaged in any of that coy negotiating. She'd just given it up. Like she wanted nothing more than him.

The minute he'd felt her leg start to move against his, he'd thought seriously about punching the button to stop the elevator. His instincts had taken over, and every one of them told him to press her back against the wall and burrow deep inside all that insanely hot sweetness. To take all of her sugar for himself.

Bracing himself on the kitchen counter, Connor took a deep breath. His cock ached just thinking about how hot she'd been. He would give it to her, every inch he had. The innocent act really did it for him.

And if it wasn't an act? If she really was that sweet and soft and naive?

An odd, almost nasty half growl caught his attention. When he looked down, he spotted a rat. No, maybe that was a dog . . . or some weird combo of the two. Whatever it was, the little animal sat at his feet, staring up at him with a less-than-menacing glare.

"You are the single fugliest thing I've ever seen." And it was irritable. Its little body shook as it unleashed a high-pitched bark his way.

"Lincoln!" Lara was back and she quickly picked up the dog. Yeah, now that he looked at it, the thing appeared to be some mix of Chihuahua and dachshund. It had a weenie-dog body but the triangular face and shaking that accompanied the poor creatures with Chihuahua DNA.

On the other hand, he kind of envied the little mutant because Lara picked him up and cuddled him to her chest.

"You named that thing Lincoln?"

Her chin came up, a sure sign she was ready to be stubborn. "Lincoln was a noble man. I want this little guy to be noble, too."

There was no way that squirming thing could ever be considered noble. "Was it homeless before you picked it up?"

Lincoln studied him from the safety of Lara's arms, still growling and yipping. Lara used her free hand to pet the thing. "He's a rescue dog. There are so many dogs who need homes. I've had him for a couple of months now but he still seems really surly. I guess it's just his nature."

Well, if Connor weighed three pounds soaking wet, he might have an attitude, too.

"Who the hell do you think you are?" Tom stalked into the kitchen from the back of the unit. He still wore the nice slacks and polished loafers he'd worn to work, but had since changed into a black T-shirt to try not to look like the lawyer he obviously was.

Kiki was still wearing the clothes from earlier, a sexy boho-chic skirt and a peasant blouse that showed off her mocha and caramel skin. "I think he thinks he's her bodyguard. With benefits."

"There are no benefits." Lara shook her head. "Huh. That's actually sad when you think about it. Bodyguards should get benefits, too. Have you thought of unionizing?"

"No." Oh, he intended to make sure she became intimately familiar with every beneficial part of him, but explaining that to her would just get him in trouble. First, he needed to deal with the two potential troublemakers in front of him, and he couldn't do that if he didn't keep Lara on task. If this had been a normal mission, keeping them quiet would have been easy, but Lara would likely throw a fit if her two besties ended up disappearing from the face of the earth. She would probably lead a search team with canines eating cruelty-free foods or some shit.

Sometimes it was way easier to deal with the dregs of the world. At least he always knew how they would behave.

"Look, Senator Armstrong and I reached very reasonable terms, so I'm doing my job. I'll be more effective if I have less interference." He put on what he hoped was his reassuring face and told himself to behave as normally as possible. And by *normal* he meant not killing them because he didn't want to listen to their whiny lawyer voices anymore.

"I don't care what her dad says. He's gone straight out of his mind. I think you should leave. There's no way you're staying here. She doesn't even know you," Tom said with a sullen pout.

Yep, not crushing Tom's windpipe with one hand was going to be an act of pure mercy on his part. "Could we all sit down and talk about what happened?"

Lara nodded. "Yes. I think that's a very good plan. Let's form a friendship circle and talk this out. That will bring Connor into the group and make him feel comfortable."

Kiki grinned impishly. She wasn't so bad. "I don't think that man has ever been in a friendship circle. Maybe we should get the drums out. Lara spent some time with a tribe in Ecuador who believes that drumming together aligns souls and makes for better negotiations."

Dear god. There wasn't enough Scotch in the world. "I think we can skip the drumming."

Lara nodded. "It makes Lincoln howl and then my next-door neighbor yells at me. He's a very unhappy man."

Oddly, Connor didn't like the thought of someone yelling at her. She would never yell back. She would likely try to "understand" the man. He pushed those thoughts out of his head. He wasn't here to protect her from herself. "Let me put this to you as straight as I possibly can. Do you two understand that someone tried to kill Lara this afternoon?"

Tom's eyes widened and he slumped down on Lara's love seat, making a place for Kiki to sit beside him. "The radio said they thought it was random or maybe some form of drug deal gone bad."

He would be honest with them—to a point. "It wasn't. The gunman stopped right in front of where we were sitting and pointed straight at her. There's no doubt who his target was." He turned to Lara. "My first question is, who knew where you were going to be this afternoon?"

It was time to start getting some real answers. Sure, the whole bodyguard thing was a cover, and once he found the information he needed, she would be on her own, but he had to look like he was doing his job.

"I met Lara at the coffeehouse, but I had to leave before you got there," Tom admitted. "I don't think she told anyone about it but me and Kiki."

"She just wanted company in case you turned out to be creepy," Kiki added. "Of course then she got a look at you and she dumped my ass really fast."

"I did not. I just realized that I was late. You totally could have come along." Lara sent her friend some seriously pleading looks.

This would be a tough group to keep on task. "So, Lara, no one else knew where you were going to be this afternoon?"

She turned to him and shook her head. "No one. I just told Kiki and Tom and only because a woman on her own can't be too careful. Anytime I'm meeting someone, I always make sure one of my friends knows when and where the meeting place is."

Something about the way she'd hesitated over the word *always* made him think she was lying.

He would bet half his fortune that her friends didn't know she was meeting Deep Throat.

"All right. I'm going to need to figure out who's tracking you and how. I need access to anything you were carrying with you today." Most likely, someone had traced her cell phone. He'd run a few programs to see if someone had tampered with her device.

Tom held up his phone. "Or you could just look on Facebook. She told all 3,274 friends of hers exactly where she was at. See? She checked in at Ebenezers."

He would always have to remember that he wasn't dealing with a polished operative. He was dealing with someone more like Miley Cyrus, and if she'd been shot, she would likely have taken a selfie of her bullet wounds and posted it on Instagram before bleeding out. He turned to Lara, who gave him a sheepish smile.

"Yeah, I forgot about that. I do little check-ins through the day. You know, in case there are any friends who happen to be in the area."

"Yes, I understand. Social networking is so important for your generation. It's how you let assassins know where to find you. Lara is . . . enjoying a latte. Please come murder her." He crossed his arms over his chest and gave her a stare assured to send the most seasoned operative into a fetal position. "You will shut down all social media today."

Lara just stared back at him. Her eyes narrowed, her lips thinning, and he wondered if she was making fun of him. "Won't that send out the wrong message? We told the press this attack was random. Shouldn't I act all normal and stuff?"

Freaking hell, she was right. "All right, but I'm in charge of your social media now. You don't put a single word out there unless it goes through me."

She coughed, but he could have sworn it sounded like *Gestapo*.

He ignored her. He wasn't the Gestapo, Nazi Germany's infamous state police. He was so much fucking worse, but she would find that out on her own. So he had narrowed down his suspects to roughly 3,200. Thank you, Internet.

He turned to Tom and Kiki. "I've been told you two know about Lara's website."

Kiki sighed. "You really think this is someone Capitol Scandals burned? Do you think those people would follow her social media?"

"If I'd had my life trashed by a tabloid and found out who ran it, you can bet I would use everything I had to track that person down," he explained.

"I told you that site would get you in trouble," Tom complained.

Lara sat on the couch, apparently expecting Connor to take the single chair since she spread out. "You didn't hate the site when I ran that article on the circuit court judge selling verdicts."

Tom shrugged. "He was a total asshole and his clerks were jerks. They kept me out of the fantasy football league. They deserved it."

It was good he had his priorities. Connor shook his head. "Your opinion of the site is irrelevant. All that matters is figuring out who's trying to kill Lara."

"Isn't this what the police should be doing?" Tom asked.

Kiki rolled her eyes. "As childish as he made that question sound, it's valid. Why aren't we letting the police handle this? I'm not questioning Connor's ability to protect you, but the police have resources he just doesn't have."

She had no idea what resources he could call to his fingertips, but he couldn't explain to her that he could count on both Langley and the executive branch to aid him. "I'm good with investigations and I'm excellent with a computer."

"But the police . . ." Tom argued stubbornly.

"Connor and my dad think that's a bad idea," Lara explained.

"Since when do you do what your dad tells you to?" Tom shot back.

"Since he ganged up on me with him." Lara was pointing his way. "They're surprisingly immune to my arguments."

Those big blue eyes were killing him. Fuck. She was cute. He didn't do cute. He wasn't the guy who liked cute intellectuals with great asses. He definitely wasn't buying into her bullshit. Professional. That's how he had to stay, which meant getting some distance between them. Except when he went to sit down, he found himself on the couch, plunking down right beside her so she damn near fell against him.

"Hey. I left that seat for you," she said, scrambling to right herself and Lincoln, who was growling again.

"I think it's best if you got used to me being on top of you," he said, settling in. "In a nonliteral sense, of course."

She would look pretty riding his cock.

Fuck, had he just thought that? He could sleep with her for the sake of the mission, but he would be in control. He would never again be vulnerable like he had with Greta.

He forced his head back in the game. "If we bring the police in, we have to tell them our suspicions."

Kiki groaned. "And then they find out about Capitol Scandals."

"The police could keep that quiet," Tom insisted.

He was as naive as Lara. "Maybe the cops wouldn't mention it, but if the press got wind of an investigation, they would start digging and it wouldn't be long before they found her out. She's got a good setup. While I'm here with her, I'll strengthen her firewalls and put some more layers of protection in, but she'll always be vulnerable."

"So you're covering up the murder attempt to keep it out of the press," Tom allowed. "What's with the lip lock? Are you trying to convince her that sleeping with you is good protection? That's kind of sleazy, isn't it? Or is that the way she's paying your fee?"

After that comment, surely rendering the kid unconscious would be acceptable. Maybe even applauded.

"Tom, are you trying to say I would sell myself?" Lara's face had turned a vibrant red and Connor finally knew what she looked like when she was actually angry.

Tom backed down really quick, his angry posture changing in a split second. His shoulders slumped and his gaze slid away from hers. "I'm so sorry, L. I would never say that. I'm just upset because I think this guy is using you. We should talk to your dad."

"I told you. Dad is all on board with Connor. Apparently Connor's in good with Hayes, and you know Dad really wants into that circle." Lara sat back.

That was a dangerous line of thought. The last thing he needed was someone thinking he was in Zack Hayes's inner circle. "Not exactly. I did some work for the president back when he was just a kid in Congress. He came overseas on a fact-finding mission. He was part of the Armed Forces Services Committee. Well, what happened after that is classified, but he told me afterward if I ever needed a reference to go to him."

Zack had actually been in the Middle East with a congressional committee, and Connor had provided security. He'd just been in the CIA when he did it and he certainly hadn't been merely muscle. He'd been responsible for evaluating any and all threats to the American delegation.

So he wasn't exactly lying. It was always best that any story he told her held a grain of truth.

"Tom, I have the skills needed to protect Lara. Her father is confident in that and so is she." He looked her way.

She didn't appear at all confident but after a few seconds, she got the idea. She nodded. "Yes. I am. He's right."

He needed to work on her acting skills. "And I kissed Lara in the elevator because it's part of our cover, one all of us need to stick to. You two and her parents are the only ones who know that she's the force behind Capitol Scandals."

"And that there's a douche bag who's trying to murder me," Lara added.

"Obviously, we don't want him in on our plan. Tom and Kiki, if anyone asks, I expect you to keep our cover. If a reporter happens to phone you for a quote, you tell them she's doing all right and she's happily nesting with her new boyfriend."

Kiki clapped her hands in what seemed like delight. "You're going to pretend to be her fiancé so the press doesn't think she has a bodyguard because then the press would wonder why she needed one and bam, we're right back where we started. I love this plan."

"Boyfriend," Connor corrected. He damn straight wasn't anyone's fiancé. He'd never even come close to wanting that.

"Fine, boyfriend with an eye to marriage because no one's going to believe Lara would just start sleeping with someone off the street," Kiki explained.

Tom huffed a little. "Right. No one will believe that."

Lara held up her left hand and those blue eyes sparkled with mischief. "I think I look best with a princess cut, but no blood diamonds. You have to make sure you don't buy conflict gemstones. We're going to be an earth-kindness home."

He held up a hand to stop that line of thought right there. "Hey, slow down, princess. This isn't real and we'll just say we've been talking over the Internet."

"Yeah, L. How are you going to explain this to your real boyfriend?" Tom sounded a little like a six-year-old on the playground. "How's Niall going to take it?"

He watched her flush again, but this time any anger or mischief was gone. In its place was something he feared. Guilt. Shame.

Fuck it all, she thought she was really in love with Niall Smith. Niall Smith, who didn't actually exist. Niall Smith—Connor's own creation—was likely going to keep him out of Lara's bed.

"I'll talk to him tonight. I'm going to see if I can get him on the phone. I don't want him to think this is real at all." The words came out in a rush.

Lara's hand drifted restlessly over the dog. Lincoln, as though sensing his mistress's deep distress, settled down and rubbed against her.

"How serious is this thing with you and Niall?" Connor asked.

"We're friends, but we've talked about trying to be more. You know what a great guy he is," Lara said.

"You know you've got a whole country between you." She had to see that it couldn't work.

"That's what I told her," Tom explained.

He hated being on the same side as Tom, but this was a problem he should have thought of. All his careful planning could go up in smoke. He reflected on everything and realized he'd played Niall far too well. He'd constructed the guy to be a savior of endangered animals, her intellectual equal, and a sensitive activist. In short, her fantasy. Niall seemed a little like a walking vagina to Connor. If he didn't work this angle correctly, his imaginary creation could screw up everything.

Fantasies always beat out reality. He needed Lara to trust him, to turn to him. Deep Throat was coming back, and Connor wanted Lara to tell him everything because he was important to her.

He couldn't be as long as Niall was in the picture.

"Who knows," Lara said with a wistful smile on her face that let him know she'd been thinking about this for a while. "He might like D.C."

Connor shook his head. "No. That is one California boy. He won't ever leave."

"Then maybe I'll like California." She stood. "I should go and make dinner. Isn't your package going to be here soon? I assume you had them deliver something that previously had a face and a mother who probably loved it very much before she was brutally murdered for her meat."

Niall was a vegan. Another point for him. Shit. He should have sucked it up and eaten whatever she put in front of him. He gave her a wink because there was nothing to do now but brazen through. "You know the secret ingredient to any burger is love."

She frowned and flounced away, her ugly dog in her arms, likely dreaming of a man who didn't exist and who would have to prove himself to be all too human very soon.

Tom leaned over, his eyes wide. "Please tell me you ordered enough for all of us because I heard her talking about tofu tacos. I can't do that. Have you ever tried to pass vegan cheese through your digestive tract?"

Kiki shook her head. "Men. I'll go help Lara while you two plan your next kill."

"I don't kill it," Tom called out. "It just shows up in a nice plastic wrapper at the grocery store. It could have died a natural death. We'll never know."

Kiki stopped in front of Connor. "If you like my friend, you should know that Niall is going to be an issue for her. I think he's too good to be true and I don't trust anyone I meet on the Internet, but she's spent weeks building some serious picket-fence dreams around him. And I've seen his picture. He is a very cute boy."

Connor had used pictures of a barely-out-of-college intern who'd once done work as a wilderness guide in Northern California. He was a twenty-four-year-old kid with too-long blond hair and a smile that could probably get him in the movies. In all the pictures on his social networking sites, Niall was climbing a mountain or river rafting.

Niall wasn't covered in scars, both internal and external. He wouldn't use sarcasm as a shield. He was bright and fucking shiny, like Lara herself. Niall didn't cling to the shadows because the darkness felt like home.

If this was a fairy tale, Niall would be the handsome prince and Connor the villain who tore him away from the fair princess and broke her heart.

Lara was going to have to get used to the fact that this wasn't a fucking fairy tale and princes didn't exist. It was time to start resetting her expectations.

"I'm afraid she doesn't know everything about him."

Kiki's eyes closed briefly, and she sighed when she opened them again. "Just let her down easy. She really likes him."

"He likes her, too, but that doesn't mean he's right for her. Or that he's in love with her." At least he'd been careful about that. He'd been flirty and nice, but he hadn't said anything about love. Even when he was playing a role, he would never have mentioned that word.

"Tell me he's an asshole." Tom seemed more than willing to talk to him now.

Kiki shook her head and walked off as the doorbell rang. "That's probably your food, carnivores."

When Connor got to the door, he realized it was so much worse.

A small army stood there. They were a motley group. A couple looked damn near homeless, but that was just how twenty-year-olds seemed to dress these days. There were two elderly ladies, one complete with a walker. A worried-looking mom with a child clutching each of her hands.

One of the homeless stepped up. "Is Lara here? We heard about her on the news."

He was just about to toss them all out when he heard a little cry behind him.

"Oh, I'm fine. Please come in." Lara threw the door wide open and the mass shuffled inside.

Tom slapped him on the back. "Welcome to her world. No one's a stranger. Good luck keeping her alive."

Yeah, he could see that he was going to need it.

FOUR

Lara shut the door on the last of her visitors and hoped they'd bought the act. She'd had to smile and pretend to adore Connor. She'd explained that they'd met through mutual friends, but he was based in California and this was his first trip to D.C.

Her friend Barb, a divorced mom of two who lived on the fourth floor, had asked if Connor had a brother. The elderly sisters from the eighth asked if he had a record. Freddy, a fellow truth seeker from the second floor, had told her bluntly that Connor was obviously a CIA agent here on a mission to silence them all.

Sometimes Freddy had a vivid imagination.

"You have an interesting group of friends." Connor sat on her couch like he owned the place. His left ankle crossed his right knee and he sat back, a glass of Scotch in his hand. The lord of the manor. She could see him as a medieval duke, staring out over his peasants before he chose a pretty servant girl to share his bed.

That was so not a politically correct fantasy. She crossed over to her bar and poured herself a glass of rather potent blueberry wine. It was organic and local and sometimes she wondered if the FDA shouldn't step in because more than one glass really got her going.

She poured half a glass. She needed her faculties against him.

Lara turned and joined him in her small living room. She sat across from him on the love seat.

"There's plenty of room here." He gestured next to him.

No way. She'd spent the last three hours practically on his lap because there had been no place else to sit. In fact, she could still feel his arms around her. "I'm fine over here. You and Lincoln seem to get along now. I've actually never seen him so calm."

He was sitting on Connor's feet, his tiny body curled up as he slept. "I figured out what his issue was."

"What? Do you have some veterinary experience? Because he has a ton of issues. He doesn't sleep well. He never sleeps for more than an hour or two at a time. I think he has PTSD. Dogs can get that, you know."

"He was hungry." Connor's lips pulled up in a grin and he tipped his Scotch toward her. "Just a hungry mongrel, like the rest of us."

"He can't be." She stared down at him. About halfway through the impromptu gathering, he'd stopped growling. Usually she had to put him in her bedroom, but tonight she'd actually forgotten he was there. Not so great for a pet mother, but Connor had kind of taken over. "I keep his bowl full all the time."

"Yes, I saw that. What's vegan dog food besides torturous for the poor animal?"

"It's a compassionate way for an animal to eat. I try to live my life with as much kindness and compassion as I can, so I put Lincoln on a vegan diet, too."

"Let me tell you something, princess. Your dog likes burgers."

Anger flashed through her system. "You fed him meat?"

"The little fucker wouldn't leave me alone. I gave him a taste just to shut him up but then he whined so I gave him more. Your friend Tom was a little like the dog. He wouldn't shut up until I gave him a burger, too. I only got two. I'm actually still hungry."

She couldn't believe he'd done that. "He's my dog. I make the choices for him. You just ruined his diet. He won't go back."

He regarded her with all the seriousness of a lazy but hungry lion, as though he was deciding if tearing her up was worth the effort. "He never was there, Lara. He's a dog. He was born a carnivore. He'll die one. It's his nature."

"He was fine."

"He was hungry and that made him angry. You say you're all about compassion, but your dog was hungry."

She knew some vets who said it could be done. Plenty of animals lived on a vegan diet, though once meat was introduced it was very hard to get them to go back. "You have all the answers, don't you?"

His face softened, but only slightly. "Not at all, but I do know that trying to change a creature's nature will only bring heartbreak for you and him. The world isn't a pretty place, and you can't change it by feeding your dog a bunch of vegetables."

"So I shouldn't try. Yeah, I've heard this one before." There was no point in talking to her bodyguard. They wouldn't be friends. She knew his type. He probably thought she was stupid and naive, that she caused more problems than she solved. Whatever. He wouldn't fit in her world and she didn't want to fit into his. "I'm going to work for a while."

She headed for her office. Until this guy was caught, she would spend as little time around Connor as possible. The last thing she needed in her life was another man who thought she was an idiot. Even though her dad loved her, he didn't understand, either. No one seemed to.

Connor caught her hand as she started past the couch. He fixed his stare on her. "They all liked you. That whole group of people. They were each different, but they got together because they like you. What do you do for them?"

She shrugged. "I don't know. I share meals with some of them. I watch Barb's kids from time to time. I help some of the college kids with their essays. I'm really good at that."

He let go of her hand and nodded as though satisfied. "So they use you. That's why they were here. They wanted to make sure you didn't get hurt so they could continue to use you."

What the hell had happened to him? "No, I'm a part of their community. Our friendships aren't one-sided. Those same old women whose prescriptions I pick up taught me how to knit. And Barb always checks in on me. She sometimes does my laundry when I'm too busy. The college kids helped me get my furniture in this unit. We help each other."

"Sure. You go on believing that." He turned back to his Scotch.

"I might be naive, but you're cynical."

"Like I said, you can't change a creature's nature. I'm going to need all their names. I have to run checks on everyone who was here."

"Why?"

"To see if any of them might have a reason to kill you."

"Yes, because my eighty-year-old neighbors own a motorcycle and a revolver."

"It was a semiautomatic," he corrected. "I didn't get a good enough look to know the model. And just because they can't physically do the deed themselves doesn't mean they didn't pay someone else to do it. People always have their secrets. So get me a list of names."

And he would start trying to dig up dirt on them. "I won't do it."

"Lara, we can't have an adversarial relationship between us. I'm not the bad guy here." He reached down and picked up Lincoln, settling him on the couch so he could turn more fully toward her. In the evening shadows, the planes of his face looked even harsher, starker. It did nothing but enhance his attractiveness. "I am sorry about Lincoln, but I think you're wrong. All dogs are different. Some might be able to handle a vegan diet. I don't think he could. If what you're telling me is correct and he's had all these issues since he's been here, they're probably dietary. Meat is easier to digest than grains, which gives him issues. So how far does your compassion go? Will you try it again and put him through this? Or will you feed him what he needs? Or does he no longer meet your requirements as a pet because he can't follow your cruelty-free lifestyle?"

"So now I'm a vicious radical?" She hated the fact that she was tearing up in front of him. "I only care about the people who meet my exacting standards? Make up your mind about me, Connor. In the course of a single day I've been a one-percenter who didn't care about poor ex-military men, an idiot who isn't smart enough to stay off Facebook, and now I'm the vegan police, shutting out anyone who doesn't follow my code. I should really pick a persona."

She broke away from him.

"I need that list."

She was sure he couldn't see her, but she flipped him off anyway.

Her office was blissfully quiet. She went over to her desk and sank into her chair. Her Mac and the massive screen she used were a welcome distraction to the fact that the most interesting and infuriating man she'd ever met was still sitting in her living room, and he wasn't leaving anytime soon.

Deep breath. Let out all the bad energy. This was her space. This was where she felt powerful, and she wasn't going to let Connor's disdain taint her sanctuary, where she really could help change things.

And damn it, she was going to have to buy Lincoln more dog food. She certainly wasn't going to let him starve and she wouldn't give him up. She had plenty of friends who weren't vegans. Hell, she had gun-toting friends who thought the world was coming to an end. She wasn't isolated. She got along with everyone.

Everyone except Connor.

She touched the keyboard, bringing the big screen to life. Forty-five e-mails to the Capitol Scandals account. She flipped through them quickly. Some were indictments of her as a human being. Several thanked her for what she did to call for accountability. There were the requisite advertisements. Somehow the Internet thought she was a married woman looking for a hookup to cheat on her husband, and a man in need of little blue pills to cure sexual dysfunction.

And then there was the ad that popped up in her e-mail.

Farmers' Market this Saturday at the Lincoln Memorial. Great deals at noon. Don't miss out! Bring your friends for all the best produce American farmers can offer.

Her breath caught. It was a code. There was no farmer's market at the Lincoln Memorial; a product would be offered. Information.

Two months earlier, a man who claimed to have information concerning the death of Maddox Crawford had contacted her. He'd given her a name: Natalia Kuilikov. She was still looking for the mystery woman, but she felt as if she was getting closer.

How did all the pieces of the puzzle fit together? Something was going on but she just couldn't see the big picture yet. She was intrigued because this Kuilikov woman had something to do with Crawford's death, and Crawford had been friends with the president. The president had a group of friends he'd known since prep school. The Perfect Gentlemen. A few of them were very high profile. Gabe Bond, Maddox Crawford, and Roman Calder were media darlings. She'd heard there were two more but they were in positions that didn't garner exposure. One, Daxton Spencer, was an active-duty military man. The sixth guy apparently had no name, at least not one she could find. But he was a rumor anyway. Either way, all of the Perfect Gentlemen were ruthlessly protected by both the White House and the nation's intelligence agencies.

She had to keep digging for information, maybe find out who else had ties to the president.

Find out who he might have hired to murder his wife.

She focused on the words in front of her. They were a code she and the informant had worked out once he'd told her he couldn't contact her in conventional ways.

The meet site was the Lincoln Memorial. Easy enough to get to. Saturday was five days from now. How was she going to get away from Connor so late at night? Lara shook her head. She had time to solve that problem. From there everything else in the message was opposite. *Noon* really meant midnight. *Bring your friends* meant come alone.

As she pondered ways to ditch Connor for her meet, her Skype pinged. She felt a goofy smile cross her face. Niall. She clicked the icon and his sweet face popped up.

Hey, pretty girl.
Hey! I was just thinking about you.
Did Connor make it okay?
Yes. He seems very competent.

She wasn't going to go into the whole "she'd almost gotten shot" thing. She had other plans. It was past time to figure out where their relationship was going. Lara started tapping on the keyboard again.

But I was actually thinking about coming out to California for a couple of weeks. How about we get on the phone and talk? Or we could turn on our cameras and see each other for once!

Seeing Niall, getting to feel like he was here, would be a balm after the crappy day she'd had.

A long moment went by and then another one. She stared at the computer, getting more and more anxious. He must have stepped away for a minute.

I don't think that's a good idea, Lara.

A nasty feeling began brewing in her gut. He wouldn't even turn on his camera? **Is it a bad time?**

Look, I talked to Connor and he thinks I need to be straight with you. Actually, the fucker told me if I wasn't he would beat the shit out of me. I guess I didn't think he would sell me out like that, but there's Connor for you. I should have known.

Yep. She was a little nauseous. Not in all the weeks they'd been talking had he used a single curse word with her. Not once. Now he sounded like all the other guys.

She sighed. **Just tell me.**

It's nothing and it doesn't have to change what we have. I want to meet you. I want to be with you, Lara. We're in synch, you and I. When I get some time off, I'll come out to D.C. and we can hook up.

But she couldn't come to California? **What's nothing? Tell me.**

I'm married, but it doesn't mean anything. I don't love her. I'm just kind of stuck. But I think about you all the time. You make everything else worthwhile. I'm going to leave her. Meeting you has really given me the courage to walk away. I just need a little time. But that doesn't mean we need to wait.

Tears blurred the screen. Married. He was a liar. He'd seemed perfect, and like all perfect things, he was a mirage.

Really, Niall had a brilliant shtick. Treat a girl like a lady and pretend to care about her causes. It sounded so simple but he'd elevated it to something like an art form. He'd sure tricked her. Likely it was something he did to a lot of women.

Don't contact me again.

Before he could ping her once more, she blocked him from her system.

She'd been ready to sleep with him, ready to move the relationship forward. And Connor knew. That suddenly seemed like the worst part. He was probably laughing at how stupid she was. If he'd contacted Niall today, then he'd known she would learn the truth soon.

She took a deep breath, then exhaled. She had to reach her bedroom without him finding out. She needed to shut the door between them and have some time to process alone.

"Hey, you all right?" And of course he was standing in her doorway.

She stared straight forward. Her Skype screen was still up. She closed it and opened her browser. "Sure. Just getting some work done. If you're tired, you can take the bed. I'll probably just stay in here."

She had a teeny tiny chaise lounge that was mostly for show and a place for Lincoln to sit while she worked. It would do. There was no way she was getting a ton of sleep anyway.

Married. He'd wanted to use her to cheat on his wife.

"You're not okay, Lara. Did you talk to him?"

"Yes. I'm fine. I broke off our little flirtation and blocked him from contacting me again. So I'm no longer involved with your friend. If you want to leave, feel free."

"Hey." Her chair turned and he stared down at her, his gorgeous eyes searching. "I'm not leaving and I didn't agree with what he was doing. Male friendships are different. I've known him for a while. I don't agree with him and that's why I told him he had to tell you or I would."

Why wouldn't Connor leave? She supposed he'd meant well, in his way. But right now, she really needed to be alone. She wouldn't be able to hold her tears back much longer. "It was good to know before I got invested. Thank you."

"You were invested. A woman like you is always invested, and that's why he can do what he does."

She turned and went right back to staring, but not before she felt a tear slip down her cheek. God, why couldn't she be stronger? Why couldn't she be cold and stoic?

"Fuck."

She hoped he would go away, but he did the opposite. He turned her chair around again and before she could protest, she found herself being hauled into his arms, her whole world suddenly filled with Connor. It was as if the minute he touched her he occupied all the space, shoving out senseless things like oxygen and light and replacing them with warmth and strength.

"Don't cry, Lara. I don't like to see you cry." He said it as though he was surprised, as though it had never really occurred to him that someone else's tears could be disturbing. If he'd tried to kiss her, she would have pushed him away. If his hands had moved down to her ass, she would have kicked and fought. Instead, he merely rested his cheek against her hair. Lara sighed.

"I'm so sorry. If I could have spared you that I would have." He sounded sincere.

The floodgates opened. She couldn't help it. The day had been spectacularly crappy and it had ended on the worst note possible. She'd almost rather have taken that stupid bullet than find out the first guy in years who had called to her heart was nothing but a cheating jerk.

She'd been so lonely. Until now, she hadn't realized just how much. She'd tried to cover it up with work and an active social life and a new dog.

Connor stood there for what seemed like hours, just letting her cry against his chest. Somehow it was easier to let go of all the pain when she wasn't alone. His warmth drove out the cold pain she'd felt from the moment she realized Prince Charming was just another asshole who wanted to use her, who didn't really give a damn.

Gradually, she calmed down.

His big hand moved through her hair, stroking it down. "I'm so sorry."

She forced herself to move away from him. She probably looked like hell, but she tilted her head up to face him. "It's not your fault. I'm sorry for crying all over you."

He shifted to cup her shoulders, moving restlessly against her skin. "It's okay."

"It's been a hell of a day. First you have to save the damsel in distress, who then turns into a crying chick. I know it's not your usual deal."

His eyes were softer than she'd ever seen them. "I don't mind, Lara. Like I said. I feel responsible. He's my friend and he hurt you. I really will kick his ass. I don't approve of how he treated you. I don't like that he made you cry."

She reached for a tissue. "I wouldn't have expected you to care. What did you say about a creature's nature? I wouldn't have thought it would be in yours to comfort a woman because she figured out how dumb she'd been."

"Don't say that." His voice sounded the slightest bit harsh, and he gripped her shoulders again. "You weren't dumb. Niall was selfish. He's known how you felt and he should have been honest." He let her go and took a long breath. "And you're right. It's not in my nature to comfort."

"I thought you couldn't change a creature's nature."

"You can't, Lara, but maybe sometimes the right person can bring out something that got buried. Maybe. I don't know. I just . . . Let's go and get a drink or something."

It was obvious he was uncomfortable and because he'd been so kind to her, she let him off the hook. "It's okay. I think I'm going to bed. I'll just stay in here for the night."

He looked between her and the chaise. "No."

"No? What does that mean?"

He didn't reply, merely leaned over and lifted her in his arms—one under her legs, the other around her back. He hauled her up as if she weighed nothing and started out of her office.

"What are you doing? 'No' doesn't mean carry me around like a sack of flour."

He flashed her that crazy sexy smile. "I wouldn't carry a sack of flour like this. And I won't let you be miserable all night. You've had a rough day and I'm putting you to bed. It's part of my job."

He seemed to know where he was going. He crossed through the living room and walked past her guest bath, straight to her bedroom. "Get undressed. We're going to sleep. We'll wake up and everything will seem better in the morning. Well, everything except breakfast. I imagine that will be a lot of tofu bacon, but I'll eat it if you'll smile again."

When he set her on her feet, she got her PJs and dutifully went to the bathroom and changed. She caught a glimpse of herself in the mirror. Wow. No wonder he was worried. Her skin was red and puffy. She could never cry prettily. She washed her face. Connor was right. Everything would seem better in the morning.

She was a delusional optimist.

He was already in bed when she walked out. True to his word, he'd taken the left side of the bed, the one closest to the door. Lincoln was already asleep in the little bed she'd bought for him and placed in the corner of her room. Now she kind of wished he slept with her. The only light in the room was from the lamp on Connor's side, and she was struck by just how intimate the situation was. He wasn't wearing a shirt, and his broad shoulders and all the defined muscles of his chest were on display. They were alone in a bedroom.

"Come on, princess. I'm not doing anything tonight but sleeping, and I'm staying this close because I genuinely believe I can protect you. I think you'll sleep better if you know where I am. And if I try anything, you can call the president and tell him what an asshole I am."

She slipped into her side of the bed, but not before she'd seen that he was wearing a pair of boxers. She shifted, trying to get comfortable. Luckily it was a queen, but Connor was really big. He took up more than half the space.

The light went out.

"I really am sorry about Niall," he muttered.

"It's okay. I'll get over him." She would. She had worse things to deal with than a boy playing at being a man.

"He didn't deserve you."

She let his words warm her and she fell asleep far faster than she'd thought possible.

C onnor came awake to the feel of something warm on his cheek. He forced himself to stay still. Whatever had touched him didn't seem to be trying to kill him, though he could be wrong about that. But he was completely awake now, not that he usually slept much anyway.

Which made him question why the sun was obviously up. Though he hadn't opened his eyes yet, he knew the difference between night and day.

He'd lain down with Lara to persuade her to drift off. If he hadn't, she would have slept in her office, the very place he'd needed to search. He'd only planned to lie down until she fell into dreamland, then he'd intended to creep down the hall and download everything on her system. He'd found himself watching her sleep and wondering how the hell anyone could look so fucking innocent. She'd headed into slumber facing away from him, but not two minutes after her breathing had turned even and deep, she'd flipped over to face him, one arm out as though reaching for him. He'd lain there and watched her, the moonlight caressing her skin and making her look like a fairy princess.

Another warm lick hit his neck.

Was it too much to beg the universe that Lara had decided she liked the way his skin tasted and was, even now, tonguing him in a sweet attempt to get him to wake up and fuck her? He really didn't want his cock to be this hard from that damn dog. He hadn't gotten a morning hard-on in forever, but he definitely felt it now. Of course, it might have more to do with the dream he'd had. He didn't like to dream since most of them turned into nightmares where he replayed all of his worst fuckups, but his most recent dream had been about him delving into Lara's little body, driving out all her thoughts of that stupid Niall and filling her with himself.

Maybe she'd been dreaming about him, too.

No such luck. He opened his eyes and there stood Lara's dog with its weird body and bug eyes.

"Lincoln, don't do that." Small hands with a pretty pink manicure scooped up the canine and carried him away. She knelt down and her face came into view. "I'm sorry. I thought he was in the kitchen with me. He seems to really like you. I'm making waffles. I have organic maple syrup. Do you like coffee? I have some fair trade beans."

He was grateful he was on his side because if he'd been lying on his back, those probably organic cotton sheets would have formed a massive tent. He needed a cold shower and a pound of bacon. He was only getting one of those here. "That sounds great."

Even without a hint of makeup and wearing blue pajamas bottoms and a tank top with a dolphin on it, she was the sexiest thing he'd seen in forever. And that was just wrong because she was wrong for him. He liked his women sultry and overtly sexual. Not soft and sweet as freaking cotton candy. He liked women who controlled their emotions, not ones who sobbed in his arms over some idiot who had never existed in the first place.

He liked women who didn't make him feel lust and guilt in the same moment.

And god knew he was all wrong for her.

"Great." Her eyes were just a tiny bit red, like she'd cried again this morning, but now she was putting on a good face. "Breakfast is in ten minutes."

She popped up and strode back to the kitchen, leaving him alone in her superfeminine bedroom.

He rolled to his back and stared up at the ceiling. He'd slept all fucking night. What the hell? He never slept for more than an hour or two at a time. He'd wake up and check out wherever he was staying, then sleep again briefly until the night was over and he rose to tackle the day.

He did some of his best work during those in-between times. What he did not do was sleep for eight hours peacefully without once waking up to do his flipping job.

Shaking his head, Connor rolled out of bed and headed for her bathroom. Just like the rest of the condo, it was decorated in sunny colors. The bathroom was predominantly a bright yellow with touches of white and blue. The shower was almost big enough for him. He shucked his boxers and turned the water straight to cold because his morning friend showed no signs of abating.

The chilly spray hit him, the temperature jarring his jaw to lock. Unlike most of the things in this town, that water was just as advertised. Cold as hell. He welcomed it as it forced him to focus on something other than his pretty pixie.

He had to figure a way out of the conundrum he found himself in. He needed to search her office, but the events of the previous day left him with no choice but to stay close to her. He might need to think about bringing in Dax. When he'd last talked to his buddy, Connor hadn't been sure Lara had a true, credible threat. Now he knew better. The proof was in the bullet.

He would keep her close today, then scour her office tonight. The fewer people he had to bring in, the better. After he'd gone for good, she would need to forget he'd ever been here in the first place. That would be easier if her only real contact besides him was to a man she now thought of as a complete dick. Even if she tried to contact Niall in an attempt to talk to Connor, she would find Niall's very leftie website and all his social media taken down.

Damn. He sounded like an asshole. He never felt guilt. He didn't have room for it in his life. He did the things he must to keep his country and his president safe. He took the responsibility for whatever that entailed. If it meant lying, he lied. If it meant killing, he killed. If it meant breaking a silly girl's heart . . . well, then he held her and slept beside her and acted like he was a fucking twelve-year-old with his first hard-on.

With a shake of his head, Connor finished washing off. The frigid water had done what he'd needed it to. His unruly cock had fled, practically burrowing back into his balls. At least that was a relief.

And then it was right back to hard as a rock when he heard her humming along to something she was playing on her sound dock. He groaned as he shoved into a pair of jeans and a T-shirt. Naturally she was playing something acoustic. Some sad dude on a weepy freaking guitar whining about his lost love. It was the type of music that was so full of estrogen it should shrivel his cock, but no. It pressed against his zipper insistently as though it had turned into a divining rod with one purpose—reaching Lara Armstrong.

Would that be so bad? He walked out of the bedroom, warring with a conscience he'd felt certain had gone numb long ago.

Damn it, he was of two minds. Well, he was of one mind and one dick. On one hand, fucking Lara would likely buy him an enormous amount of her loyalty. While he'd lain there watching her, he'd discarded the idea that she could be a con artist pretending sweetness and innocence. She wasn't underhanded enough to pull that off. She had neither the street smarts nor the experience. Lara Armstrong was exactly what she seemed. She was naive enough to believe she could save the world. Hell, he'd seen her circle of friends. She operated with conviction and a strong core of loyalty, even when the person she was loyal to didn't deserve it.

He wanted her loyalty for himself. All of it. Connor couldn't exactly explain why. But like a greedy kid with a toy, he wanted to come first with her. The only way he could do that was to seduce her. Sex would mean something to her. Hell, a flirtation on the Internet with a fictitious guy had meant something to her. What would a real man in her bed, plying her body with pleasure, mean?

His dick was all about that plan.

And then he would picture her crying again. After this mission, he wouldn't stay with her. He would move on to the next job and never look back. He couldn't explain and he wouldn't call her afterward. He would simply be gone. How used would she feel then? At least as Niall he hadn't actually fucked her. A mind fuck, yes, but somehow it seemed kinder than actually taking her when he knew how invested she probably was before she'd go to bed with a man.

"I don't think so, sweetie." Lara's words were soft over the sounds of a hipster caterwauling about his lost dick or whatever.

She'd better be talking to the damn dog.

"It's the way he moves," a masculine voice said back. "I was trained the same way. He watches everything."

"Well, he was in the Navy. I suspect they train their sailors, too. And given his chosen profession, I'm thrilled he's very observant. Otherwise, I would likely be dead. I didn't notice that man on the motorcycle at all. I was too busy talking to Connor."

Freddy. He caught sight of the man's profile. He was likely in his early thirties. Red hair. Pale face. The guy had little tics that gave Connor pause.

"Yeah. But I find it interesting that no one tried to hurt you until he came into your life. Don't you?" He spoke in a staccato rhythm, the words like rapid fire from a machine gun, and then he would halt on a dime as though he needed to reload. "There are no coincidences in life. None. The timing is too perfect. You get all those leads and he shows up? I smell a rat. We should look into—"

The man turned and spied Connor over the bar that separated the kitchen from the living/dining area.

Connor really wished Freddy had finished that sentence. What did the guy want to look into? And how bad did Freddy think he was? It was obvious Lara's oddball pal had cast him in the role of the villain.

"Morning." He tipped his head, staring Freddy down.

Lincoln barked and raced out of the kitchen toward Connor, his tail wagging.

Freddy frowned, his stare landing anywhere but on Connor. "I'll go. Talk to you later, Lara. Call me if you need me."

He shuffled out, giving Connor a very wide berth. Lara followed behind, but she didn't hug the man. She didn't touch him at all, which was odd behavior for her. He noticed the previous night that she often touched her friends. Each one got a hug as they left—except Freddy.

She would never withhold affection.

"He doesn't like being touched, does he?"

She turned after locking the door. "He can't stand it."

Unlike the rest of her friends, Freddy was clean-shaven, his hair cut in a very precise military buzz. The khakis he'd worn had a perfect crease to them, as though the man got up and starched and ironed his casual clothes. There were a couple of kinds of people who might do that. Clean freaks by nature. People suffering from OCD. Neither of those fit. Connor came to the obvious conclusion.

"He was military, wasn't he? Was he taken prisoner at some point?" The military wouldn't have accepted him with the tics, ergo the military had likely been the very place he'd gotten them. PTSD. It often came with an honorable discharge.

Lara nodded. "Yeah, how did you know that? He doesn't like to talk about it."

"I'm good at deduction. I can also deduce that he likes you a lot, and he can't stand me." He'd watched Freddy all evening. Though Freddy didn't like to meet anyone's eyes, he damn sure got an eyeful. He watched Lara constantly when she wasn't looking. He practically worshipped her with his stare.

Connor found that annoying.

She walked back into the kitchen and started pulling breakfast together. Connor noted she'd already set out two places at her little four top. "I wouldn't take it too poorly. Freddy doesn't like a lot of people. He's suspicious of everyone. You two have that in common. Your coffee's on the table."

He would have to look into Freddy's background. "Getting hauled into an enemy prison camp can certainly make you that way. Iraq or Afghanistan?"

It could also make a person obsessive if they already had that bent. Trauma like that could amplify all sorts of problems.

She returned with a plate of waffles. A big bowl of fruit and a jug of organic maple syrup sat waiting. Despite his misgivings about her diet, his stomach rumbled.

"Afghanistan. He was in the Korengal Valley."

Where some of the nastiest fighting had taken place. Connor had been in and out of there, a shadow collecting information and disseminating it where needed before melting away again. "I guess Army guys never like us sailors."

She sat down with a little sigh. "Oh, he thinks that's all a cover and that you're really a CIA agent sent in to steal my secrets. Crazy, huh? So this is a blueberry waffle. Instead of eggs, I used applesauce as a binder. I think it makes them very moist."

She might have said something else about making the applesauce herself, but Connor was thinking about how he was going to have to shut Freddy up. She didn't believe him. That was obvious—and helpful. Sometimes, it was better to hide in plain sight.

He smiled her way, hoping it was reassuring and not the look of a man who was hungry for way more than waffles. "They look great, but we need to talk about protocol."

She stabbed a waffle and dragged it to her plate, her nose wrinkling sweetly. "I don't like that word. It sounds like discipline and rules."

He would love to give her a little discipline. He could smack that pretty ass until it was a nice shade of pink and then maybe she would start listening to him. That image didn't do his cock a bit of good. "Rules are important. And the first rule is you don't open your door anymore. I open it."

"I looked through the keyhole. I knew who it was," she argued.

He took two waffles and hoped she only wanted a couple since she'd

SEDUCTION IN SESSION   95

only prepared six. He could easily eat four by himself—and still want more. She obviously wasn't used to cooking for a man with an appetite. Of course, she also wasn't used to cooking for a carnivore, so they had problems beyond her not making enough carbs.

"I don't care who it is, Lara. Even if you trust them with your life, they could still be carrying a gun or have one pointed at them. Had you thought of that? The easiest way to get to you is to bring someone you care about into the danger."

She went still and took a deep breath. It was finally hitting her that they weren't playing some game. "Should my dad do anything? He doesn't have a security detail. He's never seen the need for it."

"I already discussed this with your father. He's interviewing body-guards today. He's going to hire two I recommended so he has someone with him twenty-four seven until we clear up this threat. He's hiring a detail for your mother as well. I talked him out of bringing her home. I think she's safer on the West Coast for now."

"Why is someone doing this?" Her question came out on a sad sigh.

"You know why."

"I'm careful with the website, Connor. Almost all of my tips come through secure lines."

"No line is ever totally secure."

"You don't understand who my informants are. They're not hack-ers. They're not savvy. They tend to be people close to the subject. I talk to a lot of angry mistresses and pissed-off wives. I get tips from house-keepers who didn't feel like their Christmas bonus was enough so they turn in their employer for taking bribes. You would be shocked at what staff hears."

Because for the superrich, staff was a little like background noise. Even in Dax's home, the maids had been quiet mice scurrying in and out.

He had to wonder if they'd known how depressed Admiral Spencer had been. Had they been watchful but remained silent until the day Dax's father had pulled his own trigger?

Somehow seeing the closeness the senator and Lara shared made him think about Hal Spencer and how the man had played ball in the backyard with his son even when he and Dax had been teens. The first time Connor had gone home with Dax during a school break, the admiral had bought Connor a glove and pulled him in, too.

It still ached that the man had eaten a bullet.

He needed to get the fuck out of here. Somehow, someway, Lara brought out the emotional shit he thought he'd locked away long ago. He didn't like the muck she dredged up. Fuck. He didn't like feeling anything at all. And he kind of resented her for it. "Do you think this stalker wants you on a sexual level?"

She flushed immediately. "No. Why would he try to kill me if he wants me?"

"Did you tease some man, then refuse to follow through? You seem to have Freddy on a leash. It's barely after seven in the morning and he's already up here trying to save you from me. There were a couple of those young guys last night whose gazes lingered. And don't forget Tom. Do you dangle the promise of sex in front of him to keep him in line?"

"That's horrible. I'm not that woman." She scowled at him. "Why would you say that?"

He shrugged. "I'm merely trying to investigate all the possibilities. You said you were careful with the website so I have to look into your private life. Is your friend Kiki a jealous woman?"

"Why would she be jealous of me?"

"Because you have all those men around you."

"They're just friends. Besides, Kiki has no trouble getting men of her own. Seriously, I don't date. I thought I had something going with Niall, but you saw how that turned out." She sighed. "I don't want to talk about this right now."

"You don't have that option, princess." He was getting to her. Like any fruitful interrogation, the best way for him to get inside her head was to rattle her. Not surprisingly, she seemed easy to shake up.

"I don't like it when you call me that."

"Ah, you're one of those women who can't stand endearments. You think they demean you? Take away your feminine power? Maybe you would you prefer Ms. Armstrong so you can feel better about yourself."

Her fork clattered to her plate. "No, I don't like it when you call me that because I don't think you mean it as an endearment. It sounds like your snide way of calling me spoiled, and it hurts."

His guilt rose to the surface again. No one in his world ever admitted that someone else had hurt them, but Lara Armstrong, with her fuck-me, love-me, protect-me eyes just put it right out there. And her tearful voice made him feel like shit. What the hell was wrong with him?

"You're misunderstanding me. Have you had issues with Kiki in the past?"

She looked down at her plate. She'd eaten maybe a bite. "She wasn't happy with the way I left Tom. She thought I should have let him down sooner."

Connor had finished off his waffles and reached for another. Interrogations always made him hungry and these were good. "So she liked Tom and was jealous of your relationship with him."

"No," she replied with a shake of her head. "She'd been telling me for months she thought it wouldn't work and I put off ending it. She was angry because she thought I was being a coward and hurting a lot of people. She was right. Why do you put the worst spin on everything I tell you?"

It was time to get to the heart of the matter. "Because I'm a realist. So according to you, everything is fine in your world. Your informants are all idiots who couldn't hack a system if they tried, and no one would ever want to hurt you because you're beloved by all. So the question becomes are you so sweet and beautiful that the world simply can't handle your awesomeness? Maybe someone is so jealous of how amazing you are that they can't allow you to live. What are you and Freddy investigating?"

"The president." She stopped and sat for a moment as though really surprised she'd answered him.

It was an old trick. Speak rapidly. Ask a few emotionally packed questions but leave no time for the subject to reply. Then ask the whopper. The tactic threw many off balance and they simply answered the first moment he gave them an opening. And they usually blurted the truth.

So she was after Zack. He should have known that. In her world, Zack would be the ultimate prey. How much did she want Zack's head on her mantel? She might not eat meat, but in his book that made her a predator.

"So you don't approve of the president. Why are you investigating him?"

She shrugged and went back to her waffle. "He's the president. I run a political blog. I'm always investigating him."

"Political blog? Isn't that overstating it a little? You run one of the most salacious gossip sites on the Internet. What are you looking into? The size of his dick again?"

She pushed away from the table. All of her joy had fled and the shadows from the night before were back. "Is Connor your first or last name?"

"Why?" He shouldn't engage her. He knew damn well he should press on with his questions. Never let the subject get the upper hand, but the question was out of his mouth before he could stop it.

"Because I'd like to use your last name when we talk. It puts more distance between us." She was obviously trying to be cool, professional. The sheen of tears in her eyes and the way her hands trembled gave her away.

"It's my last name," he lied smoothly. "My first name is Spencer."

Spencer Connor. It was a horrible name, but he'd given it to her father so he had to go with it. Now he was glad because the last thing he wanted was to hear her call him by a name that wasn't his. He liked the way she said Connor. Even when she was mad at him.

She pushed back from the table. "Well, Connor, I think I'm done with our arrangement. I'll stay with my father until this is over. I'm not going to sit here and allow you to bully me. You're mean. Maybe other women would let you tear them apart because they think you're hot and society lets assholes like you get away with anything, but I don't play by those rules. I'll go pack and you can decide if you're going to be civil enough to drop me off in Arlington or if our association ends here." She turned and started to walk out.

He reached out and gripped her elbow. "I wasn't done. I need to figure out who's trying to kill you. Would you rather I was polite and kind and simply let them shoot you?"

Her mouth trembled as she looked down at him. "I would rather you not take out whatever is bothering you on me. I haven't done anything to you and yet you're trying to tear me up."

"I'm questioning you."

She shook her head. "It's more than that. I've done nothing but trust you and let you into my home, but it feels as though you resent me."

So she saw way more than he'd expected her to. She was so soft, so bubbly that he'd really believed he could break her down. It was what he did. He drove a subject past their endurance or tolerance, then built him or her back up to his liking. He'd been treating Lara like an enemy combatant, and she was having none of it.

He released her arm and she strode away, slamming the bedroom door behind her. She might be naive but she had more backbone than he'd given her credit for. Once again, she'd gone straight to the heart of the issue with no prevarication. He did resent her in that moment because he hated anything that made him feel. Sometimes he even hated his friends.

He remembered vividly standing in the Crawford building in the middle of Manhattan, dark enveloping him, his hands covered in blood. He'd killed and killed that night in an attempt to keep Gabe Bond and his girlfriend safe. He'd looked at the pair, over what seemed like an ocean of bodies between them, and he'd known that he would never have what Gabe had. No woman would ever look at him as if he was the sun in her sky. He wasn't a blessed American prince like the rest of the Perfect Gentlemen.

He was the monster who protected them. He bought his way into their world with blood.

He'd looked over and seen the horror in Gabe's eyes that night. He'd seen how quickly his friend had hustled Everly out, as though he couldn't stand to have his beloved in the same room with such an animal.

He didn't hate Lara, but she damn sure reminded him of everything he couldn't have. He'd gotten his wealth in a way she would think indecent. He could offer her a view of the Upper West Side to die for, his lonely mansion outside of Langley, a flat in London's Chelsea that not even his friends knew about. He had millions at his fingertips, but like the rest of what he owned, every cent had someone's blood on it.

She was a fairy princess who'd figured out that she had invited the beast to her breakfast table. And she was a smart princess since she had enough sense to run away.

His cell phone trilled and he looked down. Dax. The man always had the best timing. He ran his finger over the screen. "Yes."

"Hey, I've got some information on your girl. It looks like she came up to New York during the week Deep Throat was meeting with Everly. I can't track all her movements, but I think we can assume she's involved with him. I think we have to look into whether or not she's actually pulling his strings and not the other way around."

The thought was laughable. "She's not a mastermind, Dax. She's running after a story and I'm a little worried this asshole is going to box her in the same situation he did Everly. I want to find the little fucker. He damn near got her killed yesterday."

Despite his interrogation, he was certain the incident the previous day was about whatever muck she'd stepped into while fact-finding for her blog. What she did was dangerous. The men and women she reported about were some of the world's most powerful people. To think they would simply let Lara publish dirt on them without penalty was foolish, but then he had no proof otherwise that she was anything but. Tilting at windmills. That's what she was doing. The windmill was about to knock her out, and if he allowed her to push him away, she would have no one to protect her. No one understood the true situation the way he did.

Sure, she could stay at her dad's for a day or two, but then things would quiet down and she would get bored. She would tell herself that one little trip outside wouldn't hurt.

Bam. Just like that she would be dead.

He really didn't like his vision of her gone and cold. It twisted his insides.

"You sound like you care," Dax said quietly.

"I care about the case and I care about the fact that she seems to think she has something on Zack." He kept his voice low, moving into the kitchen.

"What? Is it about the nanny? Deep Throat made Everly believe that Lara had a piece to that puzzle."

"I don't know. I didn't get a chance to check her office or her computer last night."

"Why?"

"I fell asleep," he mumbled, feeling like an idiot.

"You're kidding me." A low chuckle came over the line. "Did you fall asleep from sheer exhaustion? I didn't expect you to get into her bed so fast. I have to admit, the way you described her, I kind of thought your charms wouldn't work on her."

Because he so rarely used charm on a woman. He didn't have to. Not in his world. In the shadows he inhabited, power was the key. Power and practicality had gotten him into many a bed, but none of that would work with Lara. "I didn't fuck her. I just slept with her."

There was the longest pause.

"Damn it, Dax. Don't fucking laugh at me. This is serious. I'm screwing this up. She's packing to go to her father's right now."

"Good," Dax said shortly. "Then you can break into her place, get the job done, and get back home. We can hire some PIs to trail her."

It wasn't a bad plan but Connor hated it. Logic didn't matter. Neither did common sense. He tried to tell himself he was only thinking of the case, but his dick had taken over. He wouldn't leave her. "She's too important. After the attack yesterday, I don't think we should just abandon her."

"We? Or you?"

Fucking Dax was going to make him say it. "Me."

Dax muttered something that sounded awfully like *son of a bitch*. "All right, then, brother. How bad was this fuckup?"

"I was interrogating her. Questioning her about what might have incited the attack on 2nd Street. I went too far. I might have insulted her on two or three levels."

"Her intelligence?"

"And her moral character. Probably her femininity, too. Definitely her friends. I might have implied that she likes to string men along and use them, and then I might have said something about her being a bottom-feeding tabloid reporter."

"Jeez. You really went for it." Another long pause. "Are you sure you want to do this?"

He was sure he wanted to do her. For once in his life, he could have the princess—at least temporarily. She was wrong about the way he spoke that endearment. To him, she really was a princess. In the best way. "Yeah. I have to find out what she's got on Zack."

"Sure. All right, first off I'm coming down and there's nothing you can do to stop me. You need backup."

Connor wasn't going to argue. Having another set of eyes on her would be a good thing. "Okay. Just text me all the information you found, and I'll start feeding you our schedule. I'm also sending you a list of names. Share it with Everly. They're friends and neighbors of Lara's. I need to know if any of them has cause to want to hurt her. Now tell me how to get her back."

Dax was smooth with women. Oh, he was an idiot who'd lost the only one he'd ever really cared about, but the man knew how to handle females. With his good looks and the Spencer charm, there wasn't a bar he went home from alone if he didn't want to. "First, you have to apologize and you have to make it good."

"I don't know that she's going to accept a simple 'I'm sorry.'"

"Tell her you're so used to dealing with people who lie that it's hard for you to believe when they're being honest."

That was definitely part of the truth. "Okay. I can go with that."

"And then take it a step further. Tell her you don't know how to deal with a woman like her, one you know would never give you the time of day and that hurt, so you took it out on her. Tell her you want her but you know you can't have her."

And there was the rest of the truth. Dax had always seen right through him. Had he met Dax Spencer as an adult he would have pushed the guy away as fast as he could. But he hadn't and childhood had bonded them so tightly. Now he couldn't shove the fucker out of his life, even if he'd wanted to. "All right. Call me when you get in."

"Will do. And good luck, brother."

Connor hung up. He looked to the back of the apartment, where Lara was likely cursing his name. Honesty. He had to throw her a little. He had to get her to trust him or nothing would work.

Luck? Yeah, he was going to need a lot of that.

FIVE

Lara sniffled as she pulled out her overnight bag. She kept some clothes at her parents' place. Still, she had no idea how long she would be there. Maybe she should pack for a couple of weeks. She'd have to call the vet and find a place to board Lincoln since her dad was allergic. Or maybe someone in the building could watch her little guy while she was away.

Damn it. Why had Connor turned out to be so horrible? She couldn't work the way she needed to at her parents' house. And how the hell was she going to meet her informant on Saturday? Her condo was only a couple of miles from the Lincoln memorial. If she stayed with her father, the distance to her meet point would be more than double. She would have to drive in or take the Metro. Sneaking past the new bodyguards her father was hiring might be a challenge, especially if Connor had recommended them. And her informant had been very specific. She had to come alone.

Everything was falling apart, including her composure.

"Hey."

She didn't turn around. The last thing she wanted was for Connor to see her crying again. Over another damn man. That was the worst part. She looked like a fool because she'd believed that men she didn't know well in the first place were good guys. She let herself care when she shouldn't. She'd been right to bury herself in work. It didn't break her heart.

"I'll be ready to go in a few minutes. Are you going to take me to Arlington or should I call my father to pick me up?"

"I wish you wouldn't go at all." His deep voice washed over her. He wasn't using his military, rapid-fire, brooked-no-disobedience voice now. He'd switched to the same lazy drawl he'd used the night before when he'd put her in bed.

Of course he didn't want her to go. He needed the paycheck. She was certain her father's generous per diem only lasted as long as he was actually protecting her. God, she hoped the next bodyguard was unattractive and polite. She would keep her interaction with the next one strictly professional. "Well, it's for the best. Maybe this will all settle down if I spend some time out of town."

"Arlington isn't really out of town."

"Fine. We'll call it lying low, then." The last thing she was going to do was get into another argument with him. She'd learned she couldn't win.

"It's also the first place I would look if I was the kind of predator who wanted to kill you. If you're going to run, it's a safe bet that you would run home."

"Well, I'll shut down all my social media sites and I'll figure out a place no one will look." She fisted her hands in frustration. It was a useless emotion, but Connor seemed to incite it with ease. "It doesn't matter. It's not your problem anymore."

"I'm sorry, Lara. I had no right to interrogate you in that manner."

But it was his nature, and he'd flat-out told her that she couldn't change his. She'd gotten sucked in by his beauty and the tenderness he'd shown her when he had held her as she cried. She'd been duped by how good it felt when he'd covered her body with his. He'd been doing his job and she'd been crushing, like some teenaged girl on a pop star. "It's fine."

"It's not." He was right behind her, and her stupid body reacted. It was as if every sense she had went on high alert the minute he walked into a room. "I was mean and I was wrong and my only excuse is that I acted out because I was jealous."

He couldn't have said a single thing that surprised her more. She turned around, nearly colliding with him. She had to look up to see his face. "Jealous of what?"

"I didn't like Freddy in your kitchen this morning. I didn't like those college boys around you last night, and I definitely don't like the thought that Tom feels as if he has any right to your time or attention. I want those things for myself."

What kind of game was he playing? "You don't even like me. You've said it."

"When did I say that? Did I say that when I kissed you? When I picked you up and carried you to bed? When I tricked my way into sleeping beside you?" His head shook in a sharp, definitive no. "I'm a man, Lara. I'm a one hundred percent testosterone-laden Neanderthal. You can't judge us on our words. We're not good with those. You have to look at our actions."

"Your actions are those of a man doing his job. And you can't put that on me. You said hurtful things to me and now you're telling me I misinterpreted them? It's my fault?" She wasn't going to get caught up in that. She'd had enough of that crap with Tom. Besides their lack of heat in the bedroom, Tom had a bad habit of never taking responsibility for anything.

He didn't give her any space to breathe, just kept looming over her with dark eyes. "You're going to make me say it, aren't you?"

"I'm not making you do anything, Connor."

"I want you."

She rolled her eyes. Yeah, that wasn't going to work on her. His "confession" was enough to break the spell. He'd said the words in a cold, almost hostile way, as though he resented it. She wasn't going to be resented. She walked to her closet and selected a couple of pairs of comfortable jeans. "Let me spare you the dissatisfaction, Mr. Connor."

"Just Connor, and I'm screwing up again. Tell me what I did wrong. I don't understand."

"Fine, Just Connor. You picked the wrong subject to come at me with. You should have tried to tempt me with something a little more academic like your friend, Niall. Now there was an asshole who knew how to manipulate a woman. I'm not some sex kitten who's going to go crazy the minute you touch me. Others have pointed out that I'm a little frigid."

And maybe that was okay. That's what she told herself every night she went to sleep alone. It was all right to not need sex the way everyone else seemed to. She had other gifts. As far as she could see, sex really only got a girl in trouble anyway. She'd had a high school boyfriend and Tom. Neither had praised her as a lover.

"Did Tom tell you that?"

He might have screamed it at her when they'd broken up. He might have written it in a couple of letters, but she understood he'd been hurt. "That's none of your business."

"So let me get this straight. The sex wasn't great between you and Tom, and that little fucker made you feel like it was your fault. It's not. You're just as sexual as the next woman. What you two lack is chemistry."

"Chemistry? I loved Tom." She did love him. She just hadn't been *in* love with him.

"Love has nothing to do with it. It's hard to explain but sometimes two people just click and every touch between them is electric. I'm not saying it doesn't lead somewhere else, but that spark is all about sexual compatibility. We've got chemistry, Lara. That's the whole problem. That's why your nipples are hard right now."

"Could you please stop talking about my nipples?" It was embarrassing, but she did understand what he meant by *spark*. She'd felt them flying through her system since the moment she'd laid eyes on him. Was it true? Did they have some kind of chemistry that only came along once in a while?

"Do you think this happens to me all the time? Let me tell you, prin—" He paused. "Lara, it doesn't. It's very rare that I meet a woman and want her like I want my next breath. And it's never happened this hard and fast. It's thrown me for a loop and I have no idea how to handle it. That's why I'm doing such a terrible job of dealing with you. I need you to be a little patient with me."

Her patience got her in all kinds of trouble. It was why he was here in the first place. Of course it was also likely the only reason she'd survived yesterday's attack. "We're kind of opposites. I know they attract and all but they rarely work out in the end."

"Does everything have to end in marriage? Were you thinking about the long term with Niall? Don't answer that. I know what you're going to say."

This was not how she'd expected the conversation to go. She'd been waiting for some protest on his part, but in a professional manner. She certainly hadn't expected him to initiate any kind of intimate dialogue. Was she, like he'd suggested, reading too much into his words and not enough into his actions? He'd been tender with her the night before. She would bet he wasn't tender very often.

"Yes," she admitted. "A couple of days into talking with Niall, I was thinking about a future. It's what I do. I know I shouldn't. Kiki thinks I need a few flings to loosen me up."

"And now I kind of hate Kiki, too."

"Why?"

He threw his hands in the air. "I have no idea. I am utterly irrational when it comes to you. I'm being honest with you, Lara. Why was I mean? Because I want you and I don't think I can have you. Because I'm a jealous, possessive prick who doesn't deserve you any more than Niall did."

She shook her head. "It wouldn't work. We just met and we've already argued."

"Because I'm fighting this. Because I don't want to be vulnerable to you or anyone. It's totally against my nature. I don't like the feeling. But I also know that I don't want you to walk away. I can't give up the responsibility of watching out for you. If anything happens to you, I won't be able to live with myself."

"Why? I have trouble believing that you're feeling too much for me or whatever. You just met me."

"I didn't say it was rational. I just said it was." He sighed. "Look, Niall is a player. He figured out very quickly what you wanted in a guy and gave it to you. I'm the opposite. I won't pretend. I'm just the asshole who makes you feel like crap because I like you and I don't understand why or know how to say it."

Actually, she understood that entirely. Still, his admission stirred up a bunch of girly, fluttery emotions. She'd been very open with Niall because he'd seemed so honest with her. They'd had a lot in common. At least she'd thought so. She and Connor came from completely different worlds. But that only made him more dangerous.

She tried to shove her feelings back and focus. "I thought I wrote a rag."

That hadn't been the most hurtful thing he'd said, but it was the easiest to address.

"I might not believe in everything you do, but I like that you stand up for what matters to you. And I admit I don't understand it completely. So why don't you teach me, Lara? Let me really get to know you."

She liked it better when he was being an ass. He was way easier to deal with. This new Connor had soulful eyes and she halfway believed what he said, even knowing it could all be a ploy to win her trust so he could keep his paycheck. "Against my better judgment, I kind of like you, too. This seems like a bad idea."

He invaded her space again and cupped her shoulders. "Kiss me. That kiss in the elevator meant something. You know it did. It was more than just setting our cover. Just kiss me once and if you don't want to do it again, I'll leave. If you still think I'm only here for the money, I'll walk out the door. But if you get even the slightest thought floating through your brain that you might enjoy being with me, then let me stay."

Simply being close to him messed with her mind. His touch was potentially addictive. She'd slept better last night than she had in weeks because he made her feel safe. Despite every snide word he'd tossed at her earlier, despite the fact that he was a distrusting carnivore with a worldview that ran counter to her own, he tempted her like mad. All she wanted to do was put her lips on his and explore.

She'd never done anything like that with Tom or her high school boyfriend. She even shied away from playing with herself because she liked connecting with people. So there hadn't seemed much point in masturbation. But she'd stood in that elevator with Spencer Connor and she'd wanted to wrap her arms around him, spread her legs wide, and welcome him inside her. She'd rubbed against his leg because her every instinct told her this man could make her feel.

"I don't do flings." That wasn't something she could manage, at least not yet. She needed time to think things over.

He finally took a step back, placing much-needed distance between them. "Okay. I didn't jump on you last night and I won't now. But you won't find another man who will protect you the way I can. You won't find another man who will let you work the way I will. And if you want to experiment, if you want to explore this chemistry between us, I'll let you do that, too."

In a flash, she knew she'd regret it if she didn't. She would always wonder if Connor was the one man who could have set her sensuality free. Why should she have to live like a nun for the rest of her life?

The things she was best at had always been things she practiced. Like the piano. She'd hated the lessons when she was a kid and now she found a deep peace in being able to sit down and play Bach or Chopin. She was a better writer for having done it over and over throughout the years. She could look at some of her early pieces and cringe, but she'd gotten better.

What if sex was like that? What if her supposed ineptitude really hadn't been her fault and all she'd needed was some instruction and practice?

Lara shook her head. This train of thought was stupid. She wasn't as dumb as he suspected.

Still, she had that meeting coming up and she was sure that keeping it while staying in the city would be easier than trying to rendezvous from her dad's.

"All right. You can stay, but only as a bodyguard and you have to sleep on the couch." She couldn't risk physical intimacy with him, not until she'd really prepared herself.

"Lara . . ." His face had fallen and she could see him working up to argue his case.

She shook her head. She'd let him call all the shots up to this point, and that time was over. "No. If you can't handle the couch, I'll go to my father's."

It was time to take control back. He was too different, too dangerous, but he was also her best option in a bad bunch.

He stood there and she could practically see that sharp mind of his working overtime. He wasn't slow at all. She no longer bought the "I'm a lowly sailor" routine.

Was he telling her the truth about wanting her? Did it even matter since she knew what a horrible idea sleeping with him would be?

"All right," he relented. "I'll sleep on the couch."

She held out a hand. "Then we're good."

He took it in his own, but instead of shaking it, he cupped his other hand over hers. She was surrounded by his warmth, his strength. And she definitely felt the electricity between them. "But sweetheart, we've already set our cover in motion. In public, you have to act like you're in love with me."

"Can't we break up?"

He shook his head. "No."

"I thought you'd say that." He was good at saying no. She pulled her hand from his and began putting her stuff away.

"I'll go reheat breakfast and we can start over. You need your strength. We have a lot to do today." He was gone before she could reply.

Lara stood in her bedroom and had to wonder if she hadn't just made a deal with the devil. A handsome, glorious devil, but the devil all the same.

Three days later, Connor wondered if he was going just the tiniest bit insane. He had the dog on a leash as he walked by the statue of Mary McLeod Bethune in Lincoln Park, praying the little thing didn't shit all over the place. Oh, he was prepared for it because Lara had given him a biodegradable bag to scoop up Lincoln's waste.

"You started him on the meat," she'd said earlier that morning with a wrinkle of her nose. "You can handle the consequences."

How the mighty had fallen.

Lincoln—the constipated dog—barked and strained against his leash.

"Lincoln, heel," he said in a low growl.

The little thing sat back, its bug eyes wide. If only his mistress was so easily handled.

"Nice day for a walk. Like the pooch. She's exactly what I would have gotten you," a familiar voice said. "You know they say pet owners choose pets that are very similar to themselves."

Roman Calder was right on time, but then he always was. Connor took in the sight of one of his oldest friends, dressed in workout pants and a Yale sweatshirt covering his chest with the hood pulled low in deference to his semi-celebrity status. It looked as if he was well into his daily five-mile run. Most of the time he went with Zack, but they couldn't have this conversation surrounded by ten Secret Service agents.

"It's a he and obviously he's not mine."

Roman's lips curved up even as his feet moved, keeping his heart rate up. "I never thought I'd see you domesticated."

Connor heard the laughter in Roman's voice. His buddy would be on the phone with Gabe in a heartbeat. Zack would likely know Connor had become Lara's errand boy before Roman even got back to the White House. Bastard gossiped more than any old lady. "Could we move on? I have to be back in ten minutes."

Roman finally stopped his slow jog, looking out over the park. "Where is she? I've seen pictures, but I have to admit, I would love to see the woman who bosses your ass around."

Oddly, he kind of wanted Roman to meet her. She was smart and funny and she kept him on his toes. Though if she met Roman, Connor's cover would be blown, so that couldn't happen. At least not until this whole thing got sorted out. "She's meeting with her father and a friend in another part of the park. She's got two guards I approved watching her so I figured I could break away to see you."

"So everything's been quiet since the initial attempt on her life?"

Connor nodded, his eyes never stopping their scan of their surroundings. "Yes, but we haven't left the apartment to do more than grocery shop. If you can call it that."

His fairy princess lived off berries and salad. He was fairly certain that any moment he was with Lara, birds would come to carry her biodegradable bags filled with rabbit food, and all the woodland creatures would keep the palace spick-and-span.

She was the Snow White of the tabloid world. She was idiotically naive at times, and then she would stun him with her honesty and her backbone.

He had whiplash from being around Lara Armstrong. And he definitely had a hard-on. He'd had it for freaking days.

"The police found the motorcycle the shooter used in his attack abandoned outside the city. It was stolen, naturally."

"I want a full write-up on whoever owns it." It would be simple enough to use his own ride and then claim it had been stolen. He wanted to know if there was any connection at all between the owner and Lara.

"I've got them working on it. I've explained that the White House wants updates because the victim was the daughter of a senator. They're buying it for now. I'll get the reports and send them to you. From what I understand, Everly's worked up profiles of the people in Lara's building and her friends. She's got some interesting pals."

"What do you mean?"

"Did you know Kiki Ross is having an affair with a married congressman?"

Shit. "You're sure?"

"Oh, I have the photos in both color and black and white. They should come in handy at election time." Roman wore his shark smile.

"You can't."

"Of course I can. We've been wanting that district for years and we always fall just short. This coming year, I'll release those photos shortly before the election. There's a reason we call it an October surprise."

He would handle that later. The elections were months off, but somehow he couldn't see letting those photos get leaked. Lara would be deeply upset. She would do that thing where her eyes got wide and her bottom lip would tremble just the slightest bit before she nodded as though accepting the weight of the world on her shoulders.

How could he know so fucking much about the woman in so little time?

"What about the rest of them?"

"Tom Hannigan's father was a federal judge. He stepped down three years ago. To the public it was nothing but an early retirement, but according to buried DOJ files, they were about to indict him on twelve counts of accepting bribes for judgments."

"Seriously?"

"Oh, yes. The only reason they didn't go through with it was the chaos it would have created. All of his cases would have been thrown out, including judgments against two of America's biggest corporations. It was decided that putting Hannigan in jail wasn't worth the risk of letting those FTC-violating bastards walk free."

"Who knows about this?" Had Lara been picking and choosing her targets? He found that oddly disappointing.

"It's buried. Unless she's got an informant in the high ranks of the DOJ, there's no way she knows about it. I can't be certain even her ex-fiancé knows."

Somehow that made Connor feel better. He'd kind of started looking at her as Super Fairy, protector of truth (there was none), justice (even less of that), and the American way (burying their heads in the sand and buying another Happy Meal.) It might be ridiculous, but he would be disappointed to discover her hypocrisy. "What else have you got?"

"It's all on this thumb drive. I know how freaky you are about sending things over the Internet, and I think you have good reason this time."

"Why?"

"The NSA is interested in one of Lara's neighbors. A man named Fredrick Gallagher. They believe he's hacked some important sites and might be involved in cyberterrorism. They don't have the goods on him yet."

"So?" If the NSA didn't have the balls to question him, Connor's team could do it. "A little friendly interrogation on foreign soil never hurt anyone."

Roman sighed. "We're not renditioning American citizens, Connor. He's a veteran with a tragic past. I pulled his records. It's not pretty. If it got out that we're investigating him at all, it could blow up in our faces, so keep it quiet. But if you get a chance to get into his place and collect intel, I know some people who would owe you a favor. Now, what have you found out?"

This was the shitty part. "She's clean. Everything she's said to me is truthful."

Roman's eyes narrowed. "You're kidding me."

Connor shrugged. A couple of nights on her couch had allowed him to comb through her system, downloading it quickly and then uploading it to his own computer so he could browse through at his convenience. Just yesterday afternoon they'd sat in her office together. She'd been at her desk working on some story about a company fudging their reports to the EPA. She hadn't had a clue that the whole while she was investigating her scoop, he'd been investigating her.

"She keeps meticulous records, but her e-mail contained nothing that might lead us to Deep Throat. It's either informants or friends or spam. I'm reading each and every one in case there's some code, but it's going to take me a few days. I've blocked off the time period from Mad's death to today. It's roughly two thousand e-mails to go through."

"Send a third to Everly and another to Dax. If this didn't involve Zack, I would hire an investigative team. We're wasting your talents having you read e-mails."

He didn't want anyone else to do it. Some of those e-mails were private. He'd been reading her e-mails to her mother where she talked about Niall and how much she liked him, how she thought she might find a soul mate in him. She'd written to a cousin congratulating her on her upcoming wedding and asking if she could bring a date. She'd told her all about Niall.

She would have to attend the wedding alone. Would she explain what had happened or just tell her happily married cousin that it hadn't worked out? The wedding was in three weeks. Maybe she simply wouldn't attend.

Or, Connor thought, he could take her.

"I need to get a feel for her. I'll get through them. I don't have much else to do. She spends a lot of time at her computer."

Roman was staring at him. Connor had seen that look in the courtroom right before Roman tore apart opposing counsel's argument. "You haven't managed to do anything but download her system?"

"I can't let her catch me."

"Drug her."

"I think she would notice that."

"Fine. Fuck her and keep her in bed, and let my guys come in and go through everything with a fine-tooth comb. We can do the whole place in thirty minutes and she won't have a clue we've been there."

It was actually what he needed. He'd hesitated to do too thorough a search since after that first night she'd struggled to sleep. She'd gotten up at least once each night to sneak into the kitchen and grab a bottle of water. He would watch her through hooded eyes as she tried not to wake him. In the moonlight, her skin glowed like alabaster.

"I'm not sleeping with her."

Roman sighed like it should be obvious. "Then start sleeping with her. Look, if you're not into her, if you can't get it up around her, let Dax do it. He gets a hard-on from the woman who serves him coffee every day and she's got to be eighty-two."

"I fucking do not." A surly voice reminded him that he and Roman weren't alone. Dax was watching Lara, connected to Connor by a comm system worn in each of their ears. "And she's not eighty-two. She's a very youthful fifty. You know fifty is the new thirty, according to one of her magazines."

"He's yelling at you, isn't he?" Roman was grinning again, his friendly smile taking the place of his everyday shark expression.

"Yeah, but he also told me enough to know that he fucked her. Really, Dax? You slept with the coffee lady?"

"And her daughter. I have to say it was one of my wilder nights, and now I get half off all coffee products," Dax admitted. "And you should make something up because if Roman finds out how deep you're in with this girl, he'll move heaven and earth to replace you."

"He's not my boss."

Roman's expression sharpened as though he could almost hear what was going on. "Who's not your boss?"

"Dumbass," Dax said in his ear.

He was a legend in the Agency for not fucking up. He was smooth and cool and always got the job done. He did not give up an operation because the woman he was investigating might be offended.

"I was talking about Gabe. He's been bugging Dax to persuade me to call. He just wants an update, but he's not my boss so he can wait with the rest of you." Connor reached into his pocket. He'd made a mold of her apartment key the same day she'd given him her spare. God only knew how many other people had one. He handed it to Roman. "This is Lara's apartment key. I'll tell you when to come so I can leave the dead bolt undone. You'll have to deal with the surveillance cameras."

"Not a problem. I actually know someone in her building. I'll set up a meeting with her and no one will question the president's chief of staff bringing a few security guards along." Roman looked down at his watch and his feet started moving again, jogging in place. "We'll take her down, brother. You'll see. It'll be easy. And talk to Gabe. I don't know what's up with the two of you, but I can't stand being the go-between. What are you going to do? Throw him a bachelor party and not talk to him the whole time?"

He hadn't even considered it. Gabe was getting married, and they'd barely spoken since that night at the Crawford building where Connor had taken down their enemies in a blood bath. Gabe thought Connor had put his job before their friendship. He had no idea what Connor had sacrificed. Thankfully, Zack had smoothed things over with Langley, but he was still on administrative leave pending the investigation. He could still lose his job for his decisions that night. And Connor simply couldn't forget the way one of his oldest friends had looked at him.

Like he was an animal.

"I think I'll have to skip the bachelor party and the wedding, for that matter. I'll be back on the job." He hoped. He would immediately put in for a foreign assignment. Someplace dangerous and deadly. Someplace without a single fairy princess in sight.

"Come on, man. We already lost Mad. We can't lose you, too. You're coming and don't think I can't make that happen. I made a promise a long time ago that I wouldn't let you fade off into the shadows and shit. And don't worry about your job, though I wish you'd quit and come work for us. Zack would put you in charge of personal security in a heartbeat, and then you wouldn't have to hide from the press or all the people who want to kill you."

"What's the fun in that?" It wasn't sarcastic, exactly. He'd gotten used to the adrenaline rush, and what he'd discovered was people got lazy when they weren't on the edge. And someone always wanted to kill him. Better to never forget and never let his guard down.

"I'll let it go for now. Call me. Tonight or tomorrow if at all possible. I want to know what this chick has on Zack before we go into the election cycle. I can't let the opposition sneak anything past me. So get me the intel I need, brother. Speaking of intelligence, does that dog have any?"

Lincoln was on his back, rubbing himself all over the ground, his tongue lolling around. It was what he did when desperate for someone to rub his belly.

"Nope, not a lick." Rather like himself.

Roman laughed and jogged away.

"He's right about Gabe. You have to talk to him sooner or later," Dax said in his ear. "But how are you going to get Roman into her place if you're not sleeping with her? When the hell are you going to sleep with her anyway? Don't tell me you don't want her. I see you. You don't watch her back. You watch her ass. That's got to be the world's most protected backside."

He wasn't sure where Dax was, so he held up his hand and flipped him the bird, much to the chagrin of a passing group of what looked like elementary school kids on a field trip.

"Very nice, Connor. Yeah, you taught them something," Dax laughed in his ear—then stopped. "Hey, I think I'm not the only one watching your girl."

Connor tugged on Lincoln's leash and the dog rolled back over. "Where?"

"I'm watching from a bench approximately a hundred yards east of the subject. A man in a ball cap, jeans, and a black T-shirt has circled three times around her. He wants me to think he's talking on a cell, but he's taking pictures of her. The damn rent-a-cops haven't noticed. Should I pursue?"

"Not on your life." Because it might mean hers. He didn't want to leave her unprotected for a second. "But get me pictures. Anything you can while you're still watching her back. I'm two minutes away."

He scooped up the dog and started to jog.

Lara sighed as her dad glanced down at his cell phone. He stood up from the bench she'd been sharing with him and Kiki. She was fairly sure she knew what was coming next.

"Honey, I have to take this. I'll be right back." Her father gave that expression she thought of as his sad-senator, "the world needs me" look.

"Sure." It was a good thing she'd thought to ask Kiki to come. Meeting with her dad often ended in her sitting alone while he was on the phone if her mom wasn't around. She'd managed to get her mother to stay in Napa for the week so Kiki had been her best bet.

"Good, now we can girl talk," Kiki said, leaning in. She looked around at the two guards her father had brought with him. They were very professional-looking men in their dark suits and mirrored aviators. She would bet they would never allow themselves to take doggy duty. Of course, Connor wouldn't stand around all puffed up with self-importance. Having these men screamed "Hey, look at me; I'm so important I need a bodyguard." Connor simply sat at her side, never giving away how dangerous he could be.

She knew how quick he was in the field. Now the real question was how much damage he could do to her heart. "I don't know if we should talk around them."

Kiki's nose wrinkled as she dismissed the duo. "I don't think they care. Besides, you haven't called or come by in days, and the one day I tried coming by your place, no one answered."

"Oh, my washer is on the fritz and Connor won't let me bring in a repairman because apparently they all moonlight as assassins, so I had to use the basement laundry. That was superfun. I got to fold my granny panties in front of Connor." And she'd ended up folding his sleek boxers alongside her clothes. She'd told herself she'd taken his little pile of clothes with hers because it only made sense to save water and energy. It wasn't some deep-seated cavewoman need to ensure her man wasn't forced to wear clothes he'd picked up off the cave floor and sniffed.

"You could have used mine. Next time tell Connor he can scan my apartment for assassins. Then you can do your laundry and we can gossip and drink. I'm dying to know what's going on with Hottie McHotPants, and I can't wait a minute longer. He is looking fine, by the way."

He'd looked a little mad when she'd waved him off to walk Lincoln, but she wasn't sure she felt comfortable talking about what she needed to say with him anywhere in the vicinity.

She felt his eyes on her, watching as always. When she looked up and saw him circling back around with her dog, she felt . . . comfortable. She wouldn't have imagined it, but his presence seemed to soothe her as though nothing bad could happen as long as he was around. Everywhere she went, she could feel his gaze on her and hear those words in her head.

I want you.

She'd told herself to be professional, but it wasn't working. She dreamed about him at night, like he'd managed to plant a seed in her head with his offer to let her explore their chemistry, and it had grown and shoved out all other thoughts.

She dreamed about what would have happened if that elevator door had never opened. She fantasized about him shoving her against the wall and pushing her skirt up and getting between her legs.

"He is looking well. We've come to a meeting of minds." Well, they had come to a sort of agreement. She did her job and he did his. She cooked twice a day, but she was starting to wonder if Connor wasn't a little like Lincoln. Lack of meat had made him crabby. He ate, but it was grudgingly.

How could anything ever work between them?

"What is that supposed to mean?" Kiki asked with a scowl. "A meeting of minds? That's not the part of him you should be meeting up with."

"It means that we understand we're opposites who have to work together, so we're keeping necessary space between us." Except he'd sat right next to her the night before. He'd plopped down on the couch as she'd watched the news, and their hips had touched. She'd meant to mention it to him, meant to move over, but then he'd looked so comfy that she hadn't wanted to move or disturb him. But then she'd kind of leaned closer. Only the pinging of the oven had stopped her from melting against him.

"Why?" Kiki rolled her eyes. "God, you're doing it again."

"Doing what?"

"Look, I get that you have your convictions and you think that one day your vegan prince is going to come, but you have to see that it's silly to expect a man to check every item off your list."

That made her sound like a complete idiot. "I am not trying to check off some list."

"Really? You won't explore anything between you and Connor because Niall the Great meets all your criteria."

"Niall the Great?"

"It's what I call him. Tom calls him Niall the Douche. He's, like, your perfect guy. Same political convictions, rabid vegan. Hell, he works for Greenpeace."

"He's also married."

Kiki's jaw dropped. "What?"

It wasn't right or fair, but she'd kind of been okay with Connor's edicts since they'd kept her from having to tell Kiki how badly she'd screwed up. "He's married. I bet he lied about a bunch of other stuff, too. Likely, he never worked for Greenpeace. He's probably off somewhere clubbing seals as we speak."

"Oh, honey. How did you find out?"

"Connor. He made Niall tell me. It was awful." She'd cried all evening and then slept like a baby because Connor had been there with her. Now she couldn't sleep at all. She got up in the middle of the night for water just so she could make sure he was still there, as if his mere presence reassured her.

"I knew there was something wrong with that douche bag. You can't just meet someone online and expect to really get to know them."

"We talked for hours. I thought it was better that way because we could get to know each other's mind before getting the bodies involved." She knew exactly what Kiki was going to say. She was naive.

"You're so naive, sweetie. Bodies are always involved. And a person doesn't show you who they really are on the Internet. You have to stop trying to find your perfect vegan lover and find the right one."

That wasn't exactly fair. "I've dated plenty of omnivores. They're the ones who can't bend for me."

Kiki sat back on the bench as though settling in for a nice long argument. "So Connor's been eating takeout every night?"

She'd been a little surprised when he sat down with her for dinner that first night after their fight. He'd just taken his spot across from her and asked where his plate was. She'd set another place and then they'd found a nice routine. "No. He eats what I cook, but he did buy booze. It's nonorganic and I'm fairly certain it wouldn't pass the fair trade test."

Kiki pointed at her. "There. Right there. Not everyone has the same values you do, hon. This is what you do to every single person who gets close to you. I love you, but I'm constantly waiting for you to figure out that I'm not good enough."

Lara shook her head, horrified that she felt that way. "That's not true. I would never think that way. I know I talk politics a lot, but I don't expect everyone to do what I say."

Kiki suddenly had tears in her eyes. "I don't know. I've done things you wouldn't approve of."

What was Kiki hiding? She always seemed so upbeat. Was she

really so close-minded that her best friend didn't feel as if she could talk to her? "I might not approve, but I would still love you. Kiki, people do stupid stuff all the time. God, I run a tabloid. I have no room to judge. I would just try to help you."

"But you are judging. You're judging Connor without really giving him a shot. He's trying."

"How do you know that?"

"Because he let you send him off with the dog and he's been eating vegan. Sweetie, a man like that doesn't suffer silently. He goes and does what he wants unless he wants something else more. I think you're the something he wants more. A man like Connor doesn't come around very often. You shouldn't let him slip through your fingers."

"We haven't known each other for very long. I don't really know if my fingers want him yet." She was lying, but she just wasn't ready to admit the truth.

"So? You knew Tom for years before you slept with him, and how did that work out?"

Kiki had several very good points. None of them actually solved the real problem. "I'm scared. After what happened with Niall, I'm scared that Connor is playing me to get me to do what he wants or to make his job easier . . . I don't know. I just don't trust how I feel about him."

"You've been out of the game way too long. You know, I think you stuck it out with Tom those last two years you were together. You should have just gotten out. You weren't happy with him."

She hadn't been. Tom had gotten possessive. He'd made demands on her time that didn't make sense. It all culminated in the nastiest fight of her life and a broken engagement. They'd gotten back to being friends, but she was still a little wary. Tom had changed when they started having sex. They were much better as friends. What if she had that effect on Connor, too? Although it wasn't like she and Connor had a real friendship to fall back on. On the other hand, that meant she didn't have as much to lose. "It was comfortable. Well, it was and it wasn't."

"You didn't want to admit you'd made a mistake. You thought Tom checked off all your boxes. He was politically in the right place. He was smart, attractive, supportive."

"He lied about being a vegan." Tom had claimed to convert when she'd done it. They were in college and he'd been right beside her. He'd shoved it in her face when they'd broken up, telling her he'd never believed in any of it and had only done it to get her into bed.

"Honey, very few people can live that way."

It wasn't in their nature. Like Lincoln's. It definitely wasn't in Connor's and yet he hadn't complained. Oh, she could tell he hadn't loved her tofu scramble this morning, but he'd actually complimented her black bean tacos and had a second and third helping. He was trying to fit into her life.

Maybe she should bend a little. "I'm not going to lie to you. I think about Connor a lot. But I don't know if things can work out long term with someone like him."

"Not everything has to be long term. Lara, I love you like a sister, but you have to let go of the idea that your life is going to be a model of perfection. You've always been so afraid to make mistakes. The one thing you took a chance on has become the passion of your life."

Capitol Scandals. Her baby. Sure, her baby was built on stories about the president's penis, but it had done more good than all her protesting days. She'd actually helped victims of scams and political cover-ups—real people. And when she'd started she'd been so scared she'd shut the site down three times before she calmed enough to let it work.

Was she doing the same thing with Connor? Did she think a thing was only worth doing if it was guaranteed to turn out right?

"I want him."

Kiki nodded. "You should. He's the single hottest man I've ever met."

There was more to it than that. He was electric in some odd way she'd never experienced before. Even when he was sitting perfectly still, she could practically feel the energy pouring off him. Every time she touched him she felt a connection. "It's not just about his looks."

"No, it's not. There's something about that man. When I look at him I just know he could take care of me in bed. I think if he wanted to he could pretty much take care of everything. He's a perfect specimen of alpha male."

Lara hated the flare of jealousy that sparked through her system.

Kiki pointed. "You don't like how I talked about him. That's the second time. You're possessive. I've never seen you like this."

"Because it's not something I want to be." Jealously was a useless, destructive emotion.

"What's wrong with a little possessiveness?" Kiki asked. "I can assure you if you get into Connor's bed, he's not going to share you. He's going to be a caveman and he'll club any man who tries to take what's his."

His. Her whole body seemed to flare hot at the thought. She was a modern woman. She wasn't supposed to belong to anyone but herself. And yet the idea of being Spencer Connor's woman lit her up like nothing she'd ever felt. He was everything she shouldn't want, but she was starting to wonder if Kiki was right and she wasn't overthinking things. She couldn't run her love life like she ran her website.

"I didn't expect I'd ever want someone like him," Lara admitted. "I expected to find someone who made me feel peaceful and secure. I don't feel that way around him."

"You're looking for something that doesn't exist. Or maybe it does, but it shouldn't. You want to love a man, but not too much. Not so much that you're plagued with real, nasty human emotions. Love can make you do some really bad things. It isn't always positive. You don't know that because you've never really loved someone with your whole heart, so much that you'd be willing to do anything for him. You don't want to find out that you're just like the rest of us."

Lara stared at her best friend, unsure of who she really was in that moment. "I never meant to make you feel bad. I don't think I'm better than anyone else."

Kiki sighed. "Don't mind me. I'm being a jealous bitch." She reached out and took Lara's hand. "I'm going through some things I'm not ready to talk about and I'm taking it out on you. I'm sorry. It's not fair and I'm doing it because I know you'll still care about me."

"I will."

Kiki squeezed her hand. "Sometimes I get jealous because you seem to have everything together and I'm still a mess. It's my issue and I'll get over it. In the meantime, think about what I said. Passion can be messy. You've spent most of your life spreading all that love and compassion you have around. That's easy. Those people you help aren't really a part of your life. You get to walk in and be the hero and walk back out. This is harder. Friendships aren't necessarily neat. Relationships don't always end the way you want them to, but that doesn't mean you can't learn from them. Take the leap. Live a little."

Lara thought she was living, but now she had to reassess. With the singular exception of her website, she'd done what was expected of her and tried very hard to not fail. At anything. That was why she'd said yes to Tom. She hadn't really wanted to be his wife, but saying no would mean the relationship had failed. It would have meant she'd failed.

Calling a halt to her wedding had been a massive leap of faith but it had paid off for both her and Tom. Was she ready to leap again?

Any sort of future with Connor was impossible. Or maybe it wasn't. How the hell would she know if she didn't even try?

"You think too much." Kiki forced her to look into her eyes. "Look at me. Do you want him?"

"Yes."

"Will you regret it if you don't try?"

She knew the answer to that one. "Absolutely."

"Then you know what to do."

Oh, she was so wrong. "No. No, I don't. What do I do? Do you think I should write him a note?"

"Oh, dear god. Don't. Don't write him a note."

"I don't think he'll be impressed with a song."

"You give men way too much credit, sweetie. Just tell him yes. That's really all he needs. He'll take it from there. It wouldn't hurt if you cooked him something he wants to eat. You can get some grass-fed organic beef where the ranchers massage the cows and send them on spa days and stuff."

"I don't think that exists, but I did promise him burgers tonight. He would be surprised if it wasn't a big mushroom."

"And pleased."

Compromise. It made the world a better place sometimes. "All right. But I'm getting premade patties so I don't have to touch it."

He'd told her to kiss him. He'd offered to let her explore. Was the offer even still open?

"That was the White House." Her father stepped back to the bench they'd chosen. He kept staring at his phone like he was stunned. "The president is interested in one of the projects my committee is working on and he wants to talk to me."

"That's great."

"He's invited you to come with me."

That was surprising. "I don't think I should go to the White House. Don't they have a ban on people like me? Like a no-fly list. I've protested Zack Hayes enough that I should be on that list."

A man darted past their bench, his long legs sprinting. The movement had both security guards on edge. They stepped in, wedging themselves between the runner and Lara and her dad. Kiki stepped up, getting in front of Lara.

"What are you doing?"

"I don't know," Kiki admitted. "It seemed like the right thing to do."

The man was running the other way. It looked like he was just taking a shortcut. People ran through the park all the time.

The security guards were a little oversensitive.

Connor returned, his gaze on both guards. He shoved Lincoln her way but spoke to the suits. "You two idiots, stay here. Did you not notice the asshole stalking her?"

Connor took off in the same direction as the other guy, loping away with the easy movements of a predator.

She tried to glance around the security guard. Had she just caught a glimpse of the man who'd sought to kill her at the bus stop? Lara tried to recall everything she'd noticed about that guy. It had all happened so quickly that she remembered the motorcycle and the gun and not much beyond that. Everything else had been nondescript . . . kind of like the guy she'd seen today. Maybe it had been him. And maybe it hadn't. She wished she'd been paying more attention before he'd jogged off.

Then she heard something rustle in the bushes behind her and turned, her heart racing. Was someone hiding there? Did her killer have a partner who'd distracted her security detail while he waited? Would this guy succeed in shooting her this time?

"Something or someone is in there," she whispered, pointing.

"I'll check." The guard nodded to his partner and disappeared behind the wall of shrubs.

It had seemed like a peaceful spot, serene and quiet. Now she scanned the park and all she could see were places where people could hide. The trees and bushes were more than lovely pieces of nature. They were barriers she couldn't see around. Anyone could be watching. Anyone could be waiting for her.

Then she felt someone's stare fixed on her, felt malevolence.

Her cell phone trilled as a text came in. She thought about ignoring it, but then decided she needed anything to take her mind off what had just happened. The panic that had plagued much of her childhood seemed right on the edge of her consciousness. If Tom had sent her some crazy anecdote about his job, maybe the normalcy would pull her back from the edge.

The number of the originating text didn't register as unknown until she'd already pulled it up. Already seen it.

I can get you anytime. Anywhere. He can't protect you.

A picture accompanied the text. It was a picture of her from the previous night. In her own building. She was folding her favorite T-shirt and smiling at someone off camera. Connor.

He'd been in her building—when she'd been sure she was safe.

Despite the incident the day she'd met Connor, Lara hadn't completely processed that someone was trying to hurt her. She'd wanted to buy into the cover story that the attack had been random and she'd simply been in the wrong place at the wrong time. The last few days had been so normal she'd convinced herself the shooting at the bus stop had been a fluke and met her dad in the park because she couldn't stay cooped up a second longer.

But she couldn't deny the truth any longer. Someone wanted to kill her.

By burying her head in the sand, she'd put her dad and Kiki in danger. For all she knew, the would-be assassin would shoot either of them to get to her. Or Connor, who was doing his best to hunt the gun-toting killer down right now.

What if the hunter became the hunted?

"Lara?" Kiki's voice sounded far away.

Her hands started to shake and the world just began to fade in her peripheral vision.

"It's a panic attack. She's had them since she was a kid. They used to be so bad, she took medication." Her father's hands were on her, lifting Lincoln away.

She heard a man's low curse and then she felt hands on her face, lifting her chin up.

"Hey, breathe for me, princess." Suddenly Connor stared down at her, his handsome face seemingly the only real thing in the world. His hands moved, one reaching back to cup her neck and the other wrapping around her waist. "You're fine. I told you I wouldn't let anyone hurt you. I'm not going to. You're fine and you're here with me. So take a deep breath."

What if the stranger had killed him? What if he'd died for her? She squeezed her eyes shut, feeling sick.

"Look at me." He stared down at her. "Look at me and listen to my voice. Nothing else."

She managed to nod and take a shaky breath. Then she pried her eyes open.

"He's gone. He's at least a mile away by now so he can't hurt you. I'm going to find him, princess. Then he won't be able to hurt anyone again, but I need you to stay with me."

Don't give in to panic.

He leaned forward, lowering his face to her forehead. "If you don't calm down, I'm going to kiss you. I'll do it right in front of your dad. I know how to calm you down." He smoothed her hair back. "I'll just keep kissing you until you believe me."

He did know how to calm her down. Now she wasn't thinking about anything else.

"I'm good. I'll be okay." She needed to tell him about the man in the bushes.

"Good." He raised his head, but his hands stayed on her body.

"I think there were two of them." She managed to say in gulpy breaths.

Connor turned slightly, looking to the guard to her right. "What is she talking about?"

The other guard was back. "She seemed to think someone was watching her from behind that bush. I did find tracks. They appear to be sneakers of some kind, but I'm not a tracker. They could be new, could be from hours ago. I don't know. I don't think anyone was there."

He started to let her go and she wobbled without his strength. He cursed under his breath and leaned over. Before she knew it, she was in his arms, cradled to his chest. "You'll forgive me if I don't bow before your powers of observation. You didn't even realize that fucking jogger was watching her."

"I noticed him."

"But didn't do anything?" Connor shook his head. "Get your head in the game. This is your job." He cuddled Lara close then turned to the other guard. "And you were apparently going to stand around and let her have a panic attack. You're not watching my charge ever again. Senator, I'm sorry for the rudeness but I'm responsible for Lara right now and I won't let her out of my sight again. If you want to see her, you'll have to set it up through me."

"Of course." Her dad was watching them. "I think she got something on her cell phone. She was looking down at it when she went pale. I thought she was going to pass out."

"He sent me a text," she managed to say, forcing herself to calm down. Somehow being in Connor's arms gave her the peace of mind to control the chaos.

"Kiki, hold it up for me." Connor didn't seem eager to let her go.

Kiki did and Lara turned her head away, burying herself in the softness of Connor's shirt.

He cursed. "I need to get her home. Then I'm going to find where that bastard put it."

"Put what?" she asked.

"The camera he has in the basement."

"He was there," she gasped, feeling the blood leave her head.

"No, princess. He wasn't. I checked. But I'm thinking he's got surveillance equipment set up. If that's the case, I'll find it and shut it down."

Somehow knowing that Connor was on the case made her relax. "You can put me down now."

"Not on your life. You'll wobble and fall. Then I'll have to take care of you. Kiki, could you walk Lincoln back to the building?"

She nodded. "And Lara, I'll stop by the store. I'll get you everything you need."

"Thanks," she murmured to Kiki with a grateful smile.

"Stay safe, baby girl," her dad said just over Connor's shoulder.

Lara would have loved to talk to her dad, to assure him that everything was fine, but Connor had made the decision to head for home—and was striding through the park as though he had no intention of stopping.

She noticed a man in a Navy T-shirt, sweats, and sneakers. He was tall and handsome and his lips quirked up as they strode by.

Lara clung to Connor, the panic starting to fade and a certain inevitability taking its place. Life was too short. She was going to give herself to him.

She just hoped it wasn't too late.

SIX

Connor pushed the button to the elevator with a deep sense of unease. He'd found one of the building's security cameras in the basement. Someone with great skill had hacked into the feed. Someone likely close to Lara.

He would really like to see what kind of setup Freddy had.

If that little pervert was taking pictures of her, Connor would end his miserable life. If the dude thought he'd seen some bad shit in the Korengal Valley, that was nothing compared to the hell Connor would rain down on him if he was the asshole scaring Lara.

Connor's gut knotted. He'd been sitting just outside the range of that camera like an idiot, watching her fold laundry, enjoying the fact that his clothes were mingling with hers. All the time someone had been spying on her.

Some fucking bodyguard he was. He'd yelled at the senator's detail, but the truth was he wouldn't have known about the man in the park if Dax hadn't been there. He'd been talking to Roman and trying to figure out how to get Lara in bed instead of doing his fucking job.

After that, he'd lost his target. He'd wasted precious time because he couldn't stand to see his fairy princess so vulnerable. He'd stepped in like an idiot storybook hero.

Connor didn't believe in white knights. They got murdered fast in his world. Their fair damsels had their throats slit, too. If he didn't get his shit together, Lara was going to find out way too late that there were no fairy-tale endings.

The elevator stopped at the lobby and Connor exited, wondering if he was doing the right thing. Maybe he should just introduce her to Dax. He'd been running that scenario over and over in his head since he realized she'd very likely caught a glimpse of him. Dax had been the "bad guy" in the bushes. Explaining the situation to Lara would have brought her some peace of mind, but he had other considerations.

Dax had a much higher profile. He'd tried to keep out of the press as much as possible after his father's suicide. Given his military career, the last thing Dax wanted was to be a tabloid stud like Gabe and Mad had been or on the nightly news like Roman and Zack. Still, Dax was a solid part of that world and not an outlier like Connor. Lara was smart and knew her D.C. society. If she connected the dots from Dax Spencer to the fact that Connor had used Zack as a reference, there was no way she'd continue buying his cash-strapped vet routine. She would dig and investigate. Then his cover would be blown.

And she would have to deal with the real Connor Sparks.

Would that really be so bad? The real Lara was stronger than the woman he'd imagined before they'd met. Although Connor sure would like some explanation about her panic attack earlier today. What had set her off? She'd handled some asshole pointing a gun her way with relative calm, but a stranger running away and a text had freaked her out.

Because she'd thought someone was stalking her every move?

Probably so. If Lara could see the threat, she handled it. But if the danger was hidden, the perpetrator lying in wait . . .

That was why the crap at the park had thrown her for a loop. She had real proof that someone was watching her, biding their time. She'd felt violated. She feared the unknown.

He stepped out of her building and into the last of the evening light. He needed to make this quick.

"Hey." Dax emerged from the alley on the side of the building, wearing sweats, a Navy T-shirt, and his sneakers.

"You're losing your touch, brother."

A grimace crossed his face. "I know. She saw me. I'm sorry. She wouldn't have if I hadn't been trying to get closer to her because you took off. You should have let me go after the bad guy while you watched your girl."

"She's the client. Hell, she's not even the fucking client. She's a mark." He had to start remembering why the hell he was here—and it wasn't to walk her damn pathetic dog and wallow in domestic bliss. He didn't need a woman to wash his clothes. That's what the cleaners were for. He'd lived off takeout food for years. He sure as hell didn't need a woman who only knew how to cook flipping vegetables.

Dax sighed a little but didn't push. "Fine. But she's your mark and she obviously trusts you. She nearly caught me. If she had, all that trust you've built would go straight to hell."

"Fine. Next time I'll let you handle the stalker. Have you figured out who he is yet? Because that asshole has probably been in her building. He's hacked into the security feed."

Connor wanted to believe it was Freddy. Oh, he wanted to prove it was Freddy, but the man he'd chased had been too tall, too supremely athletic and managed to outrun him. Likely if he'd been closer by even a few feet, the fucker wouldn't have been able to lose himself in a crowd of tourists.

"I got a couple of good shots before he made me. There wasn't a ton of cover in that part of the park."

"Which is precisely why those rent-a-cops should have been able to make him." Connor wished he'd beat the crap out of them.

"I think we lucked out. They wouldn't have thought to take pictures. They would have immediately scared the stalker off. Here's the thing that bugs me. You said she got a text, right?" Dax asked.

"Yeah, the bastard sent a message right to her phone. It was a picture of her doing laundry. I think that's what set her off. I have to figure out why so I can make sure it doesn't happen again. If she crumbles in the middle of a firefight, she'll kill us both."

Connor knew he sounded like a complete dick. He sounded pissed that she'd been so fragile in that moment. The truth was that watching her stammer and strain to breathe had just about killed him. He'd picked her up because he couldn't watch her shiver a second longer. Once she was in his arms, he'd felt her calm. She'd snuggled against him like a fluffy little bunny who didn't know she was cuddling a tiger, one who wanted more than anything in the world to eat her alive.

"That's a problem, Connor. He never touched his phone. He couldn't have sent her that text."

"Of course he did. You said he was taking pictures."

"Yes, with a small, old-school camera. It might have been one of those old disposables. Does that sound like the guy who sent a well-timed text? Like a guy who knows how to hack a building's security system? He wouldn't use some piece-of-crap camera. He would use his phone or a tablet or something digital."

It didn't make sense. "You never saw him pull out his phone?"

"Not once. Just that crappy camera."

"He could have had that text scheduled in advance."

"That's my point. Would a guy with a low-tech camera like that know how?" Dax shrugged, as if giving up the argument. "Well, Everly has the pictures I took and she's going to run it through the FBI's facial recognition software."

Connor grinned at that. Somehow he'd always thought Gabe would end up with a debutante, not a kickass security professional who could hack into the feds' website. Still, he would hate their wedding to be interrupted by the bride's arrest. "Shouldn't we go through legal channels?"

"Everly says she does it all the time. Besides, if she gets caught, Zack will pardon her. We have to use that get-out-of-jail-free card while we can. We've only got another couple of years to get our criminal on." Dax leaned against the building.

Connor didn't miss the fact that Dax managed to stay out of the security camera's range. Sometimes Connor thought Dax should have ditched the Navy and joined the CIA with him. He was a stealthy bastard. He would have been amazing in the field. People always talked to Dax. He would have been a seriously effective asset. Then Connor realized the shadows weren't the place he wanted his sunny friend to live. Dax might be good at avoiding detection but he'd never had to get his hands bloody, and Connor intended to keep it that way.

"So Everly is going to get in touch with me if she gets a hit?"

Dax nodded. "Actually, I was thinking Everly should get in touch with you before that. Look, you haven't managed to get anything really useful out of Lara yet."

"It's only been a few days. I need more time. It's not like I can torture the information out of her." He wanted to—sensually speaking. It would be the most interesting interrogation of his life. He would strip her down, tie her up, and bring her to the edge of orgasm time and time again. He would use his fingers and his mouth, and if she was a very good girl and told him everything he wanted to know, maybe she would get his cock.

It was all bullshit because if he had the chance, he would get his dick in her as quickly as he could. He would shove inside that hot, tight pussy and then maybe he would find some relief for the ache that had began the moment he saw her.

"Hear me out." Dax's voice pulled him from that particular fantasy and not a moment too soon. "Deep Throat mentioned Lara to Everly. Don't you want to know if he mentioned Everly to Lara? There's a connection here we're not seeing. I want to know, and so do Gabe and Ev. Let her make contact with your girl. Let's see if Lara is willing to talk to someone who's connected to her contact."

It wasn't a bad plan. He was just surprised he hadn't thought of it. Again, his brain had fled and his dick wasn't as smart as it used to be. He needed to distance himself. He needed to come to terms with the fact that sleeping with Lara was a bad idea. She would get clingy. Shit. He wasn't sure he wouldn't get clingy.

He had a job to do. To get it done, he needed to sneak Roman and his men into her place. Because Connor was still on leave, he didn't have all the right equipment. Even if he hadn't been, the Agency wouldn't have green-lighted this op, so he would have needed Roman anyway.

"All right." Connor sighed. "Bring Gabe and his girl down in the next couple of days. Have Everly make contact with her on her personal e-mail. Tell her a confidential informant gave her Lara's name. We'll find out very quickly if they've been in contact with the same man. I can't imagine she'll turn down a chance to talk to Everly. The minute Ev mentions that she's Mad's sister, Lara's investigative instincts will kick in. She'll be all over it."

"And hopefully Everly will be able to girl-talk some information out of her. Then you can get back to real life," Dax suggested. "Roman told me he's sure Langley is going to clear you in the next couple of weeks. He's speculating that they're tugging on your leash, hoping to rein you in a little."

They wanted him afraid. They had zero idea how tired he was of all of it. Of course there was always the fear deep down that he wouldn't be good at anything else, that he'd made his deal with the devil and there was no way out of hell.

A vision of Lara humming while she folded laundry played across his brain. He'd been so calm that evening, peaceful and centered in a way he hadn't been before.

It had been a lie. The whole time someone had been watching, lurking in cyberspace, waiting to take her out.

He was being lulled into some kind of domestic bliss, like a hungry tiger who thought the zoo was the solution to all his problems.

Fuck that. He wasn't buying what she was selling. He didn't need vegan muffins and constipated dogs and women who listened to vagina rock.

"Good. The sooner this is over with, the better. I have other things to do," Connor spit out. "Even if the Agency reinstates me, I think I'll take some more leave. I won't be satisfied until I find Natalia Kuilikov and get some answers out of her."

"You and me both," Dax agreed. "I'm staying in a hotel about a block away. Text me when you're on the move again."

"Will do. You coming with Roman when I let him in?"

Dax frowned. "You're really going to do that? She might be able to forgive you for snooping around if you ever tell her the truth, but I'm not so sure you and Roman have the same agenda."

"Of course we do. We're both looking for Deep Throat and Natalia Kuilikov."

"I'm worried Roman will shut down Capitol Scandals. You know he plays hardball when it comes to Zack's legacy. He always has. If he thinks taking everything away from that girl will protect Zack's right pinkie from getting a hangnail, he'll do it and he won't think twice."

Lara lived for that rag. Yes, it was a tabloid. But stories about the president's penis size notwithstanding, she never reported anything that was false or actively hurting the public. What would she do without her site?

Why did it fucking matter? It couldn't matter. He had to lay aside his odd affection for the girl and finish this mission. "Yeah, I'm going to do it. If I can spare her, I will. If I can't, well, that's politics, right?"

Dax's eyes narrowed. "Now that sounds like the Connor I know. Funny, I was really starting to like the new one. Call me when you're on the move. I'll shadow her as long as necessary. I think I kind of like her, too. I finally read the damn site. Yeah, it seems to be nothing but a tabloid, but there's substance there. She's found a way to get people to listen. Smart girl."

Dax walked away and Connor couldn't help but think that he'd disappointed his best friend.

He stepped back into the building. This was why he needed to get back to his real world. He didn't fucking fit here. He didn't belong where fairy princesses made breakfast and did laundry and tried to save the world through impassioned words. He didn't even fucking understand this world. Everyone around Lara was dirty. Her best friend was screwing a married man. Her ex-fiancé was likely hiding his father's backdoor dealings. Freddy was up to something. God only knew what he could dig up on her father.

On the ride up to the tenth floor, it struck him that maybe he should confront her with everything. He should find all the dirt under Daddy's seemingly shiny surface. Her mother probably had a couple of skeletons in her closet, too. He could lay it all out for Lara. Then she would understand his worldview, know that it was right. She would have no choice then but to admit she needed someone like him, who didn't mind getting his hands bloody or giving away pieces of his black-as-night soul to keep her safe in this nasty world. She would finally grasp that he alone stood between her and a big heaping pile of danger. After that, she would get on her knees and beg him to protect her.

He would do it, but their roles would be clear. She would pay him with that sweet body, and he could hold himself apart because she was just like the others, offering him a deal. After all, nothing was free.

Something nasty roiled through him as he stalked down the hall toward her sunny apartment.

When he headed for her door, Connor realized that if he dumped all his honesty on Lara, she would never offer him the same affection she did the rest of her friends. He cursed under his breath. Damn, he couldn't keep her anyway. Sure, he could tear her apart and force her to his side temporarily, but he would go back to the Agency because it was his home. Hell or not, it was where he belonged.

So instead of seducing her tonight, he would keep his distance. It was the only gift he could give her.

He would drug her tonight, slip something into that organic wine she liked and let the wolves in. Once Connor had the information he needed, he would disappear from her life. Eventually, she would find her pansy-assed prince. They would have 2.5 kids and he would cheat on her and she would be forty and single and miserable.

And Connor would be alone. That was just how the shit had to fall. He would stay away from her, no matter how much he wanted to sink himself inside and take all that warmth as payment for being cold for so long.

The predator inside him couldn't fucking stand that she was going to get away. But he would release her because he didn't want Lara Armstrong to be one more ghost who haunted him.

He opened the door, and the heavenly smell of meat assaulted him. His stomach growled. That was some spectacular-smelling tofu.

Lara stepped out, wearing her clothes from earlier, along with a pink and yellow ruffled apron. She was biting that full lower lip and frowning. "It's almost ready." She swallowed then took a deep breath. "Do you like it bloody? Or well done?"

"What are you talking about?" Connor growled because there was no way she could be talking about what he thought she was. Lara Armstrong didn't bend. She was constant, and that had been a wall between them, one he wouldn't climb.

She was a little pale. "The, um, meat. How long do you want me to cook it?"

That was when he noticed the spot. It was small, but his gaze caught it because he wouldn't have ever expected to see a drop of blood staining her pristine apron. She'd cooked for him. For him and not just because she was cooking. She'd given up something important in order to please him.

His fairy princess had gotten bloody for him.

He crossed the space between them and had her in his arms before she could take another breath. She was so small, he just lifted her up so he could get to her mouth.

All of his resolutions from barely three minutes ago went out the window as his mouth descended to hers. He saw a moment of surprise in her big blue eyes, and then her arms wound around his shoulders and she leaned in.

He was all over her. He took two steps forward so her back flattened against the wall and he could press in, surrounding her with himself. The need to rub his body all over her was almost primal and completely irresistible. He needed to mark her, to bury his own scent in her skin so other males understood they would be forfeiting their life if they tried to touch what was his. He dominated, his tongue surging inside and stroking into her mouth in a blatant imitation of what his cock wanted.

That quickly, the most important question swirling in his brain wasn't whether he would keep her for the time being, but whether he would ever be able to let her go.

Lara was still a little breathless hours later when she finally sat down across from Connor, a glass of wine in her trembling hands. She'd poured him a couple of fingers of his ridiculously expensive Scotch and handed it to him in a crystal tumbler before deciding she needed a little liquid courage, too.

She was so confused. First he'd kissed her like he would never stop. He'd pressed her against the wall. She'd been completely dependent on him. Her feet hadn't touched the ground and her whole focus seemed to narrow to the feel of his mouth on hers. Over and over he'd kissed her, his tongue tangling with hers, his body harder than the wall. She'd felt his erection between them as she'd wrapped her legs around him, wanting to ride that cock. She'd never thought of it that way before. She'd thought of a penis in clinical terms but that big, hard erection that had rubbed all over her couldn't be described as anything less than a cock. She'd lost track of time while he'd kissed her.

At least until the smoke alarm had gone off.

Connor had set her down, kissed her forehead, and chuckled as he silenced the loud contraption. She'd burned her first try at making him a burger. Luckily, Kiki had brought her four patties, claiming a man as big as Connor could eat them all.

He'd eaten three and a half. Lincoln had been fed the other half under the table. Yes, she'd caught that. Dinner was pleasant. Connor talked for a change. He'd told her about a group of friends he'd grown up with in small-town Connecticut. He'd asked her about Kiki and Tom. They'd talked about movies they liked. Not surprisingly, he was an action junkie. She preferred romantic comedies.

They'd done the dishes in an easy, companionable fashion, and then he'd turned on a football game. The past three hours had crawled by as she stared at her computer screen, wondering what the hell that kiss had meant.

Ten minutes before, he'd shown up in the doorway to her office and asked her to make him a drink and join him in the living room. She could feel his eyes on her the whole time. Now he was sitting on her couch, leaning back with his Scotch in his hand like a king surveying his palace.

"Why did you cook for me tonight?" he asked, the question a deep, sexy rumble.

She sat across from him. How to answer that question? Right after he'd kissed her, she likely would have blurted everything without thinking. Now, she'd had hours to worry that it was a mistake. He seemed to be in an odd mood, and she thought briefly about a pithy answer. He hadn't asked her about cooking meat. Just cooking. "I was trying to be a good hostess."

His eyes narrowed. "Lie. Try again."

He could be so irritating. Why couldn't he just be polite like other men? "Why does it matter?"

"It matters to me." He glowered.

Two could play at that game. "Why did you kiss me?"

"Because I want you very badly."

"Then why, after you shut off the smoke alarm, did you pretend like it didn't happen?" That question had been bugging her all night. Had she kissed him wrong? Was she bad at it?

He arched a single jet black brow. "I didn't do that at all. After dinner, you were the one who said you needed to work. So I tried to spend as much time with you as I could. I talked with you, cleaned up with you, offered to watch TV with you. How was that pretending like it didn't happen?"

Put that way, it didn't. "I meant, why didn't you kiss me again?"

"Ah, that's what you're upset about. I didn't kiss you again because if I had, I would have taken you straight to bed and we would still be fucking. We would likely be fucking until we passed out."

And that was a problem, why? "So that game just seemed more interesting?"

His eyes narrowed, those dark orbs pinning her to her seat. "I wasn't interested in the game. I was giving us both a little time. That kiss hit me hard. I'm not a man who normally loses my head like that. I needed time to get my shit together. I wanted you to have time, too. Now that we've shared a pleasant evening, you can decide if sex with me is something you really want. I hope you've thought about it because if you say yes, we're going to do this my way and I'm not sure you're going to like that."

His way? His way had seemed really nice when he'd thrown her against the wall. Passion had welled up and she hadn't been thinking about anything but him. It had been simple and he seemed determined to make it complicated. "What's your way?"

"I'm in charge. I'll take control and you'll either say yes or we'll walk away."

"That seems harsh." It was pretty much everything she feared about him. Spencer Connor didn't seem like a man who understood the meaning of the word *compromise*. Although he had eaten with her all those days when she wasn't cooking anything he liked. And he'd given in when she'd pushed him to let her out of the condo earlier in the day. He hadn't even lectured her about how poorly the venture had gone.

"It's the only way I'll have a physical relationship with you, and I pulled back to make sure you understand. You were saved by the bell, so to speak. I'm trying to be fair with you. I want you to walk into this clear eyed and with absolutely no romantic notions."

She didn't like the sound of that. "So what you're saying is all you're willing to offer me is a few nights of sex and then you'll leave me to the next man."

"I didn't say that at all." If it was possible, the room got cold. His eyes had turned into stony orbs. "You should understand there won't be any other men. I won't tolerate it, Lara. Maybe you believe in modern relationships where two people go to bed whenever they get an itch so they scratch it with whomever seems to be handy. When it comes to you, you'll find I'm very old-fashioned. I won't hesitate to defend what I consider mine. Don't ever use another man to manipulate me. I will end him. Do you understand what I'm saying?"

He was saying if she got into bed with him, she would belong to him. "What do you really want from me?"

His lips curled up. "Now you're asking the right questions. This is why I gave us time. I don't go into anything with a lackadaisical, hope-it-works-out attitude. I want things made plain. What do I want from you? I want your warmth and affection. I want your intelligence. I want your loyalty first and foremost. I want you to understand that I'm your lover and you owe me your trust above all others. I want your body. I want to be the man who introduces you to just how sensual you can be, and I want that to mean something to you."

He hadn't mentioned a thing about love, but asking for her warmth and affection had done something to her. He was a man who needed it. His admission had lacked sentimentality, but Kiki's words earlier were ringing in her ears. She'd spent years trying to find the perfect mate only to have it fall apart again and again. She'd been looking for someone like her. Connor was her polar opposite.

Unlike Niall, Connor was being upfront and honest with her. It wasn't perfect, but it was real.

"And if the sex meant something to me, what could I expect from you? Besides the whole 'death to any man who touches me' thing."

His head fell back and his deep, almost musical laughter filled the room. When he looked back, warmth filled his gaze. "You're the only one who can do that to me, princess."

"Make you laugh?" Her hands were shaking as she took a drink. Nerves. Anticipation. Just being near him made her both the tiniest bit anxious and thrilled. Connor was completely unknown territory.

"Make me forget a lot of the reasons why I don't laugh." He patted his lap. "Come here."

She set her glass down. She'd kissed him twice, practically humping his leg both times, and yet sitting on his lap seemed so intimate. There would be no elevator doors opening or fire alarms going off. They were all alone and would be for the rest of the night. This was why he'd given them hours. He'd let her cool down, given her space to really understand he was different. A tiny part of her resented him for it. If he'd just kept kissing her, taken her to bed, she wouldn't have to make the decision. Her body would have made it for her.

"I can see you thinking. It's got to be your choice. I'll take care of you, but I refuse to be out of control. You can always tell me no, but I want you to use that no with discrimination. Trust me to know what your body needs."

"And outside the bedroom?" She couldn't be his doormat. She couldn't be a plaything he took out when he needed physical gratification.

"I'm in charge of that too, princess, though I think you'll find I can be deeply indulgent when I'm satisfied. Now answer the question and make your choice. Why did you feed me tonight?"

"Because I wanted to make you happy." There it was, the only honest answer to his question. But it left her vulnerable.

Connor rewarded her with a toe-curling smile. He patted his knee again, offering her a place. "That's what I wanted to hear. Come and sit on my lap, Lara. I want you. I want you more than I'm comfortable admitting. I know I should let you go, but I can't."

She'd studied this man for days. The men she'd been around would have coaxed her, used their charm on her. Connor was simply honest. When she thought about it, the entire evening had been his version of seduction. Giving her time had been an indulgence, but he needed to know she came to him with her eyes open.

He wanted sex, yes. But he also sought her warmth and affection because he needed those things. If he'd just called her hot and said he wanted her body, she likely could have turned him down. He'd zeroed in on the one thing guaranteed to make her say yes. He wanted the very things she valued most in herself, so she stood on shaky legs and crossed the distance between them. She watched as he exhaled, as if he'd been afraid she would refuse him.

His way. All the way. Did he realize he'd already compromised with her more than once? When things had gone bad, he'd been nothing but tender with her. If he needed to think he was always in control, she could give that to him.

She trusted him. It was time to trust herself.

Perching herself on his lap was awkward at first, but the minute his arms settled around her, that all drifted away. This was the magic of him. When he looked at her, she felt like the only woman on earth. When he focused all that energy on her, she felt alive in a way she'd never been before.

"That's right, princess. You made the decision, and now you can stop thinking and let me take over." He set his Scotch down and dropped his hand to her knee, cupping it lightly. Her whole body seemed to soften, warming up the minute he touched her.

"It's hard for me. My mind is always racing." It was why she struggled to sleep at night. Her brain dissected the day, replayed the conversations she'd had and the correspondence she'd read, then drafted to-do lists for the following day.

"Your mind is always working. Now it's time to let it rest and let your body take over. You need this as much as I do. Tell me what you like."

She sighed with relief. More talking would be good. She wasn't sure she was ready to see what Connor's "way" entailed. "I like lots of things. I like a surprising number of pop songs. There are several TV shows I'm obsessed with."

The hand on her knee tightened just enough to get her attention. "I'm talking about sex, princess. I want to know what you like about sex."

That was a great question and one that made her antsy. "I like kissing. I really like kissing you."

"Then you should kiss me."

"I thought you were in control." He was confusing her. She'd never spent so much time building up to something everyone else in the world thought should be spontaneous.

"I am." His hand slid up her leg, tantalizingly disappearing under her skirt. "That's why you're going to kiss me. It's why in a little while you're going to stand up and take your clothes off and offer yourself to me."

"What?" That wasn't how this seduction had played out in her head. He was supposed to take over, and then she wouldn't have to worry about being sexy enough for him. He would just take what he wanted and she could follow his lead, and then he would hold her and sleep next to her. His version of control really sucked.

He nuzzled her neck. "Did the poor little princess expect me to tear her clothes off and fall on her? I'm not going to play that way. I want you with me every moment. I don't want a second where you're thinking about anything except what we're doing together. I would bet every single one of your lovers let you get away with that crap. I won't. You won't lie there and not participate because you either don't know what to do or it's too messy for you. Let me tell you something. By the time I'm done, you'll like it messy and nasty and hard. Now kiss me or get off my lap and we can watch the late news."

His words seemed to have a direct line to some secret feminine place inside her. She knew she should protest, but all she wanted to do was melt in his arms. His hand parked on her thigh, just shy of where she wanted it to go, and it didn't look like he was moving it until she gave him what he wanted.

She turned her head up to face him and realized he wasn't as controlled as he wanted her to believe. He clenched his jaw tight and she reached up, brushing her fingers along the bristles of his five-o'clock shadow. He shaved every morning. She'd caught glimpses of him dragging a razor across the planes of his face, but somehow it seemed right that those whiskers were there. Another layer of texture. He reminded her of a sensual beast, one of the big cats. He could be lazy when he wanted to, but she should never forget that he could eat her up in an instant.

Her stare caught on his lips. So firm and plump and perfect. She'd become fixated on that mouth and whether she'd see a sexy smile or that arrogant, regal frown she'd come to know so well. She leaned forward and pressed her mouth to his, feeling the velvet softness of those lips. A little zing of electricity zipped through her every time she touched him.

While he had been the one to demand that she kiss him, he was perfectly still beneath her. At first it made her self-conscious. He stayed his hand, heating up her thigh. His mouth moved, but only in time to hers. He didn't leap up and take over. Was she doing it right? She wasn't sure how good a kisser she was since she'd never really taken the time to just lie around on her lover's lap and explore him.

That was the gift he was offering her. He was allowing her to explore, exactly as he'd promised. She hadn't quite believed him. And she hadn't realized just how much she wanted it.

Lara raised her hands and cupped his face, enjoying the lines of his jaw and cheeks. She didn't need to balance. He wouldn't let her fall. He would ground her so she could touch him as she liked. Emboldened by that revelation, she did what came naturally. She dragged her tongue across his lower lip. He rewarded her with a low growl that seemed to come from his chest.

She gave him one last kiss before staring into his eyes. "You're right. I've always just done what my partner wanted because I didn't want much more out of it than the cuddling and closeness that comes afterward. I didn't like kissing much before you. It was messy and awkward, but when I kiss you I don't feel any of that. But I don't know what to do when it comes to sex. I've had exactly two lovers and not a single one in the last two years."

His hand eased up, his fingers lightly playing at the edges of her panties. "Now we're getting somewhere. And you're not awkward when you kiss. You just have to stop thinking and let your instincts take over. If it helps, I haven't slept with anyone in almost eighteen months."

That was surprising. "Why? I mean, I just didn't think a man like you would go that long between lovers."

"Such a sweet thing. I didn't have lovers, princess. I had one-night stands and casual hookups. Those get boring after a while. That's why this is going to be different for both of us. I'm not going to let you treat sex like something you have to do to keep a boyfriend. I want you to crave it, to want me so much you can't think about going a day without my cock inside you. Now spread your legs for me."

Before she could think about it, her knees parted as though they obeyed Connor and nothing so insignificant as her brain. His voice had deepened, taking on an almost musical tone that had her feeling drugged. He was using this time as part of foreplay. Her experiences before had been rushed and awkward. She and Tom had found a certain rhythm after a while, but it had never been this lush, lavish dance between them. And she would never have thought to spread her legs before the actual act was about to occur.

"I don't like these, Lara." His fingers slid over her undies, a light caress that still had her straining to get enough air into her lungs.

"I don't like them very much right now, either."

His lips brushed across her cheek. "Take them off for me. Take everything off for me. Show me what you have to offer."

She stiffened in his arms, all her insecurities crashing back in. Naturally he couldn't take her to the bedroom, turn out all the lights, and then make love under three layers of covers. No. He wanted her to get naked in the middle of her living room. It wasn't like she was a prude. She walked around in her underwear all the time when she was alone. But she didn't care that her boobs sagged a little and her hips were way too round.

"Did you not hear me? Or have you decided to be a coward?" he asked in low tones. "I can't believe that of you because if there's one thing I've figured out, it's that Lara Armstrong isn't afraid of anything. She's bold and brave, and it's past time that she took all that daring she has to stand up for everyone else and use it for herself. Show me what you're offering me."

She suddenly realized that he wasn't just talking about body parts. He wasn't merely asking to see her breasts or her legs. He wanted her to be brave enough to say "This is who I am and I would like to share that with you."

Every sexual experience she'd had up to this point had been hollow. It was easy to see that now. They had been a means to an end she hadn't even acknowledged to herself. She'd wanted love and offered her body because she thought that was the only way to get it. It was as unfeminist a trait as she could think of. She thought of herself as a strong woman. She used her voice for politics and to argue for the underdog.

Why should it be different when it came to sex? Why should she accept less than her due?

She stood, her hands on her blouse. She turned to Connor. It wouldn't be right to not look him in the eyes. He should see that she was offering herself. And she was worthy.

"Slow down. I want to enjoy this." He watched her through hooded eyes.

She spent so much time in fast forward, trying to speed her way through her checklist. His reminder to slow down resonated. She never did that because she always expected something better and brighter around the next corner. Even when she achieved a goal, she didn't celebrate. She found some reason to negate the victory.

She did want to enjoy this. She wanted to connect with him, and that didn't have to wait until after the sex. They could connect before, during, and after if she just let herself be open to the experience, if she valued it the way she should.

She took a deep breath, drawing in the scent of his aftershave and memorizing it. He smelled of sandalwood and soap. That aroma drifted around her, clung to her skin, and she loved that she didn't have to be touching him to inhale him. She let her fingers find the buttons of her blouse. Cool air caressed her skin and she didn't even mind that her nipples rasped against the confines of her bra. It seemed normal now. When Connor occupied the same room, her body came alive.

She let the shirt hit the floor, and her skirt followed. When she was down to her bra and underwear, she realized her nipples weren't the only proof that Connor had an effect on her. Her underwear was definitely damp. A flush stole across her body.

"Why did you just blush?"

"I'm a little embarrassed."

"By your body? You don't have anything to be embarrassed about. You're gorgeous." His eyes lit up and he leaned forward. "Are you embarrassed because those panties are damp? Show me."

He was going to kill her. She moved forward and he put his hands on her hips. "There, now you can see them. I believe it's a reasonable response to your touching me there. So it's really your fault if you think about it."

He was staring at her. Right there. He was looking at her undies but she felt as if he'd already pulled them off her body and was gazing at her pink parts. He took a deep breath, inhaling through his nose like he was scenting the sweetest bouquet. "My fault? Do you always respond so quickly? I doubt it. That is all for me so I'm going to take the responsibility for those undies. Take them off and your bra. You don't need either one for the rest of the night."

He sat back. She'd wanted so badly to have his hands on her. The anticipation was killing her, and she was fairly certain he liked it just that way. A riot of need drowned out her embarrassment. She slipped her bra off. He wanted to see her sex. She would save it for last. She took a long breath as her nipples tightened even further under his gaze. Her skin felt too tight, the room suddenly unbearably warm.

"Fuck, you're gorgeous, Lara. Inside and out. Show me what I really want to see." He adjusted on the couch, and there was no way to miss the bulge that tented his jeans. Seeing that made it easier for her to let go of her inhibitions.

She hooked her thumbs under the waistband and slowly lowered them, adding them to her little pile of clothes Connor believed she didn't need.

He watched her intently for a long moment before he patted his thigh, silently instructing her to climb back onto his lap.

"But your jeans . . ."

He grasped her wrist and tugged, tumbling her into his arms. She found herself sitting on his lap, her legs splayed across his. "I didn't ask you to worry about my laundry. I told you I was in charge and that means obeying me. I want you on my lap. I want your legs spread wide and your body completely vulnerable to me."

He held her legs open, spreading her with his knees. Cool air hit her slick folds and she shivered at the sensation. She'd never really paid attention to her sensual side, but now with his hands on her skin and his hot breath on her neck, she wanted to drown in it. His denim scraped her backside softly as he trapped her against his body, forcing her back to arch, her breasts to thrust up, and her head to rest on his shoulder. She felt as if he'd put her on display.

His hands began to roam the minute she relaxed against him. "This is what I've wanted from the moment I first saw you—you open for me." As he cupped her breasts in his massive hands, he pressed his hips up, letting her feel how hard he was. "And I definitely wanted to give you this."

With his cock pressed against her backside, his fingers slipped over her clitoris. Her whole body reacted, her pelvis lifting to those fingers. She'd never felt so hot, like her body wasn't really solid. She was some silky creature, writhing on Connor's lap, desperate for some sensation that was just out of reach.

He jerked his hand away. "Don't try to steal an orgasm from me. You'll get it when I say you'll get it. If you try that again, I'll go to bed and we can start this all over again tomorrow."

Embarrassment flashed through her system and she started to sit up. "I'm sorry."

His arms tightened around her. "Don't go. Give me what I need."

"I don't understand. I wasn't trying to steal anything. It just felt good."

His chest rose and fell with the force of his breaths. He exhaled a calming sigh. "I need you to let me please you. I'm at the end of my restraint and I've allowed you to lead as much as I can right now. Let me take control."

From Connor it was practically begging. The last thing she wanted was that proud man on his knees.

She relaxed against him, giving herself over completely. No more holding back. No more questions. If she was going to surrender, she would be one hundred percent committed. He'd earned her trust by saving her life more than once. Yes, the feelings developing between them had blossomed quickly, but she didn't think that taking it slow was the answer. Her connection to him had been instant, unlike the one she'd shared with Tom. Maybe it was time to trust her instincts, and every single one of them said to leap.

"You won't regret it." His arms tightened around her as though he was afraid she would flee.

She glanced at him over her shoulder, trying to meet his gaze. "I trust you, Spencer."

"Connor. I like Connor." His body had stiffened.

"Connor." So what if he didn't like his given name? She'd wanted to use it to be more intimate, but she would honor his wishes. "I trust you, Connor."

He growled a little and she could have sworn he cursed under his breath, but he dragged his hand down her body, right to that place he'd been playing with before she'd made the mistake. She wasn't going to make the same one again. When his finger teased at her clitoris, she rested her head against his shoulder again and remained still.

"That's what I want." He kissed her earlobe, nibbling on that soft flesh in a way that made her squirm. "You take what I give you. You're mine. But you'll find I enjoy making you feel good, princess."

With his knees, he spread her wider. She stifled a scream of pure pleasure when his finger invaded. Electricity sizzled through her, a jolt of shock that had her bucking with sensation. She hadn't even realized how much she needed him to fill her. He kept his thumb on her clitoris while he shoved his thick finger deep inside her.

"You're so fucking tight. God, I won't last. I'm going to make sure you're very satisfied because I'll come the minute I feel this hot pussy all around me. Tell me what you're going to do when I fuck you."

She couldn't breathe. His finger curled inside her, rubbing a sensitive spot that shot tingles down her legs, up to her nipples. Euphoria bubbled. Somehow he'd known exactly where to find that place deep inside her and he worked it until she felt like a pleasure bomb just waiting to go off. She hadn't even known such a spot existed.

Connor pressed his thumb down on her little button, exerting the right pressure to keep her on the edge. When she didn't answer him, he stopped everything. "Tell me, Lara. What are you going to do when my cock is so deep inside your pussy you can't tell where I end and you begin? What are you going to do? Let go of all your inhibitions. Talk dirty to me. I want it."

She ached. The pleasure swirled, consuming her, overwhelming her. Her heartbeat roared. She couldn't stop herself from blurting the first words that flooded her brain. "I'm going to squeeze you so tight, Connor. I'll clamp down hard and do everything I can to keep your cock inside me because I won't ever want you to leave."

"Hmm, princess. I knew you could have a dirty mouth." His finger moved faster, as though her words spurred him on. "Do you have any idea what that does to me?"

She had a pretty good notion. His hips started to rock against her backside as though he couldn't stop himself. Captured between his hand and his cock, she felt like she was riding a magnificent beast. She couldn't control anything so primal. All she could do was hold on and trust him.

"Come for me, princess. Give me what you've never given another man in your life," he growled in her ear.

Her body tightened until she was sure something would burst. Just when she thought she couldn't take another second, his thumb rubbed with the perfect pressure as his finger thrust deeper. Lara went over the edge.

In the back of her head, she realized that all her previous orgasms had been tiny bursts, inconsequential flutters of pleasure. In Connor's arms, she experienced something completely different. This orgasm flashed white-hot, blistering through her system. The pleasure seized her, possessed her. She jolted against his hand and went wild, trying to squeeze out every second of the exquisite sensation. For long moments, she twisted in his grip, like a marionette dancing for a puppet master as he prolonged the ecstasy far longer than she had the breath to scream.

Finally, Lara fell back, completely exhausted.

The world upended as he stood, cradling her in his arms as if she weighed nothing at all.

"Good. Now that we have that out of the way, it's my turn. And I don't intend to go easy on you."

She shivered at the promise in his voice. She'd been sure she couldn't possibly experience anything more earth-shattering than what he'd just given her, but Lara was suddenly convinced that he intended to try.

She didn't bother to put her arms around him. Connor wouldn't let her fall. She'd finally found the man she could trust with her body. She knew her heart was already halfway there, too.

"Anything you want," she vowed.

He carried her into her bedroom, and Lara was certain that she would never be the same again.

SEVEN

C onnor couldn't remember a time when his dick had been harder. He'd been worried about how silent the damn thing had been since Greta had nearly fileted him. She'd been a supermodel of an operative. Sex on two very long, dangerous legs. He'd had some of the world's most stunning women in his bed, but this short, curvy little sprite who'd induced him to dry hump her like a fucking fifteen-year-old had nearly undone him. He never lost control like that, and he swore as he carried her into her bedroom that he wouldn't do it again. He wasn't going to sink into her and fucking forget why he'd tracked her down in the first place. He would make sure she was taken care of but he wasn't going to lose his head.

Or anything else.

She trusted him. She'd proven it by giving herself over to him. The minute her body had fully relaxed, he knew he had her. All he had to do was reach out and take, and she would be his—only his.

That was the moment he'd decided to keep her.

Anything you want, she'd offered him.

Well, he'd never wanted anything more than he wanted her, but he could manage that desire. He could wrap her up in bonds so strong that when she discovered the truth, she would still choose him. Eventually, he would tell her his real name and that those close boyhood friends he'd mentioned were now superpowerful men, but she never had to know everything. He'd tell her that he'd acted to protect her. If he gave her enough pleasure, she would believe him and stay. He could have all that warmth and softness for himself.

He laid her down on the bed and grabbed fistfuls of his shirt. He tugged it over his head and tossed it aside. He would take care of her and provide for her. She never had to know he was anything but an analyst with the CIA. He would pull back on foreign assignments and he would make sure she stayed out of trouble.

In exchange, he would give her the family she craved, the stability she required. Hell, he would find all the dirt on her parents and bury it so no one would ever find it—especially her. He would protect her and her folks the way he'd protected his friends all these years. Surely that was a good exchange.

He shoved out of his jeans, his cock desperate to be free.

She'd managed to sit up among the myriad pillows that littered her bed. Her dark hair fell in tumbling waves all the way down to her breasts, curling around one nipple. Now that he had her naked, she seemed perfectly comfortable. She watched him, her eyes wide. She looked ethereal in the moonlit room, like any fairy princess should. The drapes were open, but her unit was up higher than all the surrounding buildings, so he didn't worry about anyone peeking in.

He liked seeing her in the silvery shadows. It made her skin glow. And as she watched him undress, her stare zipped right to his cock and a flush darkened her cheeks.

"Do you like what you see, princess?" He found himself a bit self-conscious. Every inch of her skin was dewy perfection. He was covered in scars. He was older than her other lovers. She tended toward doe-eyed idealists. He was as far from that as a man could be.

She twisted up, crawling toward him in a way that made her breasts bounce, and his dick tightened almost painfully. She balanced on her knees, ass resting on her heels, her hands perched on her thighs as she looked him over. "You're a beautiful man. I've never known anyone like you."

His gut coiled up. She didn't know him at all. He couldn't correct her, so he rationalized his every deceit. If he hadn't come after her, Roman would have sent someone else who wouldn't have even tried to protect her. He could still make this right for her. He would.

"Come here," he cajoled. "Touch me."

He needed to slow down, feel her hands on him. Now that he had her in her bedroom, he wanted to take this slow. They only had one first time together.

It damn sure wouldn't be their last.

When had he turned into a fucking sentimental old man?

As he'd been thinking in circles, Lara had risen to stand in front of him. She touched her palm to his chest and brushed over his skin, her fingers finding the scars. She caressed the thin white line on his bicep leftover from a knife fight in Macau. She traced the jagged flesh along his ribs where he'd taken fire from a double agent in Dubai.

She stopped at the newest mottled flesh, a short but nasty scar from the blade Greta had shoved into his chest. She leaned over and placed her lips there.

The moment vibrated. Sensation rushed him.

Stunned and unmoving, Connor barely dared to breathe as she kissed her way across his chest. Her hair fell against his skin, a soft touch that sensitized him. As if he needed to be more sensitive to her. His cock was so hard he was sure it would thump against her belly in a desperate bid for attention.

Finally her hands made their way to his hips.

She bit her bottom lip and cautiously brushed her hand over his unruly cock. Her fingertips found the head of his dick and she seemed utterly fascinated by the pearly drop seeping there. It was evidence he'd been so close to the edge. She swiped her thumb across it and he was right back there, fighting against the loss of control.

He couldn't do it. He couldn't take another second of her hands on him or he would lose it. "Lie down on the bed. I want your ass on the edge, knees in the air, wide apart."

"What?" She shook her head like she hadn't heard him properly.

He sank a hand into all that hair and used it to tilt her head up so she was forced to look him in the eyes. "You. Bed. Edge. Legs spread. I'm going to eat your pussy and you're going to lie very still while I make a meal out of you."

Her breath came in sexy gasps. Her heavy breasts with their hard tips pointing up, along with her pink cheeks and dilated pupils, were like a barometer for her arousal. Not three minutes after her first orgasm, she was starting to squirm.

He could seize control again by making her beg. "Now."

She nodded and nearly stumbled in her haste to reach the bed. Once she'd decided to obey him, she did it with all the enthusiasm she put into one of her causes. If she felt awkward now, he couldn't tell. Her breasts bounced as she lay back on the bed and splayed out. "I've always wanted to know what this felt like."

How could she make him laugh in the middle of something that felt so fucking serious? Or incite that twinge in his chest when he realized no man had ever given her this pleasure. There was zero artifice in the way she acted. She wasn't trying to seduce secrets out of him. She wasn't trying to gain the upper hand. She simply wanted him to make her come again, to make her scream, and she would enthusiastically comply with his every order to get it.

"Touch yourself. Stroke your pussy." He had to be very specific.

"I've done that before," she said, blushing. She shook her head, but her hand trailed down her body and she gently worked two fingers over her labia.

He dropped to his knees, putting those wet, swollen folds right at eye level. Her pink-tipped fingers were already glistening with her own arousal. He'd done that to her, gotten her wet and creamy. "No man has ever eaten your pussy? Keep stroking yourself."

Transfixed, he watched her fingers glide over her flesh.

Her voice was deeper than normal, a little husky. "Tom never wanted oral sex."

"So clinical," he tsked. "You won't get what you want until you ask for it properly."

"Please give me oral sex."

"Are you kidding me?"

"Please put your mouth there. On me. On my pussy." She was awfully cute when she fumbled. And she definitely sounded a bit breathless. "Yes, I would like you to put your mouth on my pussy and then move your tongue all around. Kiki talks about how nice it feels but only when she's had too much to drink."

"The correct term is *eating pussy*. That's what I'm going to do to you. Spread your labia for me. Tell me why Tom wouldn't want to taste this sweet pussy." He could smell her arousal, musky and pure.

"He said it wasn't natural."

"The hell it isn't." Connor leaned forward, gently grasping her wrist and bringing her fingers to his lips. With her eyes on him, he sucked her cream-coated fingers into his mouth and licked off every last bit of her essence. "He's a fucking idiot. You taste so damn good, and I'll show you just how nice it feels to have the big bad wolf make a meal of you."

He leaned forward and ran his tongue right over her clit. She gasped and nearly came off the bed.

Connor stopped. "Be still or I'll tie you down and bring you to the edge over and over again. Then I'll give you nothing."

She went completely still. "That sounds horrible. But the other part felt even better than Kiki said."

"And no more mentioning Kiki or anyone else now. You and me and no one else in the entire world. Am I clear?"

"Yes." Her body was still, but he could feel her effort in her fine trembling.

"Who's going to fuck you?" He liked hearing his name on her lips.

"Connor. My Connor."

That did more for him than he liked to admit. "Only me."

He'd never given a crap about where a lover was going after he'd finished with her. During college, he and Dax had shared women on many a night. There were women at Yale who had made a game out of bagging all six of them. Connor had just shrugged and taken his turn.

The thought of anyone else touching Lara Armstrong made him crazy. Something primal inside him had taken one look at her and decided she belonged to him—and his higher-functioning brain could go to hell.

He lowered his head to her pussy and devoured her. He licked and sucked and gave her a light scrape of his teeth. All the while she whimpered and cried out, each moan going straight to his dick. He reveled in every bit of her as he pulled back the hood of her clit. That pearl was engorged and desperate, ready to go off at the slightest sensation.

"Please. Please, Connor."

"Please what, princess? Do you remember what I said to you the first day we met? I told you it might make you feel safer if I didn't make love to you until you begged me. So what do you want me to do? I think I'll forgo you getting on your knees and I'll simply accept a very polite request."

"Please make love to me, Connor."

"Now go a little dirtier for me."

"Please, please fuck me."

"With pleasure, princess." He sucked her clit between his teeth and was rewarded with a scream that just might have the police storming the condo. She cried out his name as he drew out her pleasure. Her legs shook and spasmed, and by the time he lifted his head, her whole body was flushed and trembling.

She lay there, her eyes half closed, her body utterly spent. She wasn't thinking about anything now. That was clear. He could do anything he wanted to her. She was his, body and soul, in that moment, and all he'd had to do was give her a few orgasms. This could work. *They* could work. He could keep and protect her. She never had to know the whole truth.

In fact, maybe she was his reward for all the bad shit that had come before and all the darkness he still had yet to endure.

He fished a foil packet out of his jeans. The minute he'd walked into the condo, he'd known this would happen. He'd prepared. She hadn't seen him do it, but he'd already moved a box of condoms into her bedside table. He'd saved one because he hadn't been sure where he would fuck her first. By the time he was done, he would use every surface and room in this place. There wouldn't be a single inch of this space that wouldn't remind her of what it felt like to have him inside her.

He rolled the condom on his rock-hard cock.

"Connor?" She lifted her head to look at him.

Shit. He couldn't lose her now. "Yes?"

She wore the sweetest grin on her face, as if she'd been drugged from all the pleasure. "I thought I was one of those women who couldn't have an orgasm, but I had two. I'm fully functional."

Had Tom told her she wasn't? That's right, the prick had called her frigid because he was too fucking clueless or selfish to please a woman. Connor wrapped his fingers around her ankles and positioned her right where he wanted her. He could see her whole gorgeous body laid out, her breasts, her silky skin, that pussy so close to his cock. She gripped her comforter tightly, looking breathless.

God, had he really been looking for weapons in her hands? He'd thought he was over that shit.

Lara wasn't capable of hurting a fly, much less her lover, and he intended to keep it that way. She was going to live in a world where shit like that didn't happen.

"Wrap your legs around me." When she did, he pushed the head of his dick just inside her. Already the heat and pressure were killing him. So fucking soft. Everything about her was silky and welcoming, including the quickness with which she heeded his needy commands.

With her eyes wide and focused on him, Lara reached up to touch him. He grabbed her hands and held them down. He couldn't have her arms around him. Not yet. Maybe in a couple of years, but for now he needed this. She was utterly trapped beneath him while he assumed total control.

His eyes nearly rolled into the back of his head as he pressed forward. She was so wet. If he hadn't gotten her hot first, he doubted he could have worked his way inside her easily, if at all. Her pussy was the tightest thing he'd ever felt. Those endlessly blue eyes of hers stared up at him, widening with each inch he took.

But he needed to be deeper. "Relax. You can take me. You can take all of me."

She sucked in a deep, ragged breath and exhaled, her body melting into the mattress as she tilted her pelvis up so he slipped completely inside her. He groaned long and low.

Very slowly, he began to drag himself back out, fighting the urge to pound into her. He wanted her to love this, to need him as often as possible. He didn't have months to brand himself on her before his cover story could unravel. He had days, a week or two at most, and he needed her bound to him. So he fought his desperate desire and stroked into her, long and slow, moving his hips in a rhythm, finding that spot inside her.

"Oh god." Her legs gripped him like a vise as she panted and whimpered.

He locked in place and let himself go. Over and over he fucked her deep, providing friction to those nerve endings until her whole body flushed and she cried out his name. Her head thrashed against the comforter, the only movement he allowed her. Other than that, he controlled her body, forcing her to take each stroke of his cock, every hard thrust.

She clenched around him and he felt her body seize as she came with abandon. Her ecstasy sent him hurtling toward the edge. He couldn't hold back for more than another second or two.

Connor pounded deep into her softness, lost to the primal rhythm of mating. He hated the fucking condom. He wanted to mark her, to know his seed might take root. Hell, in that moment he wanted to get her pregnant. She couldn't leave him if she was carrying his child, right? Then they would also have a connection she couldn't deny, no matter how angry she got if she learned the truth.

His spine tingled and his brain shut down. Pure electric pleasure sparked through his system. Orgasm hit him with the force of a crashing wave. He pumped into her like a piston, using hard, rhythmic strokes to give her everything he had.

God, he was going to marry her.

It took long moments before his breathing and heartbeat normalized. Pleasure lingered in his veins like a sweetly heavy drug. Just when Connor was about to collapse, he propped himself above her, struggling to catch his breath and bring his heartbeat back under control.

What the hell was he thinking? Marriage? Babies? She had his head reeling. This was not like him. He eased back and rose to his feet, taking a long breath. His whole body was still pulsing with pleasure and he wanted to press himself against her and share the buzz, but he needed a minute alone.

"I'll be right back." He turned, but not before he saw the startled hurt in her eyes.

She'd expected him to fall into her arms and give her "after" time, complete with cuddling and praise, no doubt. Instead, he picked up his clothes and stumbled into the bathroom, closing the door between them. He disposed of the condom he'd thought about not wearing.

Deep breath, Sparks. What the hell just happened? He stared at himself in the mirror. He'd lost control in the end. He'd let go in a way he never did.

He'd utterly forgotten that he had a job to do.

After turning on the faucet to cold, he reached into his jeans and pulled out his phone, texting Roman. He'd left the door unlocked. It was a calculated risk, but his gun was on the nightstand. As soon as Roman had what he needed, Connor would lock them in again.

He was letting the wolves into the princess's castle. He was going to distract her by fucking her all over again.

Why did he already feel a twinge of guilt for doing what he needed to?

Gritting his teeth, he pounded his fists against the sink, and he was lucky he didn't crack the marble.

Lara knocked softly on the door. "Connor? Are you all right? Did I do something wrong?"

He couldn't continue dithering about her like some inexperienced idiot. He'd already made his choice and contacted Roman. There was no calling him off now. And there was no going back with Lara. He'd taken her. He could tell himself he would walk away at the end, but he made it a practice never to deceive himself. He would have her again and again and again. He would never fucking be satisfied.

So he needed to suck it up and start being the man he was. Stop trying to be worthy of her. He never would be, but that didn't mean he couldn't take her, keep her close, and do his best. Sure, he'd have to lie to her. He'd have to manipulate her. He could manage that. After all, he'd made a profession out of dealing in misdirection and falsehoods. In return, he'd protect and sate her. It wasn't much but all he had to offer. He'd never had anything to call his own, and he wanted Lara to be his. In the end, he knew he might cost her everything, but he couldn't leave her alone.

Shame that he couldn't be better for her slithered through him but he tamped the useless shit down.

And now he was being a coward because he'd closed a door between them. He would never allow her to do that to him. It was time to stop fucking around and be her man.

He opened the door and had her in his arms before he could second-guess himself again. He would do what he had to do for the operation, but he'd fight to the death to keep her. She'd given him everything she had and he wouldn't let her take it back. But he had to give a little, too. He had to get over his fucking PTSD.

Connor pulled her close and felt her arms go around him. "You didn't do anything wrong, princess. You were perfect." He lifted her hand to touch his newest scar. "The reason I haven't had sex in almost two years was the last woman I went to bed with gave me this."

She gasped and all that doubt immediately became concern as she placed her hand right over the puckered gash as though she could somehow heal him. "Was it a knife wound?"

He nodded. "She was a little crazy. So I got overwhelmed. Forgive me."

She was on her toes, enthusiastically kissing him. "Of course. I was worried. I . . . care about you. I didn't want this to be the only time. I didn't want this to be our only night."

Not if he had any say in it. "I care about you, too. We've started something tonight. I told you I didn't want some casual thing. We're together now, and I intend for us to stay that way."

She laid her head against his chest. "Do you want to go back to bed?"

He picked her up. "The answer to that question will always be yes."

He laid her out and proceeded to show her how much he wanted her.

It was two in the morning when he heard it. Such a little sound, but then he'd been waiting for the *snick* of a door closing as quietly as possible.

Roman was here.

Lara turned over in her sleep, her hair in a tumble across the pillow. He'd been right. When her tresses were loose, they went everywhere. They were like wild vines creeping softly across his body, drawing him in. All he wanted to do was curl around her and go back to sleep, pretend there wasn't a team outside trying to steal her secrets.

Yes, she still had them and he couldn't allow her to keep any. He couldn't protect her if he didn't know what she concealed. No matter what happened, he had to make sure she was all right, and that meant finding out absolutely everything he could about her.

He could justify it all day, but it didn't stop the guilt in his gut and he resented the hell out of it. This was his job. He'd never before felt guilty for protecting his president.

He rolled out of bed as quietly as he could and paused to make sure she wasn't moving. The moonlight washed over her, and his heart flipped a little. God, he was in deeper than he'd imagined. He needed some distance. He wasn't letting her go, but he had to find a way to not need her so much. Surely, he could devise a strategy to keep his soul from threatening to spill out every time he had sex with her.

It would get easier. Everything between them was new right now and she was different from any woman he'd ever met. The newness would wear off and he would be able to enjoy her the way he should. He would do his job and keep his secrets and she would be his reward.

He forced himself to look away and grab his gun off the nightstand, just in case. After all, a killer sought her. In fact, he kind of hoped the killer was, even now, sneaking through her door, rather than Roman. Connor suspected he would feel loads better after killing Lara's stalking scumbag.

As silently as he could, he opened the door and walked down the hallway. Black figures moved through her apartment. Connor slipped down the hall, staying in the shadows. He counted four of them. All big guys. No crazy stalkers. He was out of luck on the killing front. Roman seemed to hire security for their bulk as though he wanted to make sure every guard could physically cover Zack in the event of an assassination attempt.

Of course Roman had been onstage with Joy Hayes when she'd died from a fumbled attempt to kill Zack. Maybe Connor could understand, but then he could also tell Roman that bulk didn't always win. Connor managed to sneak past three of the guards and get right behind Roman, who was hovering over Lara's computer. He placed the muzzle of his gun squarely against Roman's head.

"Please tell me that's you, Con. Because otherwise I might ruin a perfectly good pair of pants for nothing."

Connor grinned in the darkness. It was good to know he could still scare the shit out of someone. He pulled away. "Safety's on. But you need new guys. I got past all of them."

Roman turned, shaking his head. "I keep asking you to come and take the whole thing over. We would all feel better if you worked at the White House. Is your girl out? Did you roofie her?"

"No." At least he wouldn't have that on his conscience. "I couldn't find an organic, cruelty-free brand."

"Was that a joke? What has she done to you, man?"

The last thing he wanted to do was talk about his relationship. He didn't really want to think about the fact that she trusted him and he was betraying her. "What have you found?"

"I downloaded her system. I'll go over it at my leisure. The boys out there are tapping her landline and duping her cell. We've also now got a feed into this building so we'll be able to see who comes and goes. And thanks for the heads-up about the senator firing his guards today. I was able to get some of my men on his detail. That will come in handy. They can search the senator's place when he's asleep. The more dirt I have on the old guy, the more leverage. Oppo research has never been more fun. You said she's close to her dad, right?"

Connor didn't like the turn of this conversation. He really didn't appreciate Roman inserting his own guards into the senator's house and life so they could spy on him for another politician. "Why do you care? And Armstrong has almost always supported Zack. How is he oppo?"

The smile faded from Roman's face. "I care about this mission, Connor. I expect that you do, too. Armstrong might be in the party, but he knows what his daughter does and he doesn't shut her down, so I don't trust him. Is there something I need to know? Dax seems to think you've got a serious hard-on for this girl. Have you forgotten what she does for a living?"

"I know what she does and why she does it. I'm committed to figuring out where Natalia Kuilikov is, but I don't see what that has to do with Senator Armstrong." He kind of liked Lara's dad. Sure he'd thought of digging up dirt on the man, but he didn't like the idea of Roman being in control of it.

Roman turned back. "I'll handle the political portion of this clusterfuck. By the way, you're welcome. I got you reinstated with the Agency starting in six weeks. You'll find yourself in the unique position of being able to choose your assignment. You can have any field job you want or you can run a team of your own."

Where was the relief? He'd expected to feel some triumph in putting one over on his director, who had thought he could use the situation in Manhattan to get rid of Agent Sparks. The old man didn't realize just how close he was to Zack. So why didn't Connor want to fist pump and start figuring out what his next move should be? He could get back into the Middle East or North Korea. He could go solo or form his own team. He would likely be given enormous leeway to do what needed to be done.

All he could think about was that he only had six weeks left to ensure Lara would still be here when he returned. If he returned. Operatives who took the kind of chances he did rarely lived to a ripe old age. What would happen to her if he wasn't around? She could get into serious trouble, and he doubted she would properly defend herself. She would try to bring out her flipping talking stick and form a trust circle around her attacker.

"You don't seem happy." Roman was studying him, likely using that big brain of his to reach conclusions that Connor didn't want him drawing.

"It's great. I've just got a lot to think about. Did Everly have any luck finding our guy in the park?" He needed to get Roman off the subject of his relationship with Lara.

"Yep. You can calm down. Your girl is being stalked by a pro. The good old Russian mob is back in play. He's a man named Pavel Sopov. According to the very top secret FBI database Everly hacked into, he's a low-level member of a syndicate."

"Let me guess. He's a Brighton Beach associate of the Krylov gang."

"Absolutely." Roman leaned against Lara's desk. "I need to figure out what Krylov wants. He's making some moves I don't quite understand. And I still want to know who the hell Sergei is. Krylov's name is Ivan, so it's not him."

"He runs much of Moscow. From intel the Agency's collected, I know he's been a big player in arming jihadists in Afghanistan and the Middle East. He plays both sides. Doesn't care about politics. If you've got the money, you can buy from him. Now we know he had an arm of the syndicate that ran a human trafficking ring. But we have no idea if Sergei had anything to do with that. There's no higher-ups in the organization by that name."

"Why do you think Krylov would spend time and money trying to terrify Lara Armstrong?"

That was simple. "He believes the same thing we do, that she can lead him to Natalia. The question is does he want to silence Natalia? Or blackmail Zack? My money's on blackmail."

A long sigh came from Roman. "Mine, too. Which is why we have to find out what she knows. Can't you just fuck the information out of her? What happened to pillow talk?"

"She fell asleep. Maybe your lovers have the capacity to talk after you do whatever you do, but mine just tend to drop off because I don't leave them with any energy to talk."

The truth was Connor hadn't even thought about talking to Lara about the case. Before she'd drifted off, he'd just wanted to fuck her again and again. If she'd stayed awake, he would likely be buried inside her again, and he didn't want those men hearing her. She wasn't quiet. She let him and likely everyone on this floor know just what a good time she was having. He couldn't stand the thought of these men knowing how she sounded when she came.

Roman shot him the finger. "Like I have time to fuck. I swear to god after Zack's second term I'm going to Vegas and you won't see me for at least three months."

Cameras were always on Roman. He walked a fine line. He dated occasionally, always some model or actress. He stayed utterly away from anyone in politics.

"I need to get back to Lara," Connor said. "She wakes up occasionally. I don't want her walking out here."

Roman held out a hand. "I'll study the information we get, but you have to start asking her questions. I get that you like the girl, but you can't forget who your friends are."

"Funny, I bet you didn't give Gabe this talk when he got together with Everly."

"Everly's family. She was Mad's sister."

And Lara wasn't family. Lara was the enemy in Roman's mind. Roman tended to take out the enemy without blinking. "I'm still in charge of this operation. You don't do anything without my go-ahead."

Roman shrugged and gave him a "who me?" expression he didn't buy for a second. "Of course, brother. We just need to find Kuilikov and then this can all be over. We can get back to our regularly scheduled lives. We'll be out of your hair in five minutes. She's got a safe I want to look into."

"A safe?" He hadn't been able to properly search her place. He'd spent that first night sleeping, and every other night he'd been worried she would find him and kick him to the curb. He tried not to let her out of his sight during the day. So the secondary team had been a necessary evil. And an effective one, apparently.

"One of my men found it. It's not standard in these buildings. She must have installed a custom job because it's in the back wall of her coat closet behind about fifty sweaters. Smart. I wouldn't have looked there but I told the boys to be thorough. Too bad for her I already found the

She wrote it in her day planner."

n amateur mistake. She went to the trouble of having a safe

and then was afraid she would forget the code so she wrote it down, thereby letting any thief with half a brain take whatever was inside. "I'll go with you and see what's in there."

He couldn't give her secrets over to Roman without even seeing them. And . . . he wasn't sure he trusted Roman to stick with the plan without someone watching over his shoulder. Roman could be ruthless when it came to protecting Zack.

"Connor?" A feminine voice cut through the quiet.

Shit. He rushed out of the office, not looking back. Everyone seemed to have melted back into the shadows. He picked out where the men were hiding, but he doubted Lara would. Still, he had no intention of letting her see a damn thing. He blocked her exit from the hall.

And the view of any fucker who might see her. She wasn't wearing a stitch of clothing. Her body was like a beacon in the gloom.

She gasped and stepped back. "You have a gun."

He let it dangle at his side and used his free hand to smooth back her hair. He tried to make sure he was covering her so no one behind them could see her and every part that fucking belonged to him. He had to force a pleasant look on his face. "I thought I heard something. It was just someone walking in the hall outside. The doors are all locked. But as long as you're awake . . ."

She laughed as he maneuvered her back to the bedroom. "You have more energy than any man I know."

"When it comes to you, hell yes, I do. Come on, princess. I'm still hungry." He backed her into her bedroom, shut and locked the door.

She looked up at him, her hands going to his chest. "I was worried about you."

He shook his head. "No need. I can take care of both of us. It's what I'm here for."

She leaned against him, cuddling up. "I just don't want anything bad to happen to you. I couldn't stand it."

He wrapped his arms around her and pondered the irony of her worry for the well-being of the big bad wolf. He'd never really had a woman worry about him. "I'm going to be fine. I've trained to combat danger all my life. Look at me."

Her head tilted up and he was awed at the trust he saw there.

He kissed her forehead. "We're going to be fine. No matter what. I need you to believe that. I'm going to take care of you. I'm going to make sure you're safe."

No matter what he had to do.

He lowered his mouth to hers and tried to forget that they weren't alone.

EIGHT

Every muscle in her body was deliciously sore. Lara stretched as she prepped breakfast. Kiki had brought her some eggs for Connor, so he could have a scramble with spinach and peppers, rather than her usual tofu. She might have given on the animal products, but she intended to sneak some veggies into his diet one way or another. She cracked another egg into the skillet. He looked like a man who could eat four eggs. Maybe more. He'd expended an enormous amount of energy the night before.

She felt a grin spread across her face. He might be a carnivore, but he was the most spectacular lover in the history of time. Now she knew why Kiki giggled when she talked about sex. She couldn't seem to stop smiling when her whole body felt alive.

He'd taken over her shower just fifteen minutes before, using his big body to trap her and kiss her until she was breathless. With her hands over her head, both manacled by one of his, she'd been utterly at his mercy and he'd had none. He'd grabbed the soap and washed her off, paying very close attention to his favorite parts. She'd cried out his name.

Apparently, she was a screamer. Lara had always thought she was very ladylike in bed, but Connor brought out her inner vixen. There was no place for decorum when his mouth was on her.

She'd even turned the tables on him, taking his erection in her soapy hands and rubbing. She'd watched him, utterly fascinated when his cock had surged and released in her hand.

She felt a little damp and flushed just thinking about it.

Lara scooped his eggs onto a plate just as her doorbell rang. She was almost to the door when Connor scowled at her from the hallway.

"What do you think you're doing?" He was back in bodyguard mode, wearing jeans and a dark T-shirt, his shoulder holster and gun on display.

In her mind, she could still see him naked, feel every muscle and indention of his body. And all the scars. What had he been through besides the psychotic ex? Probably a lot. She wanted to kiss all his scars, to let him know he was safe with her.

She gave him a little smile. "I was just coming to get you so you could answer the door."

His eyes narrowed, but he rewarded her with a slight hint of a smile. "Sure you were, princess." Now when he called her princess it made her warm and happy. He winked as he brushed past her. "Get out of view until I tell you it's safe. We're going over protocol this morning. After yesterday, I'm putting some new rules in place."

She wrinkled her nose. He loved rules of all kinds when they applied to her. In fact, he seemed to relish them. "That does not sound like fun."

"I'm going to have a ton of fun going over all the new boundaries. Can you fix me some coffee, baby?" He strode toward the door.

At least if she was stuck in the house, she was stuck with him. If he was going to restrict her routine and control her schedule, he could entertain her. She had a list of things she wanted to try. After last night, her imagination had opened up. Now her mind was a veritable *Kama Sutra*.

She poured Connor a cup of coffee and took both plates to the table. Hopefully whoever had knocked on the door wouldn't need too much attention. Their breakfast would get cold.

She'd gotten an e-mail the night before from a woman named Everly Parker. *The* Everly Parker. Maddox Crawford's sister wanted to talk to her about something and she was coming to D.C. today. Lara had already started mentally composing a list of questions to ask the woman. Her brother had somehow been involved in the plot to cover up Natalia Kuilikov's whereabouts. The conversation would be delicate, but she intended to find out what Parker knew. Lara hoped Crawford's sister could provide more information about this piece of the very large puzzle she and Freddy had started to fit together a little over a year ago.

That wasn't her only problem. She had to figure out how she was going to slip past Connor to meet her informant at midnight. He would bolt if he saw Connor there. Maybe she should think about giving up on this particular story. The idea of tricking him didn't sit well with her.

Or maybe she should tell him everything and ask for his advice. He could be her partner.

The only thing that held her back was the fact that he'd used Zack Hayes as a reference. How loyal was he to the president? How would he feel when he found out exactly why she was investigating the commander in chief?

"I need to talk to Lara." Tom's voice rang down the hall.

"We really do. There's something freaky going on with Freddy," Kiki chimed in. "Not that there isn't always something freaky happening with that guy, but this is even weirder than normal."

Despite Connor's warning, she stepped into the hallway. Freddy had issues, but she could usually talk him down. "Come on in."

Kiki set Lincoln down and he immediately started jumping up on Connor's leg. Traitor. Her dog had turned on her for a little beef. Connor scooped the pup up and then turned, giving her a stare that could

have frozen a blazing fire. That stare promised retribution for misbe-
havior.

She shivered but not in fear. Connor was rapidly turning her into
a sex-crazed woman.

"Later," he mouthed as he let her friends in.

"Your breakfast is on the table and I brewed fresh coffee." She gave
him a smile she hoped would calm his savage beast a little.

"I'll get him some water." He leaned over, kissing her right in front
of her friends. "Behave until I get back. And if you set foot out of this
apartment or unlock that door while I'm gone, you won't like what
happens when I catch you."

His dark tone sent another shiver down her spine. She watched him
until he disappeared into her kitchen.

"Holy shit, you slept with him." Kiki's eyes were wide.

Tom shook his head, his jaw hanging slightly open. "No. She
wouldn't do that. She's got better taste in men. He's a barbarian and she
knows it."

"He's wonderful," she said with a sigh. She didn't want to get too
into it with Tom. As far as she knew he wasn't dating anyone. He'd gone
through several woman right after they'd broken up, but no one in the
last year. "Yes, he's different from my normal dates, but that's okay. We
get along really well. We're very compatible."

Kiki leaned in. "How compatible?"

"Multiple times compatible." She was fairly certain the grin on her
face was a mile wide.

"I can't believe you slept with him." Tom was staring at her like
she'd grown two heads.

"I know it's soon, but we've already spent more time together than
a lot of people who've been dating for weeks. The twenty-four seven
thing can really make you get to know a person fast."

"Do you?" Tom asked. "Do you really know him? Or do you see
what he wants you to see?"

"What is that supposed to mean?"

"It means that he's obviously using you and you're too naive to know it," Tom spat.

"It isn't obvious to me." Connor sipped coffee from the mug she'd left for him, his eyes steady on Tom. "Just how am I using her?"

For just a second, she thought Tom would back down. She hoped he would. Naturally he found his backbone and squared off against the much more muscular man.

"You're using her for sex," Tom accused.

"Hey!" Lara flushed, embarrassment flooding her system.

"Maybe it's the other way around. Maybe she's using me for sex," Connor said without a hint of humor on his face. Lincoln bounded back through the door and Connor scooped him up again. He looked simply delicious standing there with her dog cradled to his chest and drinking her coffee. He didn't need to shout. His deep voice reeked of authority. "I don't see anyone standing up for me."

Kiki nodded his way. "I will. The way she's using you is terrible. You deserve so much more. It's easy to see you're more than just a hot body."

"I like to think so," he said as innocently as a man wearing a gun could.

"Don't be ridiculous." Tom had turned red in the face, his eyes narrowed. "She doesn't even like sex. You tricked her into bed."

Embarrassment turned to flat-out humiliation.

"She likes it with me and she's absolutely the best lover I've ever had in my life. She's giving and passionate and I'm lucky she's with me. Now get to the reason you came here because my breakfast is getting cold."

Just like that the humiliation fled. She moved close to him, trying to let him see how much she appreciated him. "It's okay. You go ahead and eat. I'll be there in a little bit."

"No. We had a very important night. I believe I performed heroically given your inexhaustible appetites." He winked her way. "I want my intimate breakfast for two. I'll wait."

For a man who didn't say much, he really knew how to get to her. She turned to Tom, whom she'd had just about enough of. "What did you need?"

Tom shook his head. "I can't believe you would fall for his bullshit. He's not what he seems. You think he's a good guy, but he's lying to you."

And they called her the conspiracy nut. "About what?"

"About what he wants," Tom sputtered. "And he's some kind of pervert. Don't expect me to clean up the mess when he breaks your heart."

Tom stormed out, slamming the door behind him.

Kiki frowned. "I would never have brought him with me if I'd known he would react like that. I'm so sorry."

"Why was he with you in the first place?" Connor asked, cool as a cucumber.

"I'm helping him write up a brief on a case. I know more about the legal precedent than he does. He fell asleep on my couch last night. He was there this morning when Freddy showed up." Kiki reached into her bag and handed her an envelope. "He wanted you to have this. He said it was information you need to know in case he doesn't come back."

She took the envelope, but it was in Connor's hands before she could open it.

"No," he corrected her, setting the coffee mug on the bar and letting Lincoln run free. "You have no idea what's in this thing."

"Very likely it's a treatise on ancient aliens." Freddy had a little bit of an obsession with them. Lara frowned. "What do you think could be in there? It's an envelope, so I don't think it's carrying a bomb."

"It could contain any number of lethal agents. Anthrax comes to mind first." He inspected the envelope as if it could explode at any moment.

"Freddy is terrified of all viral agents," she replied. "He likes me. He wouldn't send me anthrax."

"Or he's the one stalking you and he's just pretending to like you. Maybe he's obsessed with you. Did he know about Niall?" Connor asked.

"She didn't hide it from her friends," Kiki replied.

Lara nodded. "I mentioned him."

"And this was right around the time the threats started?"

It had been. She'd started talking to Niall a few weeks before. "Yes, but Freddy wouldn't try to hurt me."

"Discovering you had a thing with another man might have been an inciting incident. I'm taking this to the bathroom to inspect it. Do not follow me. Kiki, tackle her if she tries." He stomped off.

Freddy wasn't her stalker. Connor was being paranoid. Not once in their entire relationship had Freddy shown a single sign of wanting anything beyond friendship. Connor could do whatever bodyguard-like things he wanted with that letter. He wouldn't find anything beyond a list of the most likely politicians currently under alien control. She turned back to Kiki because her friend could give her some important information. "Was he wearing his bug-out bag?"

"Is that what you call that massive backpack? Because yes. It looked like he was ready to survive an apocalypse. He said he was heading for the woods."

He had a small property somewhere in the Appalachians. He hadn't told her where it was since then he'd have to kill her, but he had offered to take her with him if things got too hot with their investigations. "I wonder what set him off."

"He said it was men in black. He claims they were crawling all over the building late last night." Kiki shook her head like she couldn't quite believe a grown man would say such a thing. "I think I know what he saw, and they were definitely in black suits. I went across the street to the all-night drugstore to get some candy bars. I think better with sugar. I would have sworn I saw Roman Calder leaving the building with a group of men just after three this morning."

"The president's chief of staff? Are you sure? What would he be doing here at that time of night?" No wonder Freddy had flipped out. If Calder had been in the building, he'd likely been surrounded by guards or Secret Service, and almost all of them wore similar black suits. There was a reason the myth had started.

Kiki shrugged. "I'm pretty sure it was him. Superhot. I watch press conferences just to catch a glimpse of that man. As to why he'd be here, I have no idea. Maybe he has a mistress here. You know he doesn't have a girlfriend. He probably keeps a little something on the side. I can't imagine a man that alpha male hot would go without sex."

"Or he was meeting someone and he didn't want the press to find out. There are a couple of congressmen who keep apartments in the complex."

"I like my version better," Kiki complained. "Anyway, that's probably what set Freddy off and he said he came to my door because Connor is one of them."

Of course he was. "Well, there's not a lot I can do. He'll come back in a few weeks. This isn't the first time he's bugged out." She winced. "I left my copy of the investigation in his apartment. Damn it. He won't let me keep it on my system. He claims it's too important to let the hackers find. I have a key to his place. I think I'm the only person in the world he trusts. God, I hope he doesn't have the place booby-trapped."

She was going to have to go in because she couldn't leave that data behind. Things were starting to happen.

"Don't go anywhere without Connor," Kiki said.

The minute Kiki said the words, she figured out how to get what she needed. Guilt hit her hard, but she shoved it down because there was a greater good to be served. If she played her cards right, Connor wouldn't even know she'd ever left the apartment at all. "I'll leave it to him. He's the expert after all."

He was the expert who would very likely agree that the best time to break into a place was late at night when no one was around. He would never take her in with him, simply lock her in the condo until he was done.

Connor would be so mad if he figured out what she was going to do.

Kiki gave her a hug. "I think letting Connor handle everything is the best way to go. I've got to get to work. Call me if you need anything. And I'll talk to Tom."

"Thank you." No matter what, they'd been friends since childhood.

She locked the door behind Kiki and tried to come up with a way to tell Connor she firmly believed the president had arranged for his wife's murder.

Connor locked the bathroom door and opened the letter, suspicion playing in his brain. Freddy wasn't without resources. He'd read the man's dossier. Just because he believed in aliens didn't mean the man couldn't get it right from time to time.

He could hear the mumble of Lara's conversation with Kiki out in the living room. Lara was likely explaining that her new lover was paranoid and that Freddy would never hurt her.

Of course he couldn't agree with her or tell her the Russian mob was after her. That would require far too many explanations he wasn't in a position to give, especially since he didn't know precisely who was behind the hit.

Besides, being a paranoid freak allowed him to do things like "inspect" the letter meant for her. He was sure Freddy had told Kiki to deliver it as quietly as possible, but he'd misjudged the girl. Kiki was the kind of woman who actively looked for authority in her life. For all her Bohemian charms, she wanted the world to have rules that made sense and a strong leader to guide her. It was very likely how she'd gotten involved with a married congressman. If he was strong and charismatic, she'd probably believed whatever the fucker told her. So she'd come straight to Lara and hadn't thought a single thing about passing Freddy's missive to her in front of Connor.

Lara herself was another story. She usually bucked authority in her own peaceful way. He wondered if Lara would have surrendered Freddy's letter so easily if they hadn't slept together the night before. Sex seemed to put her in a deeply cooperative mood.

Or not. If he hadn't exited the bedroom at the right moment, Lara would have opened the door herself, and this letter would now be in her hands. His game would probably be over.

Connor tore open the envelope. Yep, there it was. Somehow the fucker had found a picture of him from the Yale newspaper taken during his senior year. Those photos were supposed to be history. All pictures of him had been removed from the Yale database. Of course the Agency couldn't stop people from scanning their hard copies in. This photo showed him standing next to Zack as they walked out of the student union. They were both younger, but their faces were clearly depicted, their identities obvious.

Your bodyguard is one of them. There were six. Crawford, Bond, Spencer, Sparks, Calder, and Hayes. I think your guy is actually named Connor Sparks. He's here for our data. He will protect the president at all costs, including killing us both. He works for the shadow government. He's the one Hayes would hire. There's almost certainly blood on his hands. I have to leave. I can't stay with so many of them around. They were in your apartment last night. I watched them go in. I'll pray for you, Lara. Fight the good fight.

Freddy.

Fuck a duck. He was going to have Roman's ass. The asshole had sworn they would be quiet as silence and as undetectable as air. They weren't supposed to leave any fucking witnesses.

What was he going to tell Lara? He couldn't show her the note, but he also couldn't destroy the entire contents of the envelope. He needed to use Freddy's paranoia against him.

Connor very carefully tore the picture, deleting himself entirely. He folded his half of the photo and the note, then tore both into tiny pieces before flushing them down the toilet.

It was all he could do for now. Connor couldn't deny that Freddy had figured out who he was quickly and couldn't forget that the man would be back.

This missive also told him that Freddy was investigating Zack for some reason. That meant Lara was helping him, and he couldn't have that. She needed to stay as far away from Zack as possible.

Things were getting complicated, especially his feelings for her. She was a weakness and he'd never had one before. Sure, he had his friends, but they were all savvy and played things safe. Lara was reckless. She seemed convinced that she could save the world.

Connor knew the world would eat her alive and he couldn't let that happen.

He opened the door and walked back out, wishing like hell that Kiki and Tom hadn't shown up.

"Is everything all right?" Lara was standing in the living room as he walked out. "Kiki left. I locked up and warmed breakfast."

He'd been looking forward to it. Now he was going to have to force himself to eat. "Good. I'm starving." He handed her the envelope. "Nothing scary. Just an old picture of the president. Why would he send you that?"

She opened it and looked down at the picture. "I'm not sure. He printed this. It looks like the source might have been a newspaper, but this came from his printer."

"Maybe he found it on the Internet. Hayes looks young in that picture." It had been snapped before Joy died, back when the hair at his temples hadn't been threaded with silver. Zack joked that his bit of gray made him look older and more competent to voters, but Connor remembered the day he'd first seen those signs of aging in his friend. It had been at Joy's funeral, as though his grief needed a physical outlet.

"I wonder where it was taken. I'll have to research it. If he left it for me, it must be a clue. Hey, you know the president, right?"

He hated lying to her. He tried to work his way around blatantly lying. "I've worked with him a bit."

It was true. He'd worked with Zack since they were lab partners in chemistry.

"Do you know Roman Calder as well?"

Shit. He took a sip of coffee. She'd refreshed it like the good hostess she was. He reached out and pulled her close. He knew how to distract her. "I know who he is. Kiss me good morning."

Her whole body softened against his. She responded as if she'd been made specifically for him. "I already kissed you good morning. If I remember correctly, I did more than kiss you."

"Kiss me again."

She rose up to her toes and pressed her lips to his. Every single time she kissed him he felt it in his gut, in his dick, in his flipping chest. He was in deep with her, but he couldn't make himself get out. He gave her a moment and then sank his hands into her hair and took over, delving deep inside her mouth. Arousal warmed his body. God, he couldn't seem to get enough of this woman.

After a moment he pulled away, briefly kissing her nose before he took his seat and grabbed his fork. "So what was Freddy working on? Why did he bug out?"

Connor hoped Freddy had actually left the area. It would make his job so much easier. He needed to separate the guy from Lara, and he didn't like the idea of having to silence a disturbed vet.

Eggs. Real, from-a-chicken eggs. Sure they were scrambled with god only knew what kind of vegetables, but compared to her tofu, it was like heaven. His appetite resurged.

"He thought he saw a big group of men in black. You know, the kind who silence people with too much knowledge."

"I'm well aware of the term." Hell, half the time he was the boogeyman and he did, indeed, wear black. The color not only blended in with the night, it hid bloodstains well. "So he saw a couple of dudes in black suits and decided they were here for him?"

The eggs were cooked perfectly. He didn't even mind all the veggies.

"That's how his mind works. But Kiki thinks he might have seen Roman Calder in the building because she saw the guy in the lobby on a trip back from the drugstore really early this morning."

He was going to kill Roman. Had his old pal forgotten the whole op was supposed to be secret? Had he just run around chatting up people in the hallways? "Why would he be here? Although if he was, he would likely come with a security detail. That would explain the men in black."

She settled in across from him. He loved how pretty she was with no makeup on and her hair in a messy bun. "That's what I thought. I don't know why he was here. There are a couple of congressmen who keep apartments in the building. There's also a former model on the fifth floor. Do you think he's having a fling?"

"Could be." At least she wasn't buying Freddy's theory.

"I might look into it. It's a juicy story. Of course, Freddy also told Kiki you were one of them. In fact, he thinks you not only let them into the building, you allowed them into my condo last night."

And just like that his appetite was gone. What else had Freddy told Kiki? "Really? I'm working with the president's chief of staff? I need to figure out where that paycheck is going."

"I happen to know you weren't running around with a big group of men in black last night. You were busy." She smiled. "Freddy is suspicious of any new person in his life. I still don't think he's the one stalking me."

Connor shrugged, unwilling to give her an answer. "Why would he think men in black are dangerous? Is it the alien stuff?"

"Actually, I was going to talk to you about that." Her cajoling voice put him on edge. She wanted something from him. He was starting to learn her tells. She only used that sexy voice on him and that was very likely why it would work. If he could give something to her, he would. "I told you we'd been investigating a possible story."

"About the president." Somehow he couldn't see Freddy working with her on an innocuous article about the president's lovemaking prowess.

"Yes. We were investigating a theory last week before you arrived. This was something Freddy has been working on for months. He found some supporting footage and actually traveled to three different states to get copies of the original, unedited tape. I have no idea what he paid for it, but he kept it off the Internet. He had it on a hard drive and I'm sure he took that with him, but I finally convinced him that if I was going to be able to write a convincing story about this theory, I would need a copy of whatever he'd acquired. He was making me a thumb drive so I could study it, too. I left it on his coffee table along with my notes. I need to go get that."

Connor had to admit, he was interested in whatever this "story" was, but he couldn't let her into Freddy's place until he was sure there wasn't some massive poster with his real name and job title on it. "You want to break into a paranoid ex-military man's apartment to get a flash drive?"

"Yes, but you should know I think he might have the place booby-trapped."

He sighed. "Well, it's not like I had anything better to do today."

"Good, because I have a plan." She hopped up, then chose the chair beside him, sitting so close her knees were touching his. "But we can talk about that later. First you can yell at me because I might have invited someone over without talking to you first."

"Who?" He was well aware his tone could have iced over the room. Jealousy sprang up in his chest. Was it another man? He'd explained how he felt about that.

If she felt the chill, she didn't show it. Her leg rubbed against his. "Her name is Everly Parker. I don't know if you follow the tabloids, but she's kind of a celebrity right now. She's Maddox Crawford's secret half sister."

"The guy who died in the plane crash?" Mad. He still couldn't believe Mad was gone. He still expected to open the door and find Mad standing there with a ridiculously expensive bottle of Scotch in hand, telling him that the death gig had been one big joke.

"Yes, that Maddox Crawford. He ran Crawford Industries, which was caught in this big scam with the Russian mob. As far as I can tell, Crawford didn't know his business was being used as a front for human trafficking."

Wow. She'd twisted that around more than a little. "I remember reading about that. I don't think the Russian mob was embedded in the business, just using a charity Crawford Industries supported as a front."

"Right." She nodded. "I forgot. I don't have my notes in front of me. Anyway, Everly Parker is coming here at noon and I think she's bringing her fiancé with her."

"Why is she coming to see you?" Roman had worked fast. Connor hadn't expected to see Ev for another day or two. And he hadn't been sure Gabe would come. What the hell could he say to the man who'd once thought of him like a brother? God knew he'd been silent since Connor had unleashed the massacre at the Crawford building, since Gabe had looked at him like he was a monster.

"Okay, here's the other part you're going to be mad about, but I want you to put yourself in my shoes. I didn't really know you so it didn't make sense to tell you everything."

"So it makes sense to put your life in my hands, but not to tell me about everything that could harm you?"

She sighed at his sarcasm. "Fine. I should have told you, but this could be the biggest story I've ever broken and it ties in to the work I'm doing with Freddy. I was in Manhattan a few months ago. I was visiting a friend and working on a story about businesses paying EPA inspectors to look the other way. That story got picked up by the *Times*. Oh, they won't ever admit it, but they used my source and everything."

If he didn't corral her, she would go off on a tangent about the *Times* and big business destroying the little guy. "You were in Manhattan and . . . ?"

She refocused. "I got a call from a man. I still have no idea where he got my cell number. Or who the heck he was. Anyway, he tells me he knows all about Capitol Scandals."

Now that was new information. He'd been running on the theory that she knew Deep Throat. But another person—a total stranger—was aware of her secret identity? That list was starting to get awfully crowded. "And you didn't think that information was relevant to me?"

Every time he got cold, she seemed to warm up another degree. She curled her fingers over his arm, rubbing as if she petted him. Like she meant to soothe him? "I've had other things on my mind since then, but I can see now where it's relevant. Anyway, when he called, he said he had information I needed to hear."

"Tell me you didn't meet with him." He knew she had, but accepting that was different now. Lara had put herself in danger by secretly meeting a man she didn't know, one who had valuable information about her.

She had the good sense to wince. "I would love to be able to tell you that, but I did. That's where I found out about Natalia Kuilikov and her ties to Crawford Industries. My informant thinks Maddox Crawford was killed because he knew too much about her and a man named Sergei."

A chill went up Connor's spine. That Russian name came up a lot. He still didn't know who the fucker was. And he sure as hell didn't like it. "Who's Sergei?"

"I don't know. I was told to find him. He's the smoking gun, I guess. To do that, I need to find Natalia Kuilikov first."

"Does Everly Parker know Natalia? Is that why you're meeting with her?" Everly would do just about anything to track down the Russian immigrant. She was sure Natalia would bring her closer to truly understanding why Mad had been killed by the Russian mob after he'd discovered the human trafficking ring. But Everly thought it went deeper, and every word out of Lara's mouth made Connor believe that, too.

"Apparently she was contacted by the same man. He told her to get in touch with me, that we have different pieces of the same puzzle."

"Why should we care about this, Lara?" Because it would be the kind of story that would garner her international exposure and credibility?

She frowned and took her time replying. He sat in stilted silence as she squirmed in her seat. He didn't do a damn thing to break the tension. She should feel it, understand that he was serious.

"It goes back to the story I'm working on with Freddy."

He stared, waiting for her to continue.

Lara frowned. "You know you can be very intimidating."

"I can also be very nasty when I don't get the answers I want. Tell me what you're working on."

"Joy Hayes's death."

She managed to surprise him. "Joy Hayes was killed by a whack job who was trying to get the president."

Connor should know. He had chased the man down. He had shot and executed the assassin that day. All the press reports simply stated that one of the candidate's bodyguards had killed the man. Roman had managed to keep Connor's name out of the press.

"I don't think so. I believe the president hired someone to assassinate his wife three days before Election Day because he was several points down in key battleground states and he was going to lose. I think the event was carefully orchestrated, right down to the way Hayes held his dying wife onstage, for maximum press exposure and

sympathy. Rumors are that their marriage was one of political convenience and that she intended to leave him if he didn't win the White
House. Americans poured their hearts out to him and swept him into
office." She shrugged. "I also believe that Sergei is the real assassin."

Rage threatened to pour from Connor. He'd been there that day.
He'd seen the devastation. "You don't know what you're talking about."

"I do," she said quietly, almost sympathetically. "I have proof and
you can get it for me tonight. I know you like the man, but I believe
he's all kinds of dirty. I think he might even have ties to the Russian
mob, and this Sergei person can prove it. I'm going to track down
Natalia Kuilikov and then I'm going to find this mysterious guy. Once
I dig up the truth, I'm going to make sure Zack Hayes can never hold
political office again."

She was embroiled in everything Roman had sworn she was. Lara
was actively plotting against his president, his friend.

Connor knew he was going to have to choose. There was no choice,
right? Zack had stood by him. He knew the guy, had known him since
they were just children trying to make it in a world they didn't understand. He'd seen Zack's grief. No, their marriage hadn't been perfect,
but Zack and Joy had been friends and partners. He still mourned her
to this day.

"Over my dead body."

"What?" She sat straight up, blinking owlishly as if she couldn't
quite believe what she'd heard.

"You're not going to make up shit and call it news, Lara."

A flush stole across her skin. "I knew you wouldn't like it, but you
have to give me a chance to show you what I've found. Once you see
the evidence, you'll understand."

"No, I won't. I'll just know that you're good at crafting fiction. It's
one thing to write an exposé on the president's dick, but you're not
going to drag a good man down because you think you can." He pushed
back from the table. "You're going to drop this story."

Her hands balled into fists, but she managed to keep her voice steady. "No, I'm not. And I don't make stuff up. I've never run a story I wasn't absolutely one hundred percent sure of."

Roman would crucify her. There wouldn't be any way to stop him, and Connor wasn't sure he should. He believed in very few people in the world, but Zack Hayes was one of them. He needed to look at her evidence. "I'll go get it."

She popped out of her chair. "You can't do it now."

"Why?"

"Because Freddy's place is right next to Mrs. Sullivan, and she calls the police when she sees anyone even walking near his unit. You have to wait until after eleven when she goes to sleep."

"I can handle her."

He wanted to see this evidence. He could probably take it apart forty different ways and prove it was bullshit. Once he did and he had her begging his forgiveness, he would take her back and make sure that she could not target Zack Hayes again.

"Please, Connor."

Something about the way she looked at him made him stop. Just for a second he thought she might be hiding something. He stared, but she simply looked up at him with those clear blue eyes.

"Fine. But I want to see that evidence tonight."

"Absolutely." She moved to his side, her hand slipping into his. "I'll show you anything you want to see. I'll talk you through everything and if you still have doubts, I'll listen. I know you admire him, but I want you to see everything we've collected with an open mind."

Never. But being stubborn wouldn't get him where he needed to be. Everly and Gabe would be here soon. This was a mission, not a relationship, and it never could be a relationship if she intended to spread lies about his friends.

"Of course," he managed to say.

"You're angry with me." She eased closer, pressing her body against his.

Did she think she could control him with sex? One night of orgasms and she thought she was some kind of Mata Hari?

"Make me less angry with you." If she wanted to misdirect him with sex, he would let her. He would take everything she offered and it wouldn't change his mind at all. He could fuck her for days and still shut down everything she loved to protect his friends.

The morning hadn't gone the way he thought it would. He'd had a few hours of something like peace before the world reminded him that everyone had secrets and a dark side, even fairy princesses. Especially the ones willing to do whatever it took to get what they wanted.

"Connor?"

He looked down at her. "You heard what I said. Make me less mad."

"Why are you so angry with me?"

Because it fucking hurts to know that you're willing to step all over my friends for your own gain. Because you're just like all the others, a sweet lie.

He couldn't tell her any of that. "You've kept very important facts from me. I can't do my job if you don't tell me the truth. I thought you trusted me."

"I do. I really do, Connor. I'm sorry." She plastered herself completely against him, raising her head so she could plead with him using those blue eyes.

He almost believed her. "I have to wonder what else you're keeping from me."

If he hadn't been watching her so closely, he would have missed the way her eyes tightened just slightly and she looked to her left when she replied. "Nothing."

She was lying to him again. He'd felt guilty about deceiving her, and all the while she'd been lying to his face. He hadn't realized she was playing the game, too.

"Connor, I don't want to fight with you. I'm crazy about you." She laid her head against his chest. "I didn't know you then the way I do now. I hope that you're getting to know me better, too."

He wrapped his arms around her. He told himself it was all for show, but she still felt right in his embrace. Chemistry. That was all it was. It made them good together in bed. It did not necessarily make them faithful or loyal lovers. "I think I definitely know you better this morning than I did yesterday."

"I'll tell you everything when we have the information in our hands. I promise. After tonight we won't have any more secrets between us."

He wasn't an idiot. Lara was planning something, clearly after eleven p.m. What? And why was she so specific about the timing of his so-called heist?

"All right." He kissed her softly.

No. Her lying didn't change their chemistry one ounce. His cock was hard and ready for her. "Kiss me."

Her lips curled up. "I'm already kissing you."

"Not where I want you to."

He'd been her supplicant the night before, giving her every bit of pleasure he could—and more—like a complete idiot. He'd been atoning for sullying the pristine princess. Oh, but now he knew better, and it was time to even the score. Because if she wanted to play the game, he would show her that he was the better player. "On your knees, princess."

Her eyes widened and he was pleased to see the slightest bit of panic there. She might lie about her plans tonight, but he couldn't bring himself to believe she'd lied to him in bed. She really hadn't had much experience. He'd opened a new world to her, and it was going to be his pleasure to show her some of its darker, more twisted delights.

"Here?"

"I told you I would have you wherever and whenever I wanted. I was happy earlier. Now I'm not because you lied to me."

Yes, he saw the irony of the situation, knew he wasn't being honest, either. But he was protecting his friends, his country, his president. She was looking to get ahead and make a buck.

"I didn't lie. I just didn't tell you everything." She wouldn't quite meet his eyes. Fuck, she was still lying to him.

It just made what he was about to do all the more easy. Every time she manipulated him or was dishonest, he would take it out on her sweet body. After this shit, distancing himself would be simple. Oh, he still had zero plans to leave her. But instead of the stability and affection he thought she needed to be happy, maybe all she required was sex and a very firm hand. He could give her those.

"You lied by omission and I still want you. Does that tell you anything?"

"I'm sorry." Her hand went to the fly of his jeans. "I think I understand. You want me to make it up to you."

She didn't get it at all, and he needed to shut his mouth. He'd all but blurted that she mattered to him. Clearly, she didn't grasp that fact. Better for him that she didn't. Connor certainly didn't intend to repeat the sentiment.

"I definitely think you should make it up to me."

Lara bit her plump lower lip. "What if I'm not good at it?"

He cupped her cheeks, forcing her to look him right in the eyes. He refused to allow her to glance away when she answered this question. He would dig the truth out of her if he had to do it with the sharp edge of his tongue. "Are you telling me you've never given a man a blow job?"

"I was really sheltered as a kid. I didn't date very much. I did manage to sleep with one guy in high school, but it was really hurried. Tom and I tried it once, but my teeth scraped him and he accused me of trying to bite him so we didn't do that again. That's why I'm worried I'm bad at it. Also, I think I have a small jaw so I might not be able to, you know . . ."

She was drawing him back in because he utterly believed her now. She had untapped sensuality and he intended to free it.

His cock jerked in his jeans, already anticipating the softness of those lips closing around it. "He was a pansy ass and I'm going to teach you everything you need to know about how to suck my cock. By the time we're done, you'll be an expert."

"So I'll have a new talent to share with the world?" Her voice was light and teasing.

"Never." He hated the jealous rage that threatened to take over every time she even joked about another man. "Don't play with me."

"I'm not. I was just teasing you. I don't want anyone else." She stared straight into his eyes, all open and earnest again.

No lies now. Damn, she had his head spinning. Maybe she didn't have an agenda of her own. Maybe Freddy had dragged her into some fake conspiracy because she was too naive to see otherwise. If so, Connor vowed to handle the situation and make sure she never got taken again. But if she was the one behind the story, crafting lies because she didn't like Zack's policies or some shit, then he would take care of that, too. She would learn never to cross him again.

But no matter what happened, he would keep her because he couldn't envision a world for himself where she wasn't in it.

"Undo my jeans." Maybe once he felt her lips around him, his mood would improve and he could deal with his friends showing up early.

With slightly shaky hands, she undid his fly and parted it. Her hand went straight to his erection, brushing against it beneath the cotton of his boxers. "You're so beautiful."

He'd never once in his life been described that way. "We must have different definitions of the word. Now, very carefully, roll down my boxers and let the impatient beast free."

He had to take a deep breath when she did as he asked and released his cock from the confines of his boxers. She worked his jeans halfway down his hips and then stared down at him.

"Tell me what to do. I want to make you feel as good as I did last night."

"You liked it when I kissed you and sucked on you, didn't you?" It was a test of sorts. A calculating woman would play coy, not give him too much power via her praise.

"So much. It was the best night of my life. I hate the fact that we wasted any time at all when we could have been sleeping together all along." The note in her voice held no artifice, just honest desire.

She confused him on every level.

"Touch me. Take my cock in your hand and slowly pump up and down." He wanted to come the minute she touched him. How long did they have before Gabe and Everly got here? He forced himself to talk, to get his mind off the pounding need to mark her again. "I got the feeling you didn't like me very much that first day we met."

"I was scared of you. Then I was embarrassed about Niall. I behaved very stupidly with him and I was determined not to do it again."

He tugged her chin up. "You weren't stupid. He was a bad guy taking advantage of you."

"And you're not?"

"Not in the same way. I can offer you something. It's always an exchange, princess. Besides exchanging my body for yours, I'm willing to exchange my affection for yours, though you should know I'm not great at that."

Her soft hand gripped him. "I don't know. I think you're educable."

Maybe but she had a lot to learn, too. "I'm never going to be the guy who goes antiquing with you."

She pumped his cock, her hand tightening to a pleasurable level. "So if I want to ditch you, I should go looking for some colonial American furniture."

He realized the problem with his statement and that he was caught in a trap of his own damn making. "First, don't ever try to ditch me. I won't take it well. Second, yes, I would go with you. Let me amend. I'm never going to be the guy who pretends to enjoy antiquing."

"So no romantic weekend getaways are in my future? No date nights? Just sex."

Yep, he was caught. "I didn't say that. Once the danger has passed, if you want to go somewhere, I'll take you. If you want to see a movie or eat out, I'll go with you. I'm just saying don't expect all the romantic stuff."

"I know you have way more experience than me when it comes to sex, but I know more about relationships than you do and you aren't so different from other men, Connor." Her hand kept up the hard grind while she rose to her toes and pressed her lips to his. "They'll pretend they like the stuff you do to get you into bed, but once you're there, they totally give up. No man likes antiquing, but one who thinks I'm important will go with me anyway. That *is* incredibly romantic."

Maybe she wasn't really lying to him. Maybe what he'd perceived as a falsehood was simply her guilt for asking him to break into Freddy's place. Hell, he didn't know anything except that her touch was making his head cloudy again and he was looking for any way to believe she wasn't a mercenary bitch who intended to sell Zack out.

Fuck. What was wrong with him? He was a guilty-until-proven-otherwise kind of a guy. He did not sit around and hope someone was innocent.

"Get on your knees, Lara. I need to feel your mouth on me."

She dropped down without a single protest and she wrapped her lips around him in an instant. She pressed kisses on the head of his cock while her hand moved over the stalk.

"Use your tongue. Get my cock wet."

Again, she didn't tease or try to make him beg. She simply tackled the task with an enthusiasm that made all the damn-near-professional blow jobs he'd ever gotten disappear from his memory. None of those women had her artless ardor, her boundless joy. He watched as the head of his dick disappeared into that sexy mouth of hers. This was how he would deal with her in the future. When she argued with him, he'd just give her mouth something better to do. He would kiss her or fuck her so hard she couldn't say anything but his name.

"Take more. Suck me harder." He pushed his hips out, his cock sliding deeper into her mouth.

He shoved his hands in her hair, pulling it out of the bun she'd wrapped it in. He wanted to feel all that softness in his hands. He definitely wanted a better grip. Her mouth was so small, so heated and perfect. Her tongue whirled around his flesh and he could feel himself pulsing. So good. She felt so right. Why did this woman do it for him?

He forced her to take more. Lara braced her hands on his hips. For a brief moment he thought she was going to push him away, to tell him he was being too rough. She was so fragile. But then she eased her grip around to the cheeks of his ass. Her nails sank lightly into his flesh and he couldn't stop the wave of molten heat that engulfed him.

"Princess, I'm going to come. You might want to let go."

She shook her head without releasing him from the hot vise of her mouth. She dragged her lips up his length, finally letting go with a soft pop, before looking up at him. "I want to taste you. I want to swallow you down."

Fuck. His hands tightened on her hair and he gave up. She could take what he dished out. Her fragility was only an illusion. She wanted it and so did he, so he fucked her mouth, thrusting in and dragging out and yes, he felt the bare edge of her teeth scrape against him. That just made him fuck her harder.

He held himself hard against her mouth as he bellowed out her name and came in a dizzying rush. She didn't stop, her tongue working him the whole time. She drank him down as he gave up everything he had. He hadn't thought after the night before or the shower this morning that he had an ounce of semen left, but his body seemed to produce an endless supply for her.

Only her.

She licked him clean from head to base, like she couldn't get enough of his taste.

He let his head fall forward as he dragged oxygen into his lungs and stared down at her. Through the thick fringe of her dark lashes, he watched as she smiled up at him, the adoring expression in her glittering blue eyes making his heart kick around in his chest.

Who the hell was she? Innocent do-gooder taken in by a crazy asshole? Or a calculating seductress determined to take him down?

Either way, she was his and he would deal. Tonight he would learn all her secrets and then she would find out just who was running this show.

NINE

Lara offered Everly Parker a cup of tea. She had a complete set her mother had given her for Christmas a few years before but she so rarely had the chance to use it. Kiki was more of a wine person and Tom wondered why she would spend so much time making something that only required boiling water and a store-bought bag.

Connor didn't seem like the type who appreciated a nice oolong. Her whole body warmed at the thought of what he did appreciate. And it didn't matter that he wouldn't enjoy it. He would still escort her, and she couldn't believe for a second that he would ruin her enjoyment by showing his displeasure. He'd already proven he could be indulgent.

God, she hated lying to him.

"This is lovely. I've never actually had tea like this before." Everly was a beautiful woman with strawberry blonde hair and a smile that Lara would have called mysterious a few days before. Now she recognized it. Everly Parker was well loved and it showed.

She finished pouring and sat on the couch. She'd decided to have tea in the living room because she was fairly certain it would be a while before she could be in the breakfast nook without thinking about how it felt to take Connor into her mouth. She was surprised by how much she'd loved it.

She flushed as she poured her own cup. "My mom used to take me to high tea a couple of times a year. I love the ritual of it. It's very civilized."

"I was raised by a cop. I'm afraid civilized wasn't in my vocabulary for much of my life. My dad was lucky to get me to wash my hair a few times a week when I was a kid." She smiled as though she truly enjoyed the memory. "I was something of a tomboy."

"You couldn't tell now. You look every inch the New York sophisticate." Lara had been slightly intimidated by the cool, chic woman who had walked into her condo with her gorgeous god of a billionaire on her arm. Everly Parker and Gabriel Bond made a striking couple. He'd come dressed in a tailored suit and he'd shaken hands with both her and Connor before Connor offered to take him out on the balcony so she and Everly could talk.

She'd been a little surprised, but pleased. He trusted her.

She shook her head. "That's Gabriel's doing. Well, and his sister's. Sara took one look at my wardrobe and declared we were going shopping. Bergdorf's was happy to see us that day."

"There's a rumor that Sara Bond is pregnant with Maddox Crawford's baby. Are you going to be an aunt? I can't imagine losing a brother, but a baby would be a wonderful balm, I suspect."

A chill settled in Everly's previously warm eyes. "There are rumors everywhere. Did you agree to meet with me so you could exploit my fiancé's sister? I should warn you, I wouldn't take that well."

Lara set the teapot down and hoped she hadn't gone bright red. She didn't hide embarrassment very well. She took a deep breath and kind of wished Connor was sitting next to her. "So our confidential informant told you about my . . . venture?"

"I know about Capitol Scandals," Everly affirmed, setting her cup and saucer down. It looked like her very civil meeting was over. "It doesn't really matter how. I want to know if you're planning on writing up a nasty story about Sara."

She was actually really sick of being painted as the villain. "Have you ever read Capitol Scandals? Even once?"

"I've seen the site." The distaste in Everly's eyes told Lara she didn't like what she'd seen.

"Have you read a single story?"

"I did read the one about the president's girth . . ."

Naturally. "Yeah, that was my shining moment. Maybe you should actually read some of the other pieces before you dismiss me. And no, I would never write a story about Sara Bond's pregnancy. I just thought you should know those rumors are circulating."

Everly sat back, regarding her cynically. "Why wouldn't you expose Sara? You write about all kinds of scandals. You wrote about Congressman Johnson's affair."

"I publish stories that have political ramifications and even then, I only do so when I believe releasing the information is performing a public service. Revealing the father of Sara Bond's baby would serve no purpose other than to spew hurtful, salacious gossip. On the other hand, Congressman Johnson was sponsoring a bill that would have made it mandatory for all school-age children to get a vaccine that medical specialists decried as being potentially dangerous. It caused neurological defects in one percent of the test subjects in the clinical trial. The company paid off officials in the FDA. The woman he was having the affair with was on the board of the pharmaceutical company."

Everly shook her head, her eyes troubled. "How was that not news?"

"Because no one cares until it happens to them. In the corporate world one percent failure is practically a victory, but I met those kids. Their lives are ruined and all their parents got was some cash and a nondisclosure agreement. After Congressman Johnson stepped down, the bill died and the vaccine is now being reevaluated. Is your fiancé's sister threatening to ruin the lives of a couple thousand children?"

"Of course not."

"Then she's safe from my personal brand of evil, Ms. Parker. I brought it up because I'm stupid enough to think talking about your sister-in-law's pregnancy would be a female-type bonding thing. I was trying to be friends, but I'll stop that now and get straight to the point. Are you planning on outing me as the owner of Capitol Scandals?"

"No. I came because I need to find out what you know about the circumstances surrounding my brother's death. Like I said in my e-mail, I was contacted a few weeks ago by a man who said he knew why my brother was murdered."

"The newspapers claimed it was an accident."

"I don't believe that report." Everly shook her head.

"Do you think someone influenced the FAA to declare it an accident?" Just because it looked like she wasn't going to find a new friend didn't mean she couldn't get some information.

"I know everyone will point the finger at the president or his chief of staff, but I don't believe Zack or Roman had any real reason to bully anyone into officially changing their findings. They were close to my brother. They would want his killer brought to justice. That said, I don't necessarily believe the FAA report. My fiancé swears my brother was a good pilot."

"Do you recognize a company named Harrison Chemicals?"

Everly seemed to ponder that for a second. "I've heard the name."

"It's a company with a plant roughly two miles east of the spot where your brother's plane crashed." She'd been looking into Maddox Crawford's death since that meeting in Manhattan. This was the first time she'd been able to talk about her findings with anyone who would care. "The FAA report stated that the evidence of an incendiary device in the wreckage was actually a cross-contamination from the plant and its chemicals showing up in the water table. Don't you find it odd that the EPA has rated that plant as one of the best in the country for years? Just a year before, a local environmental group did a study of the surrounding area and declared the plant to be a model of modern waste management."

Everly paused. "EPA investigators can be bought."

"So can FAA investigators, but I've found private environmental groups can't be. This particular group is known for being very hard on corporations. If they say this company is clean, they're clean. The question becomes who would want to shut down the investigation of your brother's death? Who benefitted by his crash being an accident instead of murder?" She realized what she'd just said and sat forward. "I wasn't saying you killed him."

Everly opened her mouth then shut it with a rueful smile. "Can we start over again? I think we're both a touch anxious. I'm very protective of my future sister-in-law. She's been through a lot and the idea of anyone exploiting her makes me very angry."

"Of course. I can understand that."

"And I haven't read your work. If what you say is true, you've found a creative way to get the word out. I'm sorry I dismissed your site. I'd like it if we could start over again. It seems like you have a lot of information I don't. Moneywise, there's only one person who gained from Mad's death and that's my fiancé. But Gabe had no idea he was Mad's beneficiary."

"And I've heard he's put everything in trust for the baby."

"Wow. The rumors really are out there. Yes, that's correct. He's actually going to turn Crawford Industries over to Sara when the time is right. Gabriel had no reason to kill Mad. He wanted my brother alive so he could be a father to Sara's child. My turn to ask a question. Why were you bidding on Natalia Kuilikov's diary?"

"Bidding on what?"

Everly watched her closely. "I heard about an auction on the Deep Web. Supposedly Capitol Scandals was a major player in it."

Lara felt her jaw drop. Disbelief spread through her. "I had never heard the name Natalia Kuilikov until a few weeks ago, and I certainly didn't get into a bidding war over her diary."

"Someone claiming to be a rep from your site was bidding hard."

"I am the whole site. I know what the Deep Web is but I didn't have an invitation to anything like that. It would be easy to pretend to be me." After the Niall debacle, she knew well that a person on the Internet could say whatever they wanted. "The question is why would they pretend to be me?"

"And why would Deep Throat contact you? Of all the journalists and bloggers in the country, why you? Unless it's a little like that environmental group. Maybe he chose you because he doesn't think you can be bought or intimidated. He contacted me because he knew I would do anything to solve my brother's murder. And then he suggested I contact you. So here we are, two women with nothing in common except him, from what I can tell."

She had a confession to make. "I met your brother a few times."

"You did?"

Lara winced. "I might have been the one who brought the problems with his Third World manufacturers to light."

Everly's eyes lit up. "Are you the one who sent fifty pounds of rotted rice to his office?"

Put like that it sounded terrible, but she'd learned it took a lot to get someone's attention. "That's what the factory was feeding the employees. And they were forcing them to work eighteen-hour shifts without breaks."

Everly smiled. "Oh, he liked you. You've got to understand. My brother, for all his foibles, truly appreciated passion. He talked about that prank a lot. He was really impressed with how you managed to suppress that smell until he got the package open."

"He didn't seem all that happy when he spoke to me later that afternoon." He'd yelled quite a bit.

"Maybe not, but he shut down that factory very quickly and opened a new facility even though it cost Crawford millions. And what almost no one knows is that he used his own money to set up an education fund for the village. My brother believed in capitalism, but he had a heart and sense of fairness. He might have been pissed that day, but he thanked you later on because he hadn't known how the factory was being run. His father had set up that whole system and Mad eventually dismantled it. He told Gabe that he was doing a tour of Thai brothels, but I found out he'd been investigating the factories and making sure they'd cleaned up their acts. I can't believe you're Rotten Rice Fucker." She blushed a little. "His name for you, not mine."

Lara had to laugh. She really had tried to get his attention by sending e-mails and letters. He'd been a busy man, so she'd resorted to something slightly crazy. She felt good knowing he'd done the right thing in the end. That made her feel good, yet worse about his death. Many men in his position wouldn't have cared and simply let the abuse continue.

"Someone wanted the two of us to put our heads together," Lara observed.

"I think you're right. Let's figure it out."

Despite the uncomfortable start of their meeting, she was beginning to relax around Everly. If she was going to get the other woman to talk, she would have to offer her something. "I have a theory about Natalia Kuilikov. I think she's tied in with the president. I learned that she actually worked for Zack Hayes's father as a domestic caregiver when he was the ambassador to Russia. Since the woman began working for the family shortly before President Hayes was born until the family returned to the States, it's very likely she was one of the current president's nannies."

"Are you sure you didn't win the diary in that auction?"

Lara sat forward, her heart starting to race. "There's really a diary out there?"

"Yes. I've read it but it doesn't tell me much more than the fact that she really loved Zack as a baby and she had high hopes for him. She was married herself, but she lost a baby and she couldn't seem to get over it. She seems to have put all her love into caring for Zack."

"Do you think she had an affair with the ambassador?"

Everly shrugged. "I don't know. I know she was trained at a girls' school, one created and run by the same human trafficking ring that was exposed a few weeks back. My brother found Natalia's diary some-

where at some point in the past. Someone killed him for it. I have to
know why. I have to figure out the reason this woman is so important."

"Even if it means potentially hurting one of your fiancé's friends?"

"Are you talking about Zack? I've talked to him about it. He doesn't
know anything more than we do. He remembers her from his childhood. He called her Nata and she was more of a mother to him than
his own. Apparently Constance Hayes really liked to drink."

She'd died in a car accident nine years before. The official report
was that the roads had been slick. But Lara had heard the woman had
a blood alcohol level twice the legal limit.

She had to point out the ramifications to Everly. "If Natalia came
from one of those schools, you must know what that means. The press
would go wild if the president was raised by a sex slave. It could ruin
his father's legacy."

Everly shook her head. "I think you'll find Zack has a healthy attitude when it comes to his father. He kind of hated the bastard, so he's
not terribly concerned with old Frank's legacy. If the story comes out,
he makes a big push to end human trafficking in honor of his beloved
nanny and everyone moves on. It's a flash-in-the-pan story."

It was hard to get used to the fact that she was sitting with a woman
who called POTUS Zack, like being on a first-name basis with the
president was no big deal.

"Unless Natalia knows where the skeletons are buried. Then it's possible that parts of her diary become a best-selling exposé of the whole
Hayes family." Lara didn't see any other way this journal of the family's
former domestic servant became a moneymaker, and even she wasn't
too idealistic to realize that everything came down to cash. None of this
would be happening if someone, somewhere couldn't make money.

"If she has a story, it could be worth a lot," Everly said cautiously.

"Yes, it could."

"But you don't care about that."

"No, I don't care about the money. I care about making sure no other woman gets sold. I do what I do to help make the world a better place. That is all I'm concerned with."

"I believe you." Everly leaned forward and picked up one of her cucumber sandwiches. "I think we can work together. For some reason our informant want us to, but that doesn't mean we're not calling the shots. I know we started rough, but let's keep our lines of communication open and see what happens. We don't have to play by this guy's rules."

"As long as you understand that my only concern is helping people. If the president has done something that would harm his ability to serve the American public, I would use this information to take him down."

"I know Zack. Whoever is running this show might be trying to implicate and harm him, but I assure you he's a good man."

But Lara knew something Everly didn't. She'd seen those tapes. She would have to use them at a later date to make her case, but since she couldn't get her hands on them now, this wasn't the time. Instead, she'd try to form some sort of bond with this woman since they'd been thrown together. It was time to take a risk.

"I'm meeting with him tonight," Lara admitted.

Everly's eyes widened. "Seriously?"

"Yes, but I hope he gives me some direction on how to find Natalia. When was the last time he contacted you?"

"Weeks ago. It's why I wrote to you. I've had no further communication with him and he didn't exactly leave me any way to contact him. You're my only lead, but I think we could become partners. I'll share information with you, Lara. I know you don't have any reason to believe me, but I promise that I will be your partner in this."

She could really use a partner. "I won't ask much of you. Just don't tell my boyfriend. I'm still hoping I can figure out a way to make the meeting tonight without him."

She'd agreed to keep Connor's cover with everyone who didn't know otherwise, so she hadn't referred to him as a bodyguard. Besides, after the last twenty-four hours, it was a lot easier to think of him as more than someone her dad was paying. He was her lover.

"That Connor guy is your boyfriend?" Everly looked toward the balcony. "He seems a little protective."

"Yes, but if I don't show up tonight alone, I'll miss the chance to find out whatever the informant knows."

Everly went silent for a moment. "I don't know if that's a good idea. Do you care about this guy?"

"Yes. I really do, but he won't understand. He won't let me go and if this informant even sniffs I've got someone watching, he'll leave and I'm worried he won't contact me again."

Everly took a long sip of tea. "He hasn't contacted me since it became very apparent I'm with Gabriel. I understand the whole protective boyfriend thing. Wait until you've got a ring on your finger and see how protective these guys can be. I mean guys like them. Your Connor strikes me as being somewhat like my Gabriel. Oh, they might not dress the same, but underneath that thin veneer of civilization lies the heart of a true caveman. He would love to drag me back to his beautifully decorated cave and keep me there."

"I don't think Connor even has a veneer. He's kind of all caveman."

A bright smile broke over Everly's face. "And you're in love with him."

"I wouldn't say . . . What I mean is . . . yeah. Yeah, I am and I don't know that he wants anything that serious. I'm fairly certain if he finds out what I'm planning tonight, he'll dump me." The thought brought tears to her eyes.

"All right, then we have to find a way to keep him out of it. If we're partners in this, you have to be able to count on me to back you."

"I already have a way. I've sent Connor on something of an errand to pick up an item I left in the apartment of a friend who's now out of town. His unit is in the building. It'll be tight, but I think I can get to the Mall, have my meeting, and get back before Connor finds out. He's going to want to search the whole place despite the fact that I only need one thing. I know that look in his eyes. Ever since he met my friend

Freddy, Connor has been suspicious. He'll take the time to search every inch, trying to find anything on him as long as he thinks I'm safely locked away."

"Why is he suspicious of this Freddy person?"

Maybe she shouldn't have opened this up, but if she was looking for a partner in crime, Everly should know what she was getting herself into. "I've had someone watching me for a couple of weeks. He's been a little threatening. Connor is sure it's Freddy so he'll take this chance to try to get the goods on him. I figure I'll have roughly an hour."

"Someone's stalking you?"

"I don't know that I would put it that way." She didn't want to scare Everly off.

"What way would you put it?"

She liked to put a positive spin on things. "This man simply takes a possibly unhealthy interest in my life."

"So he's stalking you." Everly's gaze trailed to the balcony. "All right. Gabriel's meeting with some friends tonight. I can bow out. I'll say I've got a headache. They won't mind. They'll love having a boys' night. When should I meet you here?"

"I have to go alone."

"You have to meet him alone, but you're not walking the streets of D.C. alone. I'll make myself scarce when Deep Throat shows. I'm not without talents of my own. Besides, I'd love to get a better look at the man. I can watch out for you."

"I don't want to drag you into this and I don't want to get you in trouble with your fiancé. Unless you think he won't mind."

"Oh, he'll mind if he finds out. You have no idea the shit storm that will come for us if he learns about this. So we have to be careful. You don't think your boyfriend has a clue?"

She thought about the way he'd looked at her this morning. Wary, as though studying her for some reason. He'd been upset about the story she was working on. That had to be it. There was no way he could know what she was plotting. He wasn't a mind reader. He was an ex-soldier. "No. He was upset with me about something else, but we worked that out. He's a good man. I know he seems gruff, but he has a soft side."

"That man has a soft side?"

Lara nodded. "He does. He's good with my dog. He's sweet with me. He tolerates my friends. He's a really good guy. I'm lucky to have met him. I just hope I get to keep him in my life for a long time."

"Do you think a man like that can be domesticated?"

She knew the answer to that. "I think a man like Connor has likely seen a lot of things go wrong in his life. He used to be a soldier. He's seen the rough side of the world. Now he needs to see the soft side. I think a man like him needs love and caring and a happy home more than anyone else."

Everly leaned over and took Lara's hand, and just for a second she could have sworn there were tears in her eyes. "I'm very happy for you. I don't know that many women who look closely enough at a man like him to see what they need. He's lucky and he better not forget it. I'm going to help you. I will be there tonight to watch your back."

"I don't want you to get hurt. There really is someone after me, but I have to take this chance to find out the truth."

Everly grinned and opened her Prada bag, pulling out a nice-sized revolver. "Don't worry about me. I can take care of both of us."

"That is a really big gun." Lara leaned away.

"Good thing I know how to use it," Everly said, sliding it back into her bag. "Are those more cucumber sandwiches? Plotting always makes me hungry."

She passed her the plate. "Help yourself."

"Thanks. We're going to need our strength, sister."

Lara watched as Everly selected a sandwich. A weird warm feeling began in her chest like something important had just happened and she'd found a place she belonged that hadn't existed before. Somehow she knew that despite their rough beginning, she and Everly were going to be friends.

She leaned forward. "So we meet him at midnight. Here's my plan."

She and Everly enjoyed tea and plotting.

Connor looked back into the condo where Everly and Lara sat, a delicate tea set between them. Lara had jumped through hoops to get the tray ready. She'd been specific about the type of bread she needed and how it had to be cut. Connor knew that Everly would be happy with coffee and store-bought cookies. She'd been raised as a cop's daughter. There wasn't a pretentious bone in her body.

Of course he couldn't say that. He had to pretend like he'd just met a man he'd known for most of his life, a man he considered a brother.

Unfortunately, Gabe Bond was also a man who'd seen him work, and that had changed things between them.

"She's pretty," Gabe said. "She's also going to wonder why you're spying on her when we're supposed to be doing manly things like drinking Scotch. Is this the best you have?"

When he glanced over, Gabe was staring at the label on the bottle. Everly might not be pretentious, but Gabe had grown up surrounded by cash and tended to expect the best. "I couldn't exactly buy fifty-year, Gabe. I'm supposed to be poor."

"Yes, I got the whole rundown on your cover from Roman. You're supposed to be some down-on-his-luck ex-soldier looking for a job. You're not supposed to own million-dollar homes around the country. What are you up to? Three now?"

He turned away from the window and wished Everly had come alone. "Yes. I have the place in New York, the home here, and a flat I keep in London. What's your point, Gabe?"

Gabe frowned. "I didn't really have one. I've always been curious. You can't make that much from the Agency. When we were kids, your

mom was broke all the time. You were on scholarship. I have to wonder where the fortune came from."

It shouldn't have surprised him that Gabe wanted to poke and
prod into his past. He likely thought there was plenty of nastiness
buried there, and he was right. "It's really none of your business."

"No, I guess it's not, but I'm curious. We've been friends all these
years, but you've never really talked about it. Does Dax know?"

"Yes." Dax pretty much knew everything. He'd needled Connor
until he'd finally told the bastard. Dax was seemingly happy-go-lucky,
but when he zeroed in on something, he could be like a pit bull.

"Good. Someone should know all your secrets." Gabe poured a few
fingers into Lara's crystal tumbler. "You want one?"

Now he'd likely go to Dax and try to turn Dax against him. It was
probably no less than he deserved. "Sure. They're plotting."

A grimace crossed Gabe's face. "I don't know about that. Everly
isn't going into this meeting with a lot of love for the girl."

"What's that supposed to mean?"

Gabe handed him the glass. "She runs a tabloid. Everly's had about
enough of tabloids to last a lifetime. We're currently trying to keep
them off Sara. Some asshole tipped off the rags that she set up a regis-
try for the baby. Her best friend wants to throw her a baby shower in
a few months, and Sara wanted to set everything up before she starts
showing. Apparently one of the clerks called it in and now they're all
speculating that Maddox Crawford has an heir."

"He does. I don't see why that would make Everly dislike Lara in the
beginning. She runs a site that specifically deals with political scandals,
and she only runs a story when it can shine a light on one of her causes."

Gabe's brows rose. "You sound like you like this girl."

He wasn't ready to talk to Gabe about Lara. He didn't want to talk
to Gabe at all. He took a slow sip of Scotch. "I simply don't think Everly
starting off hostile to her is going to help anything. Everly will come
around, and then she'll feel guilty and they will plot."

"Everly doesn't plot. And I don't know that she'll come around. She's become pretty protective of Sara. She's actually pretty protective of you guys, too. She was talking just this morning about how she needed to meet this woman to make sure she wasn't getting her hooks into you."

He laughed, well aware it was a bitter sound. "Why would she be protective of me? She knows damn well I can look after myself."

"She doesn't see it that way. She thinks you could use a good woman. Does Lara Armstrong fit the bill?"

He looked out over the balcony. In the distance, he could see the Mall and all the tourists milling about. Families. Couples. They were out enjoying the day. He never did that shit. Once or twice he'd gone places with Dax and his family. He could remember a couple of sweet summer days between his sophomore and junior years when he'd been invited to accompany Dax, his parents, and flirty sister, Augustine, to San Francisco. Connor remembered that trip so vividly. It was one of the times in his life he'd been able to forget that his father hadn't bothered to stick around for his birth and his mother had quickly found the bottom of a bottle and barely ever climbed out of it. She'd been a functional alcoholic and skank.

His time with Lara had made him feel like he could have something normal, something wonderful. Even if it was part-time, he might be able to have a family. He'd never thought he would have kids, but Lara would be a wonderful mother. Maybe children would ground her and keep her out of trouble, but the truth was getting Lara pregnant would tie her to him. She couldn't turn him away if they had a child together. She would always be in his life.

"She's a good woman." Who might be lying to him.

Gabe stared at him for a moment. "You're into this woman. Holy shit. You love her."

The word kind of made his stomach turn. "Don't be ridiculous. She's attractive and smart and I find her interesting."

"Yes, that's what I said. You freaking love her."

He turned and faced Gabe. "That is not what I meant."

"In Connor speak, attractive and interesting is the same thing as love. Most of the women you've slept with you described as brutal or vicious. When you kind of liked one, you would say she was tolerable. This is hearts-and-roses time for Connor Sparks." Gabe had the dippiest damn grin on his face. "You love her. You want to marry her. Hey, do you want to double wedding this shit?"

He shot Gabe the finger. "You suck, Bond."

Gabe leaned against the balcony. "Yeah, probably, but after all these years, you really can't get rid of me. Can we talk about it now?"

Fuck. This was what he'd wanted to avoid. "There's nothing to talk about."

"Of course there is. We went through something traumatic and I had a very bad reaction to it. I cut you off when I should have sat down and talked to you. I know it sounds ridiculous, but I'm older than I used to be. I needed time to process some things."

Connor wasn't stupid. Gabe hadn't wanted to have anything to do with him after what happened in the Crawford building that night. "Like I said. There's nothing to talk about."

"You aren't an analyst, Connor."

That ship of lies had sailed a long time ago. "No, I'm an operative."

"What happened that night?"

"You made a choice that left me scrambling, and I had to figure out a way to save your ass." His heart still raced when he thought about that night. He'd known what he should have done—allowed the Russians to take Everly and then followed them, finding where they were staying and gathering as much intel as he could.

He'd known the minute Gabe went after Everly that he wouldn't do what the Agency would consider to be the right thing. He would do whatever it took to protect his friends. Gabe loved Everly. He would be a hollow man if anything had happened to her. He couldn't let that happen no matter what the consequences were.

"Is that night why you've been suspended?"

He was sure he had Roman to thank for that. His employment was supposed to be top secret but Roman chatted about it around the dinner table. "Yes. I'm not supposed to operate on American soil. I killed several members of the *Bratva* that night and I had to call in a group that helps clean up messes."

Golchenko alone would have been a goldmine of information, but he'd threatened Everly and Gabe, and someone from his organization had shot Dax, and that was unacceptable. Golchenko could have led them to higher-ups in the Krylov syndicate, a network of Russian mobsters the Agency believed was responsible for arming many of the jihadists in the Middle East. Getting intelligence on that group was one of their prime concerns, and Connor had very calmly killed everyone who could have helped them because in this case, doing the Agency's bidding meant losing his friends.

"I was upset that night, Connor. I nearly watched the woman I love be murdered."

He'd seen the look in Gabe's eyes. He knew Gabe had thought he was a vicious animal in that moment. "I know you were upset. What do you want me to say, Gabe? I'm sorry you had to see that part of me. I try to keep it away from you guys. I understand if I'm not welcome at the next family picnic. Hell, it's kind of a relief. I'm not that guy anyway."

Gabe shook his head and sighed. "Will you shut the fuck up and listen for once, man?"

"Sure. I don't have anything better to do." The last thing he wanted was to hear all the reasons Gabe didn't want to be around him anymore, but it seemed like he couldn't avoid it. This was exactly why he needed to put distance between him and Lara and fucking everyone in his life. He wasn't the kind of man who got to have a family. Hell, he was the kind of man who made his fortune blackmailing his own biological father.

Yeah, he didn't want Gabe to know that, either.

Gabe stood right in front of him, putting his hands on his shoulders as if he needed to let Connor know how what he was about to say was important. "You're an idiot. I can say that because you're my brother.

I'm an idiot, too. I'm a complete moron because it took me so much time to figure out what really happened that night, what's been happening with you for most of our adult lives."

Killing people who needed killing. Living in the world's underbelly. Doing the country's dirty work. It was a hell of a life. "And what's that, Gabe?"

"Protecting us. Sacrificing for us. What I want to say to you is this: Thank you, brother. Thank you for saving me and Everly and Dax that night. Thank you for doing all the things you do to protect everyone in this country. They might not know what a sacrifice you make, but I understand and I'm so damn proud to know you."

Connor went still because he felt something weird happen to his face. He flushed and just for the tiniest of moments he felt his eyes tear up, as if he was about to fucking cry like a girl. "You're an asshole, Bond."

Gabe grinned like he knew what had happened. "Sorry about that. Some things have to be said. So stop ducking my damn calls, man. And if you don't tell me the next time you're in New York, I'll beat you up myself. I'm not going to let you brood in your bat cave."

Connor had seen operatives who went truly dark, who believed only in their jobs and struggled to function if they weren't on a mission. He would never be that man because his friends wouldn't let him. If he tried to hide, Zack would set the National Guard on him. Roman would hound him. And Gabe and Dax would hunt him down with a bottle of Scotch in hand.

And Mad would have hauled him off to some crazy strip club to show him life wasn't all darkness. He could hear Mad's gravelly voice. *It's boobs and body glitter, too, brother.*

Those stupid tears threatened again. "Fuck, I miss Mad sometimes."

Gabe put a hand on his back as they stared out over the city. "I'll miss him every day for the rest of my life. He was my closest friend in the world."

Even in their group, they'd had duos. Roman and Zack. He and Dax. Gabe and Mad. "I know."

"He would have thrown me a hell of a bachelor party."

"I don't even want to think about it. Mad would have made *The Hangover* look like a kiddie film."

"I need a best man, Connor. Will you fill in?"

Was the guy trying to make him into one of Lara's pansy-assed guitar strumming wimps? "I fucking hate you, Bond."

"I know, but you'll do it."

"Of course I will. And I'll do it Mad Crawford–style, so you should expect we'll need a corporate jet and likely a really hefty bail fund."

"Unless you want to go for the double wedding because this shit is getting expensive. Do you have any idea what they charge for freaking flowers?"

Connor chuckled. "You're not pulling me down with you. When I marry that girl we're going to do it right. Short trip to Vegas and then a long couple of weeks on a very isolated beach."

"You said 'when.'"

"I meant if." He shook his head. "No. I didn't. I don't know what it is about her."

"When you know, you know," Gabe said. "I knew immediately I wanted Everly and I knew it wasn't going to go away. Can you really see yourself not wanting her?"

He shook his head. He didn't want a world in which he couldn't have her. Being with Lara made him feel alive in a way that scared him, but he wasn't about to give it up. "But I think she's lying to me about something. I don't think I'm going to handle that well."

"You're lying to her about your name and occupation and friendships and past. Need I go on?"

"It's not the same. I'm doing what I'm doing to protect people I care about."

"And she's not?" Gabe pointed out. "If she's anything like you described, she's a crusader. She's doing the exact same thing as you. She's trying to protect her country. She simply does it with words and stories. She puts herself on the line to show the public the truth. You're actually quite similar. You're both fighting the good fight."

Was he high? "I fight the dirty fight."

"Someone has to. If you didn't, the nation would be weaker for it. And if Lara didn't do what she does, the nation would be less informed. So if it turns out she's lying to you, cut her some professional slack. Trust me. I know what it's like to love a woman who needs more freedom than I feel comfortable giving her. Everly wouldn't be happy as a society wife. She needs to work, and that work sometimes puts her in danger. I have to take a deep breath and trust that she won't do anything foolish."

"And if she does?" Lara doing foolish things wouldn't end in a higher credit card bill or a silly mix-up. It could end with her dead or in the hands of the very men Connor had pissed off weeks ago. Surely the Russians knew who had taken out their New York operations by now. Not only did they think Lara knew something she didn't, they would think she might be the way to get to him.

They would be right.

"Then we'll have a serious talk, but I'm certainly not going to walk away from her because she does something that's simply in her nature to do," Gabe explained. "I love Everly because of her spirit. I don't want to break her or change her. I just want to love her."

Connor turned back and sure enough, Everly had switched seats and was right beside Lara, laughing like they were old friends. "See. I told you."

Gabe looked into the condo. "I would not have bet on that."

"It's impossible not to like Lara. I think they're plotting." Now that he'd gotten all the mushy shit done with Gabe, he could return to the main problem at hand. Those women were bonding. It clearly spelled trouble for him. "I don't think Everly's going to be a good influence on Lara."

Instead of getting offended, Gabe threw his head back and laughed.

"You should totally tell her that. Because I'm not going to do it. That woman is very good with a gun."

Connor stared back in, wondering what they were talking about. He hoped it was tea and weddings and stuff. He was fairly certain it wasn't. "Is Dax supposed to go to dinner with you guys tonight?"

"Yeah, we're eating in the private residence. You should come. The Scotch is way better there." He still downed what was left in his crystal tumbler.

As much as he could use a good fifty-year Macallan, it would have to wait. "I can't and I'm going to have to cancel for Dax, too. I need him tonight. Something tells me I need to keep eyes on my girl and that means Dax is going to have to do a little breaking and entering."

Gabe took a sip and sat down on Lara's elegant bistro chair. "It's always interesting when you're around, brother."

Connor watched the women. It wasn't always fun, but it could be an adventure. He just hoped this one ended with him feeling like a fool because he was wrong about Lara's intentions. Otherwise, the evening was not going to go well for her.

TEN

Lara took a deep breath as she slipped out of the building and into the alley. The dark air held a cool bit of fall. She'd donned a black hoodie and jeans, along with a pair of sneakers, which allowed her to blend in with the night.

She thought about Connor. Even now, he was on the second floor, quietly breaking into Freddy's condo. She'd told him to be very careful because the place was probably booby-trapped. He'd promised her he could handle it.

Until now, they'd had a quiet, companionable evening. Connor had had groceries delivered. He'd grilled a steak for himself and a lovely portobello mushroom for her. She'd made a salad and followed with poached pears for dessert. She'd told him all about Everly Parker and he'd said he liked her fiancé. But beneath the comfortable calm, she hadn't been able to forget that Connor was willing to commit a crime for her. And she was repaying him with lies.

It's not really a betrayal, she told herself as she looked around the alley for her partner in crime. She was just trying to gather necessary information. He had a job to do, but so did she. If she didn't find Natalia

Kuilikov, she would never know the truth about Hayes—and neither would Connor or the public. And now she wanted to do it to help her new friend. Otherwise, Everly Parker might never really understand why someone had blown up her half brother's plane.

"Hey," a quiet voice said. "You ready?"

Everly had gotten the black-on-black memo, though she wore a coat that hung loosely around her frame. Lara was pretty sure it was more in deference to the cache of weapons Everly wore than because of the weather.

"Are you sure you want to do this? Won't your fiancé be upset?"

"I can handle it. I think in this case everyone will agree it's better I go with you than let you go alone." She glanced down at her watch. "We have fifteen minutes to make the meeting, then another fifteen to get back here and have you safely ensconced in your apartment. To be safe, you shouldn't talk to our CI for more than ten minutes, in case we run into traffic. Set a timer on your phone so you don't get lost in conversation. You remember what questions we agreed on?"

She had them memorized. "Yes. Let's go. I want this over with."

She didn't like lying to Connor but she didn't see another way.

"Come on. My car is parked around the corner. I'm sure you would rather take the Metro, but we're close and this will be so much faster. Surely at this time of night I can find a place to park."

"It's only a few miles." Even as she spoke, she was climbing into Everly's rental. It was two miles from the Capitol Building to the Lincoln Memorial and at least another two from her condo to the Mall. She had been planning on taking a bus, and now she could see where that might have failed spectacularly. The nearest Metro stop was Foggy Bottom and it was a thirty-minute walk from there. The bus would have been quicker, but it had to be timed to perfection.

Even at this hour, there were still tourists walking the streets. Everly pulled out onto Independence Avenue.

Behind her Lara heard the rev of a motorcycle. Her heart screeched to a halt as she twisted around, trying to catch a glimpse of the bike. Was it the same man on a motorcycle who had first tried to kill her?

Had he been out there, lurking in the shadows, just waiting for his next opportunity? Was he following her even now?

"You okay?" Everly asked beside her as the motorcycle disappeared from view.

She forced the panic down. "Just some old fears. I'm good."

She couldn't have an attack now. Before yesterday, she hadn't had one since she was a teenager and some of her high school friends had decided to play a prank on her. They'd lurked outside her parents' place and called her à la *Scream*. That had been a truly embarrassing visit from a couple of EMTs.

She'd been able to handle the most recent one because Connor had been with her. She'd focused on his voice and found a way to turn back the old childhood panic.

Of course if he'd been with her now, he wouldn't have been saying sweet, soothing words. He would likely be the one threatening to kill her.

"I see a spot up ahead. It's close, but not too close. I don't want Deep Throat to see us getting out of a car together. I'm going to stay behind you, but I've got eyes on you. When you're done, walk straight back toward the car and I'll join you. I had Gabe take me here after my meeting with you and I found the perfect place to stake out the memorial."

Everly parked the car and Lara heard the roar of the motorcycle again as it headed toward Arlington Memorial Bridge. She breathed a little sigh of relief.

Everything was going to be okay. Within ten minutes it would be over. Soon after that, she would be back in her condo, waiting for Connor to finish up his job.

Easy peasy.

She pulled the hood over her head. "All right. I'm going in."

Everly locked the car and fell into step beside her. "I've got binoculars. I'll be watching the whole time. What's the signal if you get into trouble?"

"Besides screaming my head off and running away?" Lara had decided Everly was really into the spy stuff.

"Yes, besides that." Everly also didn't give in to sarcasm.

"I stretch my left arm twice and you come running."

Everly took a turn to her left. "Be careful."

Lara walked on alone, deeply aware of the night around her. Up ahead, the amber glow of the lights from the Lincoln Memorial beckoned. She jogged up the path, wanting more than anything to get this over with so she could get home to Connor.

She'd lived in that condo for two years, ever since her breakup with Tom. It had been her refuge, and now she couldn't think of the place without seeing Connor in it. She would never be able to walk into her bedroom without picturing him asleep in her bed, his big masculine body so incongruous against her dainty pink and yellow comforter. She wouldn't be able to walk into the kitchen without envisioning him there, a mug of coffee in his hands.

She was in love with Spencer Connor. She had to get him to come around on the name thing. She couldn't go the rest of her life calling him by his last name, though Spencer didn't seem to fit him.

Lara hiked up the stairs that led to the memorial. She appreciated not being completely alone, though the homeless man sitting on the steps with the hood of his jacket covering his face didn't really give her a warm and fuzzy feeling. She usually stopped and tried to talk to people so obviously down on their luck, but something about this one made her hurry along. She swore she could feel his eyes on her despite the fact that she couldn't see his face.

A couple holding hands strode down the steps beside her, and she convinced herself to look away from the man in the hood and continue on. After all, Everly was out there. Even though she'd only just met the woman, they'd connected. Lara's gut told her she and Everly would be good friends.

Hopefully their closeness would come from shared adventures and not because Everly had to shoot people to save her.

She reached the top of the steps, only slightly out of breath. At this time of night, the rangers who conducted tours were gone. She looked up the length of the Doric columns of the memorial and then behind her. The reflecting pool stretched between the Lincoln and Washington Memorials. Somewhere out there Everly was watching.

"You made it. I wondered if you would."

Thank god. She was worried he'd draw her inside the monument where Everly likely wouldn't be able to see her. She turned to find her confidential informant standing near the entrance. He looked thoroughly unremarkable—average height and weight, hair a nondescript brown, probably in his midthirties. As he had the last time they'd met, he wore a tweed blazer, button-down white shirt, and khaki slacks. An old-school fedora perched on his head, as if he'd stepped out of a forties-era film. It struck her as a little costume-like, but then she suspected one had to be a bit dramatic to schedule midnight meetings at national monuments.

"Of course I came. Why wouldn't I?"

"I noticed you've been keeping some interesting company."

"Oh, you're talking about Connor. He has nothing to do with this. Don't worry. I can handle him."

"Do you think so?" He gave her a faint smile that suggested she was delusional and it sent a little tremor of unease up her spine. "Have you continued looking into Joy Hayes's death?"

She hadn't mentioned that to him before. "How did you know about that research?"

"I know a lot of things. I hadn't planned on sharing this with you. I had selected one of your neighbors to be my point person for that. Fredrick Gallagher is a very curious character. He's a big player in the ancient alien world and he sure does like his conspiracy theories."

"He's not a crackpot." Her mind was reeling with the thought that this guy also had his eye on Freddy, who had obviously been his first choice. Why? How did he know Freddy? Nothing made sense.

"Oh, he is, but unfortunately, he's a highly intelligent one and he's onto something. I started tracking his movements. After he visited three television stations in the Midwest and shared some of his findings with you, I knew you were the perfect partner to bring into this, especially since Freddy can't function in the real world."

"I thought you wanted to use Capitol Scandals."

"Not at all, but once I realized you were already involved, I decided you and your platform were the better choice. You can eventually be my go-between with many people. If you haven't yet, there's another woman I want you to meet."

"Everly Parker."

A hint of a smile lit his face. "Very good. I like to see my girls getting along. You understand that this goes far beyond her brother's death."

"I understand that Natalia Kuilikov is very important. I don't understand what she has to do with Maddox Crawford's death, and I definitely have no idea how she's tied into Joy Hayes's assassination."

His smile widened. "I'm glad to hear you using the right words. The papers all called her death a tragic accident. But we both know Zack Hayes was never the target."

The evidence haunted her nightly. "No. He wasn't. Did the president kill his wife?"

"Now if I told you that, we wouldn't need to have these charming meetings."

"I'm almost out of time. Is Natalia Kuilikov alive?"

"Yes. Does Connor Sparks have you on a tight leash?"

"He doesn't know I'm gone and I would like to keep it that way." The question replayed in her mind, and Lara realized what he'd asked. "Sparks? His name is Spencer. Spencer Connor."

The informant scoffed. "That one doesn't have much of an imagination. I assume he showed up just as the Russians started tracking you."

"Russians? It's a Russian who's trying to kill me?"

"Kill you? They certainly wouldn't want to kill you. They want to track you."

"You're wrong. Someone already tried to shoot me in broad daylight at a bus stop."

"Maybe someone's gone rogue." He shrugged. "But the Russians know I've been in touch so you have to be smarter than their organization. They want exactly what you want—Natalia Kuilikov's location. You need to beat the Russians to her and find out where she hid Sergei. She's the only one who knows. Without that information, you'll never find the truth."

"Who is Sergei?"

"Isn't that the million-dollar question? All I can say is Sergei is the man who will destroy the president someday. He will take down everything Zack Hayes holds dear. If you want to know why, you'll have to find him." He held out a slip of paper. "These are five known aliases used by Natalia. She's likely using something else now, but we're all creatures of habit. Find her. She can lead you to Sergei. And be careful with Connor Sparks. He isn't what he seems."

"Why can't you just tell me where she is? All of this cloak-and-dagger stuff is bullshit. How do I know you're not leading me away from where I need to be? How do I know you're not lying to me because you're Sergei?"

A deep-throated laugh filled the night air. "Unlike your boyfriend, you have a great imagination. I can't tell you because I don't know. That's why I need you. I'm giving you the information I have and hoping you can prove my theories true. If they're not, if I'm wrong . . . well, I don't even like to think about that. I don't particularly want to live in that world. So do what you do and make it all nice and shiny for me, Lara Armstrong. I'll contact you again."

She took the paper and secured it in her pocket. She wouldn't waste time studying it until she was safely home. "I still have questions."

He'd already turned away. "Of course you do. That's why you're perfect. You won't stop trying to solve the puzzle. Just make sure you're using the right pieces. Now hurry back or that man of yours is sure to get upset. I don't think you'll like him when he's upset. People tend to die around Connor Sparks. Ask him what he was doing that night in the Crawford Building a few weeks ago."

Her cell phone buzzed in her pocket. Time was up.

Damn it. He disappeared into the shadows and she had to go.

Before she could shove her phone back into her pocket, a text came through. Unknown. A chill went down her spine.

She opened it though she knew she should wait.

I warned you to get rid of him. This blood is on your hands.

Nausea threatened. She looked out into the night. It had seemed so peaceful before. The informant had told her the Russians were after her. The Russian mob? That part made sense, but it also made sense that they wouldn't want her dead. She couldn't lead them to Natalia if she was cold and in the ground. Why would they start this slow, mental torture? Why did it feel so very personal?

She paused on the top step. Was her would-be killer out there? Had he followed her and sent that text? Pure primal instinct sent a shiver through her. He was a hunter and she was prey. He wanted her blood on his hands and she was a sitting duck until she got back to Everly.

Run. Something deep inside her told her to take off and not look back. It was the same little voice that had told her to run as a child, to try to get to safety. She needed to stay in the light. He would be in the darkness, watching and waiting for her to make a mistake.

Her heart was racing as she pounded down the steps. She would make for the car and Everly. Once there, she could take a deep breath and think about everything the informant had said. With every word, she felt as if he'd sent her world spinning a little faster. Even now she wasn't sure where she'd landed. What had he meant about Connor? How did he even know who Connor was? Was that his real name? Lara knew she'd heard it before but where?

She ran. Why the hell were there so freaking many stairs? They seemed to never end.

She got to the bottom and a figure stepped out in front of her.

Lara stopped and fell back because she recognized him. The homeless man from earlier, the one with the hood. She saw the glint of metal in his hand and opened her mouth to scream.

H iding in the lobby of Lara's building, Connor stared at the elevator, willing it not to open. Let her stay in her place. Let her be real and honest. If she would just prove him wrong, he would spend the rest of the evening making it up to her. She would never know he'd been suspicious, but she would get a night of pleasure she'd never forget.

The elevator dinged and his heart fell.

Lara walked out dressed in all black. She strode through the lobby and toward the back exit.

Connor touched his earpiece. "She's on the move."

Dax's voice came over the Bluetooth. "Damn, man. I'm sorry to hear that. I'm approaching the door. It's been a while since I picked a lock. I hope I'm not rusty. If I get caught doing this, you better be down to bail me out ASAP. I am not spending the night in jail."

"I promise, but I happen to know you're fairly safe. I checked earlier today while Lara was showering. The units around Freddy's are all empty. Two congressmen are back in their districts for the weekend and Mrs. Sullivan is gone for the next two weeks visiting her grand-kids." Maybe Lara hadn't known. Or maybe she had and simply planned to stall him to coincide his break-in with her rendezvous. He'd been getting in good with the elderly couple next door. They liked to gossip. They also liked Lara. They talked incessantly about how won-derful she was.

Did they know she liked to lie?

"I'm taking the bike if it looks like she's not going on foot." Connor pulled the hood to his jacket over his head.

He'd traded assignments—and coats—with Dax, worried that Lara might recognize his jacket. Dax was bigger and broader than he was. The jacket hung off him, the hood drawing down over his eyes. He pulled the keys to Dax's motorcycle and headed out of the building.

He eased around the corner. Even if he lost sight of her, he could track her using her phone. He touched his own, making sure the connection was working and that she'd brought it with her. Sure enough, there was a little blue dot marking her movements.

"Are you sure you want to do this? Won't your fiancé be upset?" Lara's voice was quiet, but he could hear her speaking to someone at the other end of the alley.

"I can handle it," a familiar voice replied.

Son of a bitch. Connor knew they'd been plotting. Everly Parker was waiting for Lara.

"I think in this case everyone will agree it's better I go with you than let you go alone," Gabe's fiancée continued. "We have fifteen minutes to make the meeting, then another fifteen to get back here and have you safely ensconced in your apartment. To be safe, you shouldn't talk to our CI for more than ten minutes, in case we run into traffic. Set a timer on your phone so you don't get lost in conversation. You remember what questions we agreed on?"

They kept speaking but he was busy texting Gabe. There was no way he was keeping quiet about this.

> Your future wife is a bad fucking influence and if she gets
> Lara killed, we're going to have trouble.

They were obviously using Everly's car. He would have to find out what she was driving.

His cell trilled as he shoved the helmet on his head.

> My future wife is sleeping at the hotel.

He smiled with savage satisfaction. *Check again, buddy.*

> She's with Lara. What's she driving? I'm going to follow and
> make sure they don't die.

Lara needed to live long enough for him to get his hands on her. If anyone was going to murder that woman, it was him.

Lexus SUV. White. Shit, man, I'm so sorry. Where do you need me?

He switched over to his locator app and discovered Lara was moving west on Independence. He revved the Harley and took off after her.

"I can hear you," Dax said into his ear. "You better not kill that bike. I know the rest of you might have come into your billion-dollar trust funds or blackmailed daddy and hit it big on the stock market, but my mother is still alive. That bike set me back more than a freaking house. Don't dent it."

It was good to know he had his friends with him. "I'll try not to dent your bike. Where the hell is she going?"

"Try not to dent your girlfriend, either."

He resisted the urge to claim she wasn't his girlfriend. Dax knew better. At least he wasn't alone in the deceptive girlfriend column. "She's got a partner in crime. She's with Everly."

A whistle came over the line. "Nice. Gabe is going to be pissed. Look on the bright side. Lara probably isn't heading out for a booty call with another man."

He pulled in behind them and revved the engine just a little. Sure enough, Lara turned in the passenger seat. She was probably afraid since someone had tried to murder her the last time she'd been followed by a motorcycle. Good. He wanted her afraid. After he got through with her she would wince every time she heard one of the things. And was Dax high? "You thought she was seeing another man?"

"The thought didn't occur to you? I thought that was what we were afraid of."

The thought hadn't occurred to him once. Lara would lie if she thought she had a higher purpose, but . . . "No. Lara wouldn't cheat. She is, however, the kind of woman who would put her sweet ass in

harm's way for a fucking story. She's turning, I think toward the Mall.
She better be giving Everly a tour."

"I'm almost in. Be careful."

"You, too. Keep this line open." He pulled into a spot and locked
down the engine, leaving the helmet on the handlebars. He hustled to
get in front of her. She'd stopped and was talking to Everly, gesturing
toward the Lincoln Memorial.

The desperate need to spank that pretty ass of hers was riding him
hard. She would likely protest so he would have to find another way to
punish her for scaring the shit out of him, but he could picture it in
his mind. She would cry and beg and he would paddle that sweet flesh
until it was a shiny pink and she promised to never, ever lie to him
again.

He hit the steps at a run and then found a good place to settle in.

She was meeting her confidential informant. There was no other
reason for her clandestine shit. Despite combing through all her correspondence, he'd missed their communication somehow. So had
Roman's people. Deep Throat was here and if he got the idea Lara
wasn't alone, he would take a hike. That served no one's purpose.

He watched as Everly and Lara started toward the memorial. Everly
peeled off before the stairs and took up a position. It was a good one
from what he could tell. She was a professional. She'd picked a place
where she could see but remain unseen.

They had a good plan, and at least Lara hadn't come alone. It
wouldn't save either one of them. His cell vibrated. He glanced down.

She's stopped on Independence Avenue. I think she's close
to the Lincoln Memorial. On my way.

It was good to know he wasn't the only one who had LoJacked his
girlfriend. He quickly texted back.

Do not come in hot. Delicate situation. Silence necessary.

He slid the phone back into his pants before Lara strode up the bank of stairs on which he sat. He kept his head low but watched as she moved by him.

She slowed and for a second he worried she would recognize him. He heard her breath catch before she shot up the stairs. Prey instinct. She knew a predator who intended to eat her when she saw one.

He stood and leaned against the wall. She could run, but she couldn't hide and he was definitely going to make a meal out of her.

"Goddamn it. I'm going to fucking kill you. Why didn't you mention this place was owned by a medieval freak? I just nearly got my head taken off by an axe."

Ah, so Dax had made it inside Freddy's lair.

"I mentioned he was a paranoid prepper who probably booby-trapped the place," Connor murmured.

He watched as Lara strode by a couple holding hands. She seemed to pick up the bounce in her step, as though happy she wasn't alone with the likes of him, but the moment she walked past them, they turned to watch her.

Shit. He wasn't alone in following her. He hoped like hell Everly was packing. It looked like they might need some firepower. He slumped down. There were homeless people all over D.C. He didn't even need to talk quietly. Homeless people often had mental issues. It was one of the unfortunate realities that often led to their state.

"I thought you meant he would have trip wires that alerted him to the fact that someone had been in his house. I didn't realize the fucking wire would trip an ax flying at my head."

"You never took this business seriously, brother." He gave his head a couple of light slaps and noticed the couple utterly dismissed him. "Get the package and get out of there."

"I'm a little worried the package will explode in my face. This dude is insane. Oh, and he's got a massive hard-on for you. He's got a wall full of data about Connor Sparks."

"Tell me something I don't know." The couple drifted up a few steps, pretending to take in the majesty of the Mall, but it didn't look like they were pursuing Lara. When the man turned, he recognized him. Pavel Sopov, the assassin from the park. His associate was a blonde, but Connor didn't recognize her. She would almost certainly be with the Krylov syndicate. He wished he could take pictures, but that might give him away.

"Holy shit. He's after Zack. He's got tons of pictures of Zack on the walls. It looks like he's been stalking him for months at least, maybe a year or more. What the hell has your girl gotten herself into?"

He couldn't think now about the fact that Lara seriously believed Zack had killed his own wife.

Of course, he had been down three points in the polls, a little voice whispered. What would a man who had been groomed for one thing all of his life do if it was about to be taken from him?

People had killed for far less.

No. He knew Zack. Connor couldn't let himself believe Zack had offed Joy for his own gain. "If you've got time, take it all. If you don't, take pictures. We need to know who we're up against and what he knows. I need to go silent."

"Understood."

They would keep the line open but quiet until Connor gave the word or Dax needed serious help. Connor stood and started pacing the stairs. The Russians had moved up and seemed to have some sort of listening device.

"Она получила упаковку." The woman didn't even attempt to hide that they were watching Lara.

"Это список возможных имён. Мы должны добыть его не смотря на цену." Pavel nodded and took her hand again. He pocketed his device then started back down the stairs.

Why couldn't jihadists be after Lara? Connor spoke Arabic, Farsi, and Pashto, but not Russian. The couple descended past him. He had to think they were going to wait for her somewhere at the bottom of the stairs where there would be fewer witnesses to what might be anything from a mugging to a murder.

He ambled up the stairs, desperate to get a sight line on Lara. If she slipped past him somehow, she would be walking straight into a trap, and the odds would likely be their two guns to Everly's one. He needed to get her out of here and fast. If Deep Throat didn't like that, then he could find someone else's girl to make his Woodward and Bernstein. Lara was getting out of this business for good.

He was just about to storm the meeting when he stopped behind her.

Lara stood slightly above him, talking to a man dressed like a douche bag college professor who'd watched too much *Mad Men*.

The only problem with the scenario? It wasn't Deep Throat—at least not the one Everly had met in New York a few weeks back.

This man was a good four inches shorter and had a slightly stockier build than Everly's informant. He was also at least ten years younger.

Who the hell was he?

Lara turned and Connor realized the couple had melted into the shadows somewhere on the outskirts of the memorial. He moved to intercept her at the bottom of the steps. Damn, he should have brought Dax with him. He pulled his cell and didn't bother with texting. He needed Gabe.

Gabe answered and didn't waste time. "I'm almost there. I have a lock on Everly's phone."

He didn't have to worry about Everly. She probably wasn't on Pavel's radar. He doubted she would know who these Russians were, either. "Is Roman with you?"

"I'm here."

He hustled down the steps. "Get the police here and fast. I'm going to take Lara and run, but we've got at least two Russians on our ass and where there's two . . ."

"There are probably four more. Shit. I'm on it."

"Dax, I'm taking my woman out of town for the night." He couldn't risk leading her back to her place until he was certain it was secure. "Could you hang there and see if we have any visitors?"

"Sure. It's been an amazing fucking night. Did I mention that he electroshocked his computer? I can't feel my left arm." A long sigh came over the line. "Be careful, brother."

He traded his phone for his SIG, easing it out of its holster. He stopped at the bottom and waited. He could hear her running. He searched the periphery for any sign of movement. Everly stepped out of the shadows and he tipped his head up, making sure she could see him.

Shit, she mouthed and started to walk toward him.

He shook his head slightly and held up two fingers. She nodded, signaling that she was aware they weren't alone.

Lara hit the bottom step and he turned. She took one look at him, and a scream broke through the air.

Unfortunately so did a bullet. Connor tackled her just as one hit his arm.

ELEVEN

Lara hit the ground with a hard thud, but that didn't stop her from kicking out at her attacker. His big body covered hers, and then they were rolling to her right. "Get off me. Do you know what my boyfriend will do to you?"

She heard sirens in the distance. He stopped and pulled back his hood. "Do you know what your boyfriend is going to do to you?"

Connor stared down at her, his expression ferocious.

Lara couldn't breathe. Her heart nearly stopped. "I can explain."

There was a pinging sound and Connor cursed as something rained down on them. "Get behind the wall, damn it. They're shooting."

She scrambled to her knees and he shoved her into the shrubbery that lined the steps on the road level of the monument. The leaves raked against her skin, but her palms were already wet. In the dim light she could see it was blood. Connor's blood.

"You're hit."

He crouched in front of her, a gun in his hand. "It's nothing. And it's definitely nothing compared to what I'm going to do to you. You lied to me."

"Not exactly. You never asked me if I was going to a meeting." And why did it matter when he'd been shot? "You need to go to the hospital. Who's shooting at you?"

"Not me. You, princess. As with all things in my life lately, this has nothing to do with me and everything to do with you. The Russian mob sent a welcome party. They probably have had a man or two casing your apartment building just waiting for you to do something idiotic. You don't like to disappoint people, do you?"

She ignored his harsh words. He had every right to be testy. And she hated that she'd had more than one occasion to see how Connor handled nearly being killed. She gasped as she remembered her partner in crime. "Everly's out there. Oh, god, Connor. I brought Everly into this."

"Yes, I'm sure we'll talk about that later, but Everly can handle herself. In fact, it looks like she handled at least one of them." He stood up. "Where's the other?"

"He took off." Lara could hear Everly shouting.

"Tell me she's alive." Connor nodded at something Lara couldn't see.

"I would love to but I'm probably done with lying this evening. It was clear self-defense so don't worry about me. You should get her out of here."

Lara peeked above the line of bushes and saw the body of a woman lying at Everly's feet. She gasped and started to dash toward her friend.

Connor hooked an arm around her middle. "Not on your life."

"Put me down." Despite the fact that he'd been shot, he easily carried her along. "We have to stay and talk to the police. You don't know what they'll do to Everly. They might think she's a murderer."

"She'll be fine. She's a survivor, princess. You better hope you are, too. Put this on." He stopped and set her down, handing her a helmet.

She looked down at it. He was climbing on the back of a Harley. Had he been the one following her earlier? Had he been trailing her the whole time? "I don't understand what's going on."

He turned to her as he started the bike. "Right now, you don't need to understand. You need to obey. I'm not kidding, Lara. If you don't get on the back of this bike and hold on, I'm going to lose my shit. You don't want me to do that."

People tend to die around Connor Sparks. She stared at him, blinking, unnerved.

"Lara, if the police get here before we leave, they will take whatever evidence that man gave you into custody and you won't see it again."

She was being ridiculous. Connor wouldn't hurt her. Oh, he was going to lecture the hell out of her and she had a lot of explaining to do, but she couldn't believe he would truly harm her. And he was making a lot of sense. Since she hadn't even looked at the list, she couldn't afford to let it go. On the other hand, she'd dragged Everly into danger. Lara looked back in her friend's direction.

"Gabe is on his way. She's fine. Now get on the bike or we'll do this the hard way."

She believed him. She shoved the too-big helmet on her head and scrambled on behind him. The minute her arms went around his waist, he took off. It probably wasn't the time to fret that he wasn't wearing a helmet or remind him that was dangerous. He'd already been shot, so he probably wasn't thinking about possible concussions.

She held onto his solid frame as he roared into the night. When they got back to her place, Lara had no doubt he intended to fire off a bunch of questions. But she had a few of her own.

Her confidential informant sounded like he knew Connor very well. And the CI had called him Sparks. Had Connor really been in the Crawford Building when all hell had broken loose? Not according to him. Supposedly he'd been on the West Coast for months.

Lara leaned against him. She'd never been on a motorcycle before. They weren't the most environmentally friendly vehicles, but she liked how close she felt to him. When he stopped at a light, he balanced the bike before running his hand over her right knee as though assuring himself she was really there.

She pressed her chest against his back and dragged her hands up the ridges of his abdomen and his pectorals, stopping to feel his heart beating.

"That won't save you," he growled. "But it might put me in a better mood. It might encourage me to take my payback in a different way." His hand drifted from her knee, up to her thigh.

She cuddled closer to him. Maybe she wanted a little payback of her own. After all, he'd given her the fright of a lifetime. He could have told her he was there. He'd deliberately hidden from her. He'd been sitting there, looking homeless as she walked by.

But he'd also risked his life to save hers. Someone had been waiting to steal the information the CI had given her, maybe even mow her down with bullets. Connor hadn't thought twice, just shielded her with his big body as he'd led her to safety. Yes, he'd first come home with her as her bodyguard, but he hadn't merely saved her because she was a job. The way he touched her told Lara that.

The light changed and he took off again. She should be thinking about how her informant knew Connor, but all her brain seemed capable of was thinking about Connor and the enormity of what he'd done for her. It touched her heart . . . and parts farther south. Adrenaline pumped through her system and fed a need that seemed to flow straight to her sex.

She wanted him.

Lara always thought things through, but what she felt for him didn't have anything to do with her intellect. It was a primal thing that wouldn't be denied. What she felt now didn't care about questions. It didn't stop to second guess. And her libido didn't give a crap what someone else said or thought. She'd latched onto Connor with her heart and now she only cared about him.

When he drove right by her place, she didn't question him. She simply followed his lead.

It was time to tell Connor everything, to truly trust him.

As he drove through the night, Lara held tight. She wasn't sure how much time passed, but after a while, he pulled off the freeway. He'd twisted and turned a path through the city. She'd finally figured out he was trying to make sure they hadn't been tailed.

He pulled into a nondescript motel parking lot, stopped the bike, and eased off. "Come on."

"Connor?"

He turned, his jaw a tight line. "No questions right now. I need you to walk in and get us a room. I've got blood on my jacket. They won't rent to me. In fact if they get a good look at me, they'll likely call the police and then you lose whatever it was that was far more important than our relationship."

She managed to hold in a crushed gasp. "Connor . . ."

He shook his head sharply. "Not now. Pay cash. They will want a credit card. You can't give them one. This should work instead."

She took the bill he handed her. One hundred dollars. "You expect me to bribe the clerk?"

"If you want us both to survive this situation, yes. If he won't take it, we'll find another motel. Understand I'll be watching your every move. You don't want to make me come after you."

If he thought she couldn't pull this off, he was wrong. She could bribe people. She could get motel rooms on the down low. Hell, she was wanted by the Russian mob. If that didn't say something about her toughness, she wasn't sure what did.

And if he thought he was going to intimidate her, he was wrong.

She marched right up to the rundown registration desk, explained that she was an adulteress looking for a quiet place to cheat on her insanely jealous husband with her poor but handsome lover, and she was willing to pay to keep her name out of the records.

The clerk sighed with utter disinterest, took her hundred bucks, and handed her the key to room number four.

Maybe she hadn't needed her well-crafted fiction after all. Lara shrugged.

Once she exited the office, Connor hustled to the room, hauling her with him. He took the keycard and dragged her in before he turned, shut the door, and dead bolted it. She'd noticed he'd parked the motorcycle on the other side of the lot, so no one traveling the freeway could spot it.

Now that they were safely inside, she looked at Connor, ready to have it out with him. His dark blond hair was mussed, making him look disheveled and even sexier than usual. The urge to smooth his hair back almost overwhelmed her, but she doubted he would accept the affectionate gesture from her now. She had to make him understand that while she loved him, she also had a job to do.

Oh god, she loved him. She really, really loved him.

And then she was a little afraid of him. He shot her a narrow-eyed glare, his expression dark and predatory as he stalked across the room, closing the distance between them. Lara backed up until she couldn't anymore, until her back hit the wall. That didn't stop Connor from closing in. He pressed his palms flat beside her head, caging her against his body and invading her space. She couldn't breathe. Intimidation flowed from him like charisma off a really good politician.

"D-don't you want me to look at your arm?"

"Fuck that." He glowered. "Why?"

She couldn't possibly misunderstand his question. She found herself stuttering not out of fear but arousal. The desire she'd felt as they'd fled the Mall came back like a tidal wave. "Y-you wouldn't have let me meet him otherwise."

"You don't know that."

He hovered so close. Heat poured from his body. Her arousal picked up. Lara found herself breathing hard.

"I do. I know you. You would have locked me away. I would have missed the meeting and that source would have dried up."

His stare pierced her. "At least you would have been safe. You would have been out of this mess."

She wasn't so sure about that. That text she'd received at the end of her meeting seemed awfully personal. Why wouldn't the Russians simply demand that she give over the information or that she stay out of the situation? Instead, they had chastised her because she hadn't gotten rid of "him." The message hadn't even mentioned the information, just an unnamed "him." Connor?

Maybe the Russians hadn't sent the text at all . . .

Her CI knew most everything, and he hadn't seemed terribly worried about Connor. Sure, he'd given her warnings but nothing dire. Was this how the informant intended to keep her on her toes? Did he want to isolate her? Play good cop in real life and bad cop via text?

None of that mattered now because Connor was so close that her breasts brushed against his chest.

"I won't leave this story alone." Maybe it was time to be painfully honest with him and figure out where she stood. She'd been a coward with Tom, hiding her feelings and not letting him go when she should have. If she didn't tell Connor how she felt now, she'd only be a coward again. "I love you, but I can't give up everything I am because you want me to be safe."

He froze and she was almost certain she'd made a mistake. "What did you say?"

Coward it was, then. "I can't give up everything I am because you want me to be safe."

When she ducked her head, he snagged her chin in his grip and forced her to look at him. "That is not what I meant and you know it. Say it again."

That gruff command hadn't exactly been the response she was looking for, but she hoped the fact that he wanted to hear her confession again was a good sign. "I love you."

He pressed his body close, pinning her to the wall. His hard cock nudged her belly. "Say it again."

Connor had told her in the beginning what he wanted—warmth and affection. She could give him all she had. She rose up on her toes until her mouth rested bare inches from his. She wanted to breathe the words into his skin so he soaked them up. She suspected he hadn't had a lot of love in his life. She wanted him to know that had officially changed.

"I love you," she murmured.

She'd barely spoken the words before he slammed his mouth down on hers and pinned her to the wall with his big body, holding her beneath him to take his onslaught. He dragged his tongue over her lower lip, demanding entry. She didn't deny him. No, she opened herself up fully to the crazy, heady experience of being loved by this man. And it was love, she felt sure.

He devoured her like a starving man at a feast, holding her so tight she swore he'd never let go. The sizzling ache for him consumed Lara. When Connor made love to her, he sank himself in to the core of her being, and she felt as if they were the only two people in the world. Two who had merged to become one.

He tugged at the zipper of her jacket. "Take it off or I'll rip it off. Anything you want to keep better hit the floor in ten seconds or less because that's how long it's going to take me to get inside you."

Her hands shook as she quickly unzipped the jacket and tossed it away. He gave her just enough room to kick aside her sneakers then wriggle out of her pants and undies.

He shoved at his jeans, pushing them down to his thighs and setting his cock free. "Turn around. Hands against the wall."

"Connor?" She felt ridiculously vulnerable wearing nothing but a shirt and a bra.

He turned her. "Hands against the wall."

She pressed her palms flat and had to force herself to breathe when his fingers slid across her bare backside, traced the line between her cheeks, and ran along her swollen slit.

"You're wet." He groaned as he parted her labia, sliding a finger deep. "Is that why you rubbed against me on the bike? Were you wet and trying to steal an orgasm from me like a cat in heat?"

She knew she should be offended, but when his voice went guttural and his words turned to filth it just made her hotter. If any other man talked to her like that, she would slap him and leave. With Connor, she spread her legs so he could have more access. "I liked the bike."

"That's not all you like." He nuzzled her neck, his lips blazing a trail of fire to her ear. "That's right. Spread those legs wide for me. Get that pussy ready because I'm not waiting. You put me through hell tonight and I can take it out by punching something or by filling you so full of cock you can't see straight. Which would you like?"

She'd pushed him to the edge, and he wasn't a man who liked to be out of control. If her surrender to him would help right his world, Lara was all too happy to give in.

"I want your cock, Connor. Please. I'll do anything. Give it to me."

When he caressed her folds and nipped at her shoulder, the rest of the world dropped away. The fear that had plagued her all day melted under his onslaught. She shivered.

"Tell me this belongs to me." He plunged two fingers inside her while his thumb worked her clit.

She was already so close to the edge. Pleasure shimmered right in front of her, but she held still because she'd forced him to play by her rules up until this point. She was determined to give him what he needed now. "It belongs to you."

"What belongs to me? Be specific. I want the words."

"My pussy belongs to you. I belong to you. No matter what I do, I know I belong to you. I love you. I love you so much, Connor." She poured her heart into those words, willing him to believe her.

"And I belong to you. No matter what I fucking do. You remember that. You take those words and memorize them because no matter what happens, they're true and they're going to stay true. I won't let you take them back. Ever."

She wouldn't want to. "I love you."

"That means everything to me, princess." He withdrew his fingers and gripped her hips. She felt his erection probe between her thighs. "I've never wanted anything the way I want you. Remember that, too."

She couldn't reply because the head of his cock breached her in one hard thrust. He didn't ease into her or give her time to adjust. He gave her every inch he had, holding her hips and forcing himself inside her. She was invaded and dominated. He controlled and conquered. A shock of tingles rolled through her body. She whimpered.

"Push back against me," he commanded.

She thrust back and tossed her head at the feel of him sliding in to the hilt. It was almost too much. He held himself steady, and his left hand slid up to her breasts. He shoved the bra above her mounds and cupped her as he pulled out and stroked back in. He thumbed her nipple then gave it a twist.

"Never again, Lara. I swear to god if you lie to me again, I won't be responsible for what I do to you. I'll tie you to the bed and I won't ever let you leave again. Your whole life will be about taking my cock. You won't see the fucking outside world. You'll spend every day on your back and your knees and any other way that pleases me."

She found him endlessly amusing when he was angry. Somehow she couldn't see him actually turning her into a sex slave, but she was sure in the moment it seemed like a viable option to him.

He twisted her nipple again, and a pleasurable pain shimmered through her. She responded before he could do it again. "Yes, Connor. I won't see the light of day. I understand."

"I'll chain you to me, Lara." He anchored his hands back on her hips as he thrust in and out of her body in rough, rhythmic strokes. "I won't let you leave my sight. Fuck, you feel so good."

She let her head fall back, giving over to the euphoria of having Connor inside her. He was so big. When he filled her, she always had a moment when she wasn't sure she could handle it, but she ached to try. And once she succeeded in accommodating every inch of him . . . She groaned. There was nothing like it. There was certainly no one like him.

He caressed every bit of her skin that he could reach, her breasts and her belly, the curves of her waist and hips, before he found her clitoris again and strummed it—fucking her with force all the while.

Lara pressed back against him. If she hadn't, the strength of his thrusts would have sent her headfirst into the wall. Still, he didn't hold back. He simply picked up the pace and she moved with him. The push and pull of his strokes formed a rhythm she sank into. Over and over his cock sank deep before he dragged back out, sensitizing her flesh and drawing her to the edge.

She groaned as he toyed with her clitoris in earnest now.

"I can't hold out. You feel so good. You're so hot and tight around me. Come for me, princess."

In the back of her mind, she registered why she was so hot and tight around him, but that warning was a minor voice drowned out by the sound of her screaming his name as the pleasure detonated through her body. She bucked back, desperate to hold on to the sensation—and him—for as long as possible. Wave after wave of satisfaction rode through her body, flaring all along her skin.

Connor's hands tightened and she could feel him pulse inside her, and then a warmth suffused her as he came. He thrust in as deeply as he could, hauling her backward and up. He cupped her breasts as he thrust into her one last time. He buried his face against her neck and she knew a second of pure intimacy before reality drenched her peace.

"You didn't use a condom."

His arms wound around her as though he was afraid to let go. "I told you I haven't had any lover but you in a very long time. I've passed all my physicals. It's fine, princess. We can use whatever birth control you're on."

"I'm not using anything. I didn't need to. This isn't a great time, if you know what I mean." She quickly calculated the odds and wasn't happy with them. She tried to pull away, but he held her tight.

"All right, then we'll deal with it," he growled against her ear. "If it comes up later. Right now, we have other things to talk about, like you lying to me."

"Connor, I just told you I could be pregnant right now and that's what you want to talk about?"

"It probably takes my swimmers a while to get to your egg. I don't think it's instantaneous so we have plenty of time to talk about what happened tonight."

He was so frustrating. She pushed at him again, surprised to see that his bleeding had all but stopped. This time he let her go.

She turned, deeply aware that she was naked from the waist down. "And what do you mean by 'deal with it'?"

Instead of pulling his jeans back up, he pushed them down and off his hips, toeing out of his shoes as he did. He eased out of his shoulder holster, settling the big shiny gun on the desk near the bed before pulling his shirt over his head. "I mean we'll do what people do."

She started to reach for her pants. "So you'll take me to a clinic and drop me off?"

His hand shot out, fingers closing around her wrist. "There won't be any clinic. There will be a pastor or a justice of the peace. Your choice. If you're pregnant, we're getting married and that's the end of it. I don't care how feminist your beliefs are. We made that baby together and we're going to raise it together." He cursed and then pulled her close. "Damn it, Lara. We don't even know if there is a baby. I'm sorry. We both lost our heads."

She rested her head against his chest. Yeah, maybe her feminist beliefs should feel assaulted, but somehow knowing he intended to stay no matter what, calmed her down. "We did. I wasn't thinking. I just wanted to be with you so badly."

He smoothed her hair back and she could feel the thunder of his heartbeat against hers. "I did, too. When they almost shot you, I nearly lost it."

"Your arm." She dropped her gaze to the wound again. "Let me turn on the light and look at it."

"It's fine. It was a graze."

"I noticed that it stopped bleeding."

He nodded. "Exactly. It doesn't need stitches. I'll get some antiseptic on it soon." He settled her back against his chest. "Would it be so bad?"

"Being shot. Yes." It was just a graze this time, but what would happen next time?

"I was talking about a baby. About having to get married."

He would do the right thing, but she'd noticed he hadn't really replied when she'd told him she loved him. "I don't want to *have* to get married."

"Then do it because you want to."

She stilled in his arms. "Is that your way of asking me to marry you?"

He winced. "I might have mentioned that you shouldn't expect a whole lot of romance."

As proposals went it was horrible. Her head told her that they didn't know each other well enough. They hadn't spent enough time together and most of it had been under stress. To her heart, it didn't matter. She wanted to say yes and run away with him and never open that note the CI had given her tonight. Then Connor would never be in danger again.

"I thought you were mad at me."

He tilted her head up and his mouth covered hers. He kissed her long and slow before coming up for air. "I'm furious with you. Lift your arms."

She did as he asked and soon found herself as naked as he was. "Shouldn't we talk this out?"

He shook his head. "I would say mean things. We should definitely not talk this out. After I've fucked you a couple more times, we can have a semi-civilized discussion. You feel so fucking good. I'm already hard again. Do you know how long it usually takes a man my age to recover? You're like Viagra, princess. Even when you lie to me, I can't keep my hands off you."

"I didn't lie."

He ran his tongue along her bottom lip. "Did you or did you not send me to Freddy's apartment so you could sneak away?"

"Well . . . I knew you wouldn't let me go." She pressed her body against his. Being with him now was even better than a few minutes ago. The orgasm had been wonderful, but she loved being skin to skin with Connor. She slid her hands to his waist, then ran her palms up to his chest. Smooth muscles. Warm skin. He was perfect. "I couldn't risk you preventing me from going to that meeting, but I don't know if I want to be involved now."

He skimmed her back, his fingertips running down the length of her spine. "What does that mean?"

Earlier today this story had meant everything to her, and now she couldn't think of a single reason why. Her ambition evaporated in the face of the very real danger. "It means I can't stand the thought of you taking a bullet meant for me, and if I keep this up, I worry you might have to. It means you're more important to me than any story."

"Come again?"

He was going to make her say it. "I care about you more than I care about my elevated goal of saving America from whatever Zack Hayes has up his sleeve. I'm not an absolutist. People are more important. Love is more important. So would I sacrifice my principles for love? Yes. I will. I choose you, Connor."

He lifted her up so she was eye-level with him. It was a conscious show of strength and every time he used it, she melted a little. She always felt so safe in his arms.

"You know just how to play me." He frowned. "I don't know that I like that."

"I'm not playing you."

"Then marry me. Drop this case because I don't want you involved in it, either. Hand it over to Everly Parker. She has personal reasons to pursue it. We'll get married and you'll be safe."

She nodded. The moment felt surreal. Had she really been shot at, made love to, then agreed to marry a man she hadn't known a week ago? The whole evening felt disconnected from reality. But only the here and now existed. And her future—the one she would share with Connor.

Still, she couldn't help but wonder . . . "My CI knew about you. He talked about you."

Connor led her to the bed and laid her down, quickly following and pressing her into the pillowy comforter. Sure enough, his cock was hard and ready, already seeking between her legs. He dropped his head to her neck, pressing kisses in a line as he moved toward her breast. "What did he say?"

"Why would he call you Sparks?"

He licked her nipple and the world started to go hazy again. "It was my call sign in the Navy. I love your breasts. Have I told you how beautiful they are, princess? Your nipples knew they liked me before the rest of you. They always try to get my attention."

She tried to hold on to her train of thought, but it was hard when he drew the sensitive tip of her breast into his mouth and began to suckle. "He told me to ask what you were doing in the Crawford Building a few weeks ago."

Connor stopped what he was doing and sat up. "Is this some kind of interrogation?"

The room seemed colder than it had before. "I just thought it was weird that he seemed to know who you were."

"Obviously he's watching you. What does it matter now? I thought we just decided you were out of this. Or were you trying to throw me off so you could ask me your questions when you thought I was vulnerable?" He turned away, moving to the edge of the bed and shoving a hand through his hair with a frustrated sigh.

She curled onto her knees behind him, wrapping her arms around him. "No. I was just worried."

"I was in New York visiting my mother. I don't remember if I went to the Crawford Building. I went a lot of places a couple of weeks ago because I'm trying to sort things out with the nursing home. Just go to sleep, Lara. I'm not in the mood to become part of your story." He stood and stalked to the bathroom. The door shut and she heard the shower start to run.

At least he hadn't locked it.

She stared at that door between them. Was her CI trying to split her off from her protection? She would be easier to manipulate or harm if she was alone.

Or Connor was lying to her and he was somehow involved in all this.

It was an easy choice. She wanted to believe the man she'd agreed to marry over a stranger in a cheesy hat. She knew it made her twelve kinds of a fool, but she loved Connor.

Her cell trilled on the floor. It was still in the pocket of her pants. She grabbed it. Tom. He'd sent her a text with one word. Urgent.

Tom's version of urgent often had to do with new movie trailers.

She turned off the phone and made her choice. She would step away from this story because it was too dangerous and she had more than herself to think about now. Connor had thrown himself in front of bullets for her. He won, hands down.

Tom had set up an elaborate proposal. Her parents and Kiki had been at the restaurant. Her ring had glittered at the bottom of a champagne glass. The event had been public and she'd been the center of attention, but Lara hadn't been able to escape the nagging feeling that something wasn't right. She'd accepted. Deep down, she'd known it was wrong. She'd said yes because all those eyes had been on her and she couldn't let those smiling people down.

No one had been watching her when she'd decided to marry Connor. It had been just the two of them. It hadn't been terribly romantic, but it did feel right.

She stepped into the bathroom and drew back the shower curtain. There wasn't a ton of space in the little shower/tub combo. He was standing under the spray, his head down. His whole body seemed weary.

"I can't handle any more questions now, Lara. Go to bed. We'll talk in the morning. I'll tell you anything you want to know. I'm tired. I don't want to do this anymore."

He didn't want to feel hounded. She could understand that. A man wanted to know the woman he was going to marry trusted him. She stepped into the tub and eased a hand onto his back. "I think you were right. I don't think we should talk. I just say stupid things."

If anything, his head dropped further. "It's not stupid to ask questions. You should. You should have been asking questions the whole time."

"Only one matters. Do you still want to marry me?"

"Yes." The word came out in a low growl.

"Then let's get married and I'll turn all this over to Everly Parker. We'll move on with our lives."

He straightened up and turned, towering over her. He took her shoulders in his big hands and dropped his forehead to hers. "I love you. I'm not sure that's worth much, but I've never said it to another woman in my life."

His words filled her heart. His admission was everything. She hugged him, molding her body to his. "I love you. I'll be proud to be your wife."

"I won't let you take it back." He sounded stubborn, but he exhaled, his body relaxing against her. He took hold of her hips again and pressed her close, rubbing his erection against her belly. "You're right. Now isn't the time to talk. Tomorrow we will, but you should know I won't give you up."

He would likely push her to shut down the site, but they could argue about that in the morning. Tonight, she wanted to revel in the fact that he was alive and wanted to spend his life with her. Nothing else mattered.

"Lara, I want you again. I always fucking want you." His hands were restless on her skin. "Let me have you. Don't turn me away."

She knew what he was asking. He hadn't come prepared for a sexual marathon. He hadn't used a condom before because they'd been lost in the moment. Now he was asking for permission, this time both going into it with their eyes wide open.

It was a risk, but he was with her.

"I always want you, too." She went onto her toes and brushed her

lips against his. "I can't think of a better way to celebrate our engagement. Make love to me again. Say you forgive me for tonight. I promise
I won't ever do it again. I'll trust you. We'll make the decision together."

"I forgive you. I hope you can forgive me."

"For what?"

He shook his head. "It doesn't matter now. Come here. I don't want
to think about anything but you. You said yes."

She smiled his way. She couldn't say anything but yes to him.

"Wrap your legs around me." He picked her up and before she
could take another breath, he impaled her on his cock.

Lara let the pleasure flow over her, stronger now because they were
going to share a future.

TWELVE

Connor sat up in bed, the first light of dawn just beginning to breach the edges of the window. The curtains blocked most of the light, but enough shined through that he could make out the sleeping form of the woman next to him.

His almost wife.

His mind worked through the possibilities. Could he manage to get her to sign the paperwork without seeing his real name? He definitely wasn't going to put a fake name on his marriage certificate. He wanted it legal and binding. That was the whole point. He wanted her tied to him before she found out the truth.

Or he could tell her and pray she could forgive him and attempt to start their marriage with some sort of trust.

He'd let go of his rage once he realized he was doing exactly what Gabe had accused him of. He was expecting Lara to behave in a manner that was counter to her nature. She believed she was doing right and she'd placed that on a higher plane than telling him the truth. She wouldn't do that once they were married. She'd promised she would put him and their relationship above anything else.

She said that because she doesn't know what you are, you idiot. Once she learns the truth, she'll dump you so fast your head will spin.

She turned in her sleep and rolled up next to him with a little sigh. He caressed her back, tracing the line of her delicate spine, and she settled down. Even in her sleep she responded to him.

Fuck, he couldn't lose her.

He brushed his hand over to her belly and thought about what a bastard he was. The first time he'd taken her in this crappy motel, he really hadn't thought about anything but getting inside her. It hadn't penetrated his brain that he'd taken her bareback until she'd said something. He'd just thought about how hot she was and how she fit him like she'd been made just for him.

And then he'd seen his play. His end game. It had been a little thought in the back of his head before, but now it was all consuming. How many chances would he get before he had to tell her the truth? She'd said it was a bad time. That sounded perfect to him. If she got pregnant, maybe it wouldn't matter that he'd done nothing but lie to her. By then, he would be her baby's father and she wouldn't deny him. Even if she were mad, she couldn't cut him out of her life entirely. He would take care of her and she wouldn't be able to maintain her rage forever. Lara didn't have that in her.

He just needed to stay close and he could win her. Distance was the enemy. Whatever happened in the next few weeks, he had to keep her chained to his side.

God, he sounded like a bastard—but a desperate one. Because he worried deep down that if Lara Armstrong knew exactly who she'd agreed to marry, discovered how black his soul really was, she would never want him again.

Connor sighed. He needed to call Dax and find out what the hell was going on. They couldn't stay in this motel for long. How was he going to convince the *Bratva* that Lara wasn't involved anymore? She could choose to walk away, but until the Russians believed it, she was still a target. He couldn't stand the thought.

He slipped out of bed, away from her warmth. The minute he broke contact, he could feel the chill. He was certain it wasn't real, knew it must be more of an emotional thing, but it was there all the same. When he was with her, he was warm in a way he'd never been before. He couldn't stand the thought of losing her.

He found the table and his cell phone. He grabbed his pants and shoved into them. He didn't want to get dressed. He wanted to get back into bed with Lara and forget the rest of the world existed. He could be the man he'd told her he was and she could not be hunted by the *Bratva* and some insane duo of dueling informants who wanted god only knew what.

He shoved his feet into his sneakers.

"Connor?"

He turned back. Lara was half up, propped on her left elbow. All that crazy hair was around her. Every part of him softened with the exception of his dick. "Go back to sleep, princess. I'm just going to make a few calls and see if we can head back into town. I'll get us some coffee."

Her lips curled up as she lay back down. "And a little sugar. I like mine sweet."

She was the sweetest thing he'd ever seen. "Of course. I'll be back in a little bit. Lara, do I need to say it?"

"Don't leave the room. Don't open the door. Don't let anyone shoot me. I got it." She pulled the covers up. "Hey."

"Yeah?"

"I love you, Spencer. You have to let me call you by your first name now. We're engaged."

His heart twisted. "Call me whatever you like as long as you say yes. Be back soon, princess."

Fuck, she didn't even know his name. She was going to be so upset when the truth came out. He had to make sure she didn't hate him, and part of that was making sure she was safe. With one last glance at her, he grabbed his keycard and slipped outside.

He was already punching Dax's contact number as the door closed.

"I hate you." Despite being career Navy, Dax wasn't a morning person.

Connor couldn't worry about that right now. "I asked her to marry me."

That wasn't what he'd intended to lead with. He'd intended to go straight into a debrief about what had happened the night before. He needed to know what Dax had found in Freddy's room and if anyone had shown up at Lara's after the ambush at the Mall. But no. It was like he was fourteen fucking years old and he'd found his first girl.

"You're shitting me. That's great, man. I can't believe it." It sounded like Dax had woken up.

"Yep. I'm marrying her. I just have to figure out how to manage it without her finding out the whole truth."

"Connor, she has to know eventually."

He knew that, but it didn't have to be now. Things were delicate between them. "I just don't think this is the right time. I need a couple more days with her. She claims she wants out of the investigation. She's going to hand all her information over to Everly and then she'll be out of this mess."

"No, she won't. Not if she's marrying you. Unless you're planning on leaving the rest of us high and dry. I kind of thought we were in this together, brother." Dax's tone held a hint of accusation. "I'm fairly certain I could die of some unknown biological agent after going into that freak's apartment. I hope I didn't do that just to have you get all happy and dump the rest of us."

"What?" He had to worry because Freddy really was kind of a freak.

"I'm joking. Mostly. I opened a door and it dumped baby powder all over me. Or an unholy amount of anthrax. I'd probably be dead so I think we can go with baby powder."

"He's trying to mark you so he can see where you went while you were in there." Baby powder would go everywhere, but it would also get on shoes and trace wherever a person went.

"I don't give a fuck if he knows where I've been. I want to know if you're leaving the investigation. We were counting on you."

He would never leave them alone in this. "I'm not out. I just want Lara out."

"I don't see how that's possible." A long sigh came over the line. "I'm going to give you some advice. Tell her. Tell her now and bring her into this. We'll set her up with Everly and let them work through the problem. She'll be angry, but working with Everly will give her something to do other than hate your guts. It will also draw her in, make her a part of our group. Don't isolate her. She seems like the type of woman who likes having a circle. Show her you can provide her with one. By the way, this dog is useless."

He wasn't thrilled with the idea of Lara working with Everly. There were too many *Thelma and Louise* possibilities with that pair. "Lincoln? He's not so bad."

"As guard dogs go, he's a waste of canine flesh. Two barks and then he was following me around begging for treats, at least until he ate them all. I kind of wish I could beg someone for food, too. What the hell is a vegan meatball and why does it smell so bad? That thing shouldn't exist."

"Sorry. I should have warned you. Lara's a vegan. But she makes pretty mean black bean tacos. Did you find the evidence?"

There was a pause and then Dax replied, his voice low. "Yes."

"That doesn't sound good."

"I can't describe it. You have to see it for yourself and then we have a decision to make."

What the hell was this evidence? "What's that?"

"Whether we take it to Zack or try to bury it."

He whistled. "It's that bad? You don't think this is something Freddy trumped up?"

"No. This is evidence from three different sources. I didn't sleep much after looking at it. I don't know what to think. I just know we have to do something. We have to find Deep Throat."

In all the running of the night before, he'd almost forgotten a crucial point. "That's going to be harder than you think since Lara's informant isn't Deep Throat."

"Are you kidding me?"

It was a problem that should have kept him up all night. Instead, he'd done nothing but think about Lara. She made him soft. "Not at all. I got a good look. He's a different man. We're dealing with at least two people. I don't know how many more. We could be dealing with a group, and that scares the hell out of me. I didn't get a photo of the new guy. Did we ID the one Everly met? I don't know whether to hug that girl or threaten to kill her."

"I think she knows she's in trouble. I heard Gabe shook the walls of the Lincoln Bedroom last night, and not in a good way."

If Gabe was anything like him, he'd eventually shaken those walls with more than his yelling. Connor was rapidly discovering that no matter how angry he was with Lara, he still wanted her. He'd meant to lecture her, but the minute they'd gotten alone, the need to mark her, to remind himself that she belonged to him, had overwhelmed him. "I'm just glad she backed Lara up. At least one of them had the sense to carry a gun."

"According to Roman, the woman was a known associate of the Krylov syndicate."

Connor snorted. "Tell me something I don't know."

"Okay. She wasn't from the New York branch. She's from Saint Petersburg, and I'm not talking about the one in Florida."

She was from Krylov himself most likely. "So they're sending in the big guns."

"I think it's safe to say they're sending in people they trust," Dax explained. "The woman Everly killed is wanted by Interpol in association with at least ten hits across the globe. She was an assassin."

He was definitely giving Everly a hug. "So they're sending professionals after Lara."

"It would seem so. Listen, there's something else I need to talk to you about. I discussed it with Roman last night. He dealt with the police and they're keeping this quiet for now."

"Good. The last thing we need is press." They would hound Lara and if anyone got a hint this had something to do with Mad's death, it would never end. Lara would be exposed and that might kill her.

"I think Roman's going to make a play soon. It's another reason to tell her and to bring her into the family. As long as Roman considers her an outsider, she's a threat to Zack. This evidence of hers isn't going to make it better. You need to sit down and talk to him or I'm afraid he's going to try to crush her."

He intended to explain to Roman that Lara was off-limits. He would make sure she didn't do anything that could hurt Zack, but he wasn't going to let anyone threaten her. "I told him I would handle her."

"And he thinks she's handling you. He doesn't know her and quite frankly, Roman's a cynical bastard who believes everyone's out for themselves with very few exceptions. He hasn't spent days tailing her. I know I haven't spoken a word to the woman, but I like her. She's one of those people who sort of glows."

Like a fairy princess. "I won't let him hurt her."

"Then talk to him and soon. And come back to town. We had zero activity here."

Getting her back home was his main objective. "I want to install a new security system and change her locks. I'm pretty sure she gives away keys to homeless people in case they want a place to stay."

"I'll call and get that started and upgrade the dog. Stop humping my leg!"

Dax was going to have to get used to Lincoln. Lara loved the ugly mutt and that meant he stayed. "That means he needs to go. His leash is on a hook in the front closet, and don't forget the Baggies."

"Baggies?"

"For the poop."

"Dude, you owe me so big-time."

"Somehow, I think you'll find a way to make me pay you back." He hung up and headed across the street to the coffeehouse there, his mind whirling with questions.

Lara tried to fall asleep again, but without Connor the bed seemed too big, the room too unfamiliar. She stretched and walked to the bathroom without bothering to put on her clothes. The truth was she didn't mind walking around nude. It felt nice and Connor seemed to like her that way. When she was alone with him and they were naked together, she'd never felt more intimate with another human being. She loved being able to touch him, to lean against him and feel his strong arms surrounding her.

She washed her face and was grateful she hadn't worn makeup the night before. The little motel was sadly sparse on the complimentary grooming items. There was a little box with a tube of toothpaste and a teeny-tiny shampoo and conditioner set. She had to finger brush her teeth, but at least she felt less grimy as she walked back into the room.

She found her phone and turned it on. A barrage of messages flared across the screen.

She sighed. Most of them were from Tom, but one from her dad asking her to call him caught her attention. She touched the screen to dial him back. After a few rings, he picked up.

"Lara? Sweetheart, are you all right? You didn't answer your phone last night."

"I'm sorry, Dad. I was busy and I turned it off. I just turned it back on. Are you all right?"

He paused. The line went silent for a long moment. "Sweetheart, something's happened and I need to talk to you about it. I need you to know before the press gets hold of it."

Her heart sank and she clicked the screen to put him on speaker as she started to gather her clothes. If her dad was in trouble, she needed to be with him. "What's going on?"

"I told you I was going to meet with the president," he began.

"Yes. Was that this week? I'm sorry I missed it." She wasn't really. Until she figured out what had happened to Zack Hayes's wife, she wasn't sure she wanted to meet the man.

"I'm not. It was a setup, sweetheart. I never met with Hayes. Roman Calder was waiting for me instead." He sighed. "We had a long talk. I'm going to resign my seat."

She looked down at the phone because something must be wrong with it. She couldn't have heard what she thought she'd heard. Lara turned off the speaker and whipped the device up to her ear. "What? You've held that seat for ten years. Your constituents adore you. You can't quit."

"I'm afraid I have to. In a few days, a story will break about something that happened when I was in the state senate."

A cold chill crept across her skin. He couldn't be talking about what had happened when she was four. No one knew. It was buried. In order to dig it up herself, Lara had worked hard, called in favors, and still had to do a bit of reading between the lines. When the event had occurred, she'd been so young, but sometimes her anxiousness and terror felt fresh. It still lingered under her skin. She couldn't remember the precise details and that was almost worse. Her fear was vague, amorphous. It was precisely why she'd looked into the "incident" as her parents called it.

"Is this about the road construction contracts?"

"How do you know about that?" He sounded shocked.

She'd never talked to him about it. He'd always pretended it hadn't happened, and she knew why. But Lara had been desperate to understand why she'd been seeing a psychiatrist at eight and why she sometimes had panic attacks. So she'd investigated. She hadn't had much to go on, but she did remember overhearing her mother and father talking about it one night. She'd put their exchange in the back of her mind, but she remembered one thing. Gravely Construction. When her father had said the name, there had been bile and vitriol in his voice. She'd never heard her gentle father get so angry.

"I'm curious. I heard you mention a firm once. You and Mom were arguing. I remembered the name and a few years back I looked it up. They received a highly lucrative state contract the year I was four. They also have ties to the Mafia. At the time, there was a single holdout who didn't want to award them the contracts. You."

"I had no idea you had looked into that."

She'd spent months researching. She'd gathered data and put the clues together. Lara had always known how much her parents loved her but her father had basically sold his soul that term to get her back. "They took me."

A sob caught his voice. "Yes. They took you from your mother's arms. They knocked on the door and before she could do anything, they hit her over the head with a gun. I found her there with a note stating that if I contacted the police, they would kill you. The vote was the next day. I was promised if I granted the contract to Gravely, you would be returned to us within twenty-four hours."

How scared had her father been? He'd been placed in a horrible situation, but Lara was certain she would have made the same choice. She put a hand to her belly as though she could feel a child growing there. Hers and Connor's. She would do anything for that baby. *Anything.*

"Two days after the vote, a check was deposited into Mom's account," Lara continued the story. "That was the guarantee that you wouldn't take action after the fact, wasn't it?"

"They made me look guilty so I couldn't go to the police. I should have anyway. I should have been braver." Her father sobbed. Her heart ached at the thought of her big, strong father weeping. "It doesn't matter now. I'll deal with the fallout. I love you, baby girl. You are everything to us. You know that, right?"

Tears filled her eyes but a few things didn't add up. "What does this have to do with Roman Calder meeting you instead of the president?"

"It doesn't matter."

"And how did Calder even know about this? Gravely wouldn't have told him. The patriarch died and his son sold off the company. Why does the president's chief of staff care? You tend to vote with the party. You don't outwardly criticize the president." It hit her and her stomach dropped straight to the floor. "Oh, god. This isn't about you. This is about me. This is about Capitol Scandals."

"Like I said, it doesn't matter," her father continued. "I won't let you give in to his blackmail."

"Dad, how many people knew about what happened back then?"

"It was mob business. They keep things quiet. I never told anyone. I'm surprised you figured it out."

She'd been determined to know why she had nightmares about being watched and held in close spaces. She'd figured that finally knowing what really happened might help her sleep at night. "I had a lot of circumstantial evidence. Sometimes that's enough to get a good picture. Dad, they can't indict you. It was over twenty years ago."

"The scandal alone will crush me. It's best I step down as quietly as possible."

"What did he want?"

"A total shutdown of Capitol Scandals. A promise that you'll stay out of politics for good. Like I told him, he can bite my ass."

So she could give up doing what she loved, or Roman Calder and Zack Hayes would ruin her father's legacy and reputation. There was no choice. "Daddy, I'm shutting down."

"Lara . . ." he began.

"No. You can't talk me out of it." Especially since her ambition had landed them in this mess.

It couldn't be a coincidence that Calder had been in her building just days before and suddenly he had information that was locked away in her safe. How would he have gotten access to her building? Her unit?

Suspicion crushed Lara. Yeah, sometimes circumstantial evidence could paint to an accurate picture when it was all laid out.

"Dad, have you ever heard of a man named Connor Sparks?"

"Um, the name sounds familiar. Why do you ask?"

Because her lover was keeping secrets even while he demanded truth from her. "Something someone mentioned to me."

"Lara, we'll talk about that later. But Capitol Scandals . . . You can't give up your passion."

But he'd been willing to sacrifice everything for her. "I can. I can find another passion."

She bit back a sob because she had a feeling her passion wouldn't be a man with dark eyes and a low, rumbling voice.

Would he even come back? Certainly he would since the site wasn't down yet. She could do it remotely. She had the capability on her phone as long as she had an Internet signal. After she did that, he would likely walk out of her life and she would never see him again.

"Lara, don't," he insisted.

She needed to do it now or it would be too hard to. She needed to save her father and deal with the fact that her lover wasn't what he seemed.

"Connor Sparks," her father repeated, sounding as if he snapped his fingers. "He was one of the six."

"The six?" Freddy had said something about that. Now his words were coming back. Freddy had used the name Sparks. He'd said he thought Connor was Sparks. How could she have forgotten that? Oh, yeah. Her vagina had a bad short-term memory.

"The Perfect Gentlemen. There were six of them who went to prep school together. Connor Sparks is one of Zack Hayes's closest friends. They grew up together. They're considered unbreakable. A lot of people on the Hill credit more than just Roman for Zack's career. He's had backing financially from Gabe Bond and Maddox Crawford. Dax Spencer was the military man. Sparks was the sneaky one if I remember correctly."

Connor Sparks. Her lover. The man who had betrayed her utterly. This Dax person must be the reason he'd called himself Spencer. A little inside joke. "Thanks, Dad. I'll take care of this. Don't do anything without talking to me."

She hung up and was immediately assaulted with texts from Tom. She groaned but opened one to write him back that she was busy and would get in touch with him later. She couldn't deal with Tom when her whole world was collapsing.

Please, Lara. You have to listen to me. After talking to your father, I was suspicious. It's too coincidental that Roman Calder was in the building and then blackmailed your dad. So I checked with the doorman. Calder needed a code to get in. You can only get a code if you live in the building. He used *your* code, Lara. He had to have gotten it from that bastard you're sleeping with.

Calder had used her code to do his dirty work. Tom was right. There was only one person who could have given it to him. If Calder had gained access from the building manager, the man would have given the chief of staff a guest code. She'd given hers to Connor without a second thought since he was living with her, protecting her.

And he'd used his cover to lull her into a false sense of trust and stolen her secrets for his real boss.

She stared at the phone, looking through the texts. Her father had called Tom, it seemed. He'd been trying to find a way out of the trap Calder had put him in. Tom had always answered her dad's legal questions. It wasn't so surprising that he'd called Tom. Despite their breakup, her dad had always liked him.

Tom had gone to the mat for her dad. He'd called in every favor he had and he'd discovered Roman Calder had entered her building at just before two a.m. The elevator had been used shortly after that and had gone straight to her floor. A few hours later, it descended directly to the lobby again. Kiki had entered the building and she'd passed Calder on his way out the door.

So Hayes's right hand man hadn't visited her building in the middle of the night for a clandestine meeting with a congressman or a lover. He'd come to break into her apartment and steal her secrets, and there was only one man on earth who could have let him in.

Connor had made love to her for the first time that night. He'd kept her in bed for hours. She'd woken in the middle of the night and he hadn't been in bed with her. She'd gone to find him and he'd hustled her back to the bedroom and seduced her again.

Had Roman been in her house all the while? Had he been right there in her living room?

Apparently, he'd found the code to her safe in her day planner. She never remembered numbers so she'd written it down.

Stupid. Stupid. Stupid.

She sucked in a deep breath and pulled up the app for the software that powered her website. She'd started Capitol Scandals with the idea of doing something good.

She ended it with the same thought, only this time she would save her father.

Tears rolled down her cheeks, making the world blurry and opaque as she hit the button that took her site offline and hid it from search engines.

The door opened as she set the phone aside and Connor walked in carrying a tray. "Hey. I have coffee. I had them make it supersweet for you and I got you a fruit cup and a raw granola bar. I was promised both are vegan. Let's eat up and then get out of here." He set the tray down and stared at her. "What's wrong, princess?"

She would ignore the way he called her princess. He couldn't really mean anything by it. He probably called all the women he fucked princess. She stood up, so glad she'd already gotten dressed. "I would appreciate it if you would tell Calder it's done. He can leave my father alone now. I'll abide by his rules."

Connor went still, his body tense. "What are you talking about? You've been crying. What happened?"

Like he didn't know. He'd probably walked out to give his old friend a call. Likely he was expecting a fight and needed advice on how to handle a hysterical woman. She was going to make things easy on him. She just wanted it done so she never had to lay eyes on the man again.

"My father called. He explained what's been going on. I don't have Calder's number, so you'll need to tell him that I've met his demands and I expect my father to be safe from here on out. Tell him if he hurts my father, I'll dedicate my life to ruining his. Every good deed I've ever done, I'll turn around and work against him. Do you understand, Mr. Sparks?"

She needed to stay calm. Her whole soul wanted to scream at him. If she gave in to her rage, she would also give in to the bleak sorrow that threatened to overtake her. She couldn't let him see her cry or show him any chink in her armor. Connor had used her. He'd made her feel completely hollow on the inside, but she wouldn't give him the satisfaction of seeing her weep for him.

"Who told you?"

"My father explained who you are, but I put it together. And Tom figured out that you were the one who let Calder into the building and my apartment. How did he find the code to my safe?"

"What did Roman do?"

"I'm sure he did what you agreed to. He found a way to make me shut down Capitol Scandals."

"No. That was not our agreement. I'm here to find out what you know about Natalia Kuilikov."

So they intended to take everything from her. It made sense, she supposed. Men that ruthless left nothing behind. She reached into her pocket and drew out the paper the CI had given her. The information no longer mattered to her. She wasn't strong enough to play with the big boys. In a matter of days, she'd gone from political crusader to a stupid girl who wanted a baby with the man she loved.

Lara slapped the note on the table. "Here. That's all I've got. Anything else you need? I suspect you've taken already all the data from my computer."

He stared at her outstretched hand. "Lara, we need to talk about this."

"There's nothing to talk about." She stared at the paper on the table. He could take it or leave it. She no longer cared. She wondered how long it would be before she cared about anything again. "I'm going to call a cab. Our business is done."

She started toward the door, but his hand shot out, gripping her wrist and whirling her around to face him.

"There is nothing businesslike about this and you're not leaving. If you think for one second I'll let you set foot outside without me, then you haven't been paying attention the whole time we've known each other."

The whole time. She'd known him less than a week and yet she had the feeling he would haunt her for the rest of her life. How had he gotten so close to her in such a short time?

Well, of course. That had been a setup, too. "There was no Niall."

His face lost a bit of color. "No."

Somehow that was the cruelest cut of all. Losing Niall had hurt. Not in the way losing Connor cut to the bone, but they'd bonded that night when he'd held her while she cried.

Over him.

"You're a bastard."

"Yes."

"Let go of me." She struggled in his grip.

"No." He drew her close. "I can't. If I let go, you'll disappear and I can't let that happen. I forgave you for lying to me last night. Don't I deserve the same?"

The utter hypocrisy hit her like a slap upside the head. "Everything you've ever said to me is a lie."

"Not everything."

"Let me go. I'm not doing this with you, Sparks." She wasn't going to call him Connor again. Too intimate. He'd pretended to care about her, to love her. It had been nothing but a cleverly crafted ploy designed to make her open her doors and let him inside. "You've got what you want and now I'm leaving. And you know what? I don't forgive you, not for any of it. I hope you rot in hell."

"That's not like you. You're angry, but you don't mean a word you're saying. When you calm down, we can talk. But don't think for a second that I've gotten what I want out of this. If I had what I wanted, you would be back in bed and neither one of us would be thinking about a thing except pleasing each other."

"You must be really hard up to need sex from your mark. Next time, find a prostitute. At least she'll get paid."

"I won't need a prostitute, princess. I'll have a wife. I believe I did mention we're getting married. Just because you're not happy about how we met doesn't change a damn thing."

"Not happy about how we met? Are you crazy? You lied to me and used me and made me look like a fool."

"I lied to you, yes. But I made love to you and I saved your life twice. You're only a fool if you think you can brush me off now. I don't know what Roman did, but I'll fix it. I will handle it. You will go back and pick up that piece of paper. Then we're going to your place to pick up Lincoln and some of your things and we'll stay at my house until everything is sorted out. You and Everly can work on the Natalia situation."

Of course. He knew Everly Parker because she was engaged to his very good friend Gabe Bond. "She lied to me, too. I'm not working with her because I'm done with this investigation. And I'm done with you. Go to hell."

"I'm already there." He backed her up against the wall, looming over her like a really gorgeous grim reaper. "Did your dad tell you all about me? Did he tell you about growing up in a single-wide with a village bicycle for a mother? Did he tell you I attended one of the world's best prep schools on a scholarship and I showed up in jeans that were two inches too short for me because dear old Mom spent her money on drugs instead of little things like clothes and food for her kid? Did he tell you I kill for a living? Am I not good enough for you now that you know who I really am?"

She pushed at his chest. "Are you actually trying to play on my sympathy? Screw you. I don't care that you grew up poor. I care that you grew up to be such a massive asshole."

He stopped, staring down at her, and then the bastard threw back his head and laughed.

She shoved at him again, but he wouldn't move. "Stop laughing at me. Is that what you've been doing the whole time? Did you laugh at the idiot who thought she was fighting the good fight? Did you and your friends get together and marvel over how stupid one girl could be?"

He was a hunk of unmoving granite. His arms wound around her and he pulled her in. "You are not an idiot and you do fight the good fight. And if any of my friends laugh at you, it's because you're charming and funny and they'll be better for knowing you, princess. I really did contact you because you had a link to Natalia. But I stayed for you."

That didn't even deserve a reply. She simply scoffed and pushed at him again.

"Look, I don't know what Roman did, but I'm the one who gave him the power to do it so I'll be the one to fix it. I admit I have been trying to manipulate you but you don't fall for any of my tricks so I'll just say it. I'm sorry. I might have come in with selfish intentions, but everything changed when I got to know the real you. I even had thoughts of trying to shut you down in the beginning, but I understand now and

I'll fight for you. I'll fight my friends for you. They're the only family I have, but I'll risk it for you and you alone."

That soft spot in Lara's heart wanted to believe him. But she wasn't about to fall for the same tricks again. "Well, you tried to destroy my family so I don't really care about yours. Just get out of my face and out of my life."

"Lara, c'mon. This isn't like you. I understand that I've put you in a corner and hurt your pride, and you can't know how sorry I am for doing it. But the Lara I know cares about people and relationships too much to throw them away. Once you've had a chance to calm down and think this through, you'll see that you belong with me."

"I'll see that you go to jail if you don't let me out of here, Connor. I don't care who your friends are. You can't force me to stay in this room against my will."

He paused. "Where are you going?"

"Home. Alone."

"That's exactly what the Russians would love to have happen. Then they can take you out easily."

She narrowed her eyes at him. "I don't believe there are any Russians. You've lied about virtually everything. You probably set that up, too, in order to gain my trust."

"The Russians are real and they'll try again. I won't let them hurt you and I won't let you put yourself in danger. You're coming with me. If you want to call the cops, feel free. I'll explain the situation to them. I'll show them my credentials and have you in protective custody before you can blink."

"Your credentials?"

"CIA, princess. I'm a high-level operative and I assure you if I want you in custody, I'll have you there. I would rather not piss you off more than I already have, so please be reasonable."

She thought it was perfectly reasonable to not want to be in the same space with the lying asshole. It was dangerous. Despite the fact that he'd conned her from the minute they'd met, her body didn't care.

He'd trained her to respond to him, and his nearness made her skin heat. She felt as if her body had a memory of each and every time he'd kissed her, brought her to pleasure. She remembered and wanted him with an ache that was hard to deny.

Hard, but she was going to do it.

"Lara, it doesn't have to be this way. No matter how we started, what's between us is real and I won't let you throw it away. Then again, you might not be able to, or have you forgotten last night?"

She sagged against the wall, the true horror of her situation hitting her. She could be pregnant. An hour ago, she'd wanted to be. Now carrying the child of the man who had deceived her seemed like the worst kind of punishment.

Still, a vision of a baby with Connor's eyes swamped her.

Lara shoved down her tears. "We don't know anything, but if I am, you won't have anything to do with either of us."

His hands tightened then relaxed, and he took a deep breath, stepping back. "So you'd deprive your child of a father to spite me? I hope the real Lara comes back very soon."

That stung. "Yeah, well, I have to say I don't much like the real Connor."

He shrugged. "Not a lot of people do, princess. Is there any way I can convince you to eat?"

Why did he care? "I'm not hungry."

He hadn't reacted at all the way she'd thought he would. She'd expected him to snicker at her or shrug and walk away, maybe even get angry. She'd pushed his buttons just so she could provoke him. She'd actually physically pushed him. He'd still just held her tight.

"Do you want the coffee?" He held it out to her, his eyes steady, and she couldn't help but think about what it had meant for a poor kid from a trailer park to go to a prep school without the proper clothes. He stood there holding the stupid coffee like he was waiting for her acceptance, and she could see the little boy lurking under the man.

"Only because I'm addicted to caffeine." She took the brew out of his hand and didn't miss his grateful smile. "But I'm going to cut down on it. I'm going to kick the habit because it's bad for me."

"Not all addictions are bad for you."

She would have to disagree. "I want to go home."

"I can watch you better at my place."

"Or you're just bored because you've already stolen all my secrets, Mr. Spy."

He picked up the paper and opened the door for her. "Well, then you can steal some of mine. Did you think of that?"

She lifted her chin. "I don't steal things."

"I can think of something you've stolen."

Lara rolled her eyes. "Please tell me you didn't say that. That is so corny if you were talking about your heart."

He blushed a little. "I told you I was bad at the romance thing." He stopped her before she could make it out the door. "I don't want to lose you, Lara."

"You already did." She ducked under his arm and stood by the bike.

She drank her coffee in silence. He was furiously texting on his phone. She could only guess he was telling all his friends the game was over and they could go home soon. When she was done with her liquid caffeine, he took the cup and threw it away for her.

He settled the helmet on her head and started to secure the strap. She couldn't help but notice the lines around his eyes and the careful way he cinched her in.

"Why don't you take the helmet?"

His eyes met hers. "Because you're more important. I know you don't want to touch me, but you have to hold on. If you would rather, I can call a friend to come out and pick us up. It would take an hour or so, but he could bring a car."

And they would be stuck in that motel room together. No, thanks. She didn't trust her traitorous body parts to not jump him.

He got on the bike and held out a hand. She ignored it but she wouldn't be reckless with her safety. She climbed on behind him and wrapped her arms around his lean waist. He fired the engine up and took off.

And she finally let herself cry.

THIRTEEN

Connor held the elevator open and gestured for Lara to go through. Helpless. He felt completely and utterly helpless. She'd been crying and he wanted to hold her. At least while they'd been on the bike, she'd had to wrap her arms around him. Now that they'd arrived at her place, he felt the loss of her touch. She was always caressing him, putting her hand in his or leaning closer. She was normally a creature of affection. Now she'd totally shut down. He hadn't realized how much he'd come to rely on her affection.

He could see the red stain to her eyes and it damn near killed him.

"Thank you." She stepped out and frowned. "Oh, wow. It looks like your friends are here. I guess they all have keys, thanks to you. I suppose I'll move now that the neighborhood's gone to hell. Thank god Freddy bugged out or he'd have a heart attack."

Connor peered down the hall and cursed under his breath. Two men in black suits stood sentry outside Lara's door. He'd noticed a man outside the lobby, but there were always guys in dark suits in D.C. These two, however, meant one thing and one thing only.

Zack was here.

Damn, Elizabeth had worked fast. When he'd found out what Roman had done, he'd decided to play dirty. The fastest most expedient way to get Lara's site back online wasn't to argue with Roman because he only really listened to Zack. And Connor knew the way to reach Zack wasn't through Roman. No, it was through pretty, blond Elizabeth, his press secretary. The lovely woman had been Zack's friend for years, but in the last few months Connor had noticed Zack watched her like a hungry predator when she wasn't looking. His stare followed her constantly, and the minute she asked him to do something, the most powerful man in the world tripped over his Prada loafers to get it done.

"I didn't exactly invite anyone. Well, Dax. You'll like Dax. He's been . . ." Maybe he shouldn't explain how Dax was involved.

Lara stopped, her sneaker tapping. "He's been what?"

"He's a great guy. My best friend." Now that she was about to meet him, Connor was unaccountably nervous. What if she didn't like his friends? They could be a lot to take, especially since Roman and Zack were on opposite sides of certain political issues from Lara.

"What has he been doing, Connor? Why is he in my apartment? I get why the president is in there. He's here to completely ruin my life, so why is your bestie hanging out? Did you need a couple of witnesses to complete my humiliation?"

He kept his temper under a tight rein. He knew she wanted him to get violent or mean so she could walk away without a single regret. He wasn't giving her that easy out. He wasn't giving her any out at all. "There will be no humiliation. Roman and I will have a talk and the problem will go away. I'll make him understand. You don't have to be afraid of Zack. He's a good man."

"I don't know about that. From where I'm sitting, he's kind of a dick." Her chin firmed and a stubborn look lit her eyes as she strode past him.

Shit. She was in protest mode. He'd seen that tilt to her chin whenever she believed something unfair was going on in the world and only she could fix it.

She marched right up to the Secret Service agents. "Am I no longer allowed in my own apartment? I am a tax-paying citizen of the United States of America and you are keeping me from my rightful property. I want you to know that I firmly intend to both sue and protest you."

The agent on the right's lips fluttered up, and there was no way Connor missed how his eyes traced over her. He touched his earpiece. "Sir, I believe she's here. You said she was a cute pain in the ass. There is definitely a cute pain in the ass out here right now. Of course. You sure I shouldn't check her for weapons?"

"That would be an illegal search," Lara countered.

Connor stepped in behind her. "If you give her a pat down, it's the last time your hands will function."

"I can defend myself," Lara shot back.

The agent winked at her, then he opened the door and let them in. Connor memorized his face because he might have to kill the man. It would likely make him feel a whole lot better.

Lara entered her apartment with a judgmental finger pointing, just looking for a target. She immediately found one. Roman stood in the doorway to the kitchen, a cup of coffee in his hand. His supercool, nothing-ever-fazed-him eyes widened as Lara stalked closer. She was a good foot shorter and Roman had a hundred pounds of muscle on her, but he took a step back.

"You unholy ass. Get out of my house. Now. And put down that coffee. That coffee is fair trade coffee and you shouldn't be allowed to drink it. You should drink evil coffee. How dare you think you can break into my house and blackmail my father, then drink my coffee? I'll call the police and they will throw you out, and how is that going to look on the evening news? And who the hell are you?" She turned as Dax was walking out of her bedroom, Lincoln in his arms. The little dog perked up.

"I'm Dax."

"You're trespassing."

Dax set Lincoln down and came back up grinning. "It's so nice to actually meet you. Congratulations on your engagement."

Connor shook his head, trying to give Dax the "Stop, go no further" sign.

Lara turned back to him. "You told them?"

"I was happy about it."

She stopped and stared at him. "How could you tell them?"

He nodded. "They're my best friends. I wanted them to know."

She stood there for a moment, her mouth slightly open, and it was obvious he'd surprised her. Had she thought his proposal was some ruse? Had she thought he would leave when the job was over and not see her again?

She turned back to Dax. "Why are you in my apartment? I know what the douche bag in the bad suit is doing. He's the Grinch come to make sure all my Christmas ornaments are crushed."

Roman frowned. "This is a three-thousand-dollar suit."

Lara whirled on Roman. "Do you know how many hungry children that suit could feed?"

Roman put a hand on his suit as though protecting the precious material from Lara. "Um, none. They would likely get very sick if they ate this suit. Children aren't supposed to eat wool."

Connor stepped in behind her. The better to catch her if she decided to launch herself physically at one of them. "You have to forgive him. He's very literal. Hello, Gabe, Everly. Zack."

She gave a little gasp and turned toward her living room. He was pretty sure her eyes hadn't widened because of Gabe and Everly. Her stare fell straight to Zack. He stood in back of the room, a little smile on his face as if the whole thing amused him.

Everly moved across the living room and enveloped Lara in a hug. "I'm so glad you're all right. God, I got so scared when I realized those Russians were after you last night. Of course realizing Connor was there pretty much scared me, too. I still haven't heard a reasonable explanation of how he knew to follow us."

Connor watched as Lara froze, but Everly didn't let up. She talked about how Gabe had screamed at her and how she hadn't slept for worrying about Lara. And slowly, gradually, Lara's arms wound around Everly.

"I was fine," Lara said. "Just a little scared. I got what we needed. Well, what you need."

Everly pulled back slightly. "I'm sorry for lying to you. I didn't know you. All I knew was that you ran a tabloid and I hadn't even read it. I'm afraid I walked into this prejudiced against you."

Lara nodded. "I'm not that kind of tabloid."

"I know that now. And I'm so sorry I only took out the one assassin."

Lara gave her an encouraging smile and a pat on the arm. "Don't be down on yourself. You were amazing. You totally shot one of them."

Roman moved in next to him as Lara continued to praise her partner in crime. "I thought she was a pacifist."

Just watching her gave him a warm feeling. "She is but she's also a pathological cheerleader."

Lara proved his point by holding Everly's hand and continuing her praise. "Connor didn't even manage to take one of them out and he's supposedly some sort of superspy. Though he lies a lot. You're way tougher than him."

"I was busy protecting you," he pointed out.

Lara ignored him. "Thanks for helping me, Everly. I really appreciate it. I wish you hadn't lied, though."

"The guys thought you wouldn't cooperate if you knew who Connor was. I probably just would have bought you a drink and had a talk with you, but the guys are all about subterfuge. I think they missed something in their childhood. Too much prep school."

"You're a bad influence, Parker," Connor scolded with a grin. Maybe Dax was right and letting the girls bond was a good thing. Lara was very loyal to her friends.

"She is not." Lara took the bait, stepping in between them.

"Oh, she's a terrible influence," Gabe said with a grin. "But then I think you might be, too, Armstrong. I'm pretty sure this group doesn't do calm, sweet women."

"Lara's sweet," Connor corrected with a sly grin.

She blushed and shook her head, obviously flustered at the double entendre. He still had a chance with her if he could make her blush like that. He looked at her across the room and willed all the heat he felt into his eyes, hoping she could see his desire there.

Their gazes locked for a long, electric moment and then she broke away. Her arms crossed over her chest but it certainly wasn't cold in the room. She never could hide her reaction to him, and he'd curse the day she figured out how to.

"Ms. Armstrong, I was hoping you would do me a very great favor," Zack said, stepping up to the group for the first time. He was dressed casually for Zack. Designer slacks, Prada loafers, a cashmere sweater over a snowy white dress shirt and tie. The only time Zack didn't wear a tie was when he was jogging.

Lara frowned at the president of the United States. "I don't owe you any favors, Mr. President. I've done everything for you I possibly will. You should know that while I will honor our deal and stay out of politics, you can't force me not to vote. It's my legal right and my moral responsibility, and I have to say after today, I won't be voting for you."

Zack's brows rose. "You see, Roman. You did this. You cost me a vote."

"Will you please just tell her? This is the second time today I've had one of your women verbally beat the hell out of me. It was easier when everyone was single and all our arguments were settled with a couple of punches thrown and a round of beers. This whole new thing of setting the women on a man is bullshit," Roman grumbled.

"If I'd known what you'd done, you would have had all three of us on your ass," Everly added, then she regarded Lara. "We women have to stick together. It's the only way to survive this group."

"Ms. Armstrong, may I call you Lara since it seems we'll be family soon?" Zack asked in that oh-so-polite way of his.

"You can call me Lara because that's my name. I'm not marrying Connor."

"Yes, you are." He would take a page from Roman's playbook. Often when something negative came up about Zack, Roman just denied and denied and rewrote the story until everyone simply believed him because it was easier than arguing.

"No . . ." Lara took a deep breath and turned back to Zack. "What else do you want from me? Tell me so I can figure out what it will take for you, your friends, and your security team to leave."

Zack turned on the charm. He reached for her hand and put it between both of his. His gaze focused on Lara and softened. There was a reason he'd gone into politics. "Would you please serve as an emissary from me to your father? I need to apologize to him for the actions of my chief of staff."

"I can apologize myself," Roman said in a grumpy tone.

"You're horrible at apologizing. I'm quite good." Zack's stare never left Lara. "Roman thought he was protecting me. That's his only excuse. Please let your father know that whatever information we have on him will never be used against him. We'll destroy it immediately. The last thing I want is for a good man to leave the Senate. We have so few of them."

"And the website?" Connor wanted to make sure Lara got everything she wanted. "She took Capitol Scandals down."

"Lara is free to do as she pleases. No one in this room will reveal her identity or strongarm her into shutting down again, though, please, if you don't mind, could you stop running the stories on the size of my . . ." He cleared his throat. "While flattering, I find it takes away from serious politics."

Lara shook her head. "You would be surprised how many women those stories bring in. I actually have data that women who read stories about the size of your penis or your sexual prowess go on to read more substantial stories forty-five percent of the time, and they become regular commentators."

Connor didn't like the way she was looking at Zack. Her eyes had widened and her hand was still in his. She was looking up at him like he was some kind of rock star. Zack had movie-idol looks. He wasn't covered in scars. Zack was suave and didn't have any trouble being romantic. Would Lara forgive him if he was more like Zack? Would Lara prefer Zack?

He moved in and snatched her hand out of his. "She won't think about your penis anymore."

"I always knew he would be a possessive caveman with the right woman," Dax said with a chuckle in his voice.

Lara stood unmoving in his arms, not fighting him, but also not leaning back against him the way she used to. "I'll talk to my dad. But I have to ask why you would do this. It's obvious you don't like my site and you have the leverage to take it down. I won't stop you or fight you. So why do it?"

"Because Elizabeth threatened to tear my balls off," Roman said. He held a hand up. "Well, not in those words exactly. She said a lot of Southern things and then she blessed my heart, which I've come to realize is Southern women code for 'something bad is going to happen to a man's balls.'"

Zack sat on Lara's couch, crossing one leg over the other. "Despite what Roman will tell you, Elizabeth merely brought the situation to my attention. Roman often acts on his own. We've worked this way for years, but sometimes he becomes overly protective as he did in this case. It's true I didn't see the value of your site, but that doesn't matter now. I wouldn't have done it because it would hurt you, and hurting you would mean hurting Connor. I don't have a lot of friends. I have sycophants and people who hang on to my coattails in hopes that I'll do something for them. All of my life, I've been surrounded by people who want something from me—with five exceptions, and one of them is gone now. These men are my brothers and I would do anything for them. The minute you became involved with Connor, you stepped into my circle and that means I'll protect you, too. I'll protect you whether you like me or hate me or vote for the other guy."

Lara paced and Connor could see plainly that Zack had confused her. She'd walked into this room expecting a confrontation. Instead, Zack had given her acceptance. "All right. I'll call my father."

Zack nodded. "Good. Please tell him I really would love to have dinner and meet his wife. Perhaps you and Connor could join us."

"I'll have to see about that, but thank you for clearing this up for me." She turned to Roman. "You got the information out of my safe, didn't you?"

"Yes. If you're going to keep information like that around, you should protect it better."

Connor tried very hard not to kill Roman. "I'll upgrade the safe."

"Or I can just make sure I don't have people in my home who let their friends steal from me." Lara turned and walked back toward her bedroom.

Shit.

"Dude, she's pissed at you," Dax said, pointing out the obvious.

Connor chose to spend his anger on Roman. "Did you have to do that to her? You really thought that was your best play? What are you going to do next, asshole? You want to kick a couple of puppies?"

"That's your dick talking, Sparks, and you know it. When we started out, you agreed with me that she was dangerous. You were the one who promised to get the fucking site shut down in the first place. This was all your plan. I don't see how I ended up being the villain of the piece."

It didn't matter that Roman was right. "Things change. Even in the middle of an op, the situation can change and you have to change with it. She's not a danger to Zack."

"I don't know about that," Roman shot back. "I found a ton of e-mails where she talks about some kind of evidence she's collected on him."

"Stop reading her e-mails," Zack said quietly. "Connor's serious about her and that means we're all going to welcome her with open arms."

Connor had never thought about it, but Zack really was like their Godfather sometimes. Ever since that day they'd almost been expelled from Creighton and Zack had calmly explained to the administrator why and how he would ruin the man's life, they'd all looked at Zack as the authority figure. Connor might be the one who physically protected them, but at the end of the day, Zack was the final word.

"I like her a lot," Everly said with a smile. "It will be really nice to have another woman around."

"I don't know if she's going to be around." Gabe's gaze trailed back to the bedroom. "She seems pretty damn angry."

"I don't think she'll be able to stay that way for long." Dax set Lincoln down and the dog made a beeline for Connor. "She's a very sunny woman. She'll be angry for a few days, but as long as Connor keeps her close, she'll come out of it and find the good in the situation. She won't be able to help herself. She slept with you for a reason."

"We have chemistry."

"When I talked to her, Connor . . ." Everly began. "She glowed when she said your name. That's more than simple chemistry. She's in love with you. A woman in love can forgive a lot. Ask Gabe."

"They never forget, though." Gabe shook his head. "Be prepared for that."

Connor picked Lincoln up, cradling the little guy to his chest. Maybe she would talk to him if he was holding her dog. At least she wouldn't push him away. "I'll be right back. I'm going to have her pack a bag. We'll be staying at my place. It's more secure. Until we figure out what the hell is going on, I'm keeping her close. I can't risk the Russians coming after her again."

"I would really like to take a look at whatever the new guy gave to her. I still can't believe there are two informants," Everly muttered.

Connor nodded. Lara could work on the mystery with Everly and hopefully she would see that it wasn't so bad to be attached to them, to him. Before he could make it to the hallway leading to the bedroom, Zack stopped him.

"Could you please ask her if I could see this evidence she has against me?" Zack's face had gone grim. "Dax mentioned it was about Joy's death. I would like to know what's coming at me."

"I'll ask her." Connor shook his head. "But she's listening to conspiracy buffs and got excited about the idea of cracking some great mystery. I don't know what she has, probably nothing. I'm crazy about the woman, but she believes in the mystical healing properties of tofu, so . . ."

"Still, I would like to see it."

"All right." He walked back to the bedroom where he'd first made love to Lara. Where he'd betrayed her. He had to make her see they could survive this bump in their road together. She needed to understand that he would sacrifice for her. Somehow over the last few days he'd gone from wanting her to be a part of his life to her becoming the center of his whole life. The one thing he knew? He couldn't go back to what he'd been doing before he'd met Lara. Sure, he'd fought to get his job back and now he couldn't imagine doing it because it would mean long periods of time away from her.

"Yeah." Lara was on the phone, her back to him. "You don't have to worry about it, Dad. I promise it's over. You can keep your seat and I don't have to give up anything."

"Let me talk to him," Connor said.

She turned and he could see she'd been crying again.

"Please? I can explain. He'll just think you're protecting him, but I can make him believe."

She thrust the phone his way and then stalked off to the bathroom.

"Senator?"

"Is that you, Connor?"

"Yes, sir."

"Why did you do this to us? To her? I think she was in love with you."

"Good, because I intend to marry her."

A sigh, followed by a chuckle, sounded over the line. "Did she grow on you, son? She has a way of doing that. Even the people who don't like her at first tend to come around. Tell me something, did you really lie to her and let your friends steal her secrets? Are you the reason Calder threatened to ruin me?"

He wasn't used to having a sense of shame. It kind of made him nauseated, but he actually admired the senator and found it difficult to lie to him. "Yes, but I thought I was doing the right thing at the time. I wanted to shut her down, but when I realized her motives, I changed that goal. I have to admit, now I just want her out of the dangerous stuff. I want her safe."

"Do you love my daughter, Connor?"

That was getting easier and easier to admit. "Yes."

"I want you to understand that the choices I made, I made for her."

Connor had seen the file Roman had sent about Lara's abduction. He'd read both the information and what was between the lines. "The mob held her hostage in exchange for your vote. Then they made sure you couldn't call the cops. I knew that the minute I read the scenario."

"How?"

"Because you're her father. She got her light from you."

He could hear the senator clear his throat. "You have my blessing, son. I'm going to give you some advice about my daughter. She needs a man who trusts her instincts, who believes in her. She needs a man who will support her, and I don't mean financially."

"I fought my friends because I believe in her."

"And will your friends accept her?" Obviously the senator knew who his friends were.

"They will love her as much as I do."

"Then make yourself vulnerable to her. She can't resist that. She needs to be needed. If you want to keep her, make her feel loved and adored and tell her that you need her."

That wouldn't be hard. It was all true.

The door to the bathroom opened and she stepped out.

He held the phone out toward her. "He's good now."

Lara took it, putting it to her ear. "Dad?"

He stood and watched her as she listened to her father. She turned away and spoke in low tones, but he could tell they were discussing him. She cursed under her breath a couple of times, agreed, argued, agreed, told her father he was insane and finally agreed to disagree. She hung up and turned back to him.

"Thanks for talking to him. At least he's no longer holding a press conference so he can resign his seat. Whatever you said convinced him that I'm not sacrificing anything to save him. I don't get why he wouldn't want me to. He sacrificed to help me."

"Would you want our child to give up her passion to save us? Would you be willing to allow our daughter to give up her life's work?"

"First, we don't have a daughter and never will, and obviously, no. That's not her place. It's our place to protect her. Not the other way around. I mean, my place. Damn it, Connor. Why did you tell them we're getting married?"

"I told you. They're my family. I told your father we're getting married, too. I told them because I am utterly incomplete without you." His future father-in-law's words stuck with him. He admired the senator. It was stupid but he kind of liked it when the man called him son.

She closed her eyes and let out a shuddering breath. When they opened again, she had a sheen of tears coating those blue orbs. "I don't understand you."

He stepped close to her. "I don't understand you, either, but I know I can't live without you. I wasn't lying, princess. Not about this. If you walk away from me, I'll be alone for the rest of my life because you're it for me. You're everything I want in a woman."

"And you're nothing I want in a man. I'm not trying to be a bitch. I'm not. I want a man who's gentle and kind and interested in world peace and who never lies to me. You're the opposite of all those things. I want a man who will never betray me."

"You want some perfect saint?" He clutched Lincoln kind of close. The dog was a little piece of Lara and she seemed to be pulling away. "You want a man who never makes a mistake?"

"I want a man who always believes in me. Who puts me first."

"Good. I'm going to quit my job because I want to be with you. Because you're the most important thing in my life. I intend to be the kind of husband and father I never had growing up."

"I won't marry you."

"That's your stubbornness talking."

"That's my good sense talking because I know who you are now. I don't think I can trust you again." Tears swam in her blue eyes. "I don't want you."

She had to fight to say those words but they still cut to the quick. He wasn't good. He wasn't right. A chill settled over him. For a brief period of time he'd thought he could have her. He'd thought because he'd sacrificed, that he would get a second chance.

But after everything he'd done, all the blood he'd shed, he reached too high to hope someone good like her would love him back.

He set Lincoln down. She wouldn't want him getting too close to her precious pup. He'd already made the damn thing a carnivore again. That was the whole problem. He had bloody hands and they would never come clean.

Connor tried to push all that aside and do what damage control he could. "Zack asked to see the evidence you've collected against him. He chose not to use his leverage against you. Could you at least let him know what's coming at him?"

He was pleased with how even his voice sounded. He wanted to scream, wanted to run to the window and yell out his anger and pain, but he'd somehow managed to stay civilized. He wasn't, of course. It was all an illusion, but at least she wouldn't be able to hold any sort of crazy rage against him.

She looked up at him. "Connor, I . . ." Her jaw locked for a moment before more stiff words came from her mouth. "Just take it. I'm sure your friend found it. You can give him all the information and then go home."

Of course she wanted him to go away. She couldn't stand to look at him anymore. He'd really fucked up. Lara was polite to everyone. She couldn't hold a real grudge to save her life.

He was the exception because he didn't deserve anything else.

"I don't know what you've got. Dax retrieved the drive from Freddy's apartment, but Zack would like the explanation from you. If that's more than you're willing to give, let me know. I'll try to figure it out and explain it to him. He really is serious about not using information that was stolen from you."

"Why? Why not just use what you already have? You paid enough for it. Well, I paid for it."

She wasn't going to let up. He'd worried that once she knew who he really was, she wouldn't want him anymore. He hated being right. "Zack won't use it."

Her gaze slid away from his. "He's not what I thought he was."

Of course she was talking about Zack and not him. "He's a good man. I don't care what anyone else has said or what evidence you've collected. He's good and I'll prove it."

"That's what I meant. I didn't expect him to back off."

"He backed off because I care about you." No matter what, Connor did care. He just wasn't good enough for her. She was right about that. It just proved she wasn't as naive as he'd thought.

She leaned over and picked up her dog. "All right. I'll show him. We'll see what he has to say after he's seen what I found." She walked past him, Lincoln in her arms. "Then you'll leave?"

, this.

"When I'm confident that you're protected, yes." He turned to follow her, finally understanding that she might never forgive him.

What had she done? Lara was spitting-nails angry with Connor, but the look she'd put on his face damn near killed her. The whole ride home she'd let her hurt and anger meld into a toxic mixture. She'd let it roil in her gut and she cried, her tears seeming to fuel her rage.

Then she'd gotten home and everything had been turned upside down.

He'd told his friends he wanted to marry the girl he'd seduced only so he could steal her secrets? His superpowerful friends had been waiting in her home, acting as if they belonged there for the simple reason that Connor cared about her and that meant they accepted her.

Was he serious? Or playing another game? He totally confused her, and she didn't trust herself to recognize when he was lying to her. She'd proved that attraction and sex only clouded her logic. He knew that and probably wouldn't hesitate to use it to his advantage.

She stepped out into her living room and set Lincoln down. He immediately wagged and gave a little yip and ran back toward her bedroom, toward Connor. Her dog loved him.

Her dog would just have to get used to being without him. Like she was going to get used to it. She couldn't trust him again. No way. She would be twelve kinds of fool if she took him back.

Besides, after what she was about to reveal, he would probably hate her anyway. It was obvious Connor had very few weaknesses, but his friends were one of them. She was about to prove to Zack Hayes that he hadn't been as careful as he should have been.

She stopped before making it to the hallway. This was completely reckless of her. She couldn't just accuse the president of the United States of killing his wife. What would he do to her? If he'd killed his own wife, he wouldn't hesitate to kill her, too.

She looked back and Connor stood, watching her. Lincoln was trying to get his attention, but he merely stared at her with the same expression she'd seen on his face in the beginning. Bleak and empty.

But for a few days, she'd seen something else on that handsome face. When he'd looked at her, he'd light up.

She'd extinguished that light.

Or it hadn't been real in the first place and she'd just convinced him to stop pretending.

"How do I know there's really someone out there trying to kill me?" she asked.

"I think the bullets speak for themselves."

"Do they? You're very good at making things up, Connor. How do I know you didn't concoct this story?"

"The body should be evidence. Would you like to go to the morgue and see it for yourself? She wasn't an actor."

"Or you just didn't mind sacrificing a pawn to make everything look real to me."

His stare zipped down to Lincoln, but he didn't stoop to pick the pup up. "Yeah, that sounds like something I would do."

"So why should I believe you?"

"It doesn't matter." He shrugged. "I know the truth and I won't leave you alone while I think you're in danger."

"What if the danger is from your so-called friends?"

His eyes narrowed. "What is that supposed to mean?"

"You want me to turn my smoking gun over to them and simply believe there will be no recriminations or backlash. How do I know you haven't planned this setup all along? Maybe you plotted that, once I gave you the evidence, you'd take me back to your place and make me disappear. You've done things like that before, right?"

Her stomach turned even as she forced the words from her mouth. She hated every one of them. Lara knew she should stop poking and pushing him, but something nasty that had never surfaced twitched inside her. She had a terrible need to needle, to punish, to do anything to get him to react. In that moment, she wanted him to hurt as much as she did.

He raised his gaze and she had to force herself not to flinch and take a step back from the pain there. "Yes, I have. I like to kill little fairy princesses. Is that what you want to hear, Lara? You want to make me out to be a monster? I could give you file after file that would prove you right. I've got so much blood on my hands I can't wash them clean, but I'm not going to kill you. In fact, I will never harm a hair on your head. I'm going to protect you, on my terms, on my turf." He crossed his arms over his chest. "Do you want to know what I'm going to do when I've managed to drag you back to my lair?"

She took a shaky breath and prayed he couldn't tell how much the tone of his voice affected her. "I won't go anywhere with you."

"That's why I said dragged, princess. I'll do it. I'll drag you by all that pretty hair if I have to. Do you know what I thought about the first time you took your hair down? I thought I would get caught in it. Like a web. I would touch it just once and then I would be stuck forever because something that beautiful had to be a trap. That's what you are, Lara. A trap. You're everything I've always wanted and nothing I can have. I knew it in the beginning, but I was already reaching for all that beauty." He took a step toward her, bringing their bodies so close she felt the heat between them. "When I get you to my house, I'm going to spread your legs and fasten my mouth on your pussy. I'll eat like a man who knows it's his last meal. Then I'll pin you down and have my way with you all night long. And you're going to let me."

She shook her head even as she felt her skin sizzle at the image his words produced. "No."

"You will because you'll want it one last time, too. Because you know no man is ever going to make you feel the way I do. When you find your handsome, limp-dick, vegan prince, he'll very politely make love to you and you'll lie there and let him because you think you should. But you'll lie underneath him and wish he was me. You'll dream about my dirty hands on your pristine body. You'll imagine my mouth on your pussy and that, my love, that will be the only way you'll be able to come for the rest of your life. So you'll let me have you because you'll need one more memory to get you through all those years without me." He raised a brow at her. "Now go out there and show everyone your evidence, and cling to the hope that you can put me off with your cold stares and nasty words. In the end, you're just postponing the inevitable."

Her heart raced as she turned away. He surprised her when he let her escape into the hallway.

She no longer thought it was reckless to show off the evidence she and Freddy had gathered. Nothing was as reckless as staying in that bedroom with Connor. If he touched her once, she would be a puddle of goo at his feet, very likely begging him to take her with him. She wouldn't care that he'd lied. She wouldn't care that she was being a doormat. She would only care about being in his arms again, and she couldn't allow herself to be so weak.

Lara stalked through the living room where Connor's rich and superpowerful friends were talking quietly. She heard them murmuring about how worried they were before they caught sight of her and went silent.

She was confused and all she really wanted was to get out of here so she could think, but it didn't seem likely Connor was going to give her meditation time. No. He seemed determined to hound her until he got everything he wanted from her, even if that meant body and soul.

"Do you have the flash drive?" She looked up at Dax Spencer. He was a massive mountain of pure muscle with an all-American smile that likely got every female heart in a mile radius fluttering. Strangely, she preferred Connor's dark, brooding beauty to Dax's sunniness. When had that happened? She'd always gone for the optimistic type before. It was how she'd ended up with Tom.

"Sure. It's with my laptop." He dialed down the smile, his eyes turning serious. "You're going to show him?"

She nodded. "He wants to see it. I can throw it up on the big screen so we all have a good view. Maybe I should pop some corn and turn this into a party."

Dax scowled. "Hey, this is serious to him. This was his wife. I would appreciate it if you had some concern for what you're about to do. I know Connor hurt you. We all hurt you, but this is not the Lara Armstrong I've been following for days. She would be horrified at your callousness."

Tears threatened to well. He was right. She wasn't acting like herself, but she didn't do disillusion well. "The Lara you've been following was a dumb girl. I'll be smarter now that I've learned from the best."

She shot a look back at Connor, who clenched his jaw. Immediately, she felt bad, then forced the feeling aside. Had he felt guilty when he'd been charming her and kissing her and lying to her? Probably not. Besides, she needed to put distance between them. Otherwise, all he would have to do was kiss her and get her into bed and she would give him everything.

Lara took the thumb drive without another word and retrieved her laptop. Dax's was probably filled with top-secret stuff. Dax had likely never had to deal with someone stealing all his secrets. Surely Roman had downloaded her computer. He knew how many times she searched the web for puppy-cuddling-baby videos and how many romances she bought for her e-reader. As she set up for her demonstration, she tried not to think about how grim Zachary Hayes seemed or the way Connor had shuttered his dark eyes behind a blank mask.

What kind of man was Zack Hayes? He obviously had the loyalty of the others. He was charismatic and smart. Was he ruthless enough to have his own wife killed so he could win an election?

The screen was supersized on the TV monitor. They all gathered around. Dax apparently had already seen the file they'd put together.

He stood in the back beside Connor, arms crossed over his big chest. She saw him reach out and put a hand on Connor's shoulder as if to offer him comfort.

Had she really hurt him? After hearing the enormity of his betrayal, Lara would have sworn that Connor Sparks didn't have feelings. But his friends clearly seemed to think he did.

Roman had taken a place next to Zack. Everly and Gabe sat on the love seat, hands entwined. Everly sent a worried look her way, but Lara wasn't sure what she could say or do except get this heinously awkward meeting out of the way.

"My friend Freddy practically lives in online chat rooms. He specializes in conspiracy theories. He heard one earlier this year that he latched on to. It was about the president's wife and . . . um, the election."

"Just say it, Lara. It's not the first time I've heard it," the president said, his mouth a flat line.

"It was about the fact that you probably won the election because of the sympathy vote." There it was. She tried to be unemotional, intellectual. That was how she'd get through this. It was one thing to discuss the situation intellectually with her friends and quite another when the man in question was sitting in front of her, his eyes on the screen, his shoulders back as though he was bracing to see something truly terrible.

"Of course. The conjecture began roughly five minutes after Joy died." His voice was utterly devoid of emotion, but she was fairly certain that was an affectation on his part, a wall he'd had plenty of practice erecting.

Somewhere under all that calm, she sensed the president was actually a ball of emotion. The only question was which one? Fear of being caught? Or genuine pain because he'd lost his wife horribly?

"One of the people on the board said they'd caught something on some news footage that proved the assassin wasn't after you. Freddy did some digging and this was what he found."

"But why would anyone want to kill Joy?" Roman asked. "She wasn't even terribly interested in politics. She was interested in being first lady, but she never tried to influence Zack. She was the perfect political wife."

"What my best friend is trying to say is that Joy was sweet and everyone loved her. She didn't have any enemies," Zack explained.

"But she did have someone stalking her." Lara pressed a couple of keys, and the footage from the Des Moines rally came up. "This is from three days before Joy Hayes was murdered."

The screen filled with the image of Zack Hayes walking to the podium. He leaned over and kissed his pretty, dark-haired wife. Joy Hayes beamed up at her husband. She wore a light yellow business suit, the skirt modest and heels conservative. As Zack reached the podium and began his speech, Joy sat beside Roman Calder.

"Since these political rallies are orchestrated down to the second and they're the same everywhere, I know exactly where in the speech to look." It wasn't lost on Lara that both Zack and Roman looked years younger in this tape. There was an openness to Zack's expression that didn't exist now. How much of that was the heavy mantle of responsibility and how much was the incident that happened only days later?

"Well, it's called a stump speech for a reason," Roman said impatiently. "We can't possibly write a different speech for every town. Zack visited literally hundreds of places on the road. Of course we treat them all the same."

"I'm pointing it out because the anomaly happens at the same time every time. He knew when he wanted to take her out. This is the part of the speech where Zack talks about valuing American families." She glanced back and noticed that Connor was watching the screen intently, gripping the back of her sofa.

She wondered if he'd been there. Roman had been. She didn't remember Gabe or Maddox from any of the tapes, but she had to wonder if Connor had been lurking in the shadows, providing security. How had it felt to know he failed?

"I don't see what we're looking for." Everly leaned forward, her eyes glued to the screen.

"Watch her suit. It's coming up." She always got a chill when she watched this video. All of them, actually. They were a road map that led to this woman's death.

"What the fuck is that?" Gabe asked, pointing to the screen.

There it was. A little red dot in the middle of Joy Hayes's chest. Lara paused the file.

"That's from a scope." Connor's voice shook.

Yes, from a long-range rifle. The glowing red mark on Joy Hayes's chest was faint, but there was no way to mistake it.

"Yes, had she been wearing a darker color, I don't think the mark would have shown up on film."

"Joy liked pastels and bright colors," Zack commented, his voice a forced monotone.

Lara stopped that file and moved on. The real proof was in the sequence. One incident could be brushed off. Three formed an undeniable pattern. "This is from the following day in Wichita, Kansas. I'll fast-forward to the same part of the stump speech."

She moved the video forward. This time Joy Hayes was wearing a lovely white suit, and the red dot was very clear. It was only for a few seconds and the eye could easily miss it if one weren't really looking for it. Lara paused and pointed to the screen. "You'll see this is at the same time in the speech."

Zack Hayes had gone a pasty white, but his face was perfectly still. "How many times?"

"We've found three videos. The three days leading up to the actual act. The assassin set it up carefully and he timed it. He followed your campaign." She moved on to the final file. Kansas City, Missouri. Joy wore pale blue but the red dot showed up right on time. It hovered over her heart before disappearing. "The next day you went to Memphis and that was the day your wife was killed. She was always the target of the assassin. Not once did he take aim at you. He never meant to kill you. His one and only goal was ensuring that Joy Hayes died and America watched you mourn. Days after, they swept you into office."

Zack Hayes stood suddenly. "Where's your bathroom, please?"

She pointed to the small guest bathroom. "Right there. Are you all right?"

He turned and walked away, slamming the door behind him and then came a sound she would never forget.

The president of the United States retching in her bathroom.

"Oh, god. He wasn't behind it." That fact hit her like a ton of bricks. She stood and glanced around the room at all the shocked faces. What the hell had she done to that man?

"This doesn't mean we didn't get the right guy." Connor was staring at the screen. "I chased him down. I tracked him. I shot him. He had the rifle in his hand."

"I thought the Secret Service took him out."

"No." Connor shook his head.

The supposed assassin had been a young man with schizophrenia who had tried to kill then-candidate Hayes because he'd thought Hayes was sent from Satan and had been using television to send him messages. The news had devoted hours to going over his crazy journals and talking to all his so-called friends who claimed they should have seen it coming.

Lara knew better.

"But Troy Hill has an airtight alibi for two of the three rallies. He was being held in jail for drunk and disorderly. His mother didn't have the money to bail him out so they held him for seventy-two hours. I'm sorry. He wasn't responsible. He was a patsy. Think about it, Connor. What type of rifle was used? A hunting rifle? Something he could have easily gotten his hands on?"

"It was a Dragunov." Connor's hands became fists at his sides. "It was a fucking Dragunov. How stupid am I?"

"That sounds Russian," Gabe said, his gaze moving between the bathroom and Connor as though he couldn't decide who needed his help more.

"It is," Lara pointed out. "According to Freddy, it's the preferred weapon of the Russian mob for long-range assassinations. It's why I think Natalia Kuilikov is tied somehow to Joy Hayes's death. The Russians are all over this thing. At first I thought the president might have hired a Russian assassin and Natalia had proof." She winced at the outcry that brought. "I'm sorry. I don't know him the way you do. I don't think that now. I do think someone wanted Zack Hayes in office and they were willing to kill to get him there."

Roman shook his head, his stare fused to the screen like he couldn't believe what he'd seen. "I was right beside her during every one of those speeches. I was sitting right there and I didn't notice someone was aiming a sniper rifle at her."

"You were watching Zack, like you were supposed to," Lara pointed out. Of all of the group left in the room, Roman seemed the most shaken. She was a little worried he would need the bathroom, too. He was a pasty white and she could see the way his hands shook. He couldn't fake that. Roman Calder was known for being unflappable, utterly ruthless, and cold as ice. He didn't look like any of those things now. He looked like a man who'd had his world upended.

"I didn't even question it," Connor said. "I killed that kid because I just knew he'd meant to kill Zack and had missed. I never thought to look back over any of the previous speeches for anything unusual. Why would I when they'd seemed to go off without a hitch?" He swallowed, shaking his head slowly. "I didn't question whether or not that kid had pulled the trigger or whether Zack was the target. It seemed obvious."

Gabe stood and turned to Connor. "That guy was running from the scene. Two witnesses saw him coming down the stairs and he was carrying a weapon. He raised that rifle your way, Connor. He seemed like the natural suspect. You had no choice."

"I was behind you," Dax said. "If you hadn't shot him, I would have.

I would have made the exact same call. Why would the Russian mob want Zack in office?"

"We don't know it was the mob who wanted him there." Everly took her fiancé's hand. "We only know whoever did it very likely hired a Russian assassin. It's more important than ever to find Natalia and figure out what's happening here. It's connected somehow. Perhaps Lara is right and Natalia knows who hired the assassin, or she can lead us to the man who pulled the trigger and he can tell us who hired him. We just don't have enough pieces to see the whole puzzle yet. Lara, I would really like to see whatever your informant gave you."

Zack stepped out, his face pale, but it was obvious he'd cleaned up and calmed down. He looked to Lara. "I did not kill my wife. My wife and I were friends, very close friends. I loved her. I won't lie and say I was in love with her. Ours was a marriage of political convenience, but I cared for her deeply. The last thing I would have done was have her killed. I needed Joy. I didn't want to do any of this without her. I tried to pull out of the race after she died."

Roman stood, looking toward Zack. "I wouldn't let him. It wasn't what Joy would have wanted. I'm the one with every reason to have done this. I'm the most obvious suspect so you need to eliminate me. I'll open all my records. Every file I have is yours. I'll answer all your questions. Hell, hook me up to a lie detector or something else. Connor, surely the Agency has something."

Zack shook his head. "I know you would never have done this."

"Why not? I'm a ruthless bastard. I'm the asshole who wants to win at all costs."

"You loved Joy. You would never have hurt her," Zack said quietly.

Roman took a step back. "I . . . How did you know?"

"I always knew."

"Zack, I never touched her. I never would have."

There was an infinite amount of sympathy in Zack Hayes's eyes, and Lara realized she would never question him again. This was the man with all his defenses down. This was the private man and all he seemed to want to do was comfort his friend. "But you loved her all the same and you've mourned her all these years. I believe she loved you, too. I'm not questioning you, Roman. I would never do that. If there's one thing I know in this world, it's that you have my back, no matter what. I know what you've sacrificed for me, so no one will investigate you. But there will be an investigation. Lara, I'm going to ask something of you I shouldn't."

"No." Connor took a step toward her. "Zack, no. I want her out of this."

The president wanted her to investigate. This mystery had caused her nothing but trouble and heartache. It was the most important investigation of her life and it dangled right in front of her. She probably should say no . . . but she couldn't. "I'll do it."

"With my help." Everly stood beside her, a united front. "Don't even think of forbidding it now that it's gotten a little dangerous, Gabriel."

Gabe simply sighed and shook his head. "It's only getting dangerous now? I seem to remember plenty of danger. But I won't stop you. I'll help you, love. We're in this together."

Together. She wasn't together with Connor, but she could stay in his circle for a little while.

That shouldn't have been appealing. She shouldn't want to stay anywhere close to him. But she was ass deep in this investigation now and she had to see it through. "Mr. President, I want to find out what happened. I want to solve this. I'll do it."

"Thank you. Connor, I'm sure you understand this means I'll need you to protect her." Zack Hayes neatly sprung his trap.

Son of a bitch. He was a sneaky bastard.

Connor nodded and she couldn't miss the relief she saw in his eyes. "I wasn't planning on going back to work anytime soon. I'll watch over the women. We'll be in D.C. for a few days, but then we'll head up to the city, and Everly and Lara can work on it from there."

He would isolate her. One glance told Lara he intended to keep her close and try to work his charm on her.

Would he really go to all this trouble for a disposable woman?

"I would love to spend some time in New York. I think Everly and I will work well together." She would figure out what to do about Connor later. She hated to admit that being forced to spend more time with him was almost a relief. "But Lincoln has to come with me."

Connor shrugged. "I would expect no less. My place is on the Upper West Side. He can crap in Central Park."

So he wasn't going to fight her on bringing the dog. "I'll need to find a good vegan grocery store."

"You can find anything in Manhattan, Lara. And my place is a three-bedroom. You can have your own room. For however long that lasts." His voice was a silky promise.

"Good," Zack said, taking a long breath. "That's settled. I need some air. Don't tell the Secret Service agents."

He walked out to her balcony, the door closing firmly behind him.

"Is he okay?" She knew it was a stupid question the moment it left her mouth.

They were all looking outside.

"No. He's not all right." Roman sank down to the couch. "None of us are all right."

Gabe sat down beside Roman. He looked up to Lara. "Do you have anything with a high alcohol content?"

Thanks to Connor, she did. "Scotch. It's on the counter. I'll pour everyone a glass."

Connor shook his head. "No. You'll go and pack."

"I'll get us all a drink," Everly said, heading for the kitchen.

With a nod, Connor approached Lara. "I'm going to talk to Zack, but we're leaving in fifteen minutes. I want to be in Langley before the traffic hits. We'll call your father and tell him where you are, but no one else is to know."

"All right. I have to run downstairs. Kiki has some of Lincoln's treats. I know it's stupid but . . ."

"They're the only reason he poops. I'll go with you to get them."

Then she'd be alone with him in the elevator in which he'd first kissed her. Lara didn't trust herself. Besides, Zack needed him now. "I'll be fine. The Secret Service is here. I know you're worried about Russians, but if anyone has entered the building, they'll know. I'm only going down a couple of floors to a friend's place. I'll be fine."

He sighed, then looked out at Zack on the balcony. "All right. Be back here in five minutes, Lara. I swear to god if you run . . ."

She shook her head. "I won't. I want to solve this thing, for myself, for America, and for those grieving men. Besides, I know you're really good at finding me."

Connor crossed the space between them. "I'm serious about not telling anyone where you're going. Don't tell Kiki. It puts her at risk. Maybe I should come with you after all."

"Stop. I'll be back here in a few minutes, Connor. I'm giving you my word."

He was silent for a moment. She could see that letting go of her was hard for him. He lived in a world of danger, where no one trusted. How would a man like that handle falling in love? Lara suspected she knew the answer.

"All right. I'll be waiting up here for you. I was serious about the separate room. I've got a guest room at the house in Langley. I won't ever deny that I want you, but I won't force you into anything."

She nodded, oddly disappointed. She brushed it off. Having time and space to herself would be good, smart.

She turned for the door, he caught her arm again. Suddenly, Connor loomed over her.

"Lara, I will do everything I can to seduce you. And you'll tell me if we need to visit the justice of the peace."

Her cheeks heated. "Connor, you can't expect me to go through with that."

He leaned in and brushed his mouth against her ear. "If you're pregnant, I assure you we will get married. I had a singularly crappy childhood because my father was a disgusting bastard and my mother couldn't handle the fact that her meal ticket left her. That will not happen to our child."

"I might not be," she said, forcing herself to look at him.

God, he was the most beautiful man she'd ever met.

"I can always hope otherwise." He stepped back and his face became smooth and blank again. "I'll be waiting for you."

She practically ran out the door, brushed by the Secret Service agents, and hopped on the elevator, pressing the button for Kiki's floor.

She felt utterly overwhelmed. She'd gone from suspecting the president of murder to agreeing to work for him. And Connor. God, what was she going to do about Connor? How could she ever trust the man again? He'd lied to her, used her. She couldn't possibly marry him. The thought should have sickened her.

And yet there was a part of her that wasn't ready to let him go.

The elevator doors opened and she hurried down the corridor to Kiki's apartment. Her friend had moved into this building first. Kiki had tried to convince Tom to buy a unit, too. But he'd balked, saying he liked being closer to work. When Lara had purchased her condo, Kiki had rolled her eyes and shaken her head, commenting that, "Naturally Lara had to buy the nicest unit in the building."

Sometimes she wondered if Kiki even liked her or if they'd just been friends for so long that it was natural to stay together. Like a married couple who didn't want to divorce because it would be too much trouble.

She sighed and knocked on Kiki's door. It opened, but not because she was there. It opened because it had been left ajar.

Had she gone out and forgotten to close the door?

"Kiki?" Lara stepped inside. "Are you here?"

She stopped when the door to Kiki's office opened. She'd only been in the office once when Kiki had first moved in. Her friend always kept it shut up, claiming it was the only boring part of her eclectically furnished place. She'd told Lara once that the office was the sad part of her soul and she didn't want anyone seeing it—or the sensitive job-related documents she kept inside.

But it wasn't Kiki who emerged from the office. It was Tom.

And he clutched a knife in his hands.

FOURTEEN

Connor watched her go, his whole body heavy with the desire to drag her right back to his side and never let her leave. He'd almost been ready to give up before he'd seen that tape.

She needed him. She was getting into something even more dangerous than he'd first thought, and she had no clue how to defend herself. Zack had given him the perfect excuse to keep her close.

How was he going to prove that he was worthy of her? Hell, he wasn't. Not really, but he was good for her. She just didn't see it. She needed someone like him, someone who would burn down the world to make sure she was safe and happy. She never thought of herself, always putting others' needs first. While noble, it could be dangerous if she fell for the wrong man, a guy who would use her and soak up all that sunshine for himself, never giving her anything in return. Connor intended to see to it that no one stepped on her or used her again.

Just him.

Damn it. Maybe that made him a selfish prick, but he couldn't let her go. Deep down he prayed the times he'd had her without protection were enough. Hopefully, she would see reason and marry him and then he could show her the kind of life he wanted to give her.

"She left her phone behind." Dax handed him Lara's cell with its sunny yellow case. "She probably won't run far without her phone."

"I'm quitting the Agency." He couldn't be a good husband to Lara if he was constantly halfway around the world getting his hands dirty.

Dax put a hand on his shoulder. "Of course you are. You're going to have a wife and kids. You've done your time, man. Let someone else step up."

"Quit the Navy and come with me. We can build a business. Security solutions. Hell, between the two of us we know enough sad-sack ex-military and black ops dudes to form a small army."

Dax frowned. "I wouldn't know what to do with myself. I don't have a girl. I think I'm just about ready to ship out again. I need a vacation from my vacation, if you know what I mean."

"Go to her," Connor suggested. "Talk to her. She's not married."

Dax scrubbed a hand through his hair. "You think I don't know that? I'm practically that woman's stalker. Thank god she doesn't know it because she would kick my ass and likely get me discharged. I know she's in New Orleans. She's still the most gorgeous woman to walk the earth and I also know that she still curses my name."

"Yeah, well, Lara isn't too happy with me right now. I'm not going to let that stop me." He liked holding her phone. It made him feel oddly connected to her. He looked behind him where Everly was handing Roman a glass of Scotch. "Did you know about that?"

"About Roman and Joy?" Dax shook his head. "Hell, no. That was a kick in the gut. I didn't think Roman had ever been in love. One of us needs to go talk to Zack. Roman can't do it right now."

"I'm going. He's got some hard decisions to make."

"Knowing you're hanging around should make him feel better," Dax said. "I think I'll hit Everly up for a drink, too."

Connor looked back at his best friend. "Think about what I said."

Dax sighed. "I think about that woman every second of every day, brother."

Connor turned and stepped out onto the balcony. Zack was staring at the Mall in the distance. Secret Service would flip out if they knew he was on the balcony. But he'd swept the place for bugs and did a quick scan of all the windows around them. None seemed to be open so that an assassin could take a quick shot. Besides, almost no one knew the president was here.

Connor realized he wouldn't trade for Zack's life, not for anything in the world. "We're going to figure this out. I know I'm watching over the women, but I'm actually pretty good at stuff like this. Though I haven't proven it to you. I can't tell you how sorry I am about that."

Guilt weighed heavily on him. He should have looked deeper. He should have taken over the case himself and not given in to the pressure from the Agency to keep his name out of it. One of the good things that would come from leaving his job was not having to be so damn secretive anymore.

It struck him suddenly that Lara was his light. He'd been in the darkness for so long. She was the only one he would leave the shadows for. Not because he loved them. Not because he feared the sun. He simply knew the darkness. It was comfortable. He belonged there, but maybe with her at his side, he could make another place for himself. He could finally have a home.

"No recriminations, Connor. I've got enough of those for both of us. Just figure out what the hell is going on because I have no clue."

"Your father was the ambassador for years. Have you had any contact with Russians recently?" he asked softly to ensure no one would be able to hear them over the traffic below.

"Beyond the fucker who runs the country?" Zack laughed but it was a bitter thing. "No. If you're asking me if a member of the *Bratva* is blackmailing me for something, the answer is no. If you're asking me if my father made deals with them back in the day . . . I don't know. I have suspicions but I've always shied away from them. I thought it was better to leave the past in the past. My father only ever had one ambition for me, and wasn't suffering from dementia when Joy died."

Shit. "You think your father had Joy killed to get you elected?"

Zack turned, his eyes older than they'd been before. "When the doctor told my father I was a son based on my ultrasound, he shipped my mother back home. She was six months pregnant at the time and the doctor advised against any kind of travel. She'd had several miscarriages and her health wasn't what it should have been. He wanted his son born on American soil because he didn't want any questions about the place of my birth."

"The embassy would have been considered American soil. The natural-born-citizen clause wouldn't have held you back. You were born to two Americans."

Zack shook his head. "McCain was born on a Navy base and they questioned him. The opposition will use anything. They couldn't have kept me from running, but they could have given me hell about it. So my father sent my mother back to Maryland. She almost lost me and spent the rest of her pregnancy in a hospital bed, but by god my birth certificate says United States of America. My father told the doctor that if I couldn't run for president, I was useless anyway so it didn't matter what happened. Yes, I believe my father had the very real potential to hire someone to assassinate my wife if he thought it would win me the election."

"Do you understand that if it's true, your presidency is over?"

"I know. It won't matter that I had no knowledge. My legacy and anything I've achieved in office will be ruined."

Connor couldn't imagine it. "Maybe your father didn't do this at all. Maybe it's some outside force and we don't know what they want yet."

"Either way, it all boils down to one thing."

"What's that?"

"I'd thought about not running for a second term," Zack began. "Not because I don't think I'm doing a good job. My approval rating is surprisingly high. I've managed to work with the opposition well. The reason I want to quit is her."

"Elizabeth." No one who stood in the same room as that pair could miss the fact that Zack and Elizabeth cared about each other. "Are you sleeping with her?"

"No. I wouldn't risk it because of what the press would do to her, but if I knew I was getting out, I might. I was going to tell Roman next week and then ask her to dinner with me. We have dinner a couple of times a week, but never alone. I was going to surprise her. I'm in love with her. I've never been in love with anyone, but I knew the minute I saw her. That's the horrible part. I met her a year before Joy died. I took one look at her and knew she was the woman for me. Do you know how awful I am, Connor? I had a plan. I was going to wait until after the election. If I lost I was going to offer Joy a divorce. If I won, I was going to offer her a bargain."

What a fucking mess. "You were going to let her have an affair with Roman so you could see Elizabeth."

"I didn't see it as an affair," Zack said wistfully. "It was all about timing. We couldn't divorce while we were in the White House. Roman would have happily married her. I saw it as an anticipation of the future." He sighed. "I deserve all of this shit, Connor. And Elizabeth deserves none of it. I'm going to fire her tomorrow. I'm going to end this so she can find a good man."

"That's a mistake. What are the rumors about you two, Zack?"

"That we're having an affair. Firing her should lay them to rest."

"And if this isn't a dead issue? If someone other than your father plotted to put you into office so they could use you down the line?"

"Then she's out of it."

"Or they'll see right through that scheme and know she's your weakness. Then you'll have left her utterly alone and unprotected. Until we know what's really happening, the safest place for her is the White House under the watchful eye of the Secret Service."

"Oh, god. They could come after Elizabeth. I hadn't thought of that.

I was just thinking of how she'll look at me when she finds out what my father might have done." Zack had gone pale again. "Do you think they would hurt Elizabeth to force me to do whatever they want? Likely so. They killed Joy."

"I think that if someone wants to hurt you, Elizabeth is the easiest way. If I was the one watching you and you fired her tomorrow, I would suspect your ploy. You're not known for being cruel. Dismissing her would be out of character, so I would take a much closer look. I was working in Afghanistan a few years back, trying to track down a certain bomb maker. The intelligence I had led me to a man who supplied both sides with weapons. He was a smart man. He wouldn't break since he knew the men he worked for would kill him if he ever talked. This man had left his wife and small daughter back when he'd gotten involved in the arms business. Some people would have said he was callous for leaving them. I took a chance. I brought them in. You see, the timing was too coincidental. Just as he sets up shop, he suddenly decides he's no longer in love?"

"What happened?"

"He gave me the name of the bomb maker and we don't mourn the city of Los Angeles. He took his wife and daughter and they ran."

"Are they alive?"

"I don't know. Probably not, but that's what happens when you get involved with terrorists, Zack. You can call me a monster, but I had to weigh the lives of those three people against millions of ours. What I'm telling you is that it's too late to shove her away. Talk to her. Tell her what's happening. I would be shocked if she didn't stand by you. If she knows what's coming, she'll know to be careful. But scorned women can be reckless women. They lash out at the oddest times."

Connor frowned.

"I can't get closer to her." Zack slumped down in Lara's patio chair.

"It would be a mistake to push her away." Connor wondered what he would do in Zack's position. They weren't the same, though. If Connor walked away from this case, Lara wouldn't give up. She would keep going. She would gather her little band of misfits around her and then they would all die. He looked down at the street below. "Even if you can't bring yourself to tell her the truth, you should keep her close so you can make sure she's safe."

A motorcycle pulled up across the street from the building. Connor's senses went on high alert. He recognized that bike, though it likely wasn't the same since there were two people on it and one of them was wearing a skirt.

Kiki slid off the back of the bike, pulling the helmet off so her long brown hair flowed down the back of her peasant blouse. She smiled and leaned in, giving the man she'd been with a kiss.

Was that her married lover? Congressmen didn't usually ride around on crotch rockets. Why did he have the exact style of motorcycle that their attacker had been riding?

Connor didn't believe in coincidence.

Could the person riding the bike have been a woman? Kiki was slender but in a bulky leather jacket, in the heat of the moment, she could probably have passed for a man. Her hair would have been hidden under the helmet, her hands under gloves.

The bike sped away and Kiki pulled out her phone. She typed something in and looked up. He couldn't miss the smirk on her face before she started across the street toward the building.

Lara's phone buzzed in his hand.

"Is something wrong?" Zack rose to his feet.

Luckily Lara didn't put any kind of security on her phone. He swiped his thumb across the screen and found the text from an unknown source.

Last warning. I'm coming for you tonight. You should run, bitch. Run as far as you can and never come back.

Connor closed his eyes as his own arrogance came crashing down. He'd thought this was all about the case. He'd been so certain that only something as big as the investigation of Natalia Kuilikov and Joy Hayes's murder could bring this kind of evil into the life of a good person like Lara. He'd forgotten that evil lurked behind even the sweetest of faces.

And a woman scorned really could do massive damage.

"Yes, something's terribly wrong. Zack, I might need to borrow a few of your men." He took off, praying he could get to Lara in time.

Lara backed away, adrenaline pumping through her. "I was just looking for Kiki. I'll come back later."

Tom stared at her and then looked down at the knife. "Oh, shit. You thought I was . . . Lara, I'm not going to hurt you. I thought you were her."

He put the knife down on the table just outside the office and showed her his hands.

"Her?"

Tom nodded. "Kiki. I came here because she was writing up a brief for me."

She sighed, breathing a little easier though she was still confused. "You have to stop using her like that."

"Yeah, I fucking know that now. It seemed really harmless. She didn't seem to mind and she's really good at it. She's smart, you know. I didn't realize she was mind-blowingly cray cray." Tom's breath was uneven, his hands shaky. "I should have known it was too good to be true. No woman can blow a man like she can and possibly be sane. I'm serious. She's got the suction of a Dyson, Lara."

"You slept with her?" Even though she and Tom were no longer together and hadn't been for years, she'd thought someone would give her a heads-up when Kiki and Tom changed their status from friends to lovers.

Tom went bright red and he nodded. "I kind of wish I hadn't now. I know guys like to joke about hot psycho chicks, but damn she's scary. We should get out of here. I'm worried about what she could do."

Her brain was reeling with the idea that Tom and Kiki had been together. "What are you talking about?"

He looked back toward her office. "She gave me a key about a year ago. Even after I told her I didn't want to do the friends-with-benefits thing anymore, she told me to keep it, but she always locks her office. She told me it was because she had sensitive documents back there."

Lara had heard the same. Kiki worked for a law firm that had ties to the Department of Justice. "Why would you break up with her if she's as good as you say she is?"

"Because I'm still in love with you." His face softened. "Lara, I know I screwed up. I didn't treat you the way I should have or try hard enough. Lately, I've had time to think about where we went wrong. We should talk to a therapist. We're so good as friends, but we could be great lovers, too."

She'd learned a lot about that in the last week. "Oh, sweetie, we have no chemistry."

"How can you say that? We're great together," he argued even as he looked around Kiki's apartment. "Seriously, we should get out of here. I don't know when she's coming back."

Lara's instincts flared as she stepped toward Kiki's home office. There must be some reason Tom had been standing in the doorway, clutching a knife. "What does she have back there?"

He followed her. "I think she's been sending you the nasty texts. Lara, you have to know that I didn't realize it until now."

She barely listened to Tom. Instead, she stepped into the office. Lara only had to take in a glance before her eyes went wide. Everywhere she looked she found pictures of Tom. It looked as if they'd been taken over the years. She recognized a picture of Tom in college and one right after they'd all graduated. There were shots of him smiling at the camera, but most of the images looked like he had no idea he was being photographed. They were pictures of Tom walking into his office or sitting with friends in a restaurant. They looked as if they'd been taken with a telephoto lens. She remembered when Kiki had bought the camera three years before. The woman had even offered to photograph her ill-fated wedding to Tom.

The wedding Kiki had talked her out of.

Lara wasn't upset about that. She and Tom really hadn't worked, but looking around this room, she had to wonder if Kiki hadn't had another, more selfish reason for persuading her not to get married.

"She follows you."

Tom stepped beside her, his voice grim. "She's been stalking me. When did you start getting those texts?"

"Three weeks ago."

"Around the time you started talking to that douche online?"

"Yes. What does Niall have to do with anything?"

"When you started talking to him, I realized I had to get off my ass and get you back. I told her I was going to do whatever it took. That was when I started asking you if you wanted to go to the movies and stuff."

"I thought that was just as friends." She'd turned him down because she'd had so much work to do and she'd wanted to spend her evenings talking to Niall . . . who had turned out to be Connor.

"Yeah, but I intended to ease you back into being my girlfriend," Tom admitted. "The idea of you falling for some asshole in California really gave me the kick in the pants I needed. I even asked Kiki's advice on how to get you back. I think that's when she started sending you those texts."

"She doesn't have a motorcycle." But Lara's stomach churned as she saw a picture of the three of them. They were arm in arm, with Kiki and Tom smiling at the camera. Lara couldn't smile because her face had been viciously cut out.

"Um, that's where I found the knife. It was kind of sticking out of your face. And she might not have a motorcycle, but her new boyfriend does," Tom admitted. "She told me he lets her borrow it. Besides the congressman, she's been screwing some intern at work. In retrospect, I think she told me to see if I'd get jealous. Apparently she's not serious

SHAYLA BLACK AND LEXI BLAKE

about either of them because she thinks I'm her Prince Charming or something. You know this isn't as sexy as they make it look on TV."

Lara just blinked. Kiki had been her friend. How could the woman hurt her like that?

Tom put a hand on her shoulder. "I should have told you everything sooner. I didn't want to hurt you." He sighed. "She's always been jealous of you, you know. She talks a lot about how you get everything handed to you and she has to work for it. I thought it was just female jealousy. I don't get girl stuff most of the time. I didn't think she really hated you."

But looking around this room, Lara could see plainly that Kiki did.

"I need to call Connor." She reached for her phone then cursed when she realized she'd left it behind.

"You don't need him, Lara. Didn't you get the information I sent you? Your bodyguard is working for the White House. He has been all along. Come with me. We'll call the cops and tell them everything we know about Kiki and get her . . . I don't know, committed or something." He reached down to take her hand. "I love you. I've always loved you. I can protect you. That Connor guy is just another asshole who wants to use you."

Maybe, but despite everything they'd been through, Connor was the only person she wanted to see now. It was obvious she'd been an idiot to believe that Kiki was her friend. She'd suggested Lara stay with her parents after the e-mail threat, then she'd pushed Lara toward Connor— all after Tom had revealed that he meant to win her back. Lara could have told her that she'd never take Tom back, but Kiki had never mentioned it. She'd never given her the courtesy of knowing they were on opposite sides. Never once hinted that she had feelings for Tom.

With tears in her eyes, she turned and fled the office. Connor. She would get to Connor and he would handle this. He would take care of things and she would never have to deal with this again. She would bury herself in work.

"Lara, wait for me. I'll drive us to the police station. We need to get there before she has a chance to clean this shit up. Now that I think about it, I saw her with a phone I hadn't recognized a couple of days ago. Do you think it's one of those burner phones? Is that how she's sending you all those threatening texts? That should get her some jail time, right?" Tom was hard on her heels.

Halfway through the kitchen, Lara stopped as the door opened. They were out of time.

Kiki stood in the doorway, a gun in her hand. "I left it unlocked, didn't I?"

Tom stepped beside her. "What? The front door? No. I used my key. I came to pick up the brief. It's due tomorrow. I can't tell you how much I appreciate it. What's with the gun?"

She had to give it to Tom. He was cool under pressure. She hadn't expected that. She tried to follow his lead. "I came down to get Lincoln's treats. Connor and I are leaving town until we can figure out who wants me dead."

"I think you know." Kiki frowned and nodded toward the back of the apartment. "Someone didn't shut the office door completely."

Kiki didn't make the same mistake. She shut the front door and turned the dead bolt into place. Tom didn't even have the knife anymore. He'd left it just outside the office—too far away.

Tom took a shaky breath. "Sweetheart, why don't we talk about this? I had no idea you felt this way about me. I thought we were just casual. If I'd known, I never would have broken up with you."

"Broken up? That would mean we were together in the first place," Kiki said, her voice lower and nastier than Lara had ever heard it. "You hid me. You told me she couldn't know. You were ready to marry her, but I was your dirty little secret."

Tom stepped forward slightly, putting himself between her and Kiki. "That wasn't how it was. And that's not how it is. You were the one who always said we were casual. Lara is just convenient. I want to go places. I don't want to be one more lawyer in D.C. She's actually quite connected, but that's as far as it goes. It's really you I want."

She knew he was telling Kiki what she wanted to hear, but it still hurt. It was what she'd suspected deep down. Tom was ambitious and he thought she would make an advantageous wife.

"Then you won't mind if I shoot her, will you?" Kiki's eyes were bright, her face a mottled red as she pointed the gun in Lara's direction.

"You don't want to do that," Tom said evenly.

"Tom, I love you. I've always been the one who loved you. I'm the one who supported you while she just dragged you down. How can you pick her over me?"

"I'm not. I just don't want you to go to jail," Tom tried.

"Here's a choice for you, lover. I'm going to shoot in a minute and if you're in the way, I'll know you picked her again."

"Please, don't do this," Tom began.

"Don't hurt your precious Lara? I hate her. I can't tell you how hard it's been to have to sit around and listen to her whine about shit that doesn't matter. I did it to stay close to you. You have to see that she's not the right woman for you. She's a pathetic child who wouldn't know real love if it bit her in the ass because all her life she's been an entitled princess."

Princess. That was what Connor called her. She kept her mouth shut because none of this seemed to really be about her. If she could stall for a little more time, her five minutes would be up and Connor would come looking for her. She had to believe that. He always meant what he said. He'd lied, but he'd also kept her safe time and again. Even when he could have taken the information he'd been looking for and left her behind, he'd made sure she was safe. He would come.

"Just put the gun down, Kiki," Tom begged.

"Her or me, Tom." Kiki cocked the gun, the sound distinct and chilling. "Make your choice. If you don't move away from her, I'll shoot and I'll kill you. Are you going to be her savior and martyr?"

She was just about to beg for Tom's life when he moved—to his left. He took several steps away from her, leaving her with nothing between her and the crazy woman with the gun.

He'd told her he loved her, then left her to die.

"Sorry, Lara," he mumbled, his gaze not meeting hers.

She looked up and into the face of a woman she'd never really known. Kiki had worn a mask all the time. Lara raised her hands, though she knew they wouldn't stop a bullet. "What did I do to you?" She had to keep her talking, give Connor time to come for her. "I walked away from Tom. You convinced me to. Now I have a new lover. I would never have gone back to Tom. He's all yours."

"What did you do to me? What do all you rich bitches do? You take what you want and leave the rest of us crumbs. I've known people like you all my life. And I've hated every single one of you. You know I didn't intend to kill you."

"No, you just wanted to scare me enough that I would leave D.C.," Lara surmised.

"I wanted to scare you enough so Tom would see that under your crusading bravado, you're just a cowardly shit. I wanted him to understand that he was better off without you."

"Cowardly? I'm not the one who said I loved someone before leaving them to face danger alone," Lara pointed out.

"I really am sorry," Tom said, his gaze cast to the floor.

"Don't be sorry, baby. With her out of the way, we can be together like we always should have been," Kiki said. "You don't need her and you don't need her father. That's the only reason he wants you back. He wants to leave his job and move up. He thinks your dad can help him."

"You can't just shoot her here," Tom said quickly. "Everyone will hear. You should take her somewhere else, somewhere more private."

Tom didn't sound as if he cared much what happened next.

Just as Kiki was about to speak, a mighty crash splintered the door.

Lara dove to her right, to the relative safety of the table. She crouched down and all she could see were feet and legs. Tom's quickly dashed out of sight, but Kiki's flats remained rooted in place. Lara prayed she didn't start shooting.

All around her the air burst with shouts and screams and the sound of that door being torn off its hinges. Two pairs of dark loafers entered the room.

"Put down the gun," a staccato voice commanded.

"Put it down or we'll shoot," another even voice ordered.

"Lara! Lara!" This voice wasn't even or calm. It was panicked and she was almost certain that was a completely new experience for the man shouting. And she knew those boots.

Connor had come for her.

"I'm here," she yelled back.

She was about to risk sticking her head up when a gunshot blasted through the air. She watched in horror as Kiki's legs wobbled, and then the woman she'd thought had been her friend for years hit the ground, her dead eyes staring right at Lara, blood gushing from a wound at her temple. She clutched the gun in her hand, still smoking.

Lara stared in horror before strong arms lifted her into the air and she found herself in Connor's embrace.

"Did she hit you?" His voice was a gravelly mess, as though all his shouting had roughened his throat. "Are you hurt?"

She shook her head and put an arm around his neck. Safe. No matter what he'd done, she was safe with him. She buried her face against his chest so she couldn't see the body again. "She killed herself?"

His arms tightened around her. "She's lucky I didn't get to her."

"Lara," Tom called out to her.

She didn't look up, didn't want anything or anyone but Connor. She'd thought Tom was being cool under pressure, but now she had to wonder if he hadn't just been playing them both. He would have let Kiki kill her. She would never have let that happen to him.

"Lara, come on. You can't hold that against me," Tom whined.

"Hold what against you?" Connor's voice sounded as warm as an arctic breeze.

She brought her head up. "It doesn't matter. Get me out of here."

"What did he do?" Connor turned to face Tom. She noticed the

Secret Service agents who had previously been standing at her door were in the apartment. One of them kicked away the gun in Kiki's hand, though Lara could have told him it was useless.

"Connor, I'm going to ask you to stay calm. I can work a lot of miracles, but I would hate to have to pardon you for murder." Zack Hayes stood outside the door, another Secret Service agent at his side. "Lara, are you all right?"

"Yes, sir." She nodded his way, suddenly grateful that someone could keep Connor in check.

"We've got a team on the way, Connor," Zack said. "We'll make sure this doesn't hit the press." He turned to Tom. "Young man, do you know who I am?"

"Yes, Mr. President," he stammered.

"Then you know what I'll do to you if you don't follow instructions. If you make my friends' lives difficult, I'll do the same to you. Who do you think is better at that?"

"You," Tom replied. "I'm sure you are so much better at it than I am. I don't have any desire to ever tell this story. I swear. Any cover-up you want to use, I'm here for you."

"That's what I like to hear. Connor, I don't think Lara needs to be here. Everly is packing for her. Bring her to the limo with me and we'll get you both home. She needs rest and care. It can be a terrible thing to find out the people we care about aren't what they seem." Zack headed for the door and two of the agents flanked him.

"I can handle this. So far the cops haven't been alerted. We'll call it a suicide. Naturally since the president was visiting his friend, the Secret Service investigated." The agent looked at Tom. "You're her friend?"

Was anyone really friends when the chips were down?

"I'm whatever you need me to be, sir," Tom replied.

"You broke down the door when you heard the gunshot. You're terribly upset, of course."

"So upset," Tom agreed.

The agent nodded to Connor. "Go with the president. There's no need for her to stay."

She could tell from the set of Connor's jaw that he really wanted to say a word or two. She hugged him close. "Please, can we go?"

He immediately softened. "Of course." He looked back at Tom. "Know that while the president might be very good at threatening people, I'm equally skilled at torturing them. If I find out you've caused Lara a moment's distress, you're going to see just how good I am."

"Not at all. Lara and I were in that together. Kiki was the crazy one."

Connor started walking and she looked over his shoulder, wondering if she'd ever really known her friends at all.

FIFTEEN

Connor looked at Lara across the table. In the morning light he could see how pale she was. Despite the dark circles under her eyes, she was still the prettiest thing he'd ever seen. It had been so damn hard to leave her alone the night before. After they'd been dropped off at his house, he'd tried to talk to her, tried to get her to eat, to have a glass of wine. Anything. She'd wanted a shower and to go to sleep, but he suspected she'd been up most of the night working, researching that series of names she'd been given in connection to Natalia. He'd sat up most of the night watching the light under her door, wishing she hadn't closed it between them.

The morning had brought no sudden reversal. A cup of coffee sat in front of her, but she hadn't taken a sip. She'd simply nodded when he'd taken Lincoln for a walk. Now she was so quiet he was beginning to get worried. Gone was the chatty, positive Lara he knew, and in her place was a ghost. She responded when someone spoke and did what was asked of her, but there was no animation behind her calm facade.

"Do you want me to call your father?"

She looked up from her laptop. "Why would you do that?"

She sounded slightly accusing, and Connor held in a sigh. "Because you went through something terrible yesterday. You need to talk to someone and you won't talk to me."

"Do you talk after a mission?" A brow arched over her right eye. "Do you come in from killing a few people and feel the need for emotional closure?"

She seemed determined to lash out at him, but he understood the impulse. He was the only one here. He was also the person who'd hurt her in the first place. Despite everything that had happened, he knew at the core she was still angry with him. "I don't talk about it because no one would care. I'm a weapon. No one particularly wants to know how a weapon feels after being used. Besides, this isn't an Agency debrief. This is a man who's worried about his woman."

That arrogant brow came down and she swallowed. "You're not a weapon to be used."

"I am. I have been for a long time. I'm necessary and when I leave, someone else will take my place because this country needs weapons. I just hope there's some reward for doing my duty."

"What kind of reward?"

"I would love some peace, Lara. I've been at war most of my life so I would like some peace. And normalcy. Please talk to me. Tell me what happened. You haven't cried." That was the worst part. She was bottling it all up, shoving it deep where it would fester. "You don't know what not dealing with this will do to you."

"Maybe it didn't affect me as much as you think."

"I think you watched a person you thought was a friend turn on you in the most vicious way possible." He'd seen it before, even experienced it in a way, though he'd never thought of those people as friends. He knew who his friends were. But Lara hadn't lived in the same world. Lara looked at everyone she met as a potential friend.

"She called me princess, too. I guess you both agree on that."

His heart sank. "My feelings have nothing to do with hers."

"You both think I'm entitled and ridiculous."

He shook his head. She didn't understand at all. "I don't mean it like that when I call you princess. When I first saw you, I thought you looked like a cute little pixie. Like a fairy princess. I thought you were the kind who would jump from flower to flower and wave your little wand and make everything all right. That's why I call you princess."

Her eyes watered. "Really?"

Finally he was getting to her. "Really. The whole time I was lying to you, I thought about the fact that I was the troll in that story."

She snorted a little. "Yes, because trolls are known for being ridiculously handsome."

No one ever made him feel the way she did. He couldn't lose her. "I want to talk about everything, Lara. I want to apologize and ask for your forgiveness."

"That's not fair."

It wasn't fair. He was getting her while she was vulnerable. "I am a ruthless bastard, but if you let me, I'll be your ruthless bastard."

"Connor . . ." Her eyes found the screen again. "I can't yet. Everything just hurts right now."

"Then we don't have to talk about us tonight. We'll talk about you."

She shook her head. "I'm not ready. How about we discuss the case? I think I found the connection."

Right now, he didn't give a damn about the connection. "And we'll get to that. But I care about the fact that you went through something horrible and you're shutting down."

Her eyes zipped up and this time they flashed with anger. "This case is the entire reason you met me in the first place. I would think you would be thrilled that I've almost cracked it. You're going to get everything you want."

He had to make her understand. The mission goal had changed. At some point, finding Natalia had become secondary to securing a place in Lara's life. "The only thing I want is you."

She shook her head. "What would a man with as much power as

you need with little old me? Connor, I'm cooperating. As soon as I give you this information, you can take it, pass it off to your buddy Roman, and head right back to your bigwig CIA job."

"I quit." He'd sent his letter of resignation about fifteen minutes after they'd gotten home.

"What?" She blinked.

"I can't be a good husband to you if I'm always on a different continent. I quit the Agency and I'll either build my own business or fix up security at the White House. I have enough money saved up to support us. You don't have to worry about that. I'll take care of you."

"I'm not going to marry you," she said stubbornly and then ruined it by sniffling.

She was fighting, yes. Kiki and Tom had both betrayed her in different ways. Connor knew he'd deceived her terribly himself. All in one day, she'd learned that the people closest to her weren't who she thought at all. Lara needed time. He needed patience. If he stayed calm and remembered the senator's advice, he could get through to her. *Vulnerable.* He hated the word, but nothing was more important than her.

"Whether you marry me or not, I intend to protect you. I can't do that if I'm an operative. Lara, I don't want to be apart from you. I like the man I am when I'm with you."

She sat back, her eyes not meeting his. "I hate you."

That "I hate you" sounded stubborn and sullen and a little weepy. Still, it cut him to the quick. Normally, his reaction would be to lash out, to throw down some nasty shit that would slice her soul open. Except this was Lara and he refused to hurt her again.

For almost two decades, he'd thought he was nothing but a gun with a hair trigger waiting to mow down anyone who could hurt him. Not Lara. She was both his weakness and his strength. And, just maybe, she was his salvation.

"I can understand why you feel that way right now. But I promise

I'll make it up to you because I love you. I've never loved a woman before so I'm trying. But I need you to try, too."

"Why? I was stupid to hope for loyalty or love from a man I didn't know last week. Hell, the friends I'd known for years didn't show me any." Tears rolled down her cheeks.

Connor wanted to hold her in his arms so badly but keeping her talking was more important. "I'm not them, Lara. You can always expect loyalty and love from me. I want everything that's good for you. Don't shut me out, princess. Please. This cold act isn't you."

"Maybe it should be."

"No. I said before that the world needs people like me, but it needs people like you, too. It needs people who believe in the good. It needs fairy princesses who see the bad yet still believe in the good." He sighed. "You know what? Screw the world. *I* need you. I need you to be Lara, to find it in your heart to forgive a man who lied to you, who betrayed you, and who will spend the rest of his life loving you completely."

A little sob left her mouth. He moved to her, gathering her in his arms and dragging her into his lap. He felt better than he had all day, and he knew he was a stinking bastard because he was glad she was really crying. In that moment, he realized he was happier and more alive when he was comforting her than his best day without her. "I was an asshole. Tom and Kiki were assholes, too."

Yeah, he wasn't good at the comforting thing. He stroked her head and petted her hair, happy when she leaned on him.

Finally, she wrapped her arms around him and clung. "I don't want to cry. I want to be strong."

He shook his head. "You are, princess. You have no idea how strong. Strength isn't measured in how many people you kill or how hard it is to make you cry. It's in how resolutely you cling to your goodness. I need you, Lara. I need you so fucking bad."

"How? Why? I don't understand because you're the one with all the power."

"That's not true. I have the power to protect, but you can change things. Can't you see how important that is? I called you naive at the beginning, but maybe I'm too cynical after spending so much time with traitors and killers. I need you to keep seeing the world as a good place. I can't cry anymore." He caressed her face. "I watched one of my closest friends go through hell yesterday and then I saw something worse, the woman I love get her heart broken—twice. The only power I want now is to help put you back together. The only way you'll heal is if you cry. So cry. Cry for both of us. Cry for you and me and for Kiki and Tom, and god, please cry for Zack and his wife, for Roman and Elizabeth because everything is fucked up and it deserves healing tears. You're the only one who can give them to us."

Her arms tightened around him and she sobbed against his chest. He held her, his eyes watering, but it was in pure relief. She was finally crying in his arms.

"Let me take some of the burden, princess." He wasn't going to shy away from using the nickname he'd given her just because her best friend turned out to be a crazy bitch. She was his princess and he was working hard to go from troll to knight. His armor would likely always be tarnished, but he would change for her. "We don't have to talk about us now. Tell me what happened with Kiki. Don't keep it all in. It will be a poison in your veins."

"She hated me. She hated me so much," she whispered through her tears.

"She had issues and she hid them well. Deep down she didn't hate you. She hated herself."

"Her whole office was full of pictures of Tom."

This might be a touchy subject. Lara had loved Tom at one point. He didn't want to be the bearer of bad tidings but she should know what had been happening. "She'd had an affair with him. From the information I gathered, she started sleeping with him right after you broke off your engagement."

She nodded and he breathed a sigh of relief. "He told me. He'd been using her for a long time. I think he'd decided it was time to use me again. He wanted to change jobs and thought my dad could help him."

Connor gritted his teeth. "He's not a strong man. You were right to break it off with him. As it happens, I found out he had nearly twenty outstanding parking tickets. He might have been arrested this morning."

That sounded nice and factual. What he really wanted to say was Tom was a fuckwit who deserved to have his balls shoved down his throat.

Lara froze. "You didn't."

He shrugged. "Hey, I didn't kill him."

A hopeless little grin tugged at her lips before she fell quiet again. "I never knew them at all. I think that might be my fault."

He cupped her chin and forced her to look up at him. "They used you. It's not your fault. You saw the good in them and they weren't smart enough to know what a gift that is."

She laid her head against his shoulder. "I don't know who to trust anymore."

He had no right to ask for her trust. "Give me time. Let me prove I can be what you need me to be."

"I don't think I can be near you and not sleep with you."

His gut clenched. Was she asking to stay with Gabe, who also had great security and could surround her with guards? Gabe wasn't a constant reminder that she'd been lied to. Connor didn't know how to talk her out of leaving. "I won't push you. I promise. I'll give you all the time you need."

She cuddled closer and cupped his cheek. "Time won't work. Time doesn't make me want you less. While we finish this case, I want to have sex with you. I might need it."

It, not him. "You want to use me."

She kept her gaze steady on him. "Maybe. I need to be out of my head for a while. I need something good, Connor. Are you going to demand payment for it?"

So Lara did need him. She could call it whatever she wanted, but she needed to be made love to and he was the only man in the world who would do it.

He lowered his mouth to hers, their lips brushing. He would never deny her this. "No. I'll take whatever you give me."

She sniffled again then slid off his lap. "All right. Then we'll have that to look forward to."

He watched as she moved back to her chair and focused on the screen again. He sat back and studied her as she started typing. Her face was red but her shoulders weren't as tight as they'd been before.

Connor had always been good at reading people but he was too tangled up in this woman to see beyond his own yearning and fear of losing her. Because despite the fact that she'd asked him for sex, he wasn't sure if she intended to use it to bring them back together or work him out of her system for good.

Maybe she really just wanted to fuck. He'd taught her what her body could do. He'd shown her that she was sensual and sexy. Lara wanted more of that from him, but she wasn't the kind of woman who could be satisfied with temporary forever. Eventually she would want more than a lover. She would want a husband, a family.

Could she use him simply for sexual pleasure but not see him as a potential mate?

"You should go to the store, though," she murmured. "I won't sleep with you without a condom."

"I have some," he managed to say, his head reeling.

He'd thought if he managed to help her have a breakthrough, if she decompressed about the previous day's events, that she would fall back into his arms and be the Lara he'd come to love. So far, he'd been wrong.

Connor thought seriously about putting his fist through a wall. How long would it be before Lara decided sex wasn't enough for her?

How long before he was sitting here alone without even a job to keep him occupied?

She picked up the paper the CI had given her. "So this list is Natalia Kuilikov's aliases. She came to the States on an education visa. It had a nine-month limit. She disappeared after roughly three months in Brooklyn."

"I already have a whole file on this. After what happened in New York, I talked to some Agency contacts and compiled all the information I could find. I'll e-mail it to you. Natalia was living with a known member of the Krylov syndicate."

"What happened to her husband? I can find records of her marriage but not of a divorce."

"We don't know. She left him to come to the States, but they didn't divorce. Apparently the marriage fell apart when their only child died roughly three months after he was born. She threw herself into her nanny job in Moscow and they drifted apart. Years later, she came to America and we lost track of her."

She grabbed a banana off the counter and peeled it as she sat again, her eyes on him. "I suppose I can understand why she got into her job. Her son died of SIDS?"

"That's what the death certificate said." Whether she would admit it or not, she'd needed to cry. Now her head was clearer and she could talk about the case. "The police incident report said she woke up that morning, went to get the baby ready to go to child care, and she found him dead."

Lara sat back with a sigh. "I read the translation. The coroner's report stated that the baby died hours before. He was only three months old."

She took a bite and then ran her hands over the keys. "What was the baby's name?"

Connor opened his own laptop and pulled up the file. "Sava Kuilikov."

Lara's head came up, a light in her eyes. "That's what she's doing."

She turned the list around, handing it to Connor. There were five handwritten names on the list. "Natalia originally had four siblings. Two sisters and two brothers. Anja and Dessa were the sisters. Maxim and Konstantin, the brothers."

The five names were the known aliases of Natalia Kuilikov. Anja Maximillian, Natalia Konstantin, Dessa Konn, Anja Sava.

"So she's taking the names of her closest family members and using those?"

Lara shrugged. "I suppose it would be easy to remember them. It also forms a pattern if someone wants to find her. Maybe she wants to be found. Maybe deep down she wants to tell her story."

It was definitely a theory he could work with. "We need to compile a list of possible names. Add in her parents' names as well. We'll work through and try to match them up to people who would be roughly Natalia's age, somewhere in her midfifties. Give me an hour or two and we'll have something to work with."

"All right, but let me help." She moved her chair over as he started to type.

He began the process of matching up names and wondered if, once this case was over, they would ever be together again.

Lara looked over the parking lot of the Serenity Assisted Living Center just outside of Baltimore. It was on a quiet street, but Lara had so recently learned that quiet didn't mean safe. Just because she was with two men who knew how to defend themselves didn't mean people couldn't be hurt. She looked between Connor and his big friend Dax, whom Connor had called in as backup.

"If you're nervous, I can go speak to her myself." Connor put his big, gas-guzzling SUV into park in front of the main building.

Dax leaned in from where he took up most of the backseat with his muscular body. "I'll stay out here and watch over you. Connor can get this done without us."

"I'm not nervous." She hadn't come this far, risked so much, just so she could sit in the car with her massive babysitter.

She looked around. The parking lot was half full. In an hour or so the sun would set. It had already been a long day, but things had sped up considerably once Connor had gotten someone at the CIA involved. Their pool of names had been run and they'd come up with one. Maxine Sava of Baltimore. She was the right age. Her driver's license had lapsed but they'd found a copy with the DMV, and the picture matched 95 percent with the facial recognition software despite the years between the photos. Her cheekbones were still strong, her eyes wide and exotic. Though her skin had lost its perfection, Maxine Sava was still a lovely woman.

He cut the engine and turned slightly. "Fear is nothing to be ashamed of. It's something to be embraced, as long as it doesn't hold you back. Fear proves that you're smart."

"I'm sure you're afraid of so many things," she said, tamping down the way her heart pounded every time she looked at him.

"I didn't use to be. But then fear is mostly about loss, and I didn't have anything to lose until you so I wasn't afraid."

"And now you are?"

"Princess, now I'm terrified." He pulled his SIG Sauer out of its shoulder holster and checked the clip. "Are you ready?"

"How do we know we weren't followed?"

"We don't. I didn't pick up anyone on our tail, but that doesn't mean they're not there," Connor said in that matter-of-fact way of his. He'd been so calm with her. So patient. His gentleness was wearing her down and warming her heart. She didn't want to risk opening her heart to him again but he seemed determined to pry it open.

What had she been thinking, suggesting they continue sleeping together? Like she could really have sex with him a couple of times and not want him anymore. What a joke. Despite the way he'd set her up and the lies he'd told, she still wanted him. She wanted him today more than yesterday. More than the day before.

Where this man was concerned, Lara feared her heart was doomed.

"Let's get this over with." Dax opened his door. "I'm more concerned with them following us at night or ambushing us back at the house."

"Hopefully we talk to Natalia and end this thing. If she tells us who Sergei is, we'll take him down and be done." Connor stepped out and walked around the car. As she unfastened her seat belt, he opened the door and helped her down. She slipped her hand into his, and then he curled his free hand on her waist, easing her to the pavement. "I don't want you to fall."

Everywhere he touched her she felt heat flare. Sometimes all he had to do was look at her and she could feel his hands, stroking her, loving her.

Yeah, she was totally going to be able to sleep with him and walk away. Not.

She eased aside, hoping her feet were steady. "Well, if your car wasn't as big as a tank, I wouldn't need help."

"I'll go and buy a smart car tomorrow," he promised.

"Dude, you weigh more than a smart car." Dax shook his head. "I don't think you'll fit."

"How about I look into a hybrid SUV." He started up the path to the door. "I'm sure Lara knows the best ones. We can use a new car."

This was why staying with him was so damn dangerous. She melted when he said things like that. She just wished she could figure out why he was saying them. Guilt? Had he decided that he owed her?

Or did he really, truly care?

She was quiet as they walked inside. The front room was cheery but there was an oppressiveness that came with any place like this. No matter how many cutesy signs for bingo they hung, this was a place where people waited to die.

"We're here to see Maxine Sava," Connor said to the front desk clerk.

The young woman in scrubs gave him a long once-over, and suddenly she seemed to have some sort of back issue because she thrust her breasts out. "Sure. I can find her for you. Are you her son? She talks about you all the time. She said how handsome you are, but she doesn't have any pictures. She's right."

Lara frowned. By all accounts, Natalia had come here because she'd developed dementia a few years back and could no longer care for herself. Clearly, the woman had forgotten that her son was dead. Or maybe she simply hadn't wanted to remember. Lara couldn't imagine how devastating it would be to lose a child.

She stepped up next to Connor, just barely managing to avoid rolling her eyes at the obvious flirtation. "He's not her son. He's with the INS and he has a few questions to ask her."

"My lovely coworker and fiancée is right." Connor's arm slipped around her. "Could you please tell us where her room is? We just have a few questions for her concerning an immigration issue."

They'd decided to say they were here to ask about her visa and possible immigration law violations. Despite the fact that Connor no longer worked for the Agency, someone had kindly provided him INS paperwork to back him up.

"Oh." She sounded disappointed. "I'll need to see your credentials."

Connor flashed her a badge. She glanced at it, then looked at her schedule.

"She's in 127, but some in that wing might still be in the garden. They sit outside on warm days for an hour. I'll take you out there." The nurse's gaze slipped past Connor, who was still giving Lara PDA, and settled on Dax. She immediately perked up again. "Are you with the government, too?"

Dax gave her an easy smile. "I am, but I didn't bring my fiancée along because I'm single, darlin'. Lead the way."

Connor chuckled as they started to walk down the gray tiled hall. "Dax is a bit of a player. I should have warned you."

"Everly told me he's a manwhore," Lara murmured. "Likable, but definitely slutty. But you can't go around telling everyone I'm your fiancée."

"I haven't given up yet. We should know in a couple of weeks. I'm looking at it optimistically. I think you're pregnant and we'll be getting married." He leaned over and kissed the top of her head. "If not, I'm willing to keep trying."

That shouldn't have warmed Lara's heart. Damn it, he'd plotted to steal her secrets. He'd deceived her. He'd violated her trust. Yeah, he'd also apologized more than once, comforted her, spoken what was in his heart, and told her that he loved her. Her head warned her that giving in and giving him another chance would be stupid. Her stubborn heart wanted to throw all caution to the wind.

The nurse stopped in front of one of the rooms about halfway to the outer door. "This is her room. Looks like Maxine is still outside. This is her roommate, Mrs. Simms. She's recovering from a bout of pneumonia so she stayed inside. Do you need to see Maxine's license or her social security card? She's from Ukraine, but she's been in the States since she was a young woman. I find it hard to believe she's in some kind of trouble." The nurse stepped in and opened a nightstand drawer. "Her paperwork is in here somewhere."

"We can ask her about that," Dax said.

The nurse shook her head. "You might find that hard. Some days her dementia is worse than others."

"Hey, come over here." The curtain that separated the two sides of the bedroom shook. "Come here."

"I'll be there in a moment, Mrs. Simms. I'm helping these people right now." She moved to the small wardrobe, opening it up.

Lara glanced around the curtain. "Can I help you?"

A frail looking woman lay on the bed, reaching out a trembling arm that looked as fragile as a matchstick. "You're here for Nata?"

Lara's eyes widened and she stepped behind the curtain. Mrs. Simms knew that Maxine was really Natalia? "Yes."

"They watch her. She says she can feel them watching her. Did they kill her?" Her voice came out on a shaky breath.

Lara shook her head. "No. She's fine. Does she think someone's going to kill her?"

The old lady nodded. "She's a little crazy, but who isn't? She made me promise her if she died I would give the authorities— Wait, are you the authorities?"

She nodded vaguely. "My coworker and fiancé can show you his paperwork."

Since Connor had floated that cover story, she figured she'd better stay consistent. Not that she enjoyed saying that they were engage. Well, not much.

"Swell." The gray-haired woman looked around as if to see if they were being watched. "Nata made me promise that if she died I would give the authorities the note."

"Note?"

"Yes, but if she's fine, I can't give it to you."

Another note. Lara paused, wondering if this woman would nap or head down to dinner soon, something so she could search the room. That note had to be important. Or perhaps they could persuade Natalia to give it to them. What kind of secrets had she kept all these years?

"I'm going to talk to her now," Lara said. "It was nice to meet you."

"She's not bad. I don't know why they watch her. A woman needs her privacy. But they're always watching and looking. Perverts, I tell you."

Maybe Natalia wasn't the only one with a little dementia. She was still talking to herself as Lara walked back to Natalia's section of the room. Connor was looking at Maxine's supposed paperwork.

He looked back up at the nurse. "This isn't enough. I'm going to need to talk to her."

"All right, but don't forget I told you so. If she slips into whatever language she speaks, just wait. She comes back to English eventually." The woman in scrubs sighed and led them back out.

"What note was the woman talking about?" Connor asked, leaning over to whisper in her ear.

"I don't know. She said it was something Nata told her to give up in case she died. According to her, people watch Natalia. Why? If the Russians know where she is, why wouldn't they take her out?"

Connor led her through the door and out into the garden. There were several people in wheelchairs, a few caregivers. "Could be a couple of reasons."

"She's out by the pond." The nurse pointed to a small duck pond where a woman sat on a bench.

"Thank you." Connor nodded to the nurse.

Dax gave her a wink. "Hopefully I'll see you on the way out."

"Count on it." The nurse sighed a little as she walked away.

Dax shrugged. "She could be helpful."

Yes, she would likely be very helpful to his penis. She shook her head and started toward where Natalia Kuilikov sat. "Ms. Sava?"

The woman sitting on the bench turned slightly. "Yes? You have my tea?" She might have been in the States for a long time, but she still had a heavy Russian accent. "I hope it's not cold this time. Tea should be hot. We're not barbarians."

"I'm sorry." Lara moved to the seat beside her. "I don't have any tea. May I sit with you?"

She turned her patrician nose up. "If you must. It would have been more polite if you had brought the tea."

Lara studied the woman who seemed to be at the heart of the mystery that had upended her entire life. Her dark hair was now streaked with gray, but she kept it in a neat bun at the back of her head. While many of the other residents wore robes and pajamas, Natalia was dressed in slacks, a neat white shirt, and a tidy cardigan.

"Ms. Sava, I'm a reporter. I run a blog about politics. I came here this afternoon to ask you a few questions. These are my friends." Connor and Dax stepped from behind the bench.

Natalia's eyes widened and she stood. For a moment, she thought the older woman was going to walk away, but then she stepped forward, and she wrapped her hands around Connor's arms. "My Sergei, he send you."

Lara went absolutely still, the sound of that one name bringing everything to a halt. Sergei.

Connor had gone still, too. He looked down at the small woman and nodded. "Yes. He sent me. I hope you know he sends you his regards."

She smiled like the heavens had opened up. "I knew one day he would come for me. My sweet Sergei."

Lara started to open her mouth to ask a question, but Dax shook his head and gestured for her to move away from Natalia.

Suddenly she felt as if the situation had gotten infinitely more dangerous.

Connor glanced over at her and gave her an almost imperceptible nod in Dax's direction, silently telling her to leave this to him. She moved behind the bench and found herself in Dax's grip. He pulled her close, whispering into her ear.

"Stay quiet. We don't want anything to pull her out of the delusion. Let Connor do his thing. He's good at this," Dax whispered.

Connor sat down beside Natalia, easing her back down to the bench.

She started chatting away, patting his arm as though they were close friends. Unfortunately, she was speaking rapid-fire Russian.

He held a hand up. "Please, Natalia. You know Sergei would want us to keep our covers. In English, please."

She nodded. "His English is very good, don't you think? He is the smartest of men. It's how he can do what he does."

What does he do? The question was right there on the tip of her tongue. She wanted to shout it, to scream it out, but that would likely give away Connor's game.

"Sergei can do anything," Connor agreed. "But he's concerned about you."

Natalia's skin flushed and she sniffled a bit. "I still love him. I never stopped. How could I? I also understand that we can't be together again until he has finished the job he started so long ago. I miss him. Tell him I miss him every single day."

"I will," Connor replied, his eyes steady on Natalia. He practically radiated assurance. "He misses you as well. He wants to thank you for all the work you've put in. But we're a bit worried."

He was so subtle. He never said anything that might make the woman suspicious. He was good. He knew when to smile, when to pat her hand. He knew exactly how to play her, but then Lara had seen Connor at work before. He'd known exactly how to play her, too.

Except he wasn't always smooth. Sometimes, he could even be obnoxious. He would have played her better if he'd kept up the Niall identity, said the pics he'd shared of himself online were from a few years back and he'd taken up a personal training regimen or something. Why hadn't he approached her in that fashion? She would have fallen into his hands a lot quicker. She wouldn't have been so distant in the beginning with him.

"What does he have to be worried about?" Natalia frowned. "Everyone who could have stopped us has been taken care of. We took care of the woman when we needed to. And that bitch. Yes. It was good to take care of her. What was her name? I should remember."

Was she talking about Joy Hayes?

"This is the problem, Natalia. Your memory is fading and that could be bad for us."

"I remember the important things."

"That's for me to decide. I'm going to ask you a few questions and I want you to answer them to the best of your ability. What is Sergei's last name?"

Lara reached into her pocket and touched the button on her phone to record the conversation. She'd come prepared so they wouldn't miss anything, but she'd forgotten about it until now. Connor glanced her way and nodded to let her know they were now being recorded.

Dax's stared into the distance, scanning their surroundings. He was there to do what Connor couldn't while he was so focused. Dax was searching for a threat, ready to defend them.

"Of course his last name is . . ." She stopped. "They change so many times. My Sergei's name is always changing right in front of my face. Why do they hide him from me?" She sighed, then continued her rant in Russian.

Lara fought back disappointment. At least she could take the recording to a translator. They might not know what Natalia said now, but they would know at some point. Anything could be helpful.

"Natalia, I told you, in English," Connor said with just a hint of sharpness.

It seemed to bring her out of whatever place she'd gone to in her head. "I'm sorry. It is so hard because I want to go home. It has been so long. So long. I am getting older now, but my Sergei will still bring them all down. He will destroy this country as he was meant to do. These new people are wrong. They seek to make money, but there is a greater purpose. He will fulfill his destiny because he is a great man. When he stands over the rubble, all will know him and they will understand what we sacrifice for our people. I will watch with pride."

Natalia spoke with the fervency of a true believer. Destroy the country? It made Lara's gut clench. Something terrible was going to happen. Something they had to stop.

"Are you going to kill me now?" Natalia asked the question with all the emotion of a woman asking about the weather.

"No. Why would you say that?" Connor asked.

"Because you always watch me. Because you're never far from where I am. I do not know if you are here to protect me or to kill me.

Perhaps either, as need be. I have, how do you say, insurance policy. If I die, your secrets will not be safe."

Connor's head came up and he flashed a look Dax's way.

That was the precise moment she heard the whirring ping and saw Natalia's body buck. Connor dove to the side, and Lara found herself facedown in the grass. She tried to look around. Connor had been sitting right next to Natalia. Had he been hit? Her heart threatened to stop at the very thought. No. Connor couldn't get hit. He was too smart, too good at his job. He couldn't be hurt. She needed him too much.

"He's across the pond," Dax said, his voice eerily calm. "I saw the glint of his rifle. I think he's on the move."

"We don't know that. He could be aiming for another target."

Lara didn't need an interpreter to know that Connor meant her. If that was the *Bratva*, they'd been after her, too. Maybe she was a loose end they wanted to tie up.

Connor crawled to her, his SIG in hand. She couldn't see all of him. She needed to get her hands on him, make sure he was okay. What had she been thinking when she'd tried to keep her distance? Hadn't she had enough proof that life was way too short?

"Keep down, Lara. I'm going to get you out of this," he vowed.

"I think Natalia was the target," Dax said. "I've got a decent line of sight and he's moving west toward the parking lot."

Reason punched through her anxiety. They'd just gotten a woman killed and the man who'd done it was getting away. The only person who might be able to tell them what Natalia had meant was fleeing the scene. "No. We have to get the shooter. We have to catch him. We don't have enough information. We don't know how she's connected."

"No."

"Connor, please." The guy was likely getting away right at that moment. "I'm fine."

"I could go," Dax offered.

"Don't move, Dax. I'm calling in every favor you've ever owed me."

"This is not a move they would have applauded at the Agency, brother."

Connor cursed. "I know but she's more important than anything."

Dax stayed right where he was and Connor joined them, both men covering her.

"Don't move. We've got some cover here in case he comes back to finish the job." Dax moved his hand. She couldn't see what he was doing but she heard him a moment later. "There's been a shooting at the Serenity nursing home. Yes, you heard me right. We need police and at least one ambulance. Hurry."

Lara raised her head up as much as she could. "Natalia?"

"She's dead." Connor gently forced her head back down. "It was professional. One between the eyes."

Maybe the assassin wasn't the only person who possibly could help them decipher what Natalia had said. The odd conversation she'd had with Mrs. Simms came back to her in a flash. "We have to get back to her room before the cops get here. They'll take the evidence."

"Evidence?"

"Natalia left a note with her roommate in the event of her death. That may have been the insurance policy she mentioned. Mrs. Simms thought that was why we'd come here in the first place." Adrenaline flooded her system. "Please. We need to get it. I can convince her to give it to us."

Connor cursed under his breath. "Dax, watch my back. If I go down, you protect her. Fuck the note." He got to his knees and then lifted her up into his arms, turning immediately. He held her close and started to run.

He was offering himself as a target, his strong, broad back protecting her completely. Chaos was starting to erupt as one of the nurses realized something had gone terribly wrong. Shouts began and several residents were crying, but Connor plowed on. He simply sprinted toward the building and inside. He didn't put her down until they were in Natalia's room, and then he stood guard alongside Dax.

Lara stepped inside. Mrs. Simms's eyes widened as Lara threw back the curtain.

"I'm afraid I'm going to need that note now."

SIXTEEN

Connor closed and locked the door, feeling safer than he had in days. Passing that damn note over to Roman had been a relief. It had taken hours to get the cops off his back, but he hadn't wanted that note in his house. He didn't want it anywhere near Lara.

"I can't believe you handed it over to him," Lara complained as she picked up a very hyperactive Lincoln and hustled him to the backyard. She let him out and closed the door behind him before frowning and turning Connor's way.

If he didn't smooth things over, he would be in the proverbial doghouse right next to Lincoln. "I explained why."

"Because Roman can get a translator faster than you. You're CIA, Connor. This kind of stuff should be your stock-in-trade."

"Ex-CIA." Now he could see that it would have been more helpful to quit after this case was over, but the damage had been done. "My security clearance has already been torched and I already called in favors for the INS paperwork. I'm sorry, princess. I'm afraid I'm a civilian now."

"You'll never be a civilian, Connor. You were born a warrior."

And she was a woman who wanted peace for the world. "Unfortunately, I don't speak Russian and that whole note was written in Cyrillic."

She turned a little thoughtful. "It looked like a list to me."

"You have to be prepared that note we risked our lives for might end up being a shopping list or a recipe for borscht. She wasn't in her right head in the end." Connor had gotten a little chill when she'd looked at him. Her eyes had lit up as though she'd known him. He'd seen recognition in those eyes.

"What do you think she meant about Sergei destroying the country?"

Again, something about that speech of hers had set off his radar. "I don't know. We'll know more after we get the translations back. That was awfully smart of you."

"No, it wasn't. You handed my phone over. Now I don't have one, Connor." She let Lincoln back in and locked the door before stalking his way, her flats slapping against his marbled floors in obvious irritation. "And we didn't risk our lives to get that note. You risked *your* life. You made sure that if the assassin took another shot, he would have killed you."

Connor shrugged. "I likely would have crushed you to death when I fell on you so your life was definitely at risk."

"Don't joke about that." She stopped right in front of him. "Why did you do that? Why did you really give up the evidence to Roman?"

He'd known what he would do the minute she'd shown him that odd, handwritten note Mrs. Simms had given her. He hadn't wanted her to hold on to it. He hadn't wanted her to be the target. There was no way he would be able to keep her out of the investigation forever, but she didn't have to be the person holding the evidence. When he'd dropped Dax off at Roman's, he'd made the decision to put a couple of layers of protection around Lara. There was no way he could take her off the case completely. She would walk away from him and still be in danger. But he could make sure that she wasn't the primary target.

Roman had been more than happy to take on the task.

"I did it so they won't come after you. They can shift their focus now."

"The *Bratva*?"

"Yes, the Russian mob who keeps sending assassins your way." The minute he'd realized Natalia Kuilikov was dead, his one and only thought had been getting to Lara. It hadn't been Natalia he'd seen in that moment. He'd seen Lara's beautiful face with a bullet hole, her unique light snuffed out. He'd gone a little crazy. His first thought should have been finding the assassin and bringing him in for questioning, but nothing had mattered more than getting to her, putting his body over hers so he took any bullet coming her way. He'd been willing to die, to let Dax die, and now to put Roman in harm's way all in order to protect one woman.

Having feelings sucked. It had been easier when he didn't care.

"It begs the question . . ." Lara began, her eyes turning thoughtful.

He didn't like how focused she was on this case. She'd been perfect with the police. She'd charmed them and gotten teary at exactly the right times. Her hand had been in his, but the minute the detectives released them, she'd pounced all over the case again. It was making him crazy. "What question?"

"They knew where she was."

He'd thought about that, too. "It's possible they followed us."

"Do you really believe that? Even her roommate talked about the fact that she thought they were watching her. She said she knew they were always around her. Why would they know she was there but never act?"

"Until we showed up." He'd thought about it on the drive home.

"Why not just kill her? Why wait until she could possibly talk?"

He knew why the Agency would do it. "Two reasons. First, her 'insurance policy,' whatever that turns out to be. Second, there's a certain honor among thieves."

"What does that mean?"

How to explain it to her? "I was in the same business, just an opposite side of the coin. If an agent knew something so important that the country's stability was at stake, one of two things would happen. Either the Agency would immediately and with all due care put the operative down, or they would watch and wait. It might be a sign of respect that they've hidden her. She talked about what she sacrificed. If that's true and they respected what she did for the cause, they might let her be until such time as she threatened the operation. Me sitting beside her threatened the operation. They would have known about her mental condition. They would have understood the possibility that she could talk to someone she shouldn't. She was dead the moment we struck up a conversation with her. They let her live until she became a liability. The other thought I had was that she was important to Sergei, whoever that is. Maybe her long-lost husband, maybe a lover? He was willing to let her live until he couldn't afford it anymore. Hopefully, we'll know more when we translate that tape and her note." He took her hands. "Lara, we should sit down and talk for a while. Let me make us a drink."

She stared at him warily. "About what?"

Was she really going to push him to the limit? "Us."

She pulled away. "Talking doesn't change anything."

Did she think on any level that he would allow her to walk away without really talking about what had happened between them? "Sit down, Lara. We're going to discuss what happens from here on out."

"I don't want to talk." She moved into his space, her body slinking up to his. There was no other word to describe it. Her breasts pressed up, her legs tangled with his. "I want what I talked about earlier. It's time for bed, Connor. It's time to get what you promised me."

"What I promised you?"

"You said I could be with you while I'm here." She pressed her chest against his and met his stare. "I don't want to sleep alone tonight. I want to forget everything from the last two days. I just want to feel for a while."

She sank her fingers into his hair and leaned in, her mouth so close to his. He couldn't wait. He kissed her long and slow. She might think she didn't care about him or could fuck him out of her system, but she was fooling herself. The minute she let him in, he would hold on to her so tight. The real Lara was underneath all the hurt and he intended to find her.

Pleasure. Intimacy. They were gifts he could give her. She wouldn't be able to hold back. If she thought he would just throw her against the wall and fuck her hard, she was so wrong. He intended to show her just how good it could be between them. He intended to make it so good she would never want to leave him.

The minute her mouth softened, he invaded. He breached her with his tongue, sliding deep to find hers. She was tentative at first, almost shy. After a moment's sweet coaxing, she moaned into the kiss and gave as good as she got.

Sex had always been a bodily function. Something Connor required, but still a pleasure to be had and forgotten. With her it was as necessary as breathing, something to sink into and savor, a pleasure to build on and protect. He let himself go, forgot about all the problems they still faced, and focused on the only thing of importance—comforting her.

She wanted to be out of her head. He could give her that.

"Show me your breasts," he whispered along her lips. His cock was already hard and wanting, but he ignored it for the moment. The horny bastard wasn't in charge yet.

She sat up on his lap and grabbed the hem of her shirt. She dragged it over her head and tossed it aside. A plain white bra covered her breasts. Odd that he'd seen some of the world's most beautiful women in expensive lingerie, but Lara Armstrong in cotton called to him. It had nothing to do with the packaging and everything to do with the way she glowed. The day's events had dimmed her light, but he was going to make damn sure to stoke it back to life.

He raised his hand to the silky skin of her neck, trailing down to just above her breast. "You are the most beautiful woman in the world."

She shook her head. "Now I know you're lying."

He forced her to look at him. "No matter what else happens between us, I'm going to make you believe this. You are the most beautiful thing I ever have or ever will see. I'm crazy about you."

"Connor, my face is puffy. I know what I look like when I cry."

"You look like a real woman." He cupped her breast through the bra, her nipple already hard against his palm. It was good to know her nipples still liked him. "I know you're confused about what happened yesterday and you want to lump me in with Kiki and Tom, but I've never hidden the real me from you. Yes, I didn't tell you my real name or why I was there. But the man falling in love with you was absolutely real."

Her lower lip came out in the sexiest pout. "And Niall?"

She was never going to forget that. Gabe had warned him . . . "That was the Internet. It doesn't count. Even then I think I knew. That's why I didn't come to you as Niall. I wanted to come to you as me. I wanted you to like me, to need me."

"You can be an asshole." But her chest was rising, forcing her breast into his hand like a kitten begging for a stroke.

"Yes. See, no lies there. I would have had an easier time if I'd put on a mask, but I wanted you to see the real me in all my fucked-up glory. Take off the bra."

She sat up in his lap, reaching to the back of her bra. "You're very bossy."

At least she was starting to relax. He could see it in the way her lips had begun to curl up when she spoke. "I like being the boss of you."

She let the bra drop and almost immediately her back arched, offering up those gorgeous breasts to him. "You're so not the boss of me."

He reached and tweaked one of those perfect nipples. "I am here."

"What if I want to be the boss?" Lara asked on a shaky breath.

Just the idea made his gut twist. There was emotional vulnerability and then there was the primal fear of being truly, physically vulnerable.

She cupped his face. "I was just joking, Connor."

There was his Lara. She was looking at him with such openness. He took a breath to ease back into the moment. She'd talked to him.

Maybe it was time to really talk to her. "Take off your pants and I'll tell you what happened to me."

She was off his lap in a heartbeat, her eagerness a balm to the wounds of the day. "You said your last girlfriend hurt you."

Oh, she was so good at making things sound better than they really were. "She wasn't my girlfriend, princess. She was a coworker and she turned out to be a double agent."

Her eyes were wide as she kicked off the rest of her clothes and stood naked in front of him. "Double agent?"

He adored how unselfconscious she was. Most women would be posing to their advantage or begging for compliments, but for Lara, nakedness was just another state of being. He intended to keep her naked as much as possible. Just being able to look at her, to know he was the only man in her life, soothed in ways he hadn't thought possible. "Come here."

He tugged her into his lap and breathed in her scent.

"Connor? Double agent? Like she was spying for someone else?"

"Oh, yes." Now that she was naked in his arms, he didn't want to talk about his idiocy. But he'd promised. "We were tracking down an urban terrorist cell in Europe. We posed as a couple for about six months."

"So you had a relationship with her."

He toyed with her nipples. Such pretty pink buds. Everything about her fascinated him. "Take your hair down for me. I like it down. And no, I didn't have a relationship with her. We fucked. It was nothing but an itch to scratch. Nothing like what I feel for you."

Her hair tumbled around her shoulders and down her back. "I'm not an itch?"

He gathered her close, her hair tangling them together. "You're my everything." He slid his hand between her legs. "So just before we busted the cell in Berlin, she seduced me. She said she wanted one more night and I didn't notice the knife in her hand until she carved up my chest with it. She was on top of me, riding away. I watched her climax. After she'd stabbed me."

"Connor." Gaping, Lara tried to sit up.

"Don't move. I'm only getting through this story because you're soft and sweet in my arms. Spread your legs and let me touch you." She complied and he stroked down her thighs before continuing. "The only reason I survived was she left the knife in. If she'd removed it, I would have bled out. She didn't and I played dead. I managed to hold that knife in until they got me to the ER. Five months later I tracked her down. I ended her. I still need to be in control during sex but I want to give you everything you need."

She shook her head. "Right now, I don't need anything but you."

And later? Stubborn thing. "You have me for as long as you want."

"Then make me forget, Connor. I don't think I can sleep tonight without replaying what happened today in my head."

He stood up, sweeping her into his arms. "Then I'll give you something else to think about."

He carried her to his bedroom, ready to pour himself, heart and soul, into her.

Lara didn't have much time to look around. Connor practically raced through his mansion of a home. She'd purposefully not studied it before. She hadn't wanted to see the real him, didn't want to know any more about the man. She'd been afraid to get too attached. Now she had no idea how she could possibly escape it.

She really was an idiot.

He strode through French doors and into what had to be the master bedroom. It looked to be bigger than her apartment. She had a glimpse of a sitting area before he moved to the bed. She would bet he'd hired an interior designer. The space was utterly masculine, with dark woods and deep tones. It reminded her of a very elegant lair. The perfect home for a predator.

But this particular predator had been awfully sweet to her tonight.

He laid her out on the bed. "Put your arms above your head and keep them there. No moving allowed."

She looked up at him. She was completely naked while he was still in his T-shirt and jeans and boots. "I thought we were going to . . ." She'd started to say *make love*. She wasn't sure that wasn't exactly what they were about to do, but she wasn't ready to use the word *love* around him yet. ". . . have sex."

The look in his eyes told her he suspected what she'd thought, but he was letting it go for now. "You want me to take you out of your head for a while. I'll do that, but I'll do it my way. Hands over your head. Don't move. If you can't keep your hands to yourself, I'll find a way to tie them down."

Her body was already heating up in anticipation of what he intended to do to her. She was surprised she didn't hate the idea of being tied up by him. It was all a question of trust. She trusted him with her body, her life, her pleasure.

Could she trust him with her heart?

She let her arms drift overhead, her fingertips brushing the railing of the headboard. Cool metal flashed against her palms as she gripped two of them. She had a feeling she would need to hold on to something.

"Bring your knees up and spread your legs. I want you open for me." She did as he asked. "What's going on, Connor?"

"Stay like that. I'll be right back." He stepped away.

She stared up at the ceiling. What was he doing? He was giving her too much time to think. She turned slightly and looked at the nightstand. It was empty with the exception of an elegant table lamp. It was obvious he'd bought the best of everything, but there was something cold to his furnishings. There were no pictures or knickknacks. No gifts or souvenirs proudly displayed.

"Close your eyes," he commanded.

A little panic threatened. It was still so close. She could still see

Kiki, still hear the gun firing off, still hear Natalia slumping to her death and smell the acrid scent of blood. "I can't."

"You can." His tone was deep and dark, cajoling her to do his bidding. "I don't want you to think. I just want you to feel."

She took a deep breath and closed her eyes. Maybe if he kept talking, she could concentrate on his voice. "Why did you buy this place?"

The bed dipped as he sat beside her. The anticipation was going to kill her. "I needed a place near work."

"Your work was all over the world." She could feel her body tightening, waiting for that moment when his warm hands would stroke across her skin. "It would have been easier to get an apartment. Less upkeep."

"I wasn't worried about the upkeep. I was worried about showing my father how well I've done and just how much I could buy with his money. Don't scream, princess."

Something cold touched her right nipple and it nearly took her breath away. She couldn't help it. Her eyes flew open. Connor was running a piece of ice around her areola. She shivered. "That's so cold."

"But this isn't." He leaned over and sucked her nipple into his mouth, giving her the hard edge of his teeth. The sensation raced along her skin, flaring out and making her squirm. He licked her and then lifted his head, dark eyes staring down at her. "Are you thinking about anything but me right now?"

She shook her head.

"Then stop complaining." He brought the ice cube to her lips, dragging it across her mouth. "I have a couple of fun things to do before we get to the main event, so to speak. Everly packed for you. I asked her to make sure she didn't miss the very important items in your nightstand."

She gasped as she realized what he was talking about. "Oh my god, how did you know about that?"

He winked and reached down to the side of the bed, coming up with her small pink vibrator. "Princess, I snoop. It's my job and my nature. And do you have any idea what kind of fantasies I had about you and this little wand? I like it. It's your fairy princess wand. I'm going to use it to grant a wish."

She was fairly certain her whole body was on fire with embarrassment. He'd known about her little wand. She'd bought it on a whim. She'd gone to her cousin's bachelorette party. There had been a woman selling erotic toys and after a couple of margaritas, she'd ordered a little pink wand vibrator. She'd only tried it once and had discovered it didn't really work on her.

She wasn't going to tell Connor that. For some reason she didn't want to stop him. He was relaxed, happier than he'd been before. That made her happier. And she wanted to know the rest of his story. He never talked about himself. Anytime she asked, he cleverly turned the conversation back to her.

He skated the ice cube down her torso, every inch making her shiver and groan. He grazed it down and she stiffened when it hit her clitoris and he stroked cool circles around her little bud.

"Did your dad like it? This house, I mean." Every word was a pant. She had to force them out because he was slowly driving her mad.

He slid the rapidly melting cube along her labia while his free hand brushed her nipples. "He never saw it. Once he'd given me what I asked for, I never actually talked to him again. He died a couple of years back."

She watched as he pulled the ice from her pussy and brought it right to his mouth. He licked it and sucked it like it was the richest ice cream ever. "What did you ask for?"

"Twenty million." He brought the vibe closer, twisting it and putting it on a low hum. "My father was a congressman. Unfortunately, he started life as a drug dealer. That's how he met my mother. By the time I found him, he'd turned his life around and his father had sold the family ranch for a hundred million. Turns out it was sitting on prime development land and on top of one of the largest natural gas reserves in the country. He'd gone legit and married and had his two-point-five kids. I blackmailed him."

From what she understood, he'd been left in a terrible position. His mother had been a drug addict. He'd been a child trying to make his way in the world. So smart. So ambitious, but other than his friends, so alone. He'd had to teach himself. She'd had two loving parents. She'd had a family to support her and teach her how to love.

The last day or two, she hadn't been putting her knowledge to good use.

How would Connor love? Would he stumble and fall like a child needing guidance? The love would still be pure, but there would be a learning curve. Could a man like that make a terrible mistake and try to correct it with all his heart?

The vibrator hummed in his hand, but when he looked down at her, his face was blank. "Are you shocked by that? I took twenty million dollars from him. I signed a document stating that I wasn't his son and would never contact him again."

How much of his heart had that cost him? Her poor, sweet Connor. He had a cold home, bought with blood money. He spent his life protecting without ever receiving an ounce of warmth. Only his friends had given him a safe place.

It struck her quite suddenly that was exactly what he sought. A safe place. He'd been a lonely boy and then an outsider even among his friends. He'd found a place in the world with the CIA, but it had pushed him further to the outside.

Peace. He'd said he wanted peace in exchange for the work he'd done.

He'd quit his job and asked her to marry him. He'd offered her the one thing that was very likely sacred to him. A child who would never know want the way he had. A child who would need a father.

She looked up at him and realized that if she rejected him again and pushed him away for what he'd done in service to his friends and country, they could very likely be over. They would go back to being polite strangers who went their own ways after the case was solved.

Lara had hit a fork in the road. She could protect herself. She could ensure that he never had the ability to hurt her again. In some ways, she could have her revenge on him for hurting her in the first place.

Screw the world. I need you. I need you to be Lara . . .

He'd said he needed her, all but pleading for the parts of herself she'd always valued. Warmth and affection. Forgiveness. Kindness. Love. She'd found an endless well for people she barely knew. Didn't the man she loved deserve all those things from her and more? Yes, real love, intimate love, was so much harder than giving charity to a stranger or even hugging a friend, but she'd never been one to shrink from a challenge.

"Baby, I think you should have gone for an even thirty million," she replied with a little smile. "Though I do hope you gave some to charity. I know some really nice people who help recovering addicts get back on their feet."

He stared down at her and she could practically feel his relief. "Whatever you want, princess. It's all yours. And next time I blackmail someone, I'll make sure to talk to you before I set a price. You're quite ruthless."

Okay, maybe he'd misunderstood. "Connor, I was joking. You can't blackmail people." She started to talk about how he could achieve his goals without blackmail, but he flicked the vibrator on and placed it against her clit until she could barely think anymore.

"What was that?" Connor asked with a decadent grin as he moved the wand in soothing circles. "I couldn't hear you over the hum. See, when you start lecturing me, I'll just ensure you're too busy to speak."

"I'll find a way," she managed on a shaky breath. "I'm very determined. I chained myself to a park tree when I was eight years old. They were going to tear it down but I knew a family of squirrels lived there. Actually, they were trying to tear it down to build a public water park, and I argued so well at city council that they changed the plans. Yeah, I was unpopular in school."

He laughed, one of those rare, genuine Connor laughs that she hoarded like gold because he only ever seemed to laugh like that around her. "I can imagine it's difficult being a preteen crusader." He moved the wand all around, upping the hum and causing her whole body to tighten. "I was a preteen pessimist, so we're an odd pair."

She couldn't miss the way he relished saying those words. Her hands tightened around the bars of the headboard. Her feet dug into the comforter. So close. She was so close.

And then he pulled the vibe away.

Her eyes flew open. "You're a sadist."

He moved between her legs, settling himself on his belly, his face hovering over her pussy. "No. I'm a patient man and you are a very impatient woman. I think I'm going to do the adult equivalent of your squirrel rescue. I'll chain you to my bed until you promise to marry me."

"Why marriage?" She watched as he lowered his mouth and placed a reverent kiss on her flesh. "We could date for a while. We haven't known each other very long."

"Because when it's right, it's right. Because I've waited my whole life to find you and I want to start our future now." He licked at her, and her skin seemed to fire off, pleasure building like a grenade about to explode.

She could read between the lines. He'd waited his whole life for someone to call his own. He'd likely not even thought it would happen. He'd assumed he was cursed to be alone and now that he'd found the woman he wanted, he would move to secure her like the ruthless tactician he was. He wouldn't feel safe in a casual relationship. He would want her bound to him in every way possible. It was simply the way Connor Sparks was built.

"Tell me you love me," she murmured.

He jerked his head up, his hands tightening around her legs like he was a little worried this was a trap. Still, he didn't shirk or shy away. "I love you. I love you so fucking much. I love every inch of you, and the next time you want to save a family of bushy-tailed rodents, I'll take care of everyone who tries to stop you."

They were going to have to work on his violent tendencies. "I love you, too."

"Marry me." He wasn't a man to take a small victory when he could push for the end of the war.

And it was a futile battle. "You know I will."

"You won't regret it." He smiled, a wolfish expression, and then the wand was back. He placed it right on her clit and turned that sucker on. "I'll make sure you don't."

He speared her with his tongue, fucking up inside her while he stimulated her little nubbin. She went off like a rocket, her whole body bowing with the pleasure.

After a moment, he kissed her one last time and she felt him leave the bed, turning off the wand. She kept her eyes closed, reveling in the way her body felt. Only one man could ever make her feel like this—languid and beautiful, weak for him, but oh so strong.

She'd made her decision. It might be silly, but she didn't want to live in a world without him. Love required a leap of faith, and holding out on him wouldn't change the fact that she was hopelessly, irrevocably in love with Connor Sparks.

Had he been standing with her in Kiki's apartment, there would have been no negotiation. There would have been no playing the odds and deciding he couldn't save her. He would have placed himself between her and that bullet, and nothing would have made him move. Tom might have thought he loved her, but Connor had been right. With men, actions spoke louder than words.

"I forgive you." He needed to hear the words. "I won't hold the way we met against you. We'll move on from here together."

She felt the bed dip again and then heard an odd *snick* of a sound.

"And I trust you, Lara. I trust you more than anyone in the world. Help me get past my fear. I don't want anything between us."

She sat up and found Connor laid out beside her, his gorgeous body on display. His hands were over his head and he'd locked them to the headboard with a pair of silver handcuffs.

He was utterly open and vulnerable to her.

She looked at her gorgeous man, at every scar he wore on his body and the ones no one could see.

She would prove to him that he was safe with her.

SEVENTEEN

Connor hated being vulnerable and thought about the fact that he could probably break the bed, but he'd gone too far with the cuffs. Way too far. He couldn't pull them apart. He couldn't drag himself out and that made him damn near crazy. What had he been thinking?

Lara looked down at him, her eyes wide, and his dick didn't seem to have the same PTSD he had. His cock was straining, preening under her hot gaze. The damn thing reached almost to his navel and he could feel it weeping, wanting to come.

She'd said she would marry him. He'd won her back. Both his relief and his joy were epic. But he knew they wouldn't be complete until he gave her something she needed: his trust. Lara Armstrong needed to know she was the only one in the world he would give control to.

She placed a hand over his chest, her lips curling up in the sweetest smile he'd ever seen. "I think you picked me for my belief in nonviolence."

He'd never really known anyone like her. She was unique in his world. "I picked you because you're you."

She leaned over and pressed a kiss to his chest, just above his nipple. "You don't ever have to worry about me hurting you, Connor." Her tongue laved over his skin and he bit back a groan. "Though I will admit I've come to have a fondness for certain forms of torment. What does the Geneva Convention say about sexual torture?"

"I think they're for it," he murmured as she ran her hand down his chest toward his waist. He wanted to drag her down and force her to grip his cock hard and pump him while he branded her with his mouth, but this wasn't his show.

She licked his other nipple, turning them into erogenous zones he hadn't known he had. Her hair flowed around her, creeping across his torso. It tickled and tormented him, and he wouldn't have had it any other way. He loved being trapped in her web. It was a safe place to be.

"I also have to say I've come to believe that nonviolence isn't always the best way," she said.

"Why is that, princess?" He was very still under her ministrations. Her little tongue darted over his skin, tasting and licking and lighting up his flesh like a butterfly flitting from flower to flower.

"It's been a rough week, babe. We've been shot at a whole bunch. It might take me some time to get back to totally peaceful thoughts. I'd kind of like to shoot Tom."

His hands tightened at the sound of the other man's name. "He didn't love you, Lara."

She kissed along his jawline, her hand brushing up against his cock. "You're right. I was never safe with him. Even when you were lying to me, I was safe with you."

He groaned as she ran her tongue along his lower lip. "Always."

"I think I figured out that we all wear masks sometimes." She got to her knees, staring down at him. "Kiki blindsiding me was partially my fault. I never really scratched below her surface or I would have seen her anger."

Now he really wanted use of his hands so he could tug her close.

"It wasn't your fault and she wasn't truly angry with you. Baby, why don't you let me out of these cuffs and we can talk about it."

His cock would have to wait.

A little frown crossed her lush mouth and she shook her head. "No. This is my time." She shifted, throwing a leg over his hips and straddling him. "She harbored some definite anger at the world. I didn't really listen to her the way I should have, or I would have heard it and tried to get her help. I definitely wouldn't have let Tom use her the way he did. He used us both." She paused. "You used me, too. But you didn't do it to advance yourself. I'm trying to tell you that I know you're not like Tom. The things you've done in the past have been to protect other people, Connor. It was noble."

He could feel her heat and it was killing him, but he couldn't lie to her. He never wanted to lie to her again. "I wasn't, Lara."

She looked over him, her hands splaying over his chest. "You are a beautiful man, Connor Sparks. And you are a noble man, too. Some of the things you had to do were likely very unpleasant."

"Princess, I killed people."

"Bad people. You didn't run around randomly shooting anyone, Connor. You took out threats to the country. I understand. We're similar. I wanted to shoot the guy who chucked his foam coffee cup in the park the other day."

"That is not the same."

"It was. I wanted to shoot him. Well, maybe just force him to eat the foam and see how it tastes, but I digress. In our own way, we both want to make the world a better place. Tom didn't." Against him, she started to rock her hips, rubbing her slick flesh against his cock. "He just wanted to get ahead."

"It's not too late. I could kill Tom for you. That would make the world a better place."

She wrinkled her nose. "You're out of the killing business. And I might be out of the tabloid business. I think I can find a better way to make a difference. I liked the whole detective thing. I think we can have a family-owned firm. I can investigate on the computer and you do what you do best, go out and take down the bad guys."

She was wrong about him. What he'd done hadn't been noble. He'd gone to the CIA so he'd have a better life than his shithole childhood. But that didn't mean he couldn't change. In fact, he could feel himself changing now. He'd looked for a home all his life, bought grand houses and told himself he'd made it. Home wasn't a place. It was her. It was her and her fugly dog and her fairy princess ideas that were making him a better person. For so long he'd been the Agency's operative. It was how he'd defined himself.

Now he had a new definition. He was going to be Lara Sparks's husband. And that was all he wanted in the world. If she wanted to use his skills to make the world better, he would be her operative, her protector, her everything.

"I think that's a great idea, princess. You know what's a better one? Penetration." He flexed his hips because he was almost there.

She slid down his body. "Not yet."

She was really going to kill him. "You should know I intend to get you back. I'll have you screaming for me."

Her mouth hovered over his straining cock. "I always scream for you. I thought I'd be more ladylike. Let's see if I can get you to beg."

His eyes rolled back as she sucked the head of his cock between those gorgeous lips of hers. Her tongue whirled around, lapping up the fluid that collected on the slit of his cock. She apparently thought he had way more pride than he did when it came to her. "Please, Lara. Please fuck me, princess. I need you."

She licked his cock like she couldn't get enough. All the while he could feel her against his thigh. She was wet and hot and so ready he was aching for her. "I need you, too. The problem is you taste really good."

Her words hummed along his skin, making him quake. "I don't want to come in your mouth."

She cupped his balls with one hand while she gave his cock another lick. "Then don't. Don't come until I'm ready."

Definitely she was trying to kill him. This was punishment for all the times he'd taken her right to the edge and refused to allow her to go over. And he wouldn't have taken back any of it. He liked her dirty and a little vengeful. "Do your worst. If you want to make this a game, I'll make sure both of us win."

She sucked his cock between her lips, and heat engulfed him. He wanted to sink his hands in her hair and force her to take more. She was being thorough, suckling him an inch at a time before moving back up and starting the process all over again. She eased down between his legs, settling in. He groaned as she took him deeper, laving him with her tongue and giving him the barest hint of her teeth.

He hissed at the sensation but didn't really think about telling her to stop. That little pain flared through his system, and then she eased it with her lips and tongue. Lara would never hurt him. She didn't have it in her. He was absolutely certain her newfound appreciation for violence in select situations would fade in a few days and he would get to listen to her lectures again.

By then he would be out of these cuffs, and he knew just how to distract his girl and get into her pacifist panties.

"Take more. Your mouth feels so fucking good."

She worked her way down his cock, her tongue teasing him until his whole body was taut with the need to spill into her soft, sweet mouth. He held back. He wasn't going to lose this game. He wanted to be inside her when he came, wanted to mark her again and know that when she slept beside him, a piece of himself was still with her.

"Ride me, princess. It's been so long. I want you to fuck me hard. You're the only woman I'll ever make love to again. I want to give you everything I have." He knew how to get to his girl. She liked it dirty and sweet. She liked to hear the truth, and his truth was that he needed her. He'd been incomplete until the day he'd met her. "I love you, Lara. Take me. I made you mine. Make me yours."

He was already hers and he rather thought he'd been hers all of his life. He'd simply been waiting to meet her.

She got to her knees, her breasts bouncing lightly as she straddled him again. This time there was purpose to her every movement. She took his cock in hand.

"If you want, the condoms are in the bedside table." He was going to trust her. She'd given her word that she would marry him. If she needed time, he would give it to her.

She slowly started to lower herself down. "I think I'll take everything you have to give me. You're not getting any younger."

He flexed up. Even without use of his hands, he could still take a little control. "I'm young enough to handle you, princess."

She gasped as his cock invaded. "Yes, you are."

He loved how her eyes went slightly glassy, as though making love with him was a drug. He was already addicted to her. She seated herself, her pussy clenching all around him. So good. She felt so fucking good and there was nothing for him to do but enjoy her. He couldn't really take control so he was forced to focus on what she was doing to him, to really see her.

His future wife leaned back slightly as her hips rolled. Connor took her in. She looked wild, her hair rolling in waves, breasts peeking out from behind the dark tresses. Her torso flowed to a shapely waist and feminine hips. His eyes focused on the juncture of her thighs where that gorgeous pussy was currently sucking at his cock, taking him in and squeezing him tight.

She took control, setting the pace. In and out. Taking every inch of him until he couldn't think about anything except how perfectly they fit together. She bounced on top of him, pushing him further and further. He could feel her clenching all around him.

She leaned forward, using his chest as leverage as she fucked him hard. "I love you."

He wondered how long it would be before he didn't catch his breath every time she said it. "I love you, princess. I'm not waiting. We're going to Vegas."

She nodded as she pressed down against him. "We should beat Gabe and Everly to the altar."

He grinned. "I can see you're going to be very competitive. Game nights should be a blast." He bucked up, needing her so badly he couldn't wait. "I'm going to come. Now."

She ground down on him, her mouth opening on a cry as her pussy clenched all around him and he went over the edge. The orgasm exploded like a supernova and he released inside her, every pulse a pure pleasure until he had nothing left to give.

Gasping, panting, heart rate slowing, Lara fell on top of him, nestling close. "I liked being in charge."

Her hands eased over his body, soothing him.

"Don't get used to it." Bliss pulsed through his system and he could have sworn their bodies were in perfect tune. "You're going to get me out of these cuffs and then I'm going to take my turn."

She gave him a little scowl. "You already had your turn."

"The turns never stop, princess." They wouldn't as long as he was alive.

"Bossy." But she was already moving off him, grabbing the keys and releasing his hands.

The minute he was free, he pulled her close, flipping her over so he was on top. He pressed his lips to hers. "You like me bossy."

"As long as you're mine," she agreed, her arms wrapping around him.

"Always." He would never be anything else. He kissed his soon-to-be wife and proceeded to show her how good always could be.

The Oval Office
One week later

Dax Spencer stepped into the outer office with a sense of satisfaction. Connor hadn't answered his phone. Connor always answered his phone. If Dax needed something, Connor was there in a heartbeat. It had been that way since they were kids. But Dax knew it wasn't good for him to be Connor's first priority. This morning when he'd called, he'd gotten a text back explaining the honeymoon was starting early and asking if it was important.

It hadn't been. Dax had wished his friend well. Connor had found his real purpose and it wasn't the Agency. Dax could breathe easier knowing Connor wasn't off at the ends of the earth putting himself in danger.

It was time to think about heading back to work. It was time to say good-bye to his friends and hello to his ship. Maybe when he was cruising the Persian Gulf he wouldn't think about *her* every minute of every day. Maybe he wouldn't beat himself up over how completely he'd fucked up his life.

"Hello, it's Captain Spencer for the president," he said with a wink to the older of the two secretaries who ran Zack's appointments with the ruthlessness of a warrior protecting her city from the barbarian horde.

"You don't have an appointment." Mrs. O'Neal frowned his way. "And he's busy right now with his press secretary."

Dax glanced down at her desk. There was the latest edition of a tabloid sitting there with a huge picture of the president and a gorgeous brunette on his arm. He recognized her as an actress of some repute. She was stunning and just about as plastic as a woman could be without being considered a cyborg. She was so far from Zack's type.

What the hell was going on?

"He won't be with her for long," the younger receptionist said with a huff.

Mrs. O'Neal shushed her, but it was obvious neither woman approved of the president's actions.

The door opened and Elizabeth stalked out, her eyes red.

"Elizabeth, do not step foot off these grounds without a guard. Am I understood?" Zack stepped to the doorway, his eyes on Elizabeth and his tone cold enough to freeze the reflecting pool on the Mall.

Elizabeth didn't look back, merely took a deep breath. "I understand, Mr. President. I understand that you're not the man I thought you were."

"Then we're on the same page. I expect you at the two o'clock meeting. Don't be late." He looked up at Dax. "Come on back. Mrs. O'Neal, if you would tell Roman we're ready for him."

Dax managed to wait until the door closed. "What the hell was that?"

Zack was always gentle around Elizabeth. He never raised his voice to her. Dax had expected the two of them had simply been waiting for Zack to leave office before they started dating publicly.

"It's nothing," Zack said, moving to one of the two couches before the fireplace. He gestured to Dax to take the other.

"She looked really upset. And since when do you date overly Botoxed actresses?" He sat, wanting the world to shift back to something he recognized. Zack wasn't a playboy. He'd had a few girlfriends and they were always serious. He was monogamous, and the women were smart and discreet.

Zack's jaw turned into a stubborn line. "It's none of your business."

"Don't pull the president crap on me, Zack. It might work on Elizabeth, but I remember why we call you Scooter. I'm the one who carried you to the nearest ER to make sure your dick still worked so don't tell me it's none of my fucking business."

Zack stared at him for a moment and then his mouth split into a grin and he laughed. It was good to hear his friend laugh.

After a moment, Zack shook his head and sat back. "Sometimes I think my father was right to have one child and only one child. He told me when I was a kid that he wanted to put all his effort and energy into making me successful. Brothers, he told me, are just distractions. He should have mentioned that they're also pains in my ass."

"You're the dipshit who let Mad rope you into this weird family. Now tell me why Elizabeth was crying."

The smile fled in an instant. "I can't risk her."

Shit. "You think whoever killed Joy might use Elizabeth as leverage."

"Or they might just kill her outright. Until we know who this Sergei is and what he wants, I can't be too close to her. I wanted to fire her and get her as far away from me as possible, but Connor pointed out a few problems with that plan."

"If they don't believe you, she has no protection. You need to keep her close so the Secret Service can watch her. Shit. So Plastic Woman is for show?"

Zack nodded. "I'm taking a page out of Mad's playbook. I met her at the White House Correspondents' dinner a while back. I'm going to escort her to a couple of functions. Lara has promised to put it front and center on Capitol Scandals for the next few months. I'm afraid Elizabeth misunderstood my affection for her."

Bullshit. Dax ached for his friend, but he understood. "And when this is over?"

Zack sighed. "I'm afraid I just burned that bridge. But she'll be alive at the end of it. That's all I can give her."

The door opened and Roman walked in with a handful of papers. "Dax, thanks for coming on such short notice. How was the wedding? Connor's a bastard. He finally gets married and all we get is a text from Vegas?"

Dax smiled, remembering his best friend's very hasty wedding. Only Dax, and Senator and Mrs. Armstrong had been invited to the quickie wedding in Vegas, but it had still been lovely.

It had reminded him of everything he lost when he'd lost Holland.

"It was a great wedding and the senator plays a mean Texas Hold'em. Connor didn't want a lot of press. Now that he's quit, the Agency won't hide his identity anymore. But he promises to have a small family reception the next time we're all in town."

Roman sank down beside Zack. "I heard you're going back to your ship."

"It's time."

Roman slapped a piece of paper on the table between them. "I don't think so. Not yet, brother."

"What is that?"

Zack leaned forward. "The translation of the note Lara retrieved from the nursing home. Natalia's 'insurance policy.' We've also managed to get some reports on the woman now that she's dead. It appears she was working with high-level Russian intelligence at one point."

"I thought this was about the Russian mob."

"After the fall of the Soviet Union, a lot of Russian intelligence shifted to the *Bratva*. They took over much of the country. We believe at one point Natalia's husband was KGB. She was found in one of the girls' schools and turned into a prostitute at a young age. I don't know how it happened but she married, probably because she was pregnant. Then we believe her husband used her to spy on my father and everyone who came through our home in Moscow."

"Did you get translations of Lara's recording?"

"Yes. They confirm a few things we know. She talks about being moved from place to place and always having a new identity. She was tired and she says something about the regime. Apparently she didn't like the new guys. I have to assume that's the *Bratva* she's talking about," Roman said.

"She thought she knew Connor." It had been there in her eyes. The minute she'd seen Connor, they'd lit up.

Zack shrugged. "No idea. Her memory wasn't what it used to be. We'll never know. For now, we're operating on the idea that someone in the Russian mob knows something about my father that could potentially hurt me or the country. Given what a bastard my father is, it could be anything. I'm waiting for a blackmail demand."

"And the note?"

Roman turned it around. "It was a bounty list going back almost thirty years. You see the name is listed on the right. On the left is how much would be paid out to the assassin. There are twenty-three names worth over fifteen million dollars, and we believe they all have something to do with whatever is coming our way."

"You want me to investigate this?"

"Dax, look at the fourteenth name," Zack said grimly.

Dax picked up the list, a chill going through his system.

ADMIRAL HAROLD SPENCER

"My father committed suicide." He sat back, his whole world spinning.

Roman shook his head. "Did you ever really believe that? I didn't. Your father was murdered by the same people who killed Joy. Her name is the last on the list."

"And my mother's name is number eight." Zack stood up, rubbing at his head. "She died in a car accident. At least I thought she did. Now I don't know a damn thing."

Dax stared at the paper, his eyes not quite focusing. His father had known something and he'd been killed for it? The bastards had made it look like a suicide, very probably setting his father up for the scandal that made everyone believe that good man would take his life.

Maybe it was time to investigate again. Maybe he could clear his father's name.

Dax stood up. "I'm going to need you to pull some strings for me, Zack. I'm due to report in a couple of days."

"I'll handle it. You're on a special assignment for me now. I'll have credentials made for you. Anything you need, you'll have clearance for it. Dax, if we can find out why they killed your father, maybe we can figure out who killed my mother and Joy. And what their master plan might be."

Dax nodded. "And we can stop whoever's coming for you, brother."

Three hours later, he had his paperwork and his bags packed. He turned his bike to the southwest. He had a stop or two to make, then he was off to find his father's killer. He had to talk to the NCIS agent who'd investigated the admiral's death. Special Agent Holland Kirk.

He was probably the last man she'd ever want to see again . . . but too bad for her.

He revved the engine and headed home, to New Orleans.

Dax and all the Perfect Gentlemen will return in

BIG EASY TEMPTATION

available soon from Berkley.
Keep reading for a special preview . . .

Y ou're sure you want to do this?" Connor stood beside him outside
the condo he now shared with his wife, Lara.

"I have to find out." Dax set his helmet on the seat of his bike and
pulled his gloves on. "My father's name was on that list."

Only days before they'd tracked down the mysterious Natalia Kuilikov, a Russian woman connected to the Hayes family when Zack's
father had been an ambassador to the Soviet Union, before the fall of
the Wall. She'd written a diary people had died for, including his dear
friend Maddox Crawford. All clues led to the *Bratva*, the Russian mob,
being responsible for the murder. Connor and Lara had recently spoken to the older woman. Moments after a bullet ripped through her
forehead, they'd discovered Kuilikov's handwritten notes in Cyrillic.

The translation had come back as a dead pool—a list of assassination targets.

Joy Hayes had been on that list, as had Constance, Zack's mother.

Admiral Harold Spencer had been on that list as well. Dax damn sure wanted answers.

His father had been gone for three years. His death had been declared a "suicide." Dax hated to think about any of it—not the scandal that had come before his father's death, nor the horrible time after it, and definitely not the investigation that ended with him losing Holland Kirk—the woman he'd long idolized—forever.

Until he'd seen that translation, he'd never intended to set eyes on her again. She'd betrayed him in the cruelest fashion possible by closing her investigation after giving it as much thought as someone opening an umbrella on a rainy day. In the blink of an eye, she'd made a judgment call that gave the press free license to vilify his father. She'd torn down his family to further her career. Oh, he'd paid her back. Now nothing lay between them but anger and regret.

But he couldn't let this case rest in peace anymore. Things had changed. *He* had changed. Armed with new evidence, Dax intended to personally make sure Holland opened the investigation again—and give the facts the due process they deserved.

"Yes, his name was on the list," Connor agreed in that tone that let Dax know he was being handled with care. "I'll look into it. Lara will help. You know we can do a lot. You don't have to go back to New Orleans. Zack pulled strings and got you placed on a special assignment here in D.C., but you have a little time left. Why don't you spend it with us?"

Connor knew damn well what was waiting for him in New Orleans. Or rather, who. "Thanks, buddy. But I think I'll spend it with her."

Connor grimaced. "Yes, that's exactly what I'm trying to avoid. You two will only tear each other up. You've done some stupid shit over that woman."

Like waking up after a bender to find himself married to someone else? Connor had a point; some of the worst moments of his life had been because of Holland Kirk.

Dax shook that reality off. "I'll be fine. I'm certainly not going to drink myself into oblivion and marry whichever woman happens to be next to me."

"Her best friend. You married her best friend," Connor pointed out. "Don't expect her to be helpful. Hell, I half expect her to bite your head off."

"Yeah? Well, I expect her to finally give me the truth." He picked up the helmet before pulling his best friend into a manly hug. "I'll call you if I need anything. I'm going to get to the bottom of this. For my dad. For Zack."

Someone was playing a dangerous game with his friend, the president. Unfortunately for whoever it was, Zack was one of Dax's closest pals. They'd already lost Mad to this nasty business. Dax refused to lose anyone else.

Holland Kirk was either a pawn or a power player. He would damn sure find out which.

With a nod to Lara on the balcony above, he hopped on his bike and revved the engine. He headed southwest, toward New Orleans and the only woman he'd ever loved.

ABOUT THE AUTHORS

Shayla Black is the *New York Times* and *USA Today* bestselling author of more than forty sizzling contemporary, erotic, paranormal, and historical romances produced via traditional, small press, independent, and audio publishing. She lives in Texas with her husband, munchkin, and one very spoiled cat. In her "free" time, she enjoys watching reality TV, reading, and listening to an eclectic blend of music. Shayla's books have been translated into about a dozen languages. She has also received or been nominated for the Passionate Plume, the Holt Medallion, Colorado Romance Writers Award of Excellence, and the National Readers Choice Award. RT BOOKclub has twice nominated her for Best Erotic Romance of the Year, and also awarded her several Top Picks and a KISS Hero Award. A writing risk-taker, Shayla enjoys tackling writing challenges with every new book. Find Shayla at ShaylaBlack.com or visit her Shayla Black Author Facebook page.

New York Times and *USA Today* bestselling author **Lexi Blake** lives in North Texas with her husband, three kids, and the laziest rescue dog in the world. She began writing at a young age, concentrating on plays and journalism. It wasn't until she started writing romance that she found success. She likes to find humor in the strangest places. Lexi believes in happy endings no matter how odd the couple, threesome, or foursome may seem. Find Lexi at LexiBlake.net.